THE REMAINING
AFTERMATH

THE REMAINING
AFTERMATH

BOOK 2

D.J. MOLLES

www.orbitbooks.net

Copyright © 2012 by D.J. Molles
Excerpt from *The Remaining: Refugees* copyright © 2012 by D.J. Molles
Cover design by Lauren Panepinto, cover photo by Arcangel Images. Cover copyright © 2014 by Orbit Books.

Orbit
Hachette Book Group
1290 Avenue of the Americas
New York, NY 10104
www.orbitbooks.net
www.orbitshortfiction.com

Originally self-published by the author: May 2012
First published by Orbit as e-book: January 2014
First Orbit print edition: June 2014

Orbit is an imprint of Hachette Book Group. The Orbit name and logo are trademarks of Little, Brown Book Group Limited.

The publisher is not responsible for websites (or their content) that are not owned by the publisher.

10 9 8 7 6 5 4 3
OPM

Printed in the United States of America

To my wonderful wife—the best person I know.
And to Chris Adkins—a true warrior-poet.
Thank you both for everything.

ONE

CAMP RYDER

WHO ARE THE REAL victims in all of this?
The infected or the survivors?

Gunshots perforated the darkness of Lee's dreams, yanking him violently out of sleep.

He sat upright on a cot in almost complete darkness, his sleep-blind eyes struggling to focus and make sense of what was going on around him. Half in and half out of sleep, Lee's mind conjured up the nearest memory of darkness and gunfire: the dim stairwell in the Petersons' house, the haze of cordite hanging in the air, the stench of the infected.

His breath caught in his chest. Dread hammered at the back of his mind. Something horrible had happened in the Petersons' house. Something terrible and irreversible . . .

Jack had just been bitten!

But no. That didn't make sense.

Because wasn't Jack already dead?

He had to shake his head to clear the images of the Petersons' house and Jack in the bedroom, covered in blood. He knew they were false. This wasn't the Petersons' house. It was . . . someplace else. *Someplace safe*, he thought. *But maybe not so safe anymore, because there's screaming and gunfire coming from outside.*

Another gunshot rang out, this time very close to him.

Adrenaline pumped like a piston in his guts. His heart rate quickened.

Slow down. Evaluate your situation. Try to remember.

Try to remember what the fuck you're doing here.

He took a moment to look around and work through what he was seeing.

He was not in complete darkness, as he'd first thought: A single gas lantern glowed dimly against dull corrugated-steel walls. He was completely naked, save for a thin white bedsheet that had been spread over him from the waist down. He lay on a cot in what looked like a shipping container and his back was in excruciating pain, though he couldn't remember why. His tongue felt thick and pasty. And he had no weapons.

Where's my damn rifle?

From somewhere outside he heard Tango howl.

Tango! he thought, almost jumping off of the cot, but stopping himself as the sound of it reverberated and echoed. *That's not right. That doesn't sound like Tango.* The howl tapered off into a throaty snarl that didn't sound much like a dog anymore. It was human.

It couldn't be Tango, anyway.

Because he was dead too.

And with that thought, the rest came back with sudden and overpowering force. Tango was dead.

Jack was dead. He'd lost his rifle at Timber Creek. Someone named Milo had ambushed them. He remembered crawling through a boarded window, nails carving through the flesh of his back. Red and Blue saving their asses with Molotov cocktails. Angela and Abby and Sam just barely making it to Camp Ryder...

The survivors. Camp Ryder. Wasn't there a ten-foot-high fence around the compound? How the hell did the infected get inside? It was an infected he'd just heard; he was sure of it. But who was shooting at them? The questions all struck his brain in rapid succession.

I can't just lie here, he thought. *I've got to move.*

He ripped the white sheet off of himself and stood, staggering through a flash of light-headedness. The questions still rolled around in his head, but he couldn't answer them now. Most of his thoughts were still muddled, but two things were coming through with piercing clarity: He needed a weapon—anything would do better than his bare hands—and he needed to get out of the shipping container. Running on instinct, these desires became a white-hot need, as real to him as his need to breathe.

That howl again, this time just outside the shipping container.

A shotgun boomed and the pellets struck the steel walls.

Flashlights from outside played across the wall, casting the wavering shadow of a man running straight for Lee. The movements were unmistakably wild and animalistic.

A short, sinewy form lurched around the corner

of the shipping container just in time for another blast of buckshot to scoop its legs out from under it like a rug had been pulled. The infected hit the ground hard on its back and attempted to stand again without any regard to its injuries. Its wide eyes glistened feverishly in the lamplight as its shredded right leg twitched about, pulled in different directions by rearranged muscle fibers. It collapsed with a hissing sound and began to drag itself toward Lee, leaving a thick trail of blood behind.

Like a car with a faulty transmission, Lee's mind finally dropped into gear. He lunged for the table with the medical equipment. He wasn't sure what he was looking for, but if anything was to be a weapon, it would be something on the table. He swept his hands back and forth like a blind man feeling in the dark, knocking over a metal tray with a few scalpels and forceps soaking in alcohol. The tray clattered to the ground and sent the instruments skittering across the floor. He thought about diving for one of the scalpels, but it wouldn't bite deep, and given infected people's pension for not even registering flesh wounds, he decided he needed something with a little more stopping power.

Lee grabbed the heaviest object he could find—a big microscope that felt like it was solid metal. He spun toward the infected and found it nearly close enough to grasp his legs. Lee shouted in surprise and jumped back, grabbing the microscope by the eyepiece with one hand and smashing it down as hard as he could on the head of the infected. The heavy base of the microscope made a wet cracking noise as it dented the skull.

The crazed man on the floor thrashed and drew in a loud, gasping breath. His eyes turned skyward and he began to convulse violently. The sight of it soured Lee's stomach almost instantly. He stared, frozen, for several of his rapid heartbeats before swinging again. The bludgeon struck his attacker in the temple. His eyeballs bulged and the top of the skull mashed into a strange, cone-like shape.

Lee swallowed hard against gorge in the back of his throat. He dropped the microscope and took a faltering step back, trying to catch his breath while his pulse ran away from him. The pain in his back, all but forgotten for those brief few seconds, suddenly spread over his body like he was soaked in kerosene and playing with matches.

He staggered toward his cot but didn't make it. He lost his feet and planted his hands and knees on the floor as he felt his stomach suddenly reject whatever was inside of it. He felt the splatter on his arms and then hung his head, breathing hard and spitting.

Pounding footsteps behind him.

Still keyed up, Lee turned toward the sound and lashed out with both fists.

"Hey! Whoa!"

Lee focused on the face, kneeling down next to him.

A broad face with a wild man's beard. A Colt 1911 in one hand, the other gripping Lee by the shoulder and shaking him gently. "Can you stand up?"

Lee wiped vomit from his lips and searched his mind for this man's name. "Uh...Bus?"

"Yeah."

Lee became suddenly aware that he still had no clothes on. He stood up shakily, with Bus supporting him. "Can I get some pants?"

The big man pointed toward the foot of the cot where a pile of clothing was folded neatly beside Lee's old Bates M6 boots. "It was all we could rustle up for now."

Lee nodded and stepped to the cot, straddling his puddle of vomit—*rice and beans*, he remembered. It was a pair of athletic shorts and a green T-shirt with a yellow smiley face on the chest. It was a far cry from his trusted MultiCam pants and combat shirt, but at least he had his boots back. The harsh reality of his last four days had only strengthened his opinion that these were the best boots ever made.

Inside one of the boots, he noticed someone had stashed his GPS device. Before Doc and Jenny had begun to operate they had tried to take it from his hands, and Lee had refused to give it up. It appeared either that they had succeeded in removing it when he'd fallen asleep or perhaps that Lee had dropped it and they had been kind enough to put it back for him. Either way, finding it snug in his boot immediately increased his trust for these strangers. He'd made clear one simple wish and they'd abided by it.

At the entrance to the cargo container, a younger man appeared holding a big hunting shotgun. He was skinny, but he had a round, childlike face and a patch of blond hair that stood off of his head like a halo. Despite his cherubic features, Lee guessed him to be about twenty years old. As he entered, he looked first at Lee, then to Bus, then to the mess of what once was a human being on the floor.

"Holy shit..."

Lee pulled on the athletic shorts and spoke to Bus. "How'd they get in?"

"I guess they found a hole in the fence. Or made one somehow; that's the only thing I can think of." Turning to the young man, Bus said, "Josh, give Captain Harden your pistol."

Josh pulled a Ruger LCP out of his back pocket and held it out toward Lee. It was a tiny pocket pistol that could fit in the palm of his hand, and essentially worthless on a moving target past a range of about twenty feet. Just as Lee was about to take it, Josh jerked his hand back and looked at him suspiciously, an expression that didn't quite fit on his face. "I'm gonna get this back, right?"

Lee honestly didn't know, so he just looked to Bus for clarification.

Bus shrugged back at him. "I'll get you something better when we have time."

"Then I guess you'll get this back," Lee said to Josh and accepted the gun. He pulled the magazine out of the well. It was a .380 caliber with only four rounds left in the magazine, plus one in the chamber. He would have to get in close to use the thing effectively. Still, it was better than a microscope. He shoved the magazine back into the gun and stomped his feet into his boots. The

GPS device he slipped into the pocket of his athletic shorts.

Josh pointed out to the darkness of Camp Ryder. "I think we got most of 'em."

Bus just shook his head. "We don't know that. Get everyone in the square."

"A'ight." Josh spun on his heel and ran off into the night.

Bus looked Lee over. "You okay? Didn't get bit?"

Lee gave himself a quick once-over before answering. "Think I'm good."

"Let's get moving."

Lee followed the big man out of the cargo container at a jog. "What's 'the square' and why is everyone going there?"

"This ain't the first time we've been attacked," Bus said cryptically.

Lee found himself just rolling with it, the way you roll with the nonsensical facts in a strange dream, simply accepting the unacceptable because there are no other options. Lee felt like he was about to understand, anyway. He was about to get a crash course in how Camp Ryder dealt with attacks.

In a way, Lee felt strangely at ease being the follower. Over the course of the four days, it hadn't just been about his own survival but the survival of everyone in his little group. Angela, Abby, Sam, and until recently, Jack and Tango, had all depended on him to survive. Now it appeared that Bus was the head honcho, the man with a plan, and the absence of responsibility was like dropping an eighty-pound rucksack off his shoulders. And Lee had to admit, while he didn't know Bus well enough to say he trusted him completely, the man had a rock-steady attitude about him. There was something hard and unbreakable inside of him, and Lee could respect that.

Outside of the shipping container, he could see the stretch of gravel and dirt that made up the center of Camp Ryder, like some Main Street in an old Western movie but much narrower. To either side of the gravel stretch, the survivors had used anything and everything they could find to construct small shelters for themselves and their families. It reminded Lee of the shantytowns he'd seen in third-world countries.

Who am I kidding? Lee thought numbly. *This* is *a shantytown. And America is a third-world country now.*

Lee noticed that the shantytown was beginning to churn with bodies, like an anthill after you scuff the top layer off. People in raggedy clothes were emerging out of cars and shacks and tents. Everyone carried flashlights or lanterns in one hand and a weapon in the other. A few had firearms, but mostly it was axes, shovels, crowbars, and baseball bats. It felt like a lynch mob. The townspeople heading out to find Frankenstein's monster.

They ran past Lee and Bus, toward the center of Camp Ryder where a large but shallow pit had been dug and lined with bricks and stones. A fire pit, perhaps? It appeared to be full of ash. Lee guessed correctly that this was "the square."

Suddenly remembering something, Lee stopped

and began craning his neck around, trying to see through the jostling crowd and the darkness. To Bus, he spoke with a measure of urgency: "Where're Angela and the kids?"

Bus motioned for him to keep walking. "Josh is telling everyone to gather in the square. They'll be there."

As they walked, Bus snatched an ax handle from where it was leaning up against a tent. It was thinner toward the base of the handle and thicker at the top where the metal ax-head was missing, which made it perfectly weighted for a striking weapon.

"Harris!" Bus yelled.

A man in the growing crowd of people looked up.

"Captain Harden is borrowing your ax-handle."

The man nodded and gave a thumbs-up.

The ax handle was pushed into Lee's arms. He noticed that someone had written on the handle in Magic Marker: BRAIN BUSTER.

Cute.

Lee cinched the drawstring of his shorts up tight and stuck the little Ruger LCP in his waistband. Bus stepped in front of the crowd and looked like he was hurriedly counting heads. Lee estimated about fifty, which was close to the number Bus had given him last night. As he looked out over the crowd, he could see a tangled mess of blond hair on the other side of the crowd. In the glimmering lamplight, he could see Angela's face, etched in worry. As the crowd shifted, he glimpsed the two children, standing to either side of her.

A fear he hadn't realized he'd been harboring released its vise grip on his stomach. He thought about calling to them but decided against it. They were here with the group. They were relatively safe. For now.

Josh ran up beside him and stopped to catch his breath for a brief second. "That's everyone."

"Hopefully," Bus murmured.

"So…" Lee looked around at the gathered mass of people. He noticed that everyone had their backs to the fire pit and had placed their flashlights at their feet, creating a bright, noisy gathering. Lee was about to ask what the plan was but suddenly managed to figure it out on his own. He turned so his back was also to the fire pit and got a solid grip on the ax-handle.

He looked at Bus and shook his head. "I can't say I like this idea."

Bus only shrugged and then shouted to the crowd. "Alright, folks, call 'em when you see 'em!"

Lee saw stony faces, all etched in harsh light and deep shadows. Glimmering and fearful eyes stared out into the darkness. Weathered hands twisted tighter and tighter grips on an assortment of opportunistic weapons. Those with firearms were at the front, pointing their hunting shotguns and deer rifles out at the suspicious stillness.

Circling the wagons.

The quiet of the night felt forced. Like a breath taken and held for fear of someone hearing. Even the night birds and chirping crickets were conspicuously absent.

Lee shifted his weight and tried to focus on anything that lay beyond the ring of light created by the dozens of flashlights.

The silence stretched uncomfortably.

Someone whispered, "Why aren't they attacking?"

And another: "This is weird."

And still another: "Are you sure there are more?"

Someone's dog began barking.

Then a shout: "I see movement!"

The group collectively tensed.

"Over by the trash bins!"

Heads turned, everyone simultaneously spinning in the same direction. Lee followed suit because he didn't know where the "trash bins" were. He saw a collection of old steel shipping containers, identical to the one that held Doc's medical station. The tops of the containers had been removed so that they looked like big, open sardine cans. Several of them were filled with the monumental amount of trash that came from refugees all jam-packed in and living together.

In the murky shadows of the trash bins, Lee strained to see the movement.

A couple of the stronger flashlights probed the darkness, but didn't reveal anything. The darkness was becoming disorienting. He realized he still wasn't thinking clearly, wasn't operating like normal. The injury and the lack of food and water had taken more of a toll on his body than he'd thought, and he was only just beginning to recover. He kept repeating in his mind, *It's time to do work. It's time to do work.* Because that was what he used to tell his squad when they had to focus on completing a mission.

It's time to do work.

"There!" someone shouted.

A flash of movement between two trash bins.

"I see it!" A man with a deer rifle stepped forward a bit, but then hesitated. "Why isn't it coming at us?"

A chunk of trash suddenly shifted and that strange, unearthly screeching sound echoed out at the band of survivors. Lee couldn't see any details of the figure, but it ran straight at them. Just as it was within twenty-five yards of them it suddenly stopped and veered off. For a moment, it trotted along the edge of their lights, like a wolf probing a herd for weaknesses.

The entire crowd seemed frozen and perplexed, like everyone was trying to figure out what the hell this one was doing.

"Shoot it!" Bus shouted at the man with the deer rifle.

The rifle barked.

Lee watched the dirt at the infected's feet explode. Sympathetic gunfire followed the rifle shot as the tension became too much for some trigger fingers to handle. The night was abruptly engulfed in a volley of shotgun blasts and rifle fire. A scattershot of rounds caught its legs, then ripped into its shoulder, pummeled its chest, and finally split its head open.

It wasn't until that moment when Lee watched the miserable thing collapse to the ground that a small, familiar voice cut into his brain, dissipating the fog of disorientation and reminding him of who he was, and how he had been trained.

Watch your lane.

When learning to operate in a squad, each member would have a designated "lane of fire" to watch for enemies. If you were constantly checking to make sure that your buddy wasn't missing things in his lane, then you were probably missing things in your own lane. In other words: Stop worrying about everyone else and do what you know you're supposed to be doing.

Squad Tactics 101.

Watch your lane.

Lee spun around just in time to see two clawlike hands latch onto a young teenage girl and yank her backward. Lee watched the girl's dark hair fly up like it was suddenly in zero gravity as she was pulled to the ground. Her eyes locked onto Lee, and he saw a scared indignation, as though she were thinking, *This isn't supposed to happen to me.*

The infected was an older female. It hunched over the younger girl and lunged for the neck. The girl let out a small cry and her hands came up, trying to block the infected's mouth from reaching her jugular. The old woman bit down hard on the girl's wrist and Lee heard tendons snap.

He managed to yell, "Behind us!" and then swung for the fences. The ax-handle connected just behind the ear and left a deep hollow in the old woman's skull.

It was only then that Lee realized there was a second infected. It lunged out of the darkness and seized hold of the teenage girl and began to backpedal, trying to drag her away from the crowd, looking at the other survivors and hissing aggressively. It pulled her by the shirt collar with one hand and hammered the girl's face with the other, knocking her unconscious after two or three blows.

Lee jumped forward and wound up for the swing. A gun went off just to the right side of his head. The infected's throat exploded and it collapsed into a writhing ball. Lee instinctively recoiled from the noise of the gunshot so close to him. As Lee clenched his jaw against the ringing in his ears, the crowd swarmed around him, yanking the girl away from the infected and then bludgeoning it to death.

He looked to his right, where the gunshot had just come from, and saw a man drop a small revolver to the ground. His face was ashen. He rushed past Lee and slid to his knees next to the girl and began to wail.

The gathering erupted in confusion.

Everyone was yelling and pressing forward to hover over the girl. A younger man in the crowd turned and looked at Lee with accusatory eyes, as though Lee had done something wrong, as though it was *his* fault that the girl had been attacked. In a flash of anger, Lee thought about using the ax-handle on him too. But in the back of his mind he thought, *Isn't it your fault? Shouldn't you have been paying attention? You're the professional here...*

Over it all he heard Bus yelling, "Steve! Steve!" and the man who had fired the revolver wailing: "Oh Jesus! Oh fuck! Come on, baby! Wake up! I'm so sorry, baby!"

The girl's father?

Bus tried to push past with the rest of them, but Lee was thinking a little bit more clearly now, thinking about how those infected had hid from them and flanked them. There could be more. And if they didn't find where the intruders had come through, there *would* be more. He reached out and caught Bus with a firm hand to his chest. "Are there any others?"

Seeming to ignore him, the big bearded man craned his neck to see the girl on the ground, then abruptly realized that Lee was speaking to him. "What?"

Lee pulled the man closer, speaking low so as not to be overheard and start a panic. "Are there any other infected?"

"Uh…" He tapped his Colt 1911 against his thigh and wiped his sweaty brow. "Shit. God. I don't know."

The group was already scattering to the wind. Doc and Jenny were pushing people out of the way and Doc's skinny voice was needling at the crowd: "Everyone get the fuck outta the way! Someone help me lift her!"

More people than necessary to carry a 120-pound girl stepped in. Everyone was trying to get a hand in to help and becoming more of a hindrance. The girl's father cradled her head in his arms as they moved her quickly toward the medical trailer.

Bus was staring at the girl again, so Lee shook him gently to get his attention. "Grab a couple guys. We need to close whatever hole those fuckers came through and then do a perimeter sweep."

TWO

INVESTIGATION

BUS SEEMED TO GAIN his senses again. He reached out with a thick arm, coarse with wiry black hair, and grabbed Josh as the young man attempted to run past and join the crowd as they whisked the bitten girl off to Doc's medical trailer.

"You're with us," Bus said, and when he spoke he had returned to his normal steady tone. "We gotta find where they're coming through the fence."

"But what about Kara?" Josh's eyes were wide and concerned.

Bus looked the young man in the eye. "Let Doc handle that. You can't do anything for her right now. We have other things to take care of. Now let's go."

Josh didn't argue further. He nodded once and then both men turned toward Lee.

He quickly surveyed his surroundings and made a decision. "We need a fourth..." Lee spotted a familiar face. Miller, wasn't it? The man in the red bandanna who had helped them escape Timber Creek with the use of some Molotov cocktails. Lee waved him over. "Hey! Borrow you for a second?"

Miller took a second to recognize him in the darkness, but after shining his light a few times in Lee's face, he came running over, hand on his holstered .38 Special to keep it from flopping around on his belt. "Yeah?"

He was roughly the same age as Josh, but taller, and his features were more gaunt. While Josh gave the impression of someone much younger, everything about Miller was older, from the squint of his eyes to his confident-but-not-cocky stride. There was something else there too. Something in the tilt of his head, in the set of his jaw. Miller liked to fight.

Lee pointed to the fence behind the trash bins, as it was the closest section of fence to their current location. "We'll both start there. Run the fence line in opposite directions and see if we can find where the infected are getting through. If you find the hole, post up and secure it as best you can until we all meet back up."

Three heads nodded quickly.

"Bus, you and I will go clockwise. Miller and Josh, you guys go counterclockwise." Lee and Bus took off for the fence at a trot and began walking briskly along it, inspecting the integrity of the chain links as they went.

Lee had asked for Bus to team up with him because he wanted a chance to talk to him. There were things about their most recent encounter that disturbed him and he wanted to get Bus's thoughts on it.

While they walked, Lee spoke. "What happens to the girl now?"

"Kara?" Bus mumbled absently. "Doc will amputate and hope for the best."

Lee almost stopped in his tracks. "Amputate? Are you kidding me?"

Bus shook his head, looking briefly run-down. "No. The faster they cut off Kara's arm, the better chance she has of not contracting FURY. Doc figures it works about half the time, which is better than a hundred-percent chance of infection. Only problem is that most of the time the amputation goes septic. Or they lose too much blood." Bus swore bitterly. "We just don't have the medical equipment. It's like the fucking Stone Age again. Like Civil War surgeons just hacking off limbs with saws and crossing their fingers."

Lee couldn't think of anything else to say. The concept of amputation to prevent bacterial infection through a bite or open wound seemed to be a reckless medical maneuver, but when faced with the certainty of turning into one of *them*, the amputation had a cold practicality.

Lee pressed on. "Did you notice anything about those last infected?"

Bus didn't answer immediately. He stalked along and painted his flashlight over the length of fence before them but found it to be secure. When he finally spoke, he seemed to be choosing his words carefully. "I remember how they were a month ago." He stopped walking and turned to look at Lee. "They were disjointed and confused. Lost. Insane. They attacked each other just as often as they attacked us. I don't know what the hell is going on or how it's happening so fast, but the groups are changing. Learning. And they're doing it quickly."

Lee pictured the dark shape darting out of the trash bins and circling the edge of the lamplight while they sat in their encirclement, weapons pointed out. The cold, blood-crusted talons dragging that young girl to the ground and the other trying to carry her off.

"Like a wolf pack," Lee said, almost more to himself than to Bus. "Adaptation. Evolution. It doesn't seem like they're mindlessly attacking anymore. It seems like they're hunting us."

Bus stopped and looked Lee in the eyes. "Bullshit," he said.

Lee shrugged. "Think about it. That's the first time you've ever seen them come from both directions. Usually they're in one solid group and they just charge you. This was different. It was like they were trying to distract us so the other two could get in close."

Bus didn't answer. He just started walking along the fence line again. The truth was that the words were bitter. It was not an "aha" moment, it was an "oh, shit" moment. The infected were bad enough as a mindless herd. The thought of them in small packs, hunting them like prey, was a hard pill to swallow.

But Lee wasn't willing to ignore the situation either.

"This is the first time we've seen them maneuver like that." He followed along with Bus while he spoke. "When the situation changes, your tactics need to change along with it. If they're getting smart enough to get past your chain-link fence, we're going to need to think of something else to keep them out."

Bus shook his head fiercely. "Even a dog can dig himself under a fence. That doesn't mean anything. They're mindless shells of what once were human beings. They're just running on autopilot now. There's no evolution in this."

He sounded distraught, as though he were attempting to convince himself. *I reject your reality and substitute my own.* Lee decided not to push it. He just hoped Bus had other things on his mind and wasn't this unreceptive all the time.

Lee had to admit to himself that it was difficult to tell with the infected. Sometimes their actions seemed like the result of logical thought, and other times it just looked like instinct. Most of them appeared to be able to manipulate tools, but they weren't using them properly; they were simply using them as blunt objects to strike out with. Just because a monkey can strike somebody in the head with a wrench doesn't mean it can fix your sink. They all seemed to hold on to some rudimentary intelligence, but it also seemed to vary from individual to individual. Just as some were more aggressive than others, some were more intelligent than others. But then the question arose again, was it intelligence or instinct? Lee kept coming back to the example of a wolf pack. When a pack hunts, singles out the weakest prey, and then flanks it to take it down, is the success of their hunt based on a premeditated plan or ingrained animal instinct?

A voice came hollering across the compound. "Bus!"

Bus and Lee both looked and saw Miller running up, breathing heavily. "I think we found where they came in." He took a big gulp of air. His eyes darted back and forth, carrying grave meaning. "I think you should take a look at it."

Miller turned on his heel and started jogging back across the compound. They followed behind him, their flashlights strobing up and down as they ran. Lee took a sidelong glance across the center of the compound and saw the crowd at the medical trailer being pushed out by a man Lee didn't recognize. From inside the trailer Lee could hear screaming, high-pitched and wretched. Doc had begun the amputation.

"Right here." Miller had stopped and was pointing.

They turned the corner of a shanty made out of aluminum siding and blue tarp. Lee and Bus looked forward as they slowed to a walk and approached what Miller pointed at. Confusion passed over their faces followed by a deep, dreadful uncertainty. They looked at each other and then back at the object of their attention.

An opening had been peeled back from the fence, from top to bottom. The chain links had been pulled away and rolled up like two sides of a scroll. Only they weren't pushed inside, but pulled outward and tucked in so neatly to create the man-size breach in their defenses that it left little room for question about who or what had done this.

It was then that Lee and Bus both noticed a low, husky voice, quietly intoning some strange narrative: "... *but only slowly they neared the foe. As*

*they neared him, the ocean grew still more smooth;
seemed drawing a carpet over its waves…"*

"What the fuck is that?" Bus glared and shot his
flashlight toward the sound of the voice. The flashlight played around a bit and then found the cul-
prit. Nestled in a patch of overgrown grass at the
corner of the shack was a small black CD player,
round and glistening like an insect's head; the two
bulbous speakers stared up at them like compound
eyes.

*"…the breathless hunter came so nigh his seem-
ingly unsuspecting prey, that his entire dazzling
hump was distinctly visible…"*

Bus moved swiftly forward, raising his foot as
though to stomp the thing out of existence, but
Lee's hand shot out and grabbed him by his arm,
hauling him backward. Bus looked at him like
he was about to turn that foot on Lee, but then
understanding dawned.

Lee nodded. "Might want to check that out
real good before you go stomping around it.
Depending on who put it there, it could be
booby-trapped."

Bus managed a halfhearted smile. "That's why
I keep you around." He gestured toward the CD
player. "I'm guessing you have much more experience with booby traps than I do. You tell me."

The voice, supremely ignorant of the circumstances, continued its droning: *"…the blue waters
interchangeably flowed over into the moving valley
of his steady wake…"*

Lee gave the big man a humorless smirk and
leaned forward with extreme caution. He shined

the flashlight first around the immediate area of his feet, then lit up the patch of overgrown grass. When he saw nothing to alarm him he stepped forward and peered down into the nest of grass, working the flashlight around at different angles.

"...the hunters who namelessly transported and allured by all this serenity, had ventured to assail it; but had fatally found that quietude..."

Lee let out a long breath and relaxed a bit. Then he knelt down and stabbed the top of the CD player with his finger. The black cover popped open and the disembodied voice went silent. Underneath, a white disk spun madly at first, and then came to a gradual stop. Lee reached his hand in and plucked the CD from the tray, looking at the title and reading aloud: "*Moby-Dick* by Herman Melville. It's an audiobook."

Bus's face was made of granite. "Hilarious."

Lee shook his head. "I don't think it was a joke."

Miller chimed in, pointing to the neatly clipped ends of the chain links. "Pretty sure someone cut his way through this...looks like bolt cutters." Bus regarded Miller with a dubious look, to which Miller responded drably, "I wasn't always the upstanding citizen I am now."

"Milo?" Lee suggested.

Bus crossed his arms. "I don't see who else would be interested in fucking with us, and given our recent tiff, I think that's a pretty good deduction."

"Why not just attack us?" Josh finally spoke.

Lee offered a possible answer. "Because a day attack is too easily defended and they know they can't be out in the woods at night because of the infected. So they use the infected. Cut a hole in the fence. Put a CD player with just enough volume to attract the infected but not get noticed by us."

"Kind of clever if you think about it." Bus stared grimly out at the dark woods. "Audiobook just sounds like some guy talking. Music would have caught our attention."

Everyone who had survived up to this point seemed to know that the infected had nearly superhuman hearing at night when they became more active. Lee had to assume that because of this, Camp Ryder enforced noise discipline at night. Even at the low volume it had been set at, the CD player had probably been the loudest noise coming out of the camp, though it probably would have gone unnoticed by regular ears or dismissed as a quiet family discussion.

Lee stood up and stepped to Bus's side. "I think maybe you should tell me about Milo."

Bus nodded, then pointed to Miller and Josh. "You two patch up that fence. Only one of you working at a time; the other keep watch. Don't let anyone else sneak in. I'll send someone else down to help you." Bus turned to Lee. "Walk with me."

The two men walked through the darkness, their flashlights casting a dull glow off the ground before them and just barely illuminating their tired faces. Most everyone had gone back to their makeshift homes, but a few stragglers still made their way through the dark. Unlike the deep silence of early morning, there was still a whisper of excitement—quiet voices echoing out of wood and tin shacks, holding furtive conversations. Lee had to wonder: How many other infected were in the area to hear those barely audible whispers?

Lee looked up at the sky and saw the faint glimmer of dawn to the east, or perhaps it was his imagination. It wasn't until you spent time outside of the comfort of civilization that you began to realize why people in ages past feared the night. The night was long, it was uncomfortable, and it was dangerous. The dawn marked the end of the dark misery and the return of warmth and safety.

"You know what time it is?" Lee looked briefly at Bus.

"About four in the morning."

Lee felt his heart sink. The light to the east was just his imagination after all. Dawn was two long hours away and there would be no sleeping after this. The pain in Lee's back was beginning to catch up to him.

A dark figure strode up to them as they crossed the center of camp. All Lee could see was the figure's right side, illuminated by the cold blue light of an LED lantern. As the figure approached, it raised the lantern up to eye level and Lee recognized the pursed face and the balding dome of his head, washed out and pale in the glow. The angle of the light cast shadows that made his face look weirdly severe.

Lee thought he remembered Miller calling the man Bill.

He was the one who had resisted bringing them back to camp, only to be convinced by Lee's arguments and Miller's pleading to give them a chance. He was of average height, and probably average weight before he had been forced to ratchet down on his belt during these lean times. He was probably in his forties and going bald on top, with a ring of wiry gray-brown hair. Overall, his body language and his facial expression communicated to Lee that he was not a pleasant person to be around.

"Bus." He nodded to his superior with respect then turned a somewhat disdainful eye on Lee. "Are you supposed to be up? I thought Doc wanted you recuperating."

Lee was about to respond, but Bus cut him off, and Lee was grateful. He was too tired to argue. With a dismissing wave of one meaty hand, Bus said, "Harper, we have a problem. Captain Harden is just helping me out, and then I will let him go straight back to bed."

The man's cold silence said enough.

Lee quirked his eyebrows. "So is it Bill or Harper?"

"Bill Harper," he said with a grumble. "Miller's the only one who calls me Bill. Everyone else calls me Harper."

Lee nodded. "Harper it is."

Bus led the trio toward the Ryder building. The larger structure towered over the shantytown like a castle amongst the villagers' mud huts. It was a two-story cement structure with very few windows that Lee could see. Purely industrial, with very little to beautify it. Lee wasn't sure what it had been used for prior to the arrival of its current occupants, but he immediately began looking for its strong points, its weak points, and how it could be improved as a defensive location. If a firefight occurred, the thin walls of the shanties would provide very little protection. This building would have to be their defense.

It had a lot going for it. In addition to no windows and concrete walls, Lee could only see one entrance, which was two steel doors flanked by narrow sidelights—too narrow for a man to squeeze through. The roof looked like it was easily accessible, and Lee imagined some sandbags and a few machine-gun nests up there could lay a pretty damn good field of fire on any attacking force.

Infected or otherwise.

Lee pointed up toward the big building. "What do you guys use it for?"

"When we first got here, we all lived inside," Bus explained. "We very rarely left. The security of the fence was no big deal, because the building was our security. We welded the cargo-bay doors shut, which left only two sets of double doors to worry about—the ones you're looking at now and another set on the opposite side. We had everyone in there, but it was only about twenty people."

They reached the double doors and Bus pushed them open. Lee noticed the smell first. It was the smell of the refugee camps outside Al-Waleed and the smell of a homeless shelter he'd once visited in D.C. It was sweating bodies and grimy clothes, exacerbated by the warm air. Lee could only imagine how much worse it smelled during the day.

After the double doors, a short hallway opened

into the main portion of the building where Lee could see that the Ryder trucks had once been serviced. But instead of trucks and tools and lifts, Lee only saw another collection of shanties, these built less sturdily than the ones outside and more for the purpose of privacy. Lee thought there were about fifteen different dwellings crammed into the space, most of them with a lantern glowing inside. All the lamplight eking through wooden slats cast a kaleidoscope of light on the ceiling.

Bus guided the three of them to the right and they began to ascend a metal staircase. "After the shit officially hit the fan and FEMA tucked its tail and ran, we started getting a steady trickle of survivors. We tried to take in only people who had something to contribute, but..." Bus trailed off. "It was tough. A lot of tough decisions had to be made."

As they reached the top of the stairs, Lee spied a panel of glass to his right: a large window belonging to an office that overlooked the floor. In the dark window, Lee could see his reflection staring back at him and it almost stopped him in his tracks. He was thinner than he remembered; his neck and arms just bundles of taut cords with flesh stretched over them. His once-tidy crew cut was slightly overgrown and four days' worth of beard had grown in thick.

He was shocked to discover that the once gentle set of his face had turned into hard angles. His lips were pressed, the corners in a slight downturn, his jaw set as though preparing for a blow. The eyes that his last girlfriend, Deana, had always told him were kind now shone cold and savage. He forced his face to relax, and there he could see some semblance of the person he remembered. But it was only a grim parody. That person didn't exist anymore.

Lee realized Bus was still speaking and tore his attention away from the harsh visage in the window, refocusing on the conversation.

"I've always believed that we shouldn't turn anyone away—more manpower, you know? But a lot of people don't agree with me." Bus opened the door to the small office overlooking the floor. Lee supposed it had once housed a foreman or supervisor. Inside, it was sparsely furnished with a few folding chairs, a large desk, and a big corkboard with a county map pinned to it. Bus stepped behind the desk but didn't sit. He continued speaking as he stood there, fishing through one of the desk drawers. "Even being selective, we eventually got too crowded for everyone to fit in the building, so we allowed people to start making their camps outside. Seeing that it was safe, some of the people who were living in here decided to move out too. You think it looks cramped now, you should have seen it before." Bus sighed. "Pretty soon, we'll have too many for that, and then we'll have some real problem-solving to do."

Bus finally found what he was looking for and pulled out a bottle of whiskey. He smiled wanly at it and gestured his two companions toward the folding chairs. "Have a seat, gentlemen."

Harper and Lee both took a chair facing the desk.

Bus snagged the chair behind the desk and hauled it over to the front, so the three men were positioned in a small circle. He took his seat with a sigh, adjusting the straps of his holster. He leaned back and unscrewed the cap off the whiskey. "Wish I could say it was good stuff, but it ain't." He took a swig and offered the bottle to Harper, who accepted.

"So..." Lee tapped his fingers on his knee.

There was a long, awkward silence as Bus stared at Harper, who stared at the bottle in his hands. Harper seemed to take notice of the silence and looked up at Lee. "Did we have a problem you were going to help us with?"

Bus leaned forward, elbows on his knees. "Harper, we found a hole cut in the fence. Someone had put a CD player on the ground, playing an audiobook to attract infected. We think it was Milo."

Harper deflated with a single long sigh. He leaned back and finally took a swig of the whiskey with a violent grimace on his face. Then he passed the bottle to Lee. "Yeah...Milo."

Lee smiled unsurely. "What's the backstory on this guy?"

Harper looked to Bus and seemed to be waiting for him to take the reins.

"Uh-uh." Bus folded his arms. "You tell him. Milo's *your* brother."

THREE

Blood Ties

LEE EYED THE PLASTIC bottle in his hands as he waited for Harper to collect himself. It was a fifth of whiskey—bottom-shelf stuff, which was a shame, but Lee didn't want to offend. He took a sip and swallowed fast, trying to avoid letting the harsh liquid sit on his tongue for longer than necessary.

He managed to get it down without too much of a grimace and passed the bottle on, then leaned back in his chair and looked at Harper. In the well-lit room, there was much more to see than just the harsh lines that his lantern had thrown on his face. Lee noted his dirty hands, blistered and torn up from hard work but lacking that permanent, calloused thickness of a lifetime of manual labor. The wrinkles on his face that seemed unpleasant in the darkness now looked like old smile lines and laugh lines that had simply fallen into disuse. A scowl seemed to be his predominant expression now.

Having the full picture, Lee realized it wasn't so much that Bill Harper was a naturally unpleasant person but that he'd become unpleasant due to his circumstances. And really, who could blame him?

Maybe he'd once been a happy, soft man, living a soft life, with a soft job. But now, in the harsh reality of the new world, he had to fit in, had to find his place, and most of all, had to survive. Harper was in the process of turning into a colder, harder, more pragmatic version of himself.

Harper seemed to gather the story and then began speaking with a loud exhale. "Milo and I were born ten years apart. I'm older. Our mother was raising us by herself, so by the time Milo was starting school, she wanted me to get a job. So I got a job. I finished school. Got a scholarship. Worked my way through college. But Milo . . . he never cared to be committed to anyone, let alone to his family. He was the wild one. While I was working, he was partying, getting locked up, and costing me more goddamn money. I can't remember how many times I had to wire Mom money to bail him out.

"Milo just never grew up. He lived with my mom in their shitty-ass trailer until she died a few years back from lung cancer, thanks to sixty years of Virginia Slims. Then he sat in that trailer and continued being the shitbag that he is. Meanwhile, I'd become successful. I worked for a bank, made a 100K-plus salary, and I owned some land outside Wilkesboro. Even though he never worked for shit in his life, I think Milo resented my success.

"When all this went down, Milo shows up out of the blue at my property and starts talking about family and how we're blood and we owe it to each other. Just a whole big chip-on-the-shoulder bullshit speech. I know my brother, even though we were never close, and he's a manipulator. But damn me, I'm a weak man and I didn't want to rock the boat. He was family, after all, so me and my wife took him in.

"Then they evacuated us. First to Wilkes County Airport, and from there they bused us and choppered us over to the camp in Sanford. That lasted less than a day before it got overrun by infected." Harper stopped there and laughed bitterly. "At the time, they didn't really know much about noise discipline around the infected, so you have the camp in Sanford, with almost no perimeter defense, bright lights on twenty-four/seven, choppers landing and taking off at all hours of the night. Seemed like they attracted every fucking crazy in the eastern half of the state.

"Anyway"—the bitter smile fled from Harper's lips and now there was only that slate-gray scowl—"Milo made it out, but not my wife. Not a trade I would have brokered. But me and him were alive and we started walking. Didn't know where we were going. Just surviving. Eventually we came across Camp Ryder before their requirements became a little more stringent, and Bus here let a fumbling banker and his asshole brother stay.

"After about a week, Milo started getting stir-crazy. Started talking about how we needed to fight the infected. You'd have thought he woke up one day and believed he was in a war movie, the stupid fuck. He disappeared for a day and came back riding a goddamn Hummer with a machine gun on the back, driven by two other worthless shitheads he'd found—he's always been a magnet for shithead friends. He just pulled right into

Camp Ryder like he owned the place and laid down an ultimatum: We could join him and fight the infected or we could get in his way and suffer the consequences."

Harper's eyes darkened. "Naturally, we told him to go fuck himself. He drove off without a word, but just as he was about to drive out of sight, he let a burst loose from that .50-cal on his Hummer." Harper rubbed his face. "Hit a ten-year-old girl and her mother. This was before Doc came here, so we lost the mother almost immediately. Thought the girl was going to pull through, but her wound went septic and she died."

Harper straightened up in his chair and planted his hands on his knees. "Ever since then, he has been collecting other people like himself—criminals and lowlifes—and running around pillaging everything and everyone. And that is why there is no love lost between us, and why I will put a bullet in his brain the next time I see him."

Lee raised his brow. He thought of the people who had attacked them at Jack Burnsides's house and later burned Lee's house to the ground. They had a Humvee, and the description was very similar. The thought put a flash of heat down his back. "Any other group out there causing problems, or is it pretty much just Milo?"

Bus fielded the question. "From what we can tell, if there were any separate groups, they've all been absorbed into Milo's. We estimate he has about thirty men, but they're kind of scattered around the county. He usually only keeps ten or so with him."

Lee took a long moment to lean back in his chair, stare at the floor, and consider the ramifications of this new information. At first glance, Milo was an enemy to be defeated. At second glance, Milo was the leader of another group of approximately thirty survivors. It seemed pretty obvious that Bus wanted Milo and his group wiped off the face of the earth, but Lee had to consider what was best for his mission. Granted, given their previous actions, Lee didn't think they would be very open to the concept of allying with him, but the only way to find out would be to talk to them.

Lee kept those cards close to his chest.

Bus took a sip of harsh whiskey and shuddered. "Okay...now that we have our history lesson behind us, I need to steer this toward the meat of the conversation: the breach in the fence." Bus capped the whiskey and set it behind him on his desk. Then he crossed his arms and allowed a sour expression to push through his heavy, bearded face. "Someone cut that fence up, and I need to know who and when."

Harper puffed out air and looked around the room, without much to say.

"Well"—Lee looked between the two other men—"I'm going to say it happened at night. Probably sometime within the last two hours."

"Okay..." Bus waited for elaboration.

"I can't imagine it taking the infected that long to track down the source of the noise. Even with their hearing at night, they would still have had to be pretty close by," Lee explained. "I think if we say it happened any earlier than maybe an hour or two, we're being unrealistic. In all likelihood, they were at the fence within minutes."

Bus looked skyward as though trying to figure something. "That doesn't make any sense. If it was placed recently, it would have been nighttime. Milo's men would have had to travel through the woods at night, which kind of defeats the whole purpose."

"If I was them, I would have had someone set up in the woods before dark," Lee said. "Somewhere close to the fence, so when the time came, they could cross the distance without too much noise."

"They'd still have to get out," Bus argued. "And if you're sending in one man, why not send in twenty and take the place over?"

"Because no matter how quiet they are, twenty men will make more noise than one," Lee answered. "As for getting out after setting the trap, all the guy would have had to do was run along the fence to the dirt road and he'd be home free."

Bus considered this, then looked to Harper. "Who was on watch?"

"Sue and Stan," Harper replied.

"You may want to speak to them," Bus put in.

Lee leaned forward. "How often do they check the fence? Once an hour? Once a half hour?"

Harper seemed to resent having to answer Lee's questions, but he squinted and did some arithmetic in his head. "Takes about ten minutes to walk the perimeter, then they spend another ten or fifteen minutes on their sentry points . . . Yeah, probably between twenty and thirty minutes."

"Plenty of time to *snip-snip* and plant the talking box," Lee said. "Then run to the dirt road and make a good escape. May have had a car waiting out at the road. If the guy moved fast enough, he would have avoided the sentries and the infected."

Harper seemed to be coming around to Lee's point of view. "And at that point, there's no harm in running, even if it makes more noise. In fact, it may have just increased the odds of attracting infected to the area. The guy running doesn't care because he's about to get in a car and drive away."

Bus took a breath to speak but someone started banging on the office door, causing the whole thing to rattle. Lee looked up and could see a dark figure standing on the walkway outside through the smoky glass. Bus let his breath out in a slow, defeated huff and Lee got the feeling that Bus already knew what the person wanted, and it wasn't good.

"Come on in," Bus said, just loud enough to be heard.

The door swung open and a boy's face on a large man's body stepped in. The big kid easily stood over six feet and probably weighed more than two hundred pounds. He wore dirty old overalls that made him look like a farmhand and wrung a tattered-up baseball cap in his hands. His eyes were red and strained and his whole body shook.

"Uh...Bus..." The kid looked at the floor. "We lost Kara. Doc tried, but..." The kid sobbed once then shamefacedly stared at the floor with his mouth closed tight.

A low, miserable noise came out of Harper as he

leaned back and set his gaze on the dingy ceiling tiles. He bared his teeth as though experiencing some deep physical pain. Bus stood up suddenly and stepped over to Harper, putting a big hand on the other man's knee and patting it slowly. To the kid, who appeared on the verge of losing himself again, Bus gave his shoulder a quick squeeze and thanked him for coming to tell them. The kid nodded and hurried out.

Harper stood, shaking his bald head.

Steady as usual, Bus spoke calmly. "We should go down there."

The medical trailer was a mess of gore.

The infected that Lee had brained with the microscope had not been removed but simply pushed to the side, like a pile of dirty laundry. A dark stain ran from the coagulated pool where the creature had first fallen to where it had been shoved aside. It lay up against the wall now, half on its side, half leaning on the wall, with one dead arm slung limply over its face. Lee could still see those blank eyes, as lifeless as a doll's, staring at the ceiling.

Doc had used Lee's cot to conduct the operation, amputating Kara's arm in a futile attempt to save her life. No anesthetic. No blood transfusions. Not even a real operating table. Just a dirty cot draped with thin plastic sheeting, now streaked and dappled with blood.

Outside, the sound of grief was like fingernails on a chalkboard to Lee. The weeping of families always made him feel strange and tense, and he thought of Afghani mothers pulling their limp children out of the ruins of a hut that a misguided JDAM—a Joint Direct Attack Munition—had nearly disintegrated. Bus and Harper were with the people as they groaned and wept for another one lost. Not the first. Certainly not the last. But another one.

Only Doc remained in the tent. The younger man sat on a crate at the table where all his medical equipment lay, his scraggly brown hair hanging over his face. He stared straight ahead, perhaps at his bloody hands that lay like dead things on the table, or perhaps simply at the wall.

The sounds of grieving began to move away from the medical trailer. Lee took a few steps over to the table where Doc sat and put a hand on his shoulder. The skinny medical student cringed and shrugged it off.

"Wasn't supposed to happen like this." He shook his head slowly. "It wasn't."

Lee didn't immediately respond. He felt awkward, like a bull tiptoeing through the proverbial china shop. Finally he decided to forgo the platitudes and stick to the facts. "Doc, you're barely even equipped to stitch someone up after a bad fall, let alone perform major surgery. It had to be done, and you were the one who had to do it. No one blames you that it didn't turn out well. It's just the way that one went."

Doc's head tilted back and a strange, humorless chuckle escaped him. He met Lee's gaze and there was something intense and disturbing in it. Something that immediately made Lee uncomfortable. "You don't get it, man. It's my fault. And they *will* blame me. Maybe not now, but they will. They will eventually blame me."

Lee opened his mouth to speak, but a heavy hand fell on his shoulder.

He was preparing to turn and address the person, but then the hand was suddenly pressing down on him and spinning him around. Lee had just enough time to see the incoming haymaker and throw his left arm up to block. His arm absorbed most of the blow but whoever the hell it was had thrown his body into it and the fist still bounced off the side of Lee's head, causing him to stumble.

What the...?

Subconsciously, Lee's feet spread wide and his elbows tucked in. He didn't recognize the face, only the dark, aggressive shape, narrow slits of eyes, and a grimace broadcasting the next blow, this one a stiff right uppercut aimed at his solar plexus. Even as he saw the incoming strike, Lee's mind raced, trying to explain what was happening. It couldn't be an infected—it displayed too much control. But why would anyone in the camp want to hurt him?

Was it one of Milo's men?

Lee pivoted to avoid the blow, but it still caught him in the side and had enough steam behind it to send a bolt of pain into his ribs. Lee managed to trap the arm against his side and held it tight. His attacker tugged back, attempting to free himself. Lee got low and sent a swift knee into the side of his attacker's thigh, crunching the common peroneal nerve and toppling his attacker almost immediately.

Lee went down with him, still holding his attacker's arm. He cocked his free hand back and was ready to deliver a hammer blow to the larynx and end the fight instantly when he took a breath and looked down, only to find a kid staring back up at him. Maybe a little more than a kid. But definitely less than a man.

Lee stopped himself.

The moment seemed to stretch awkwardly as he stared, shocked, at the eyes of his attacker and saw nothing but pure loathing. The only thought circling in Lee's head came tumbling out of his mouth: "What the fuck's wrong with you?"

There was shouting and Lee realized he was surrounded by a crowd that had poured in through the mouth of the medical trailer during the brief struggle. The shouting had a distinct sound to it that told him the crowd was not on his side.

A voice broke through the background noise. "Get off my son!"

Lee looked up in time to see a boot catch him in the shoulder and shove him backward. Lee didn't resist the force but rolled with it. He felt the cold steel floor across his back and then white fire from his stitches. He winced as he recovered and got his knees back under him.

More shouts: "Did you see what he did?"

"He's one of them!"

"He let those fuckers in!"

Are they talking about me?

Then Doc's voice, stressed and high-pitched above the others: "Would everyone get the fuck out of my trailer? Get the fuck out! *OUT!*"

Lee fought off the blazing pain in his back and focused. In front of him he could see Doc's back, his arms spread wide. They swooped rapidly back and forth as though the crowd that had gathered was a flock of birds that might be shooed away. Over the tops of Doc's shoulders, Lee caught the stares of several people and he didn't like what he saw.

Anger.

Mistrust.

Hatred.

The man that Lee had earlier identified as Kara's father stepped forward quickly and pulled the kid up off the ground. *Get off my son*, he'd yelled. Which meant that Lee's attacker was Kara's brother.

They were all family.

The crowd absorbed Kara's father and brother as they backpedaled, all eyes still on Lee while Doc raved at them to get out. Watching those people stare at him, Lee thought that he had never felt so abundantly alienated, so obviously on the outside. Did they truly blame him for what had happened? Was it just because he was a stranger to them? Or was there something else that he was missing?

Bus made his way through the gathered people like a ship's bow cutting through water. He did not look happy. The man was nearly a head taller than everyone else, and Lee could see his eyes glaring from underneath furrowed brows.

"What the hell is all this about?" he shouted.

Lee wasn't sure whether the question was directed at him or the hostile crowd. The big man now stood between Lee and the crowd, with both arms stretched out as though he were holding the two parties away from each other by the sheer force of his will.

Kara's father stepped out of the crowd but didn't try to get past Bus. He just pointed one finger at Lee and began shouting. "He's with Milo! He's gotta be! We heard about the breach in the fence! He did it! It had to be him!" Spittle flew from his mouth as he screamed, his cheeks and forehead becoming red with rage.

Lee could tell that Bus hadn't expected that. He stood there, looking taken aback.

Doc sounded like he was on the edge of panic. "I don't know what you're fucking talking about. The captain has been in the medical trailer all night."

Kara's father—Steve, wasn't it?—directed his ire at Doc. "How do you know he was here? You were in the Ryder building for almost an hour. He could have done it then."

Bus tried stepping in. "Steve, this is ridiculous..."

"Ridiculous?" Steve shouted. "Ridiculous that I don't want to trust the guy who just got here? Is it so crazy what I'm saying? Have we ever had a breach like that in our fences before? Someone cut that shit—Miller said so himself. And here we are, harboring strangers. So who do you think did it, Bus? One of us?"

Bus floundered for a moment. He could say that it was Milo's men who cut the fence, but Steve and his supporters obviously believed that Lee had allied himself with Milo. It was also clear that they were so incensed at this moment, nothing Bus could say would sway their opinion. Bus needed time to let the people calm down. And he needed

Lee to speak with them. If Lee could do that, he could convince them, just like he'd convinced Bus.

Forced to ride the fence, Bus nodded curtly. "Okay. Everybody out. Let me handle this."

"How are you going to handle it?" Steve demanded.

"Steve," Bus said with a quiet warning in his voice. "You know me. You know you can trust me. Now go. Let me handle this."

Steve seemed to consider the words as he stared at Lee with barely controlled anger. His fists, balled at his sides, his lips a thin gash across his face, tears welling up in his eyes. But eventually he nodded to Bus, and he turned away from them.

The hostile grumble of the crowd died to a low murmur as everyone followed Steve out of the trailer. Lee stood up, feeling weakness in the muscles along his spine, and then a brief chill washed over him that stung at the wounds on his back and then quieted. The two men faced each other a few feet apart, and Lee waited.

"Are you okay?" Bus spoke quietly and for the first time Lee sensed the complicated depth of the relationship between Bus and the people of Camp Ryder. The strong man, yes. The figurehead, yes. Their brave spokesman, yes. But he was not in control in a situation like this. When fear was the dominant emotion, he issued orders and people listened, because fearful people needed a leader. But when anger took over, the mob became more powerful, and the leader became just a mouthpiece.

Lee nodded slowly. "I'm assuming that was Kara's family."

"Yes." There was a long silence, in which Bus looked deep in mental calculations. After a moment, he looked to Doc. "How long until his stitches heal?"

Doc, flustered and sweating now, raked a finger through his natty hair. "Uh...six weeks until I take them out."

"How long until he's healed enough to go out?"

Doc looked at Lee, his jaw muscles bulging and a vein beginning to stand out under his left eye. "Probably a week before I could be sure the wounds won't get infected. But they won't be properly healed and they could tear open and renew the chance for infection."

Bus let a slow, deep breath hiss through his teeth. "Captain, is there any proof you can give me that you aren't with Milo's men?"

Lee's stomach dropped.

Was this for real? Were they all serious about this? An hour ago, he was their friend, and now they were accusing him of being a spy for Milo? It bordered on absurdity. But as absurd as he thought it was, he had no way to refute it. No way but to simply deny the charges. "No. I don't have any proof. Just my word."

"Okay. We'll figure something out." Then Bus turned. "Miller! Harper!"

The two men appeared suddenly out of the crowd, appearing red-faced and uncomfortable. They walked awkwardly into the medical trailer, flanking Bus. Miller on the right, Harper on the left.

Lee tensed. He eyeballed the two men, finding himself evaluating them as he would an enemy combatant. He did not want to harm these people, but if it came down to violence, he intended to be the one walking away. Harper looked mean but Lee was confident in his earlier assessment of the man. As hard-assed as Harper had become, he'd still led a cushy life prior to the collapse of society. Lee could probably overpower him easily. Miller posed a bit more of a problem. He seemed like he enjoyed a fight and had the look of someone who got into his fair share of them. While he might not have any formal training, experience was more important. Lee hedged his bets that Miller was a stand-up fighter. He would need to take his legs out.

Bus looked at Lee but spoke to his men. "Watch the captain while Doc tends to him." Bus swiped a quick hand across his brow. "I'm sorry, Captain. But I don't think you should leave the trailer for right now."

Lee's shoulders pinched up slightly. "Am I being arrested?"

His eyes traveled back and forth among Bus, Harper, and Miller. None of them had an answer for him, because it was the truth, but they didn't want to admit it. He was being arrested. He had come to Camp Ryder and promised them supplies and assistance, and rather than accept his help, they were holding him in a trailer against his will.

Looking the gift horse in the mouth.

Lee had the urge to tell them to go fuck themselves. He could make a break for it, still in possession of the GPS. He could continue his mission with another group, one less paranoid and less hostile. But the nagging thought occurred to him: *What if there's no one else?*

And what about Angela and Abby and Sam?

And what about the mission?

He had to focus on the mission.

In this surreal situation, the concept of the mission was, for once, a comfort. It grounded him and gave him a sense of the big picture. This was not personal, it was business, and his business was the completion of his mission. This was a community that he could render aid to, a community that eventually could not only provide stability in the region but a waypoint for him to base further operations out of. This was the first step.

But he had to earn their trust.

It would not be given.

The only alternative was to abandon them. If he abandoned them they would conclude that they had been right about him all along. Either their group of survivors would wither and die, or eventually Lee would have to deal with them again. And they would be much harder to convince the next time around.

If Camp Ryder was going to be an asset to him, it was now or never.

Lee very slowly raised his right hand. With his left, he pulled up the smiley-face T-shirt, exposing the small pocket pistol he'd stuck in his waistband. He watched them all stare at the pistol, even some of the people outside. The implication Lee made was obvious. A guilty man, someone spying for Milo, would have kept the weapon so he could later escape with it. Instead he was choosing to cooperate.

Lee nodded to Harper. "Go ahead."

Harper glanced up at Lee's face, his eyes sharp as arrowheads.

Lee thought that maybe Harper would get some sort of satisfaction from this, considering he had not been a fan of Lee's to begin with, but he did not appear to be enjoying himself. In fact, he looked even more miserable than usual.

"Miller," Harper spoke quietly. "Take the gun from Captain Harden, please."

Miller stepped forward cautiously. Lee could see that Miller was at odds with himself. Part of him wanted to believe in his friends and family, that Lee was the enemy, that the untrustworthy outsider had been the cause of all this great misfortune. The other part of him knew that this was wrong, that Lee was there to help.

A third part was just scared that Lee was going to snap his neck if he got too close.

But Lee remained as frozen as though he were sculpted of marble. Miller stepped forward slowly, his eyes meeting Lee's, and in them Lee could see a silent apology. He plucked the gun from Lee's midsection.

Someone from the crowd yelled, "What about that thing in his pocket?"

And another: "Yeah, take it away from him!"

Miller and Lee both glanced down at his right front pocket and the handheld GPS unit bulging awkwardly from the athletic shorts.

Miller didn't move for it. He looked at Lee as though asking permission.

Lee shook his head slightly and said, "Don't."

The younger man nodded and retreated.

There was a disapproving grumble from the crowd and Bus spun on them. "That is his personal property and we won't be taking it from him. He's been detained based on your accusations but we're not treating him like some common criminal."

The gathering remained silent this time.

Bus turned to Doc. "See to him, Doc." Then to Lee, "I am truly sorry, Captain. But the situation being what it is, you may have very limited time to recover. I think you may have to produce what you promised sooner than either of us expected."

FOUR

COMMITTEE

DOC GAVE BOTH HARPER and Miller a grim look and then stepped to where Lee still stood, mulling things over. "Come on. Have a seat. Let me make sure none of your stitches popped."

Lee allowed himself to be led back to the cot. Doc stripped the bloodstained plastic sheet off and threw it to the side with a snap of the wrist. Then Lee sat down on the edge of the cot, elbows to his knees, feeling the skin stretching and tugging against the stitches. It was an odd sensation but not quite painful.

Hunched on his cot, with his chin resting on his folded hands, he looked at the open entrance of the medical trailer. Outside, the world was painted in the slate-gray tones of predawn. Gray like a corpse. Like putrefied meat. And in that dead half-light, Lee could see the last of the crowd scattering to tend to their morning duties.

The cot shifted behind him as Doc settled his weight on it and rolled up the back of Lee's shirt. He pulled at the old bandages. Parts of them had stuck to the wound and stung viciously when he tugged them off.

"Not too bad," Doc murmured. He continued replacing the dressings.

Lee glanced up and found Harper staring at him. He seemed to be considering Lee in great mental detail. Lee waited for a long moment in silence, but Harper's eyes never left him.

Lee decided to break the silence. "What do you think, Harper?"

The man's jaw clenched, tensing up muscles high on his balding temples. "Doesn't matter what I think."

"It does," Lee stated. "It matters to Bus."

"I don't think Bus blames you," Harper deflected.

Lee smiled without humor. "But what do *you* think?"

"I think you're in the wrong place at the wrong time."

Lee laughed suddenly and earnestly. "Yeah. You got that one right."

Everything he'd done for the past four days had seemed to be an uphill battle. Nothing on the outside of his bunker had been what he'd thought it would be. At every turn it seemed that something went wrong and it began to instill in him a deep sense of impending doom, as though no matter what his future decisions were, he would never be able to avert disaster. It seemed Murphy had a hard-on for him.

Footsteps crunched on the fine gravel outside. Four faces appeared from around the corner, three that Lee recognized and one that he did not.

"Lee." Angela quickened her step, ushering Sam and Abby into the medical trailer. Behind them, the guy that Lee didn't know stood with his hand on the butt of what looked like a small-caliber pistol. "What happened? What's going on?"

Lee didn't answer her question immediately. He caught the eye of the man who had brought Angela and the kids into the trailer. This one was not like Harper and Miller. This one had the look of distrust and resentment that he'd seen in Kara's family.

Lee gestured to the woman and two kids. "Really?"

The man with the pistol shrugged coldly and turned out of sight. It was becoming clear to Lee that, like any other group, Camp Ryder had its divisions. Different people formed different alliances. Some groups sided with Lee and others sided with Kara's family. Lee could only hope that the majority of the camp still wanted to work with him instead of crucify him.

Sam stood at the edge of the cot now, his eyes wandering over the room, his jaw set, and his arms crossed. "They think we're the bad guys. Because of what happened. They think we caused it."

"What?" Angela's mouth hung open. "No..."

"Yes," Lee confirmed. "From what I can tell, some of the people in camp think I'm working for Milo. And I guess they're just lumping you and the kids in with me."

Angela looked lost. "Who's Milo?"

Behind Lee, Doc chuckled bitterly and patted his shoulder. "You're good, Captain." The young man with the shaggy hair pushed his scuffed-up glasses farther onto his nose and began to gather up the discarded dressings along with the plastic sheet soaked in Kara's blood. Then he tossed the whole bloodstained mess into a fifty-five-gallon drum in the corner. Lee noticed the blackened edges along the mouth of the drum. They regularly burned the contents.

What was left of a young girl was now just a biohazard.

Doc fingered his hair behind his ears and stood in front of the small group: Lee, Angela, and the two lost-looking kids. His mouth was open as though he wanted to say something but was waiting for the right words to land on his tongue. He eventually snapped his mouth shut and turned quickly away from them, mumbling as he left the trailer, "I'll see about some breakfast."

Lee turned his attention to Angela and the kids. Sam was sitting dejectedly on the opposite side of the cot, slouched with his hands working between his knees and scowling at the wall. Abby was standing with Angela, her little arm wrapped tightly around her mother's leg. Her eyes looked distant and indifferent.

Lee reached out and tentatively touched her arm. "How you doin', sweetie?"

For a moment so brief, Lee thought he might have imagined it, Abby's eyes became ice-cold and focused points, like icicle tips. Then they melted into that same absent look.

"Okay." She nodded and looked up at her mother. "What are we doing, Mom?"

Angela brushed her daughter's hair and guided her to the cot in between Lee and Sam. "We're just going to sit with Captain Harden for a little bit."

"We're in trouble." The words seemed odd coming from Abby's mouth because her face showed so little concern. "The people here don't like us."

Lee cast a glance toward Harper, who avoided the eye contact now. "No, they're just confused about some stuff. Once they understand the situation, then everything will be okay."

She shrugged. "Okay."

Lee leaned back and squeezed Sam's shoulder. "What about you, buddy?"

Sam turned toward him, angry. "Why don't we just go?"

"Because they need our help," Lee stated simply. "And because this is my job."

"You come here to help them and they treat you like a prisoner. And what about us? What if we don't want to be here? There must be somewhere else we can go."

Lee shook his head slowly. "I don't know if there is anywhere else right now or how hard it will be to get there. We all nearly died out there. You should remember that."

Sam huffed and turned back to staring at the wall.

Angela took a seat on the cot with Lee, and Abby slid into her lap, looking tired. Lee could feel Angela next to him, a warm presence. If he had known Angela better, he would have found comfort in her nearness. As it was, he found it awkward. She seemed to place some importance on him that he didn't understand. Perhaps it was the trauma of the last few days or the shock of losing her husband. Did she think that she was going to hold onto Lee, just because he rescued them from the rooftop? Like he was some knight in shining armor, and she, the damsel in distress?

There's nothing personal here, he thought. *For Christ's sake, I shot your fucking husband.*

She just wasn't thinking clearly right now. She hadn't had time to decompress.

Maybe it was Lee's problem. Maybe he'd been alone so long he didn't know how to operate any other way. On the other hand, maybe he just understood that a relationship based on trying to survive together for four days wasn't a relationship at all.

When he turned to take a furtive glance at her, he found Angela looking at him. Her eyes were very sad, and it seemed as though she pitied him. He felt a bit of relief along with the indignation at being pitied. *She knows there's no relationship. She just thinks she can help me. She's that type of person—always looking for someone to help.*

"You're not bothered by any of this?" she asked him.

Lee met her gaze. "What makes you think I'm not?"

"You never seem bothered." She straightened out Abby's dirty shirt as the younger girl began falling asleep in her mother's arms. "Sure, you get a little intense every now and then. But it's like it all just doesn't matter to you. Like you know something we don't know."

Lee smiled ruefully. "No. I'm finding out I know very little."

"Then what? Are you not scared?"

"No." Lee leaned back a bit to take the stress off his stitches. "That's not it, I assure you."

"Hmm." She looked thoughtful. "I thought you were too well-trained to get scared."

He had to chuckle. "You know, they did a study one time. They strapped heart monitors to two Special Forces soldiers about to make a combat jump. One soldier was brand-new, fresh out of training. The other soldier was a six-year veteran. So, as they're approaching the drop point, the younger soldier is pacing back and forth, checking and rechecking his gear. He's nervous. He can't stand still. All the while, the veteran is just sitting there with his eyes closed like he's sleeping. Like nothing is bothering him.

"After the mission, they found that there was virtually no difference in the heart rates between the veteran and the rookie. They were both scared. The only difference was that the veteran was used to being scared, so it didn't show as much."

Lee looked at her again. "So, yes. I get scared, whether it shows or not."

The six people sat in a tense but thoughtful silence. Harper and Miller guiltily watched the four outsiders as they sat quietly and contemplated their strange situation. Eventually Doc returned with four small bowls of oatmeal. He explained with a shy smile, "It's all that was left in the pot."

Due to sparing supplies, whoever did the cooking had mixed more water and less oatmeal, creating a thin gruel with a little salt to give it some flavor. Despite the odd taste, the group still ate hungrily. Only after Lee finished his small bowl did he realize how hungry he was and remembered losing last night's dinner during the attack.

Rice and beans. Thin oatmeal.

No meat to speak of.

These people are starving, Lee thought.

Supplies were low and nearly unattainable with Milo's gang running amok outside the gates. The hordes of infected kept hunting from being practical. Lee thought about the possibility of trapping, but to feed the entire community, snares and traps would have to be set for something large, like a deer or wild boar. This was not impossible, but trapped animals created a lot of noise and Lee thought that even if a trap were sprung successfully, the infected would get to the animal first and rip it to pieces. Even if they left anything behind, it would be tainted.

His thoughts wandered from hunting and trapping to water. The community seemed to have enough to get by. Lee wondered about a stream in the area or possibly a large rain cistern, either preexisting or built by the community. Any streams in the area were likely contaminated with industrial pollutants, but the heavy summer rains would come soon, riding the tails of whatever hurricanes were spinning up the coastline and rolling inland to central North Carolina. That would probably wash most of the pollutants away and make the streams slightly more potable, at least after a good boiling.

In the back of Lee's mind he knew he forced himself to think of these things. The business of survival kept the mind occupied while the fear of failure swam like unseen sharks below a rickety lifeboat. Lee was determined to just keep rowing. It was impossible to be lost at sea forever. Eventually you had to make landfall.

But the fear escorted him wherever he went.

It waited for him to give up and give in, and then it would consume him completely.

An hour passed. The light outside the trailer went from that dull slate-gray to the bright and lively glow of the morning sun. Lee noted that the temperature was staying fairly mild for late July, and he guessed it would be a mid-eighties day.

Harper and Miller exchanged quiet small talk. Angela and Abby curled up on another cot. Abby fell asleep quickly, but Angela lay with her eyes open, staring vacantly at nothing. Sam got up and paced irritably.

People passed by and looked in with furtive glances. Lee watched them from the edge of his cot and saw a range of emotions. Some were angry. Most were curious. All were suspicious. When they walked by alone, they quickly looked away. When they walked by in pairs, they whispered among themselves. In groups, they stared brazenly and spoke loudly.

"Is he a spy?"

"He killed Kara."

"He let the infected in."

"Why would he do that?"

"He promised us supplies."

"That's bullshit."

Lee began to notice the trickle of passersby

thickening, everyone going in the same direction: toward the square. The steady bustle of people conducting their everyday business began to meld and grow into the semi-excited rumble of a crowd and Lee could not shake the image of an old Western town where all the ladies in their pretty dresses showed up to watch a guilty man hang.

It wasn't long before Bus appeared.

He nodded to Harper and Miller, who both stood up languidly and stretched. Then he walked to Lee and stood before him with his hands clasped neutrally in front of him. He looked at Angela and her daughter, and then Sam, who now looked defiantly back at him. Then his gaze found Lee again.

"You need to understand something," he said. "I don't run the show around here. These people, they don't know what the fuck they're doing. But they like to think they do. So when the shit hits the fan, they all look to me to tell them what to do. I'm a security blanket. They think, *If all else fails, Bus will know what to do.*"

He looked bitter. "But I don't control them. And right now there are fifty people outside who are making up their minds about you. Kara's family is convinced that you're with Milo and you sabotaged our fence—"

"That's ridiculous!" Angela hissed.

Bus looked at her. "I know it is. I'm not saying that's what I believe; I'm saying that's what is being said. A lot of people are buying it because … well, it's easy to blame the new people. I just wanted to let you know what the sentiment was like out there."

"Is this a trial?" Lee said quietly.

Bus shook his head. "Just a meeting. Not everybody has had a chance to speak with you. Most of the people in camp are forming their opinions from word of mouth. I figured having you stand up in front of everyone would be best—that way they could form their own opinions."

Lee nodded. "And what should I do?"

"Answer their questions. Hopefully they believe you."

"No one's going to believe me, Bus." Lee lowered his voice. "Not unless someone inside Camp Ryder sides with me."

"Captain, some of the people already believe you. Most of them *want* to believe you. You give them something to hope for." Bus scratched his neck. "But I can't take sides right now."

"Why not?" Sam suddenly appeared by Lee's side. "You said you believe us!"

"It's complicated," Bus said flatly. "This place isn't as unified as it may seem. There are people here who don't agree with how I'm doing things, and they will use my siding with you as a sign of disloyalty and turn the camp against me." He sighed. "I don't like playing political games. I've never been good at them. But I also can't just stand by and watch someone destroy us from the inside. I'm sorry, but I have to stay neutral."

"Bus." Lee stood up from his cot. "Just promise me that we can leave unharmed, if it comes to that."

Bus thought for a little longer than Lee was comfortable with. He eventually nodded, but despite the gesture, Lee didn't think it was a promise that Bus was going to be able to keep.

The people gathered in moody silence. They stared with stony faces as Lee approached, flanked by Harper and Miller and led by Bus. Behind them, Angela, Abby, and Sam followed with Doc and Jenny.

Lee scanned the crowd and found Kara's father and brother conspicuously absent.

Standing before them, Lee felt silly in the hand-me-down garb. It was difficult enough to convince people of his mission when he was wearing his full battle rattle, let alone when he was clad in only a smiley-face T-shirt and some athletic shorts. It did not add to his credibility.

Bus stood between Lee and the people of Camp Ryder and shifted his weight to one leg. "Alright, folks. Regardless of what you believe, let's try to keep this orderly and decent. This is Captain Lee Harden, and the woman there is Angela and the two kids are Abby and Sam, if you haven't met them already. I know there's been a lot said. Rumors tend to fly pretty quickly around here, but we need to be reasonable. This man has offered us something, and we need to figure out whether we're going to trust him and accept it or whether we want him to leave our camp."

Bus took a moment to moisten his lips and scratch his beard. "Now that everyone knows what we're doing here, y'all can ask what you need to ask, but let's do it one at a time."

Almost immediately a hand shot up and Lee thought, *Oh boy...here we go.*

"Yeah." Bus pointed to the raised hand. "Go ahead, Keith."

Keith was an older man, possibly in his mid-sixties, with just bare wisps of gray hair clinging to his head, a craggy face, and thin features. He wore a pair of canvas overalls that looked like they'd seen better days even before the FURY pandemic.

Acknowledged, Keith lowered his hand and stuck it in the pocket of his overalls. He gave Lee a scrutinizing stare, up and down, as though he were learning everything he needed to know about Lee simply by his body language.

"I guess I'll go ahead and say it, since most of us are thinking it," Keith said. "You don't strike me as some secret government super-soldier sent to save us all. You look...pretty normal. S'pose what I'm getting at here is, if you're such hot shit, where're your guns? Where's your uniform? Where're all these supplies you're supposed to have?"

There was a murmur of assent from the crowd.

Everyone wanted an answer to that one.

"That's a fair question," Lee said, trying to take it in stride. "I'll be completely honest with you. I'm no super-soldier, but I am good at what I do. If you want to know where my equipment is, I will tell you. It's in a bunker twenty feet below the ashes of my house, which Milo burned to the ground." He quickly added, "I have access to more supplies, I just—"

The crowd grumbled disapprovingly.

A new speaker stepped forward, this one a woman with pale skin and dark black hair pulled back into a ponytail. "But you haven't given us any proof. Where are these supplies you keep talking about?"

"I've been here for a day," Lee said, trying not to show irritation. "I haven't exactly had a chance to make the trip just yet, but when I do—"

"Why didn't you just take them with you?" It was a male voice. "Why didn't you bring your supplies here?"

Lee began to feel uncomfortable. He didn't like being put on the spot, and despite what Bus said, it didn't seem like many people believed him. "Part of my job is to help survivors. Angela and her daughter were trapped. When I set out to help them, I didn't bring all the equipment with me because it would have weighed me down. When I returned home, I found my house burned to the ground. I couldn't go get a refill on supplies because I needed to find a safe place for them first."

Angela spoke up this time, hesitantly. "It's true. Abby and I, we were trapped on the roof of our house. Captain Harden saved us, but when he was doing that, some men took his truck and they found his house. We hiked back, but Captain Harden's house had been burned to the ground." She paused for a moment and nodded at Lee. "I didn't believe it at first either. But Captain Harden knows what he's doing. If you'd seen him fight, you'd believe him too."

"How do we know you're not with Milo?" someone shouted.

The crowd got louder, everyone clamoring together.

"What if you're spies?"

"Is this all just a trick?"

Lee took a deep breath while Bus cast an icy stare out into the crowd but remained silent. Eventually the gathering quieted, and another person said, "Did you sabotage our fence?" This time the question was met with more of a murmur than a shout.

"No," Lee said simply, because he knew any other, more complicated answer would be seen as dodging the question.

"Can you prove you're not with Milo?"

Lee was about to answer when Miller stepped forward. "Can I say something?"

Bus nodded and the people looked at Miller expectantly.

Miller turned to address them. "I don't know where this rumor started about the captain being with Milo. I don't know whether the captain has all the things he says he has. But I was there when he and Angela and those two little kids were runnin' from Milo. I know I saw Milo's guys tryin' their damnedest to shoot the captain. I know I saw the captain pull himself through rusty nails just to get away. So if you were to ask me whether he's with Milo or not, I would hafta say no."

There was a moment of silence as everyone seemed to mull this over.

Lee watched the faces as they exchanged looks and murmured among themselves.

"I guess what everyone's concerned with," a new voice said, "is whether we can trust this so-called captain to follow through with what he has promised."

The new speaker was a tall man, this one the polar opposite of Keith, who looked like he'd been blue-collar all his life. This was a businessman, someone who fancied himself a politician. He had the bearing of someone who came from money and the soft, pleasant face of someone who had seen less of the hard times than those around him.

Lee immediately disliked him.

The speaker stepped out and then turned so that the crowd was to his left and Lee was to his right. His stance told Lee this was practiced stage presence. A glance over to Bus confirmed that the big man also did not buy into the speaker's bullshit. However, to Lee's dismay, the crowd seemed to find him enchanting.

A manipulator.

A politician.

Perhaps this was the person Bus had suggested was attempting to wrest control of the camp from him. Lee had to agree with Bus's assessment that the camp would not be in good hands if that were to happen.

To Lee, the man said, "You do recall your promise? In exchange for us taking in you and your group and providing you with what we could, you claimed to be able to produce food, water, weapons, and medical supplies." The man smiled disarmingly. "I know that Bus had the best of intentions when he let you into our camp. However, I think I speak for everyone here when I say that, in light of the security breach, we're going to need something more than just your word if you want to continue to stay here."

There was a chorus of "yeah," "that's right," and "you tell 'em!"

"Excuse me! Hold on!" Doc flapped his arms. "No. No. If you're trying to say that Captain Harden should leave to get supplies, that is out of the question for at least another week. The man has muscle damage and is probably in a lot of pain—in fact, I'm surprised he's holding it together as we speak. Plus, there's still the chance for gangrene to set in and I need to monitor—"

"I can leave tomorrow," Lee said.

Doc looked at him. "No, you can't. You won't be nearly healed enough to—"

Lee crossed his arms. "I fought today. I can fight tomorrow. If that's what it takes to get this done, then that's what I'll do."

Even the politician's mouth closed as he processed this. No one had expected him to answer up so readily. The truth was, Lee despised the idea. The cuts on his back still burned and stung with every movement. Lee had also hoped to enjoy the relative safety of Camp Ryder for longer than a day before being thrust back out into the dangerous wilderness that America had become. There was safety in numbers here, and there was water. The thought of leaving that made Lee's stomach flip-flop, the same as it flip-flopped when he hadn't received that check-in from Colonel Reid so many long days ago.

No amount of training or experience made death any less frightening.

You just learned to work around it.

So he found himself once again stuffing that

feeling down. Forcing himself to do the job that needed to be done, no matter how uncomfortable, no matter how dangerous. That was Lee's lot in life, and while sometimes it nearly overwhelmed him, he would always make his peace with it. It was built into his DNA, just as much as the color of his eyes or the shape of his face.

Bus spoke up. "You can't go out alone. Someone will have to go with you."

The politician cleared his throat. "I'm sorry if I am being too blunt, but I don't think anyone here trusts the captain enough to accompany him when we don't even know where his loyalties lie. We've just lost one of our own under suspicious circumstances, and while we can't prove Mr. Harden had anything to do with it, we can't disprove it either."

A woman in the front of the crowd put her hands on her hips. "If I remember correctly, Jerry, Captain Harden was the one who tried to help Kara, not you. I also recall that we were all facing the opposite direction until Captain Harden had the brains to look behind us. Seems like more people would have been hurt if he hadn't been there. Frankly, I think we should thank him."

Jerry the Politician knew not to argue a good point, so he raised his hands in mock defeat and tried a different tactic. "Marie, if you trust him so much, perhaps you should volunteer to go with him."

Marie's eyes became sharp daggers. "I have responsibilities here, Jerry. Unlike yourself."

Jerry ignored the jab and turned to the crowd with a smile. "Does anyone else trust the captain so much that they would like to accompany him on this trip? Anyone?"

Under the ear-ringing silence, Lee regarded Bus, who stood like an angered god with his brawny arms crossed over his chest and a deep redness taking over his olive complexion. It was obvious there was no love lost between Bus and Jerry.

The silence stretched on.

"I'm goin' with him."

Lee was surprised to find Harper stepping forward, staring at Jerry with much the same look as Bus. Harper was loyal to Bus, and an enemy of your friend is your enemy too. Lee could tell that Harper volunteered less because he believed in Lee and more out of spite toward Jerry.

Whatever the reason, Lee appreciated it.

It didn't take long for Miller to follow. "I'm going too."

Jerry looked first shocked, and then sour.

Lee nodded at Harper and Miller and felt gratitude, regardless of their motives.

Bus smiled fiercely at Jerry. "I guess it's settled, then. Harper and Miller will accompany Captain Harden. They will leave tomorrow."

FIVE

PREPARATIONS

SAFELY INSIDE THE PRIVACY of Bus's office, Harper, Miller, and Bus himself stood on one side of the room while Lee stood on the other, studying the map pinned to the corkboard on the far wall. He had already consulted his GPS device in private and now circled a large area approximately thirty miles east-southeast of the red pushpin labeled CAMP RYDER. The spiderweb of roads thinned as they drew closer to the spot Lee indicated and eventually faded to a simple blank area on the map.

"That's where we need to be," Lee stated, tapping the center of that blank spot.

He turned to find three very grim looks regarding the map.

Thirty miles had been a quick trip two months ago.

Now it was almost suicidal.

"Can it be done safely?" Bus asked.

Lee shook his head. "I can't give you a guarantee, Bus. You know that." He drew a finger along the thick line of Highway 210 coming out of Angier. Their destination was in the center of a triangle formed by I-40, I-95, and I-795. "You guys will know better than I do. How are the road conditions? Is it feasible to take the highways, or should we take the back roads?"

Harper moved both hands up and down, indicating a similar weight. "If you take the highways you hit roadblocks. You take back roads, you're more likely to run into infected."

Miller looked like he was remembering something distasteful. "I wouldn't touch the interstates, even if I was driving a tank."

"A tank would be nice, though." Harper smiled wistfully. "Got any of those up your sleeve, Captain?"

Lee looked back to the map with a snort. "Wouldn't that make life easier?"

Bus stepped forward and indicated the same line of Highway 210. "I came through this way from the other side of I-40. It was pretty clear, as I remember it. Of course, that was a few weeks ago."

Lee pointed to a small town nestled on the northwestern side of I-95. If they took the highway, they would be passing through—or at least very close to—that town. "Any information on Smithfield?" While Lee had a general rule about staying away from population centers, a small burg like Smithfield might well be a ghost town. In a situation where more time on the road meant more danger, sometimes it was better to take the more direct route.

"Last I saw of Smithfield was a big column of smoke," Bus said. "You could see it from the road we were on."

"Something bad happened there," Miller stated with a chilly sort of certainty.

Lee looked at the younger man. "What do you mean?"

Miller shrugged it off. "I heard there was an explosion. Or a fire or something. Just rumors."

Smithfield interested Lee only because it was likely to have supplies that could be pilfered. On the off chance that it wasn't a ghost town, it might have pockets of survivors who Lee could make contact with. While he didn't want to bring Harper and Miller into any unnecessary danger, he also had to keep in mind his overall mission, and if he thought he could safely reach another group, he meant to do just that.

"Alright." Lee nodded. "If there's no objection, we'll make it a straight shot down 210. We'll evaluate once we get to Smithfield if we think it's safe to go through or better to go around." He traced a smaller line that branched southeast away from Smithfield. "Once we get on this farm road we can take it almost all the way to our destination. I'll leave the finer points of navigation for when we get there."

"If all goes well," Harper said quietly. "Which is a big 'if.'"

"That brings me to the next bit." Bus sat on the edge of his desk. "Jerry can try to act like he runs things around here, but I'll be damned if he's going to control the weapons and supplies. That's my domain and I aim to get you boys everything you need." Bus looked each of them in the eye. "I'll rustle up the best weapons we got and as much ammunition as I can get away with."

Lee put a hand on his shoulder. "Thank you,

but don't leave yourself undefended. We will at least be mobile, so if the situation arises, we can always run. Plus, the more supplies we take with us from here, the less we can carry from my cache."

Miller broke in. "That reminds me, whose truck we takin'?"

"Biggest one you got," Lee said.

Bus scratched at his beard. "Keith Jenkins has a big Dodge Ram. Probably the most cargo space you're going to get. Nice off-road tires too, if you need to take it around some traffic jams."

"How will Mr. Jenkins feel about us using his truck?"

Bus pointed to the door. "You'll have to go ask him."

Keith Jenkins turned out to be the same Keith in the worn-out canvas overalls who had eagerly gotten the ball rolling on Lee's inquisition. When Lee first realized this, he instantly began thinking of who else he could persuade to loan him a truck for his expedition. However, once in private, Keith seemed far more amenable than when Lee had first met him.

Now, Keith was chewing on a straw and gazing with a sort of forlorn love at his Dodge Ram 2500, as though he might never see it again. Lee and Harper had gone to speak with him while Miller assisted Bus in rounding up what other supplies could be spared for the trip. The old man leaned against his old dually with a hand on the bed that drew back and forth, as though caressing the flank of a well-loved draft horse.

"So..." Harper ventured.

"Shit." Keith Jenkins spat. "It's kinda tough, fellas. Me and this truck, we been through a lot. You see that big ol' dent on the front fender? That shit came from two infected I knocked the Jesus out of 'fore I got here. Yeah...we been through a lot."

"Mr. Jenkins"—Lee eyed the beast of a machine—"I can't make you any promises, but we only got sixty miles to drive in this thing and I will do everything in my power to return it to you, no worse for wear."

Keith's savvy old eyes scanned along the truck, then poked at Lee. "You know, I was in 'Nam, '67 to '69."

"Tough years," Lee said, wondering where this might be leading.

"Sometimes when things go down, I start looking around for my old rifle, but alls I got is a shitty-ass deer rifle. Couple 30-06 cartridges to load it." Keith crossed his arms and lowered his head. "You want my truck, I'll loan it to you. But I get first dibs on one of them rifles you bring back. You got M16s?"

"I got M4s," Lee admitted. "A carbine version of the M16."

Keith nodded. "That's good. Yeah. I'll take one of those." He sniffed. "You promise me first pick on one of those puppies, you can take my truck and do whatever the fuck you want with it."

Lee and Harper smiled and were about to extend Keith a hand when he cut them off.

"Just one more thing," he said. "Tank's almost

empty. Doubt you'll get to your destination and back, especially the way this thing guzzles gas. You wanna use it, you're welcome to it, but you're gonna hafta come up with the fuel on your own."

Lee's smile became reluctant, but Harper's faded completely.

Harper put a hand to Lee's shoulder and turned him so they were both facing away from Keith. "That's a tall order," he mumbled quietly.

"Can't we just siphon some from other people's cars?" Lee answered in turn.

"Yeah, we can. But there're only a few other vehicles here. Most everyone came in on foot, and the people with cars were almost empty by the time they found us." Harper sighed. "Gas got pretty hard to come by at the end there. The stations are all tapped. We can siphon, but we're going to have to go outside the wire to get enough to fill the tank on that thing."

Lee swore quietly under his breath. "Well, we don't have much of a choice, do we?"

Harper looked uncomfortable. "Not really."

"Fine." Lee turned back toward Keith and extended his hand. "One rifle of your choosing, and we provide the gas. You got a deal."

Keith shook Lee's hand vigorously, with a big smile plastered across his weathered old face.

Lee and Harper eventually decided that filling the Ram's monstrous thirty-five-gallon tank was being overly optimistic. Working by the same calculations as he had when he'd appropriated the Petersons' truck, he figured on the thirty-five-gallon tank getting them approximately 350 miles, if it was full. For their needs, they settled on rounding up to forty miles both ways, with a forty-mile buffer...just in case.

This left them at 120 miles, or approximately a third of a tank.

Which still meant they had to come up with at least twelve gallons.

Coming up with a few five-gallon gas cans was the easy part. Almost everyone who had come to Camp Ryder in a vehicle had packed a few extra cans of gas and had since used them up. They now sat around, as useless as their fuel-less cars. However, Harper felt that given the edgy climate of the camp, begging and borrowing from others would prove to be troublesome. As luck would have it, he knew of a supply shed around the back of the Ryder building. When the survivors had first made camp there, Harper had been tasked with looting everything inside the compound for useful supplies, and he recalled the shed having a few empty gas cans.

While Harper went to retrieve them, Bus met Lee at the rear of Harper's old Nissan Frontier, which they planned to use for their gasoline-finding mission. Lee greeted the big man with a reserved smile and leaned against the side of the pickup's bed. Bus carried with him an olive-green duffel, much like the stuff sack Lee had been issued in the army. Hopefully it contained something worth smiling about. "Turned up anything good?"

Bus pulled the tailgate down and set the duffel on it. The bag made a heavy clank as it hit the rusty bed. "Well, it's not an arsenal, but it'll get the job done."

Lee peered into the truck bed as Bus opened the duffel and pulled out a Mossberg 500 shotgun, a Savage Axis in .308, a black revolver, and a small black pistol. Judging by the tiny bores of both handguns, Lee guessed they were both .22-caliber.

The Mossberg was a no-frills ass-beater, designed to put rounds downrange and not much else. The tube held five rounds of 12-gauge ammunition, of which Bus had managed to scrape up ten rounds of buckshot.

The Savage Axis was a reasonably accurate rifle chambered for an excellent man-killing round. The .308-caliber round was rated to take down any animal in North America, and that included humans. Bus had managed to score thirteen cartridges of .308 in mix-and-match brands. Most of them were full metal jacket, but a few had little red ballistic tips. The FMJs were pretty standard issue, but the ballistic tips were designed to expand on impact, increasing trauma to the target.

The revolver held eight .22 rounds, and the small pistol held ten. For the ubiquitous .22-caliber, Bus had been able to gather fifty rounds. While the .22 wasn't a showstopper in terms of power, the cartridge was small enough that anyone could carry a massive amount of ammunition on them without truly weighing themselves down. In reality, while the round wouldn't stop anything bigger than a squirrel past a hundred yards, in close quarters it was known to have just enough power to get inside the body cavity but not quite enough to get out, causing the projectile to ricochet around a bit and rearrange a few organs. The .22-caliber projectile was the same size projectile as in the 5.56-mm cartridge Lee used in his M4, just with much less *oomph* behind it.

Bus slung the empty duffel over his shoulder. "Keep in mind, that's what I was able to scrounge up, so don't waste it all today when you guys go out to get your gas. Avoid a fight if you can."

Lee smiled. "Goes against my nature, but okay."

Harper came walking up lugging two red five-gallon fuel cans. He set them on the edge of the pickup's bed and slid them in. He looked at the four firearms in front of him. "You choose your weapons already, Captain?"

Lee gestured politely. "You first."

"Okay." Harper rubbed the back of his neck. "I'll take the shotty and the pistol. You take the rifle and the revolver."

"Sounds good," Lee agreed.

Bus had turned and was now looking out beyond the perimeter fence. There was about thirty yards of overgrown weeds that built up into old-growth forest with a wide dirt road meandering through it toward the highway. "Where are you guys gonna look for gas?"

"Well." Harper sighed. "We usually hit up all the abandoned cars in Timber Creek for gas, but I don't think it would be wise to go back there so soon. Place was probably about tapped, anyway."

"Gotta be some big wrecks and leftover traffic

jams from when everyone was trying to get the hell out," Lee observed. "Probably would be easy pickings along a main highway."

"Highway 55 is close," Harper offered. "I remember there being a nasty wreck up closer to town. Of course, no tellin' how much gas is left in those cars—I'm sure we're not the first to think of draining them."

"It's a start." Bus looked nervous. "How long do you guys think you'll be?"

Lee didn't like being pinned down to a time frame, but he knew how nerve-racking it was for someone to be in the position of waiting an undetermined amount of time in a possibly life-threatening situation. Lee had worked on both sides of that coin and had come to the conclusion that it was simply a shitty coin.

Still, Lee felt obligated. "Ideally, a few hours. I'd say...four o'clock, latest?"

Harper seemed to agree with a bob of his head. His hairless scalp was beginning to bead with sweat and glistened as he moved. It wasn't until Lee noticed the sweat that he realized he'd begun to sweat himself. The air was a comfortable temperature if you could find shade, but the sun was hot.

Bus plucked his own shirt away from his sweating skin. "You and Harper and Miller, right?"

Lee shook his head. "Just me and Harper for the gas. Miller will join up with us for the trip to the bunker."

"Okay. Good luck, then." Bus nodded and was about to turn, but he seemed to remember something he had left in the bottom of the duffel bag. He plunged his hand in and brought out a pair of old army fatigue pants and offered them to Lee. "I got these for you. Figured you should have some real pants, rather than just running shorts."

Lee felt truly grateful, as he'd felt ridiculous in the shorts. He accepted them with more excitement than he'd felt about a pair of pants in quite a while. "Damn, Bus. You made my day."

"Well, it wasn't really up to me." Bus pointed to Lee's bare legs. "I was receiving complaints."

Harper snickered quietly and Lee pulled the pants on with a grin. They were too large and too long but Lee didn't hesitate to make do. He rolled up the pant legs so they weren't dragging on the ground and then pulled the drawstring from his running shorts and threaded it through the belt loops on the fatigues.

Presto, a field-expedient belt.

"Thanks again, Bus." Lee slapped the big man firmly on the shoulder.

"Don't mention it." He pointed to both of them. "You guys be careful."

SIX

―――――

TWELVE GALLONS

THE WIDE DIRT ROAD leading away from Camp Ryder emptied out onto two-lane blacktop. Lee cranked the passenger-side window down to allow some airflow in the stifling car and to set the muzzle of the .308-bolt gun against the side-view mirror for quick access. The warm wind gusted through his open window as Harper drove at a steady pace out toward Highway 55.

Harper hadn't said much since leaving camp. He nervously chewed on the inside of his lip, steered with his left hand, and kept his right hand on the shotgun that lay between him and Lee. His squinted eyes scanned the roadway, back and forth, then checked his mirrors for anything coming up behind them.

Lee kept his eyes on the woods and pastures that framed the roadway. A few houses, but mostly they were still on back roads. He looked for anything out of the ordinary, even kept his nose in the wind and his ears perked for the telltale howl of the infected. The signs of devastation were less evident here. There were no burned-out apartment complexes or looted businesses to disturb the picture of life as usual. For brief moments Lee felt normal, but this sensation was fleeting, gone as soon as he tried to grasp it.

His new reality was survival. It was looking over your shoulder at all times. It was waking up in the middle of the night with your heart pounding. It was tensing at a rustle in the grass or the snap of a twig. It was the dull throb of fear that underscored every waking minute. But underneath all of that was something clearer and sharper that kept Lee focused.

He felt justified.

Complete.

Purposeful.

Like he was born for this fight.

The Nissan's brakes squealed a bit and the vehicle slowed. Before them stood a four-way intersection. Here, the trees stood farther back from the roadway. The stop sign facing them was canted to the right and bent at the base, as though someone had run it over. A signal light that had once flashed red swung dormant from the power lines that crossed the intersection. From a telephone pole, someone had nailed a poster board that had crinkled and weathered in the elements. Though they were faded, Lee could still read the words written boldly in black paint.

THIS IS GOD'S JUDGMENT

Harper looked both ways at the intersection. "This is 55," he said. To either side, the road stretched away from them, empty and devoid of life. A gust of wind blew up a short-lived dust devil that twirled across the road and dissipated on the shoulder. "Which way should we go?"

Lee pointed to their left. "Is that toward town?"

"Yeah."

"Probably have more cars that way."

Harper seemed hesitant. "More infected too."

Lee shifted in his seat, getting a good grip on his rifle. "Don't go far from the truck, and keep an open line of sight both directions."

Wordlessly, Harper turned the steering wheel to the left. The power steering groaned against his grip and Lee wondered how long their machines would last without parts and maintenance. On his list of valuable people to rescue, he mentally highlighted "mechanic."

The small pickup moved slowly through the intersection and headed northwest toward downtown Angier.

Harper kept it at a steady but cautious thirty miles per hour.

Nothing but trees and power lines on both sides.

The wind bore no scent but the stale baking smell of the blacktop.

The tires whined, the engine hummed along, settling into third gear. Beyond that was the hypnotic slur of nature's constant background noise, louder now for man's lack of interference. The cicada call, rising and falling, the chatter of birds, a million other life-forms acting out their daily existence, oblivious to the changed world around them and the plight of the one species on the planet that seemed to doom themselves at every turn.

A glint of unnatural color ahead.

Lee focused at the road before them, gently

curving to the right. In the bend, just coming into view, a small white vehicle had run off the road and mired itself in the ditch on the far side of the shoulder.

"Slow up," Lee mumbled, but Harper was already pressing the brakes.

The vehicle was a little more than a half a mile away. A sniper's arithmetic produced facts in Lee's mind without even thinking about it: the vehicle was roughly a thousand yards from him. The shimmering mirage of the roadway was running right to left, caused by a strong westerly wind. They were just inside the effective range of anyone with a rifle, but Lee was less concerned due to the wind. Only an experienced marksman with a good cartridge would be able to take them at this range.

Lee leaned into his rifle, resting his cheek on the buttstock. The scope mounted on the Savage was overpowered for almost any application but punching holes in paper at long distances. He guessed it was somewhere between thirty times and forty times magnification. During scout sniper school, Lee had trained with a variable power scope that topped out at nine times magnification. The less the magnification, the easier it was to track a moving target, so Lee preferred low-magnification scopes.

Still, the overpowered scope gave Lee the ability to see details, even at this distance. Anything that might tell him about the car in the road: a moving shadow, the dark shape of feet underneath the vehicle, or even someone looking out from the backseat. But Lee saw nothing but an abandoned vehicle. A Chevrolet Cavalier, with the front right hubcap missing and a white cloth draped in the window that stirred occasionally in the breeze.

Lee turned his suspicious eyes to the nearby tree line.

The bright midday sun cast the forest in dark streaks and mottled shadows. Beyond the first screen of leaves glinting in the sunlight, Lee could see next to nothing.

About a minute ticked by.

The pickup rumbled slightly at idle.

Lee looked up from the rifle. "Looks okay."

"You want to check it for gas?" Harper was already easing the Nissan forward.

"Yeah. Pull up right next to it."

They moved forward, covering the half mile in just a few seconds. As they drew closer to the abandoned vehicle, more of the road farther down became visible. A little more than a quarter mile more from the Chevrolet Cavalier, the sun glinted off of several windshields.

Harper pointed. "Accident?"

Lee nodded. "Some sort of pileup." He then turned his attention back to the woods.

As they pulled up alongside the Chevy, Lee felt a small measure of disappointment. The gas cap was removed and hanging down. Someone had already tapped this vehicle for gas.

Harper made a face. "Sonofabitch..."

"We can still check it out." Lee opened his door. "Might be a little left."

Harper didn't argue. He exited the vehicle and grabbed a gas can and a short section of black tubing. Lee let the man set up the siphon as he swung into the back of the pickup truck. The metal roof of the cab was uncomfortably hot against his skin as he settled his elbows on it, using it to prop himself up and survey the area around them.

Harper began coughing and then gagged.

Lee gave the man a sidelong glance. "Anything?"

Harper was bent over, hands on his knees, with a thick trail of saliva coming from his mouth. He shook his head steadily, the saliva swinging from side to side. "Just fumes. God, I forgot how much I hate doing that."

"Let's roll on," Lee suggested. "I'll stay back here."

Harper yanked the black hose from the barren gas tank of the little Chevy and tossed it and the gas can into the bed with Lee. He grumbled as he settled into the driver's seat, "Good thing I didn't have anything to eat this morning. I would have lost it."

Lee took a firm hold of the roof and gave it a tap to indicate he was secure. "You're a trouper, Harper."

The older man mumbled something unintelligible and unpleasant sounding.

The pickup moved farther down the road, toward the new group of cars. Lee had scoped it while he had been waiting for Harper and it did not seem like a man-made barricade, nor did Lee see anyone around it. As they closed in on the cluster of cars, Lee got a better picture of how they had gotten there.

A large SUV had crossed the grassy center median from the opposite direction. Twin gouges in the grass could still be seen, despite the untrimmed overgrowth. A box truck had swerved to avoid the head-on collision and tipped over on its side. Three smaller vehicles had piled up on the undercarriage of the box truck.

A chain reaction of idiots following too closely.

But their poor driving habits meant good pickings for Lee and his partners. Surely one of the five vehicles would have some fuel left in its tank. Perhaps they would be so lucky as to fill up all twelve gallons.

The body of the box truck lay across the roadway like a felled beast and created a perfect defensive position. Lee kept a wary eye on it as they approached. No one jumped out and started shooting. The wrecked vehicles remained still and silent, like statues depicting a single moment of some violent scene.

Harper swung wide to the right and then cut it to the left so their passenger's side was facing the vehicles. Lee hopped out and swiftly began clearing the vehicles while Harper snatched his hose and gas cans from the bed again. The vehicles were all empty. In two of them, the air bags were deployed. One of them had a broken passenger window. To the left and right, the grass on the median was worn down to the dirt. Lee thought that explained the lack of gridlock behind this accident. Everyone heading inbound toward Angier had just gone around the accident.

Lee wondered if they had gone around it when the people were still trying to drag themselves out of the cars. What happened to the drivers was a mystery. Maybe they just wandered off. Or maybe a horde of infected had taken them.

Harper coughed and spluttered. "Goddamn..." He wheezed.

"Eureka?"

"Oh, yeah." He spat. "Gonna be a minute, though."

Lee nodded and turned his attention to the box truck. He scanned the woods and farther down the road as he moved to the roll-up door on the back end. It was emblazoned with a bread company logo and showed pictures of various freshly baked loaves and rolls. Just looking at the pictures made Lee's mouth water and his stomach growl at him.

Taking another long look around to make sure no one was sneaking up, Lee bent to the latch of the roll-up door and found it unlocked. He flipped the latch and then grabbed the canvas strap at the bottom of the door and yanked it up—or sideways, as the truck was now horizontal.

The door stuck at first and Lee pulled harder.

It finally gave way and slid about halfway before jamming again.

Lee peered into the darkness.

He noticed the smell almost immediately. Not rancid like rotting meat or overpowering like the shit-and-body-odor smell of the infected. It was a strange musty smell, like an old house that hadn't been cleaned in years.

Lee wrinkled his nose.

All the bread in the back of the truck had gone

bad—he was certain from the smell—and he had little desire to investigate further into the dark cargo area. He was about to turn away, but thought better of it and pulled the door shut again. He was pretty sure nothing dangerous was inside. But not positive.

"Anything?" Harper called over to him.

Lee looked back and saw Harper standing over his slowly filling gas can, one hand on his hip and the other shielding his eyes from the sun. The shotgun was resting against the car while it transfused its fuel into the big red canister. Lee shook his head. "It's all moldy."

"Figured."

Yes. Lee should have figured that as well. A month in the dark of the box truck, with heat and humidity to boot, and not much was likely to be unspoiled.

Lee faced away and leaned against the box truck. He sighted through the scope again. The overly magnified image forced him to strain his focus. He saw the middle of the road. In the hazy distance, an overpass? Perhaps. The image jumped and quivered with the tiny unconscious movements of his body. He swept to the left, across the median where everything was empty and the overgrown grass nearly blocked his view of the opposite lanes, then up the shoulder to the wood line on the far side of the road.

All clear.

He swept right, back across the median, back across the road that he now stood on, saw the cloudy, shimmering silhouette of the overpass. Up the shoulder. Up the embankment, to the woods. And there he saw a dark shape, hunched low to the ground, disappear into the woods.

Lee jerked back like he'd been touched by something hot.

Was that...?

He was about to call behind him but decided to double-check himself. The movement had been so rapid and sudden that it could have been a mirage, could have been an animal, could have been sunspots in the lenses of the scope.

He put his cheek against the rifle, hard this time, his focus intense. He sighted at the farthest point in the road before it dipped out of sight on a gradual downslope. There, on the embankment, not fifteen feet from the road, just at the hillcrest, he had seen something.

Something crouched down low.

And human, he thought.

He felt his heart quicken its pace, like a worried horse moving from a walk to a trot. He stared at the woods with obsessive focus, but the sunlight reflecting off the leaves blocked his view of what was beyond them.

"Uh...Harper?" Lee called behind him.

"Yeah." Harper sounded gruff and unconcerned.

Lee tried to make himself sound level but that bad feeling was putting a tourniquet around his gut and tightening it down. "You might want to speed it up."

He didn't take his eyes off the woods. Behind him he could hear the light metallic *click* of Harper taking up his shotgun.

"Did you see something?" Harper blurted in a harsh whisper. "What did you see?"

"Just..." Lee took a deep breath, forcing relaxation into his muscles. "Just get the gas. Focus on getting the gas. But hurry."

"It only goes so fast!" Harper snapped.

"Can't you start on the next can?"

"I only have one hose!" Harper growled. "Shitfire..."

Then from the woods rose a bloodcurdling howl that seemed to go on for minutes on end, searing through Lee like a white-hot fire that started in the sudden dump of his adrenal glands and radiated outward like a shock wave until it stung his fingertips and dried his mouth and throat.

"That was..." Harper started.

"Better fucking hurry." Lee lowered the rifle and scanned the woods with his naked eye. Now the roadway seemed like a horrible place to be and the woods seemed closer than they had been just seconds ago. If something burst from those trees, it would be on them in seconds. If there were more than one, Lee and Harper might not have time to react.

Slow it down and think...

Lee began to back up toward Harper, scanning slowly left to right. While he watched, his fingers checked the safety and pulled the bolt back to check that the chamber was loaded. He pushed the bolt back into place and tapped it twice so he knew it was seated.

The Savage Axis with its four-round magazine suddenly seemed like the worst possible weapon to have outside of a stapler. The scope was too ridiculously magnified to use on anything inside a hundred yards, and with only a four-round capacity before reloading, each one would have to be a hit and a half to count.

While the first howl still echoed through the woods, another call came from the opposite side of the road, this one shriller. Lee swung in that direction, but the woods still yielded nothing for him to target.

Are they boxing us in?

"Where we at, Harper?"

"First one's almost full, but this tank is tapped."

"Keep it moving; I'll let you know when I see 'em." Lee backed up to the bed of the running pickup and quickly vaulted himself in. Being a few feet higher in the bed gave him a better vantage point over the box truck's big frame.

A third call, this one very close to them, just inside the nearest section of woods. Lee looked to that section of woods and remembered the disaster of the night before—the one limping haphazardly through the trash bins while the others sneaked stealthily up from behind.

Pack instincts.

Lee turned in a slow circle in the bed, his rifle pulled tight to his shoulder, the muzzle held at a low-ready. As he turned to the woods across the road from them, he heard the crackle and swish of someone moving swiftly through the leaves and bushes.

Lee wanted to leave, but he needed that gas.

He did not relish the thought of a second trip out to finish what they could have finished right here and now. But he also did not relish the thought of losing another member of Camp Ryder. He had already taken the blame for what was clearly not his fault—how much more would they blame him if Harper died when they were out here alone and without witnesses?

Harper hacked and spit and began to siphon the next tank of gas.

Just give it a minute…

Another screech, farther back toward Camp Ryder. Though the distance was greater, it did nothing to comfort Lee; they were now coming from all directions.

A crack of twigs, very close.

Lee broke down and gave in to his instincts. "We gotta move, Harper."

Harper didn't need to be asked twice. With the black tube still spewing gasoline, he ripped it out of the car it was in, spraying gas all over himself and the ground. He snatched up the red cans and sprinted for the truck.

There was a *whoosh* of leaves.

From the nearest tree line, a figure burst through, loping toward them with a strange sideways gait. Lee brought up his rifle as a small part of his old self murmured in the back of his mind the many rules of engagement he had been taught. It questioned him with righteous indignation: *Is he a deadly threat? You can't engage him unless he is a deadly threat!*

But Lee sighted through the riflescope, saw the moving, mottled shape and a mouthful of blood-stained teeth, and pulled the trigger. The rifle boomed and bucked and the creature's left hip exploded in a shower of meat and gristle and bone shards.

Maybe not dead, but immobile.

"Lee!" Harper shouted as he threw both gas cans and the siphon tube into the bed. "Other side!"

Lee swung about, even as gas sloshed out of the can and onto his legs. From across the road, two, and then three more had exited the woods and were sprinting toward them in a staggered line, closing the gap fast. Lee cranked the bolt hard, up and then back. The brass shell sprang from the chamber, leaving a ghostly smoke trail behind it.

Lee slammed the bolt back into place.

Two of the three sprinters were leading at an angle, cutting off their prey's escape route. The other was heading straight on. Lee chose that one because he knew his chances of hitting the others with the overpowered scope as they moved laterally were slim to none.

He raised the scope to his eye, but the sight picture was not there.

He moved it around, trying to get his target.

Grass blades.

Leaves.

Blacktop.

Fuck this stupid scope!

The pickup lurched as Harper threw it into gear and slammed on the gas.

Lee lost his footing, not expecting the sudden acceleration, and fell, slamming his back into the bed of the pickup truck. Every stitch in his back was a hot branding iron held to his skin and he cried out and swore violently.

The tires were spinning, trying to gain traction.

Something hit the side of the bed.

Lee rolled toward the sound, bringing the muzzle of the rifle around. Two sinewy arms, black with blood and grime, gripped the side of the bed as the pickup started moving. Long, stringy hair, beyond which a man's face peered out, the mouth crusty with gore and set in a fierce, toothy grin, the yellow teeth snapping and gnashing wildly at him.

Lee put the muzzle to the man's mouth and pulled the trigger.

The head snapped back, but the clawlike fingers did not release their grip from the bed. Blood began to spew out of the creature's nose and mouth like a faucet had been turned on inside his head, gushing down the white paint of the pickup's bed. Lee reared back to kick the hands loose when the last instinctive muscle spasms faded and the thing slid off the side of the pickup with a wet scrape and a *thud*.

Lee reached for the back glass of the pickup and pounded it. "Drive faster, motherfucker!"

He let the rifle drop as he tried to get up on his hands and knees, wavering like a drunken sailor on a violently pitching deck. He groped for the .22 pistol he'd stuck in his waistband but it wasn't there. As they accelerated, Lee caught sight of it in the bed of the pickup, clattering back and forth.

The pickup swerved; Lee heard and felt the heavy *thump* of flesh striking the front bumper, accompanied by a breathy grunt.

Lee got his hands and knees under him and peered up over the side of the bed. The one he'd shot was still rolling on the side of the road, and another was in the process of stumbling back into the grassy median. The third attacker was just clearing the median and still sprinting straight for them.

For a moment, panic tightened Lee's throat and he just knew the Nissan would break down now, at the worst possible moment. But the straining engine found third gear and dropped to a steady rumble, and the blacktop kept blurring by underneath them, punctuated rapidly by the white lines flying by. The wind rushed loudly in Lee's ears but couldn't overcome the thundering of his own pulse.

As they turned into the curve past the white Cavalier, the infected disappeared around the corner, still running madly after them.

SEVEN

LIMITED PROVISIONS

THEY RETURNED TO CAMP Ryder's gates in a cloud of dust. Harper had put the pedal to the metal getting back and hadn't let up until he slammed on the brakes in front of the chain-link fence, causing the sentry on the other side to stutter-step and nearly jump out of the way.

When the dust settled, the sentry—a thirty-something-year-old with a rifle slung on his shoulder—was standing with his arms raised. "What the hell?" he shouted.

Harper stuck his head out of the open driver's side window. "Just open the goddamn gate!"

The sentry shook his head with irritation but complied, pulling the stop-bar out and swinging the hinged gates inward. The Nissan lurched forward, letting out a tiny spray of pebbles as Harper brought it back safely into the middle of camp.

Lee had situated himself in the bed, holding both gas cans in his arms to keep them from tipping and spilling. The first was still full, though a little had sloshed out. The second had been more haphazardly tossed and Lee thought there might be only a half gallon or so left in it. The ride back had been herky-jerky the whole way, and Lee didn't want to risk getting toppled around again. He waited until Harper turned the engine off before standing up.

Bus approached them, his black hair wet with perspiration and fresh sweat rings standing out on his white tank top. A small crowd of curious survivors followed, looking to see what the flying gravel and yelling were all about.

Harper stepped out of his vehicle and slammed the door behind him.

"Captain." Bus nodded to Lee as he hopped out of the bed. "Harper. What happened?"

Harper seemed to consider his words with the eavesdroppers still standing around. The other two men picked up on the cue and leaned in, creating a loose huddle.

"What's wrong?" Bus asked. "Did you get the gas?"

"We got *some* gas." Harper nodded. "But man, I gotta tell you...those things..." He pointed out beyond the gate and made a face. "Those things are getting smarter."

Bus lowered his voice. "What do you fucking mean, 'they're getting smarter'?"

"They boxed us in."

Lee clarified. "We were getting gas, and they did the same thing they did last night. They circled us up, had us surrounded. Then one started running toward us, while three more sneaked up from behind." He looked at the leery faces surrounding their small group and heard the ripple of hushed conversation. "I don't know if *smarter* is the right word. They still lack self-preservation. But I think the ones who stay in groups are developing some kind of pack instinct."

"They're turning into hunters," Harper mumbled.

Bus rubbed his eyebrows and swore under his breath.

Harper crossed his arms and looked resolute. "I'm telling you this because I don't think it's prudent for us to go outside the gate with only three. The captain and I barely got away with our skins and there were only four of them that we could tell. If we run into a bigger pack, we won't be able to stop them. And if we hadn't been able to drive away, we would have been fucked."

Bus's voice was harsh. "What do you want me to do about it, Harper? I don't see a whole lot of people volunteering to go outside the gate except you and Miller, and I sure as shit can't order anyone to do it."

Doc suddenly appeared in their huddle and Lee wasn't sure how long he had been standing there. "I'll go."

All three heads turned his way.

The skinny medical student had his long hair pulled back into a loose ponytail. His skin looked sweaty and pale, and his face was a dreadful mask of fear, like a trapped animal. The expression belied the willingness with which he spoke and Lee wondered what the kid wasn't saying.

"No." Bus sounded final. "Absolutely not."

"Why?" The kid's voice was flat and without conviction.

"Because you're the only doctor we have!"

Doc's face was suddenly animated with frustration. "That's bullshit! I'm not a fucking doctor, Bus! I'm a med student with no goddamn supplies to help anyone with. Without the supplies I'm fucking useless. Plus you have Jenny, and half the time she knows more about what she's doing than I do."

"Why do you want to go?" Lee asked. He wanted the extra man, but he wasn't sure if Doc would be a help or a hindrance, and he couldn't help but wonder why he'd volunteered. He didn't strike Lee as the daring type.

Doc looked at him and Lee could see some hidden machinations rolling through the younger man's brain. "You say you have medical supplies?"

"Correct."

"Unless you have more medical training that I don't know about, you don't know what we need or what's first on our list of priorities. You have a limited amount of space in that truck and most of it needs to be filled with food and water. I know what we need. I can make sure we get the vital stuff first. Otherwise you might waste your cargo space on shit that will go to waste."

Lee had to concede that his limited medical training made him less than qualified to make a doctor's shopping list. He could also see a desperation in Doc's eyes, and in the moment felt he couldn't tell him no. He wanted to know why Doc felt so strongly about accompanying them, but he knew that Doc wouldn't say. Not here in public, anyway.

In the end, he nodded. "Doc makes a good point."

The look on Doc's face was one that Lee found hard to distinguish between thankfulness and deep regret. "Thank you, Captain."

"So that gives you four total." Bus hadn't given up the fight. "And you think adding Doc to your crew is going to keep you safe? No offense, Doc, but you're not exactly Special Forces."

Lee spoke up. "Neither is Harper. Or Miller. Or you, for that matter."

The group fell silent.

"I've worked with a lot of third-world farmers and shepherds. People with goat shit on their hands who tended flocks during the day and grabbed an AK-47 and fought at night. If I can teach an Afghan goatherd to fight, I can teach anyone." Lee looked at each of them in turn. "I know we don't have a whole lot of time, but if you all give me the rest of the evening to teach you what I can, it will at least give us an edge."

"I want another one," Harper said suddenly. "I want to ask Josh. I'm sure he'll come along. Then we'd have five. All five of us can fit in Keith's pickup truck and if Lee can teach us how to work together..." Harper looked much more confident. "I'd feel a whole lot better about this thing."

Bus considered for a long moment. "Fine."

"Good." Harper met Lee's gaze. "I'll get Josh. Where do you want to meet up?"

"You tell me," Lee said. "I just need a quiet place."

Harper nodded. "Behind the Ryder building."

"Gimme a few and I'll meet you over there."

Harper and Doc departed the small huddle.

Miller, who had been waiting nearby, fell in step with them and began barraging his older counterpart with a slew of questions.

"Before you go." Bus motioned toward the gas. "How much did you get?"

"Maybe six gallons."

Bus grimaced. "Not quite enough."

"No, but it'll get us going." Lee grabbed the two gas cans and began walking toward Keith's big Dodge Ram with Bus alongside. "It should be enough to get there and back, but it doesn't give us a lot of room for error. I'm sure we'll pass more abandoned cars on the way. We'll just have to keep siphoning on the go."

Lee placed the two gas cans in the bed of the Dodge Ram and took a moment to grit his teeth against the sting in his back.

If Bus noticed the pain, he didn't mention it. "You remember Marie from earlier? The lady who took up for you?"

Lee smiled. "How could I forget?"

"She's kind of the cook around here. Puts together our meals. She's in charge of our food stores, as well. I would like for you to get up with her and see what she needs. Most likely, she needs anything and everything."

Lee nodded. "I'll check in with her."

Bus left something unsaid and forced a smile across his broad features. "Thank you, Captain. She'll be in the storage room right below my office. Just to the right when you walk in."

Lee left Camp Ryder's leader without another word and headed for the big Ryder building. He had questions, but he didn't ask them. He had the feeling he would find the answers soon enough.

He found Marie before he reached the Ryder building. She was carrying a five-gallon bucket full of water around the corner of the building. She wasn't a big woman, but Lee guessed she was a little taller than most. She wore a faded pair of tan Dickies that fit her loosely and a blue denim shirt with the sleeves rolled up. Sweat matted down the hair on her temples and the rest of it was pulled back in a dark bundle that looked on the verge of falling apart. Lee noticed the set of blank determination on her face and the lean cords of muscle that stood out on her forearms as she hauled the heavy bucket. This wasn't gym muscle but hard-work muscle. The kind you got from years of tossing hay bales out of pickup trucks, pounding fence posts in the ground, and turning up dirt for planting.

She didn't notice Lee step up beside her as she began to mount the steps to the front of the Ryder building. "I'll offer to help you with that if you don't take it as an insult."

Marie jerked a bit when he spoke and turned to look at him. She cocked her head to one side speculatively, and puffed a stray wisp of hair out of her face. Finally, she shrugged and set the bucket down. "You go right ahead, Captain."

Lee stooped and grabbed the pail, doing a good job of masking the raw feeling that it sent down his back. "Where to?"

"Go ahead and take it inside." She followed him up the stairs. "So what brings you to me?"

"Well, first I'd like to thank you for backing me up earlier," Lee said earnestly.

"Hmm." She didn't show much of a reaction, positive or negative. "You're welcome, I suppose. You can thank my granddad for that. He always told me to speak my mind or keep my mouth shut."

Lee appreciated her forthrightness.

"And the second thing?" She opened the door to the Ryder building for him and they stepped inside where it was slightly warmer and a little musty.

"The second thing is up to you. Bus sent me to ask you what you needed."

"Uh-*huh*…" She stopped and regarded Lee with her hand on her hip. "Bus sent you to see me."

Lee nodded.

She started moving again.

"He told me you were in charge of the food and to see what you needed."

"Okay." She guided them right, and then into a dimly lit space that was noticeably warmer than the rest of the building. The room was originally some type of storage closet and was lined with shelves that now sat empty. It smelled faintly of wood smoke and largely of bland, unseasoned food. Marie stepped to a shelf where a kerosene lantern was glowing and turned it up.

"By the way," he continued, "where'd you get all this water?"

Marie took the bucket from him and set it down. "Well, water is the one thing we're not desperate for. We've been busy over the last month, trying to build ourselves a life out here. I got enough scrap wood together with some tarp and built a big rain basin at the back of the building. It's getting low now, but with August coming on, I'll be hoping it fills up again."

"You're quite resourceful," he observed.

She smiled. "It's a team effort out here. Most everyone contributes. Most everyone except Jerry." Her lips flattened out as she poured some of the water into a large stainless pot. "I shouldn't be uncharitable. Jerry has his place: He knows how to organize people and is good at moderating our meetings and keeping us on track. But at the end of the day, when muscle and sweat counts, Jerry doesn't have much to offer."

Marie put the half-empty bucket down and pushed it off to the side with a foot, then stooped and hauled up the large pot and placed it on a big metal box that appeared to have been constructed up against the outside wall. Lee noticed that it seemed to be the source of the stifling heat in the room.

He pointed to the big box. "That a wood-burning stove? Did you make that too?"

"Nope." She reached over to another five-gallon pail, picked it up easily, and looked inside. "One of the guys put that together for me after we figured out why we were having extra dinner guests every time we cooked outside. The smell of the cooking food brings 'em in like moths to a flame."

She turned to the stove, then paused. "Captain, you said you were here to check out our supply situation?"

Lee stepped forward, sensing that she held those supplies in the single five-gallon pail. "Yes, that's what Bus sent me over here for."

Marie turned to him and tilted the pail so he could see inside.

It was a little less than a fourth of the way full of white rice.

Her face was grim. "This is it. You're looking at my supplies, Captain. I figure on getting about thirty cups of cooked rice out of this, and then we're done. No more food." She poured the rice into the pot already sitting on the stove. She put the bucket down and gestured to another, smaller pot sitting on a wire rack near the stove. "I got some beans left, but not a whole lot. I'll mix them into the rice and tonight everyone gets a half cup of rice and beans, and that could be the last meal they have."

"I'm bringing back food supplies. In fact, now that I know about the rain catch around back, that'll save me a lot of room I would have wasted on water." Lee sensed that there was something else that neither Bus nor Marie was saying. "Is there anything else I should focus on?"

The look on her face was guarded. "Captain, I've got a list longer than your arm of things that would make our lives a helluva lot easier. But as far as *necessary*, I think food is the big one. Besides, I don't really know what you have squirreled away, so I don't really know what to ask for."

Lee stretched his neck and looked thoughtful. "Why don't you give me the top items on your list, and I'll let you know if I can get them for you."

"Hmm." She smiled hesitantly. "Not something most men think about, but feminine products would be great. Most of the women have work to do around here. We can't have them being out of service for a week every month. Also, a lot of the women in camp are in relationships, which makes me worry about pregnancies. That is something we can't afford to worry about right now, and some form of contraceptive would be helpful." She sighed. "And of course, winter is going to be here soon. A lot of folks around here just feel the heat and don't even consider it, but I was raised on a farm, so I'm always thinking about the weather. No one has any cold-weather gear, no blankets, no sleeping bags. Everyone was dressed for summer when this happened."

Lee was impressed with her foresight, something uncommon in an average civilian. "You're a very practical thinker, Marie. I think Camp Ryder is lucky to have you looking after them."

She didn't respond. Lee felt the silence turn into that awkward expectation, like she was waiting for him to give her an answer.

"The feminine products should be in with my medical supplies. As far as winter supplies, I will be bringing back some field jackets. As many as we can fit." Lee smiled ruefully. "Speaking from experience, they won't keep you comfortable if it's below freezing, but they will keep you alive...at least in this climate. The contraceptives I don't have, but I will keep an eye out for them. I imagine that they aren't high on the list of looted items, so they probably won't be hard to find."

Marie looked relieved, but only slightly.

Lee raised his eyebrows. "And there's something else that doesn't have to do with supplies."

She regarded him for a long moment and Lee could see storm clouds brewing in her face. With her wiry build and lean features, she wouldn't have attracted many men, but she had eyes that showed a depth of concern and intelligence long forgotten in the old world of vapid beauty. It didn't bring forth desire, but respect.

Finally, she nodded. "I talked to Harper after you first got here. He said you claimed to have communications equipment, like radios and stuff. Do you have those things?"

"I can get them, yes."

"Then I have a very big favor to ask of you. It's probably why Bus sent you to me in the first place. I understand if you don't want to or if you just can't. I won't hold it against you."

Lee waited for her to spit it out.

She turned and busied herself with mixing the rice into the pot of water, steam finally beginning to rise from it. "I know that you guys are going to be passing by Smithfield. I have family there—a sister, brother-in-law, and two nephews. They lived very close to the downtown area and I know people have been saying that something bad happened in Smithfield, but no one seems to know what it was. I need to know if my sister survived." She paused. "If *anybody* survived."

"So you want me to look for your sister?" Lee's eyes narrowed slightly. "What does that have to do with communications equipment?"

Marie swiped quickly at her eyes before turning back to him. "Before we lost contact, my sister said they were bringing everyone in town to the First Baptist Church. It's a big church, with the tallest steeple in town and big columns out front. It should be pretty easy to pick out. If you find any survivors, I know you can't bring them back here, but if we could establish communications with them, then we might be able to help each other. Her name is Julia." The ghost of a smile passed over Marie's lips. "She looks nothing like me."

Lee realized that this was not only a personal favor for Marie, but excellent information for him to work off of anyway. If there was a band of survivors in Smithfield, as he'd originally suspected there might be, and Marie was family to part of their group, that might be the tie that could bind the two groups together.

Lee nodded. "Okay, I'll go into Smithfield. I can't promise that I'll find anything, but I will try."

"Thank you." Marie smiled, this time genuinely. "You're an answer to prayer, Captain Harden."

Lee didn't feel like an answer to prayer, but linking the Smithfield and Camp Ryder groups would be a massive step toward reestablishing order in the region. He kept his more pragmatic thoughts to himself and smiled back at Marie. "We'll see what we can do."

Lee spent the waning hours of daylight with Harper, Miller, Doc, and Josh. None of the four men had any military experience, though everyone except Doc had at least some experience with firearms, either through hunting or recreational shooting. Somehow, the young medical student had managed to survive six weeks of complete social collapse and devastation without firing a weapon.

Good for you, Lee thought.

Ammunition was scarce, and firing off rounds would only attract unwanted guests. So instead Lee taught what basics he could about safety and squad tactics. He focused on what he felt were the three biggest components to a successful team: do your job, communicate with one another, and don't be a hero.

While there were many other things to learn about being a member of a tactical team, Lee wasn't trying to train Special Forces soldiers. He didn't need them to be able to shoot a moving target from the bed of a pickup moving at forty-five miles per hour or fast-rope out of helicopters. He just needed them to survive the supply run.

He helped them with some basic pointers on weapon handling and moving as part of a squad. They also broke up who would be doing what when the trip was made. None of them came out and talked about the dangers of the trip because none of them knew what those dangers might be. It could turn out to be a few hours in a truck with no trouble at all, or all hell could break loose and they could have to fight their way back.

Lee knew all too well how horribly things could go wrong.

It was decided that Harper would drive, while Lee navigated from the passenger's seat. Doc would sit in the rear passenger side and Josh would sit in the rear driver's side to watch their flanks. Miller would be in the bed, covering the rear. The last thing he told them was to drink plenty of water and get hydrated, as they would be heading out with minimal supplies to save cargo room in the truck.

As they were finishing, everyone began to form a line at the front of the Ryder building. Marie was inside with her big pot, scooping a half-cup of rice and beans for each person. Lee felt a deep, hollow ache in his stomach and swallowed hard against it. He watched the line forming and looked at the faces of the people gathered there. They were too thin.

The longest Lee had gone without food in the field was about seventy hours. He felt he was well within that range and knew that his body could continue to operate efficiently, despite the pain in his gut. Knowing this, he decided not to enter the line.

He did, however, help himself to some water. It was hot and still cooling down from when Marie had boiled it, but he knew that warm water metabolized and hydrated faster than cool water, so he didn't mind. The rainwater was probably okay to drink directly from the basin, as it was not runoff from the roof but caught directly from whatever rain cloud it came out of. But since it was standing water, boiling it was a good precaution to protect against dysentery.

Lee drank his water by the old turkey fryer Marie had boiled it in and watched the line dwindle as everyone passed through. They gathered inside the Ryder building where all the indoor shanties were made and found places to sit and socialize. Despite their desperate circumstances, the sounds of the conversations filtered through the open door and Lee thought it sounded hopeful.

It seemed that even though most of them had held Lee in suspicion only hours earlier, they now found themselves with their backs against the wall, and the only hope they had to look forward to at this very moment was Lee. Perhaps when he had returned Harper safely to them after gathering gas, he had gained some trust with the community.

If he had been willing to risk his life to get gas to make the trip, and if Harper believed in him enough to go along, perhaps there was something to his wild stories after all. Perhaps he wasn't a spy. Perhaps he was truly there to help them.

After all, what else did they have to look forward to?

Lee felt that responsibility settle heavily around his neck.

The darkness closed in fast and Lee refilled his water bottle and took a seat on the front steps of the building. In the blue twilight, the late-July fireflies were putting on a show and the heavy thrum of nature in the hot sun settled into the evening sounds of crickets, frogs, and the occasional night bird.

There was a scuffle of footsteps behind him and he looked back to see Angela, Sam, and Abby coming out of the front doors. Sam's face brightened as he saw Lee, and the three of them took a seat on the steps with him, the two kids between the two adults. Lee was glad to see them but felt strangely edgy at the same time, as though he and Angela were acting out the motions of a family, and the kids were just going along with it.

The need to be with other people was always greater than the need to actually know them.

Sam looked up at Lee with one of his enigmatic expressions. "I heard about what happened earlier. I'm glad you're okay."

Sounds like an adult, Lee thought to himself but only offered a smile.

Playing the part.

Angela had her arm around Abby, who remained very quiet. "Yes, Sam was very worried about you today."

"I wasn't worried," Sam protested quietly. "I know he can take care of himself."

The kid looked like he wanted to say more, but he looked down at the ground and pinched his lips together. Lee thought he knew how the rest of the sentence would have gone: *It's just that I've already lost everyone else.*

"Did you guys get some food?" Lee asked, hoping to move the conversation off of himself.

"Yes." Angela nodded. "I didn't see you in line."

"Oh, I got some earlier," he lied, because he didn't want her trying to convince him to eat when he'd already made up his mind.

"I'm still hungry," Abby said in a subdued voice.

She was still detached, Lee noted. Just like her mother had said.

"So if you could eat anything right now, what would it be?" Lee leaned back with a thoughtful look on his face. He wanted to keep the kids talking, maybe turn their thoughts to more pleasant things, even if those things were only memories.

"McDonald's," Abby said instantly.

"Oh, really?" Lee sounded fascinated. "And what would you get from McDonald's?"

Abby smiled and seemed to come alive a bit. "I'd get some chicken nuggets. And some French fries!"

"That's it?" Lee looked shocked. "What about a cheeseburger?"

"Yeah!" She nodded. "In the Happy Meal. With the girl toy."

"And some ice cream?" he added.

"Uh-huh. With chocolate syrup."

"Mmm." Lee put on a dreamy expression for the kids' benefit. "That does sound good. What about you, Sam?"

Sam was more thoughtful. "I miss pancakes. With butter and syrup. On my birthday, Mom would make chocolate chip pancakes. Those were really good." He closed his eyes like he was tasting them again. "I want a big stack of chocolate chip pancakes."

Lee smiled at the two kids and found Angela looking at him, though he couldn't see her expression in the darkness. Feeling suddenly awkward again, Lee sat up. "I probably need to get to bed. Got an early start tomorrow."

Angela stood. "Some of the folks were nice enough to help me set up a little room of our own over by the medical trailer."

Lee must have looked hesitant because Angela

continued quickly. "I think it would help the kids sleep if they knew you were there with them."

"Of course," Lee backpedaled into graciousness. "Thank you for offering. Didn't want to be in that medical trailer again anyway."

The dinner gathering was beginning to disperse and those who did not sleep inside the Ryder building were making their way out into the shantytown. Everyone's conversations quieted as they neared Lee and his little group, and then picked up again once they were passed. But the feel was not one of ostracism, as it had been earlier. Now it seemed they were just more interested in what Lee might be talking about and were taking a moment to listen in, though Lee and Angela said little as they walked to her shack.

The makeshift room was hastily thrown together with some two-by-fours, a few pallets, and some blue tarp, which covered the structure and provided the doorway. Inside were several large pieces of cardboard laid out as beds and a small, windup LED lantern casting a sharp glow over everything. It reminded Lee of a homeless camp, but he supposed that's what they were.

Homeless.

The kids settled in quickly and were asleep almost instantly. Angela took off her daughter's dirty tennis shoes, and then removed her own. Lee followed suit and removed his boots, wondering if the four of them miraculously didn't stink or whether he just didn't notice anymore. As he pulled off his left boot, a piece of thick paper fell out onto the ground. Lee picked it up with a furrowed brow.

It was the scratch-off lottery ticket that Jack had given him just before he died. Jenny or Doc must have taken it from his old pair of pants and put it in his boot for safekeeping. Lee stared down at it thoughtfully until he realized that Angela was watching him with that same soft look that made him so uncomfortable.

He forced a smile. "Jack made me scratch the lottery ticket. Said I should keep it for good luck." Then he stuffed it into his cargo pocket without another word and began stripping off his socks.

As he laid his socks out over the toes of his boots, he noted that Angela kept hers and Abby's on and that they were about as filthy as the shoes they wore.

Lee nodded to their feet. "You should take your socks off. Feet can catch some pretty nasty things if you don't let them breathe. Air your socks out too, especially if it's the only pair you got."

Angela nodded as though what he'd said made good sense and took off her and Abby's socks. The little girl slept through it all, her legs flopping around limply while her mother worked. "Thanks," she said simply.

Lee lay back on his cardboard mattress and rested his head on his arms. For him, the silence grew thick and strained, but Angela was soon asleep and her breathing was even. He felt that strange sensation of living someone else's life, but despite whatever he felt about it, Angela and the two kids seemed to draw comfort from him.

Eventually he did fall asleep. And when he did, it wasn't dreams that followed him through the night, but memories of all the things he had lost.

EIGHT

ROADBLOCKS

THERE WAS NO FANFARE for the volunteers as they huddled around the pickup truck at dawn. Cool morning dew had settled on everything and Lee had woken up damp from head to toe. Around them the camp was slowly coming to life, but most of the people were quiet. They gathered water and boiled it. Some of the families had personal items such as coffee and tea that they made themselves in the morning to stave off the hunger.

One such family—the Burkes, Lee remembered—kindly gave a small cup of hot instant coffee to each of the five men. They all thanked the Burkes profusely and drank the brew with relish. A few individuals walking by to collect water or visit the latrines behind the Ryder building wished them good luck and told them to be careful.

There was no breakfast to be had, so after the coffee, the five men grabbed what little they were bringing and piled into the truck. They each brought a few extra bottles of water. Harper had his shotgun and .22 revolver, and Lee had his rifle and the .22 pistol. They put the ammunition Bus had gathered for them in a small knapsack in the backseat. Miller was armed with his .38 Special and a few extra shells in his pocket. Doc had a 20-gauge shotgun someone had given him for the trip and a small box of shells. Josh carried his Ruger LCP and an ancient bolt-action .22 rifle.

Lee put the six gallons they had siphoned into the truck's tank and then tossed the two gas cans and the siphoning tube into the bed with Miller. Harper cranked the engine and it started up with a throaty rumble.

By the time Lee had seated himself in the passenger's seat, Bus was there, looking bleary-eyed and tired. He leaned into Harper's open window and looked at the group. "You guys don't do anything stupid, okay? Do what you gotta do and come right back. We need you and we're all counting on you."

Bus received a few silent nods.

Lee met the man's gaze and gave him a thumbs-up. "I'll get 'em back safe, Bus." Though he knew it was a promise he couldn't necessarily keep.

Bus backed away a few steps and someone opened the gate.

Harper put the pickup in drive and they left the relative safety of Camp Ryder just as the sun cleared the treetops.

They drove slowly.

As he had the day before, Lee kept his window open so he could rest his rifle on the side-view mirror and scope out any potential hazards. They stopped frequently when Harper or Lee spied something in the roadway. Mostly it was abandoned vehicles or accidents that had not been cleared. Each time they stopped, Lee spent a few minutes surveying the vehicles and the surrounding landscape for signs of an ambush.

Checking these vehicles for fuel ate up more time. The job of testing and siphoning fell to Miller, since he was already in the truck bed and strangely didn't seem to mind the taste of gasoline fumes. Smartly, he didn't try to siphon each vehicle to see if there was fuel. Instead, he would insert the tube and feed it down into the bottom of the tank, then blow through it. If he made bubbles, he would siphon. If the air blew freely, they would move on.

They had managed to glean only a little more than a gallon so far. Most of the vehicles in the roadway were abandoned because they were completely out of gas. The ones from pileups and accidents were close to empty or had already been siphoned by other passing motorists in the six weeks since the collapse.

After clearing another cluster of abandoned cars with nothing to celebrate fuel-wise, Lee broke the silence. "So, Doc...you're a medical professional, right?"

"Fourth-year medical student," he replied flatly.

Lee honestly didn't know whether that was good or bad. He plunged forward. "Can you tell me anything you've learned about FURY? Have you been able to do any research?"

"Research?" Doc smiled. "Like spinning up some blood samples in my high-tech laboratory?" He laughed. "No."

Lee craned his neck and looked back at the younger man with a blank stare.

Doc got uncomfortable and stowed his attitude. "No, I haven't really been able to do any research because I don't have the equipment. However, we can draw certain conclusions about the bacterium from what we observe in our personal experiences."

Lee turned back around. "I'd like to hear it."

"Well, we begin with what we know." Doc gave a lengthy sigh. "We know it's a plague, which means it's borne from bacteria, not a virus. We know bacteria are a little bit larger and a little clumsier than a virus. A virus can't reproduce by itself, but bacteria can. Also, bacteria are living organisms, while a virus is just a bit of genetic material floating around.

"We can safely assume that FURY is not air-borne, because bacteria usually are too heavy to float around in the air like viruses do. Which isn't to say that someone coughing on you can't give you FURY, because the bacteria will cling to mucous and spit globules that are coming out of the person's mouth. Generally, a bacteria means we have to get it from physical contact. But physical contact doesn't seem to be enough with FURY because we've all seen people fight hand-to-hand with the infected and not contract the plague. It seems to only want to transmit from one bodily fluid to another. Blood to blood, spit to spit, mucous to mucous, and every other combination therein. So, from that we can infer that the bacteria doesn't like to be dry."

Miller looked thoughtful. "Seems like it's very selective. If it needs such a narrow avenue to spread, why did it spread so fast?"

Doc shrugged. "There's a lot we don't know. Maybe somebody out there had time to get some answers before things fell apart, but it wasn't me." He regarded his hands with great interest. "I would venture a guess that it has less to do with the virulence of FURY and more to do with how the infected people act. Normally when people get sick they stay in their houses and avoid other people. In this case, the sick ones are seeking out the healthy ones. Imagine if someone with the flu wasn't sitting in bed and sipping chicken noodle soup but intentionally going out and coughing on everyone he could find. Imagine how fast that would spread."

Josh's eyes widened. "Do you think that's a biological mechanism of the bacteria? To spread itself?"

Doc looked at him as though he'd just asked if the moon were made of cheese. "No. I think a bacterium is a single-cell organism incapable of desiring to extend its life. I think the spread of the plague is an unfortunate coincidence based on what the bacteria do to our brains and the base instincts of aggression ingrained in our DNA."

Josh spoke in a dramatic, breathy voice. "It's like a perfect storm of biology."

Doc's eyes narrowed. "You're fucking weird, man."

Josh laughed and looked out the window.

"Any other inferences?" Lee asked.

"Not really." Doc shifted in his seat. "Based on our collective experiences, those are pretty much the conclusions I'm willing to come to. Perhaps a bacteriologist or maybe even someone with a complete PhD might know more."

They came upon another pileup, this one made of two cars and an SUV.

Fifteen minutes after spotting it, they left it behind—no gas to be had.

"So I answered one of your questions," Doc said. "Can you answer one of mine?"

Lee thought for a moment. "Sure."

"Why are you doing this?"

"Doing what?"

"This whole thing. This 'mission' of yours. I mean, what's in it for you? There's no government anymore; there's no one to pay your salary or recognize your work."

Lee actually found himself laughing. "You know, for all your sarcasm and pessimism, Doc, you're guilty of doing the same thing."

"Oh?"

Lee turned in his seat and made eye contact. "Why do you heal people? You get nothing from it. You're not getting a big doctor's salary or driving a nice car or being recognized by the medical field."

Doc turned away from Lee's gaze. "I just do what I can do."

"And *I* do what *I* can do." Lee faced forward. When he spoke again it was quiet and sober. "This is no way to live. No one wants to be afraid for the rest of their life. We all want to get our old lives back. Of course, our old lives are gone. We'll never get them back. What we can get back is our sense of pride, our sense of decency." He sighed. "It's difficult to explain. Sometimes I think I'm just fighting so I can have a chance to stop fighting."

Harper smiled. "Makes sense in a twisted sort of way."

Lee shrugged. "That's my answer."

"And you're stickin' to it," Harper finished.

Doc didn't say anything. He appeared lost in thought, staring out the passenger's side window.

"Roadblock," Harper murmured.

Lee sat forward and peered over the top of his rifle as Harper brought the pickup to a stop and angled it so that Lee could gain a better view of the roadblock. This one consisted of two cars completely blocking the road and one in the ditch to the right, as though it had tried to go around and gotten stuck. On either side the road, a steep embankment rose up with trees at the top.

Lee put his eye to the glass and scoped out the roadblock.

"Back up," he said quickly.

"What?" Harper asked but was already putting the truck in reverse. "What'd you see?"

Lee watched the roadblock with his naked eye until it was nearly obscured by a bend in the road. "Stop."

Harper obediently stopped the truck.

"I didn't see anything. Yet," Lee said, sighting through the scope again. What he noticed was the way the two vehicles in the roadway were positioned. They were nose-to-nose, taking up both lanes, but didn't appear to have the significant damage that one might expect from a head-on collision.

Someone had parked them there to block the road.

He watched the two cars in the center with a

steady, unblinking eye. Seconds ticked by, turning gradually into a minute, then two. Then, just as Lee was about to give up and look elsewhere, he saw the top of a blond head poke up and peer over the top of one of the hoods.

"Got one." Lee called it. "Doesn't look infected. Two now. Two men."

"They look hostile?" Josh was almost climbing over the center console.

"Definitely looks like they're trying to set an ambush, but I don't see any weapons yet. Wait…" From out of the car in the ditch emerged a female. She was younger, possibly late teens or early twenties, and somewhat pretty, with dark hair, jean shorts, and a thin white tank top.

Bait for the trap, he thought.

The woman stood in the roadway, faced them, and began waving her arms.

"Is she waving at us?" Harper squinted.

"Back up more," Lee said. "Until we're out of sight."

The pickup lurched backward and put more distance between them and the roadblock. When the roadblock was comfortably hidden by the bend of the road, Lee opened his door and stepped out. He pointed to Harper. "Give me five minutes to get in position, and then I want you to very cautiously approach that roadblock. If they start shooting, I want you to get down behind that engine block and haul ass away from here. Just remember: Door panels don't stop bullets."

"What about y-you?" Harper stammered.

"I'll catch up with you guys." He gave him a

thumbs-up and hoped this wasn't a huge mistake. "Don't worry."

He turned and dipped down into the ditch on the side of the road, slinging his rifle as he went. Then he scrambled up the embankment and disappeared into the woods.

Harper watched the captain vanish into the woods, moving with a feral intensity that creeped him out a bit.

Doc snorted. "Who does this guy think he is? Fucking John Rambo?"

"He knows what he's doing," Harper said quietly.

Miller stuck his head in through the open back glass. "Uh...what the hell we doin', Bill?"

"Sorry." Harper realized no one had explained to Miller what was happening. "Roadblock ahead."

"Why's the captain runnin' off by himself?"

"Because he's a secret government operative," Doc said, putting on an official voice. "Capable of overcoming all the evil in the world."

"Would you shut the fuck up!" Harper suddenly shouted. "You were the one who asked to come on this trip, but all you've done is sit there and bitch! If that's how you're going to be for the rest of it, you can get the hell outta the truck and get to steppin' back to camp!"

Doc shut his mouth.

"So..." Miller trailed off.

"Roadblock." Josh took over for Harper. "Captain Harden told us to give him five minutes, and then we're going to approach the roadblock."

Miller nodded coolly and then pulled his head out of the back glass and stood up, looking over the top of the cab.

Time stretched.

The clock on the dash had only passed about two minutes.

The silence in the car was absolute as everyone intermittently stared at where the road disappeared into the bend, and then back to the little green digits of the clock. Legs bounced and fingers tapped. Everyone held their guns with sweaty hands and bloodless knuckles.

Finally, five minutes passed.

Harper let his foot off the brake and the truck started rolling forward again.

They all craned to see the farthest visible point in the road.

The roadblock came into view, and this time the girl was leaning against her car with her head in her hands, the picture of distress. Harper kept the truck rolling slowly, not accelerating and not slowing down. After a brief moment, the girl seemed to sense that the truck had come back into view. She turned to them and began waving frantically.

"Maybe she's really in trouble." Josh sounded concerned.

"Just watch for the two guys behind the cars." Harper felt the hairs on the back of his neck beginning to stand up. They were committed now. They were rolling into the roadblock. If it was indeed a trap, Harper had the feeling they wouldn't get away before the two guys behind the roadblock opened up on them.

He hoped the captain knew what he was doing.

As the truck drew closer to the roadblock, the girl ran up to the driver's window. Her face was a mask of despair, but she was attractive nonetheless. As she approached, Harper couldn't help himself from noticing the two dark nipples under the thin cloth of the white tank top. Nor could he help noticing the purple and yellow bruises on the sides of her arms and around the base of her neck.

"Please! Please help!" She was pointing to the car in the ditch. "My dad's hurt! He needs help. Please!"

Harper swore under his breath.

Everyone in the truck was in complete vapor lock. No one knew what the fuck to do.

Should we get out of the truck?

Should we drive away?

"Please! He's hurt!" she pleaded.

"Harper." Doc sounded stressed. "Just let me take a look."

And then several things happened in such quick succession, an outside observer would have seen them as simultaneous. But Harper saw each thing individually, like they were all snapshots laid out in front of him, one after the other.

The girl was backing away from them, hands down at her sides, shaking. The look of desperation was gone from her face and had been replaced by a hollow expression. Regret?

Perhaps guilt.

He blinked, and then there were two men standing behind the roadblock, pointing guns at them.

His stomach tightened.

To his left came the sound of leaves and branches

parting, and then the same noise to his right. He looked and saw a man running out of the woods, coming straight at the passenger's side of the truck, pointing what looked like a Russian-made SKS rifle at him and screaming, "Get out of the fucking car!"

And all Harper could think of were Lee's words: *Door panels don't stop bullets.*

Harper put his hands up, not daring to go for his shotgun or the revolver in his pocket.

This guy had him dead to rights.

His door opened and he felt someone grab him by the collar, and then he was being pulled out of the vehicle. He couldn't get his feet under him fast enough and he tripped and sprawled onto the pavement, his chin striking the concrete and leaving flesh behind.

Rough hands grabbed him up.

His own warm blood trickled from his chin down his neck.

The guy with the SKS was still yelling at Doc and Josh and Miller to get out of the car.

Harper found his feet and stood, holding his chin. Josh got out of the truck, looking terrified. Harper was sure he wore the same expression. Doc just kept yelling back, "I'm a doctor! I'm a doctor!" Harper tried to count how many there were. Two behind the roadblock, covering them with rifles. One on either side of their vehicle.

Four armed gunmen?

The man with the SKS grabbed Doc by the shoulder and spun him so he was facing the bed of the truck. Over the top of the bed, Harper could see

Doc's eyes were shut tightly. The gunman seized the scrawny guy by the back of the neck and slammed him hard against the side of the truck while screaming in his ear, "Shut up! Shut the fuck up!"

Doc closed his mouth. Then he opened his eyes.

His gaze fell on Harper and there was a horrific certainty hanging in the air between them: *We're gonna die now. This is it.*

And then Harper heard a sound he'd never heard before in his life. If asked to describe it after that moment, he would have struggled to compare it to anything he'd ever experienced and would have eventually settled on the description that it sounded like someone hitting an overripe watermelon with a baseball bat.

That sound was so distinct and unexpected that when the rifle report cracked through the woods a second later, Harper didn't put them together. Everyone seemed to stand motionless after the rifle report. The only body moving was that of the man with the SKS, pitching forward with the right half of his head missing. He struck the side of the truck and then collapsed to the ground.

Then all hell broke loose.

The girl started screaming.

Josh made a break for the truck and his rifle inside.

The man who had pulled Harper out of the truck shouted something unintelligible at Josh and began swinging his weapon toward him. Harper thought it looked like another SKS, but this one had a long and wicked bayonet attached to it and all Harper could see was that rusty-looking blade swinging toward Josh.

Without thinking, he lurched out and grabbed the rifle.

The man turned toward Harper and began frantically pulling at the rifle, trying to break Harper's grip on it. The "man" wasn't much older than Josh, Harper thought, but his face was lean and savage, like the difference between a lap dog and a coyote.

The rifle bucked in their hands as they struggled, the bullet punching a neat hole in the door panel of the pickup truck.

"I'munna fuckin' kill you!" the savage shouted repeatedly, furious at first, and then terrified as he began to lose his grip on the rifle. "I'munna fuckin' kill you! I'munna fuckin' kill you! I'munna..."

Harper twisted his body, pulling the man-boy off his balance, and then planted a foot in his midsection and ripped the rifle from his hands. They both toppled backward—Harper into the truck and his attacker to the ground.

He tried to tell the kid to stay down, but his wind was gone from his lungs and the only thing that came out was a hoarse croak. In his mind the words circled manically like flies around a corpse: *Don't get up! Don't get up! DON'T GET UP!*

In the background, another wet *smack* was followed by another delayed rifle report.

The kid reached for his belt, still laying on his back, and produced a buck knife. For a second, Harper thought maybe he was going to throw it down and surrender, but instead he leaned forward and tried to get up.

Harper moved fast, with a shout of rage and

horror that came out of a place inside of him he hadn't known existed. Rage at the kid's apparent willingness to die and horror at his own ability to oblige him. But he didn't stop himself, and he rammed that bayonet straight down into the kid's stomach. He felt the initial resistance from clothing and taut skin, and then the sudden, sickening release as the rusty blade slipped inside.

The man-boy's eyes went wide and panicked and he made a choking, gagging noise. Then he found his breath and started screaming. Harper screamed along with him until his lungs were empty, but the kid would not stop. He just kept going, kept screaming, endlessly, *stop screaming stop screaming stop screaming please please stop screaming!* And through it all, like a wild animal stuck in a trap, he kept thrashing around underneath the blade and trying to pull it out of himself, but Harper leaned his entire weight down on it so that he could feel the tip of the blade scraping concrete.

Finally, Harper could take the screaming no more. Overwhelmed with panic, he pulled the trigger twice in quick succession. The muzzle blast obliterated the kid's chest and punched the life right out of him. He collapsed very suddenly, eyes half open.

Harper just stood there, unmoving.

What do I do now? And then, absurdly: *Am I gonna get arrested?*

Someone was still screaming.

NINE

THE HARD ROAD

LEE RACED THROUGH THE woods, downhill toward the roadblock.

He'd taken the first man out with a well-placed shot to the head. The second shot had taken one of the two men behind the barricade in the chest, after which he saw Harper take the third one, and Lee could hear the screams even from his perch high on the hilltop. They sent a chill down his back. The fourth man had fled after firing off two rounds of birdshot that skittered harmlessly across the front of the truck, doing little but nicking the paint.

Now, as the trees lashed Lee's face, sprinting toward the road with his rifle in his right hand and his left unsuccessfully warding off the branches in front of him, he could hear someone else screaming, though he couldn't tell who it was.

When Lee burst through the trees a moment later, he found the scene in chaos.

Doc stood at the side of the truck, staring down at the first man Lee had shot. The bullet had so cleanly removed the interior of the man's head that the inside of the skull was a nearly perfect white, hardly stained by blood.

Lee's thought was singular and strange: *Melon baller...it looks like it was scooped out by a melon baller.*

Harper stood on the other side of the vehicle, holding the SKS with one hand, the other running repeatedly over his bald head. He stared down at the body, and then looked up to the source of the screaming, as though he didn't know whether he should stay with the body or go help whoever was yelling.

Breathing heavily, Lee jogged around the front of the pickup truck and saw what the commotion was.

The girl lay seated on the ground, back against one of the cars in the roadblock. Her skin was pale, her lips gray. Blood was pooling under her right leg and a trail led from the middle of the street to where she was seated now. A sheen of greasy sweat had broken out across her face and she stared at the men, terrified and taking quick, shallow gulps of air.

Miller had his pistol out and was trying to get to the girl, screaming that he was going to kill her. Josh tried to hold him back, tried to get him to calm down.

"It's her fucking fault! I'm gonna fucking kill that bitch!"

"Chill out, man!"

Lee moved in quickly and snatched Miller's wrist, torquing the joint and pulling the pistol smoothly out of his hand. Miller spun, his eyes full of blind rage that seemed to instantly dissipate when he realized who had taken his weapon.

"C-captain..." he stammered.

Lee was stern but not harsh. "You need to breathe. Go take a break."

"But she..." Miller looked rapidly between her and Lee. "She was the one..."

Lee grabbed him by the collar and pulled him in close so he could speak quietly into his ear. "She's gonna be dead in a minute as it is, Miller. You really wanna be the one to shoot her in cold blood? You really wanna be the one to take that on? Just leave it be."

Harper's voice came from behind Lee. "It was me. It was my fault."

Lee released Miller and watched Harper moving slowly toward the girl, holding the SKS by the muzzle, the buttstock dragging on the ground. His face was blank and his speech hazy. He seemed in shock.

"Harper." Lee moved to his side.

"The gun..." He seemed to be having trouble forming words. "It went off when I was fighting over it."

Lee only nodded. Harper stopped about five yards from the girl and stared at her. She was barely clinging to consciousness and took a moment to realize they were standing there. Her wounded leg was as still as a dead fish, but her good leg began jerking around like she was trying to backpedal away from them.

Lee laid his rifle on the ground and held up his empty palms. "It's okay. We're not going to hurt you anymore."

Her leg stopped moving, but she still stared at

Lee with wide, fearful eyes. He knelt down beside her, felt the wetness of her blood soak through to his knees. She must have seen some softness in his face, because the fear fled from her eyes.

Her voice was thin. "I'm sorry. I'm sorry."

Lee nodded slowly. He took her wrist gently and felt for the radial pulse with two fingers. Nothing. Then he reached across and pushed his fingertips into the crease of her hip and thigh, feeling for the femoral artery. He readjusted twice and felt only a faint, thready pulse that might have come from his own fingers.

She didn't seem to notice his prodding. She spoke like she was asleep, in the throes of a nightmare. "They made me. They made me do things…"

"Shh," Lee spoke quietly. "It's okay." He put two fingers to her carotid and felt the pulse there, but only weakly. Rote memorization of medical training rolled through his brain: Radial pulse equals systolic blood pressure of at least eighty. Carotid plus femoral equals between seventy and eighty. Carotid only equals between sixty and seventy.

With only a carotid pulse, her blood pressure had dropped too low.

He took both of her hands in one of his. They were cold and clammy.

"I didn't want this," she whispered.

Lee forced a reassuring smile, feeling drained. "I know. I know you didn't."

"I didn't want this," she repeated.

Behind him, the other four men had gathered and now silently stared on, their faces as ashen and hollow as Lee felt.

She looked around. "Can you take me home?"

Lee thought about what was best to say to her, then finally nodded. "Sure I can."

"You can take me home?"

"We're gonna go right now, okay?"

"Okay."

"What's your name?" Lee wished he hadn't asked, because he didn't want to know.

"Rebecca." Her eyes were moving around restlessly. "Rebecca Stilwell."

"Okay, Rebecca. We're gonna take you home."

"Yeah."

"Why don't you go to sleep now, Rebecca?"

"Okay."

"You'll be home in just a minute."

The girl closed her eyes and the smile on her lips was as faint as her pulse. "I'm sorry. Thank you."

And then the girl lying in the middle of the road simply ceased to exist.

They left the bodies where they fell.

They took the guns and ammunition. Two SKS rifles, one with seven rounds in the magazine, the other with a full ten. Two 12-gauge shotguns, one a nice over-under Beretta with two spent shells in the tubes, and one busted-up Remington with a loose barrel and five live shells.

Miller was able to siphon out another gallon of gasoline between the two cars in the roadblock. The one on the side of the road was empty. This brought them up to about eight gallons total, two gallons short of their comfort zone.

Just inside the woods where the two young

men had lain in ambush, they found a duffel bag that contained wads of cash, jewelry, watches, and eight cans of chili. Their hunger drove the brutality of the last half hour out of their minds, and they immediately divvied up the entire eight cans of chili and ate until they were full.

Josh puked most of his up a few moments later.

Miller made an effort to appear unfazed, but he was quieter than usual.

Doc didn't say a word.

Harper and Lee packed up the guns and left the duffel bag full of worthless cash. Harper made the joke that they could use it for kindling, but no one laughed. They took their seats in the truck and drove on, leaving the roadblock behind them.

Harper would never admit it, but he could not stomach chili after that day.

They left Highway 210 to avoid passing through downtown Smithfield. The small backstreets kept them turning and kept them wary. More roadblocks mired their progress, and they approached each with extreme caution, slowing them down even more than before. No one wanted a repeat of earlier that day.

It was late afternoon and the sun was a few hours into its downward slope when they crossed a bridge that passed over I-95. The interstate was a mess of accidents and abandoned vehicles, both creating small traffic jams behind them. People had attempted to drive their cars around the blockages only to get stuck in a muddy median, or they had slipped into a ditch and created an impassable wall of cars. With no way to clear these vehicles, the traffic was a gridlock in both directions.

They found their first good luck of the day directly across the overpass. On the left side of the road was a used car lot that appeared largely untouched by the general looting and property damage that had ravaged everything else around it. The serenity of the parking lot did not set any of them at ease, but rather caught their attention as suspicious and caused them to stop their vehicle nearly a block back and observe the car lot for a long stretch of time.

The cars were all in pristine shape, as untouched as Lee had imagined they were when a sleazy car salesman was still hawking them to witless consumers. Their windshields were emblazoned with colorful paint that advertised 0% FINANCING !!! and NO MONEY DOWN !!! The glass windows all around the dealership's main building were completely intact. An American flag stirred restlessly in the breeze, the metal grommets tapping an uneven rhythm against the flagpole.

Harper's eyes were narrow slits. "What you thinkin', Captain?"

"I'm thinking there's gotta be some gas in those cars."

"Don't you think it looks a little too good to be true?" Josh sounded unsure.

Lee nodded. "But do you want to leave it without checking?"

"No."

Lee leaned into the back and retrieved one of the SKS rifles they had taken from the roadblock.

"Josh, why don't you hop up in the bed with Miller and cover him with the other rifle while he works."

Josh traded his shotgun for the other SKS and stepped out.

Lee kept his eyes on the car lot but felt the truck list slightly as Josh climbed into the bed with Miller. The two exchanged words that Lee couldn't hear, then tapped the roof to indicate they were good.

Lee pointed to the main entrance. "Take us up to the gate right there, Harper."

The older man nodded and eased the pickup forward.

The main entrance to the car lot was gated off, chained, and locked. But it was constructed to keep cars in, not to keep people out. As the truck came to a stop, Miller grabbed an empty gas can and the siphon tube and jogged quickly over to the nearest car. It took him a moment to jimmy the locked gas cap with a pocketknife, but when he fed the tube into the gas tank and blew air through it, he looked up with a smile and a thumbs-up.

"Good." Harper seemed to relax a bit. "Hopefully we'll get what we need."

Lee heard him speaking but wasn't paying attention. He was leaning forward in his seat, looking up through the windshield at the flagpole in the center of the lot. His face was focused and thoughtful.

"You see something?" Harper asked, immediately going back to high alert.

Lee broke his stare to glance at Harper. Without

answering his question, he opened his door and slipped out, taking the SKS rifle with him. Over his shoulder he said, "Just sit tight for one minute," and then closed the door behind him.

Miller watched Lee moving purposefully toward him and straightened up, his eyes moving around as though something was wrong but he couldn't figure out what it was. "Everything okay, Captain?"

Lee was still staring to the center of the car lot. "Lemme borrow your pocketknife for a second."

Hesitantly, the younger man produced the knife and placed it in Lee's palm. "Sure."

Lee didn't say anything else. He took the knife and walked into the parking lot toward the flagpole. His gaze lifted steadily as he neared it, until he was staring straight up the metallic shaft, fixated on the banner that wavered at the top. After a moment's regard, Lee opened the pocketknife and cut the rope holding the flag in place.

He lowered the flag slowly, as ceremoniously as any member of an honor guard, and gathered it in his arms, taking care to not let it touch the ground. It was not a large flag, and it rolled up easily. He turned his back to the flagpole and walked directly back to Miller.

"Do you know how to do this?"

"I was in the Scouts," Miller said, by way of an answer.

"It should only take a second." Lee offered him the grommeted base of the flag, where the white trim met the deep blue background in the field of stars. He backed up a few steps so the flag was stretched taut, then folded it in half longways, then in half again. Making careful triangles of the red and white stripes, Lee worked his way up to Miller so they were facing only a foot apart and the stripes turned into stars.

He tucked the loose end in snugly. "Thanks."

With the flag folded properly, Lee took it back to the pickup truck.

Climbing back into his seat, Harper regarded him with a curious smile. "A little something to remember America by?"

The look that Harper received in return was sharp, but Lee spoke evenly. "The United States is an idea, Harper. The best one we've ever had." He looked down at the folded flag in his lap. "The only way to destroy an idea is to kill everyone who believes in it. And I'm not dead yet."

Harper didn't respond, because he had nothing to say.

Miller finished siphoning the gas tank, which yielded a full five-gallon gas can and brought them into their twelve-gallon comfort zone with a little extra to spare. He put the gas in the tank and the can and tube in the bed. Josh hopped out, Miller took his place, and the group was on its way again.

TEN

BEANS AND BULLETS

As I-95 FADED IN the distance, Lee finally pulled the GPS unit out of the cargo pocket of his pants. It was a thick handheld device, built specially for the Coordinators stationed in each of the lower forty-eight states. They all had access to a series of supply bunkers, the number depending on the populace of the state they were in. The GPS unit was designed to help the Coordinators keep those bunkers all to themselves.

Only the Coordinator to which that device was assigned could access the GPS unit, and therein the location of his bunkers. There was much discussion during the planning stages of Project Hometown about whether or not to allow all of the Coordinators to access all of the bunkers. The argument that ended the debate was a simple observation: If they all had access to all the bunkers, it would only take one Coordinator to be captured and tortured and turned to destroy the entire mission. In the end it was decided that they wouldn't place all their eggs in one basket, so to speak.

The unit was a black box with a five-inch screen. Below the screen was a small, glossy black square, which Lee placed his thumb on. The little square depressed slightly when he applied pressure, activating the thumb scanner. It took the device a moment to verify his print and also to check for the presence of a pulse, so interested parties could not access the device simply because they possessed Lee's thumbs.

Oh, military industry, you've thought of everything.

The screen lit up into a ten-by-ten grid, each square containing a letter and a number. The grid was randomized each time the thumbprint was verified, so the same grid never came up twice, keeping prying eyes from copying Lee's code simply by pattern memorization. Lee carefully tapped out the appropriate alphanumerics.

The screen changed and displayed ten options: Bunker #1, Bunker #2, and so on to Bunker #10. He selected Bunker #4 and the screen changed once again to a topographical map of the area. At the very borders of the screen, Lee could see the framework of the triangle created by I-95, I-795, and I-40. A small red arrow was in the center of that frame, pointing southeast. A short distance from that red arrow was a blue dot.

"Gettin' close." Lee raised his head and watched the road roll slowly by them.

They had not come across any roadblocks since passing over I-95, which was a stroke of good luck and would hopefully have them in the bunker before dark. Now the sun was dipping down closer to the horizon, just beginning to lick at the treetops. They had perhaps an hour before it was dark.

Lee instructed Harper to slow down a bit so that they did not miss their turn. After another long mile cruising at about thirty miles per hour, Lee found what he was looking for and waved at Harper to stop. To their right, a narrow gravel road led away from the blacktop. The front was barred by a plain red gate with a big padlocked chain wrapped around it. The whole ensemble was very low-key.

When Project Hometown was in its planning stages, it was decided that a simple, nondescript gate would probably keep more people out than a ten-foot-high fence marked GOVERNMENT PROPERTY. The thinking was that, in an event of social and governmental collapse, people would seek out abandoned government facilities, believing that food and water and medical supplies would be more easily found in these places. With no personnel available to guard the gate, people might find something marked as government property more attractive.

The pickup truck pulled into the mouth of the dirt road and Lee hopped out. He carried no keys, but approached the padlock with purpose. Though the large padlock looked like just another piece of rusty metal, Lee placed his GPS device against it and it popped open with a tiny whir of electronic servos. Lee pocketed the GPS and pulled off the big lock, letting the chain fall with a metallic rasp. He swung the gate open and began walking back toward the truck.

And that was where he stopped.

Everyone in the truck stiffened when they saw him freeze.

He turned his face into the breeze and lifted his nose, taking a few quick sniffs. Then he looked back to where the dirt road disappeared into the trees. There was a distinct smell coming from the direction of his bunker, a pungent odor Lee had not smelled in a long time. It was a nauseously sweet smell that set his hairs to standing on end and his stomach to churning. It was the smell of burning hair mixed with charred meat.

He looked through the passenger side window at Harper. "You smell that?"

Harper's nose wrinkled slightly and he nodded.

Lee swore quietly to himself, then stared off into the woods for a moment. When he looked back, that hard edge had set on his face again. "I don't know who's burning bodies over there, but we need to approach cautiously. We gotta go in on foot."

The other four men did not appear thrilled, but they kept their opinions to themselves.

Lee quickly scouted far enough out that they could pull the pickup truck out of sight of the roadway. He rechained and locked the fence, then jogged back to the four men, who now stood at the tailgate, looking nervous and gripping their rifles like talismans to ward off evil. They were all thinking about the roadblock.

Josh, in particular, looked pale, and an unhealthy sweat had broken out on his face.

Lee approached him and put a hand on the back of his neck. "You gotta buck up, Josh."

"I don't wanna kill any normal people," he mumbled to the ground.

"Well, that ain't up to you." Lee shook him. "If things go down, you gotta do what has to be done to stay alive, you hear me?"

Josh nodded.

"You guys remember tactical spacing?"

There was a chorus of "Uh-huh"s.

"That's what I want. I'm gonna be point and take you guys through the woods. You all stack up behind Harper." He looked at the older man. "Harper, just keep me in sight. You don't have to be up on my ass, you just gotta be able to see me. And if I start shooting, you all hit the ground and don't engage until I tell you to, understand?"

"Got it."

"Alright." Lee had traded the Savage .308 for an SKS. He put a palm to the base of the magazine and then pulled the chambering lever back an inch to make sure there was a live cartridge in the chamber. The other four men followed suit.

Five rifle bolts snicked into place.

Locked and loaded.

He jogged out ahead of them and then dipped into the woods. Behind him, he could hear the soft movement of his companions taking to the forest. They moved well for civilians, but noise discipline and woodland movement were not just for tactical teams and hunters anymore. Everyone had to learn how to survive, and those who didn't, didn't.

He ducked under the arms of trees and slipped quietly over logs. He kept his profile low and small—bent at the waist with his head down. His feet moved deftly, choosing the softest ground that would hide the sound of his approach. His eyes scanned up and down, deciding which path to take through the woods, and then looking ahead for threats. He listened carefully for anything out of the ordinary.

The smell of burning flesh became stronger,

though it still only came in jarring whiffs. Just when he would begin to think he had lost the scent, it would roll across on the wind and slap him in the face again. Every time he smelled it, he felt that dull ache behind his eyes and his stomach went weak. The smell had always given him headaches and made him nauseated.

As Lee approached the clearing where his bunker was buried deep in the earth, he saw the flickering flames and stopped, taking a knee. Behind him the constant soft rustle of the other four ceased.

Ahead and in the clearing, Lee could make out three tents. Two of them were factory-made dome tents that you could find in any sporting goods store, and the third was a crude construction of rope and tarp but was the biggest of the three. The tents formed a loose *V* shape around a burning jumble of sticks and dry branches with flames glowing deep inside and licking out at the air. Protruding from the fire, Lee could see the charred claw of a human hand. A foot jutted up, stiff and erect like a piece of a mannequin, smoke curling off the flaking skin. Lee couldn't see any other body parts, but due to the size of the fire, he suspected more than one body was burning.

A middle-aged man with short brown hair and thick glasses stood at the edge of the fire, leaning on a shovel and staring vacantly into the flames. He wore Dockers that Lee imagined had once been clean and pressed but were now a wrinkly, sooty mess. Tucked into those Dockers was a short-sleeved button-up shirt that was in about the same condition as the pants. The man's face was naturally lean but sported a good growth of beard. Lee thought he looked like a straitlaced kind of person, or at least he might have been before all of this. He looked like he might have been an accountant or a bank teller. Something boring. The kind of guy who ate plain oatmeal for breakfast along with his black coffee. The kind of guy who never drank more than three beers at a time.

Lee looked past this strange contradiction of man and activity and could see movement in the large tent made of rope and tarp, though he could not count how many others were there. Beyond the tents, Lee could see the hulk of his bunker's door, jutting up out of the earth like a half-buried monolith. It was still locked and secured. It did not appear that the straitlaced man or any of his friends had gotten inside.

Lee slunk quietly back into the woods.

He found the others still kneeling down a few yards back. They stared expectantly at Lee as he sidled up to them. They bombarded him with hushed questions.

"Is there someone there?"

"Are they dangerous?"

"What do you want us to do?"

Lee shook his head. "I don't know if they're hostile yet."

Harper gritted his teeth. "Like we didn't know if the people at the roadblock were hostile?"

"What do you propose?" Lee turned a flinty glare on him.

"I say we just take them out," Miller mumbled.

Josh looked squeamish.

Lee poked a finger in Miller's chest. "We can't just take them out, Miller! They could be survivors!"

"Or," Harper hissed, "they could be fucking assholes like at the roadblock."

"Fine." Lee wiped sweat from his eyes. "You guys take positions at the wood line. I will approach with no weapon and my hands up. I will try to feel them out. If things go badly, I'm just gonna drop to the ground and you guys hose 'em."

Everyone looked grim. But it was the best plan they had.

It was the *only* plan they had.

"Here." Lee offered his SKS to Doc. "If trouble starts, this will give you a little more bang for your buck."

Doc looked up at him and Lee could see a level of resentment that he wasn't sure he had done anything to deserve. But it was there nonetheless. Doc snatched up the rifle. "Does it get easy?"

"What?" Lee's face tightened.

"Killing people. Does it get easy for you?"

Lee just stared at him. He didn't glare; he didn't sneer. His gaze was even and blank, because behind his eyes he was actually considering the question. Though Doc had clearly meant it as a jab, Lee shrugged off the childish insult. Like so many others before him, Doc relied on tougher men than himself to stay safe, and when forced to raise his hand to protect himself or those around him, he resented those men for not being able to solve all of his problems.

"Yes," Lee stated truthfully. "It does get easier."

The party broke. Harper took the center with

Doc, while Miller and Josh split out to the left and right. Lee gave them a brief moment, and then began to follow. They moved into position as though they'd drilled on it a thousand times, and Lee had to admit, he felt a faint level of pride in them. If they could accomplish this after a few hours of practice, imagine what a few months of drills would do for them?

When each man had settled into his position, Lee stood up fully; raised his arms high above his head with his hands open, palms out; and stepped from the trees.

The man staring into the fire jumped like he'd had a cattle prod shoved up his ass and he snatched up the shovel, bearing it like a club. He began shouting, "I got another one! There's another one!"

"Whoa!" Lee stood at the wood line and didn't come any farther. "Calm down! I'm not infected!"

People were suddenly pouring out of all three tents. Lee thought there might be at least a dozen of them. They were young and old, men and women, and a few children. They all were lean, as everyone was these days, their faces dirty and hard, and they all were brandishing some form of weapon, down to the smallest child, which was a little girl Lee guessed was not much older than Abby. She held a hammer.

Lee tried to sound calm and in control. "I'm not sick. I'm not here to hurt you. No one's going to hurt you."

The straitlaced man didn't let his guard down, but the group's instant aggression kind of stalled out and everyone just stood around for a moment, trading hesitant glances. When he spoke again, his voice came out stronger than Lee had expected.

"Who are you?"

Lee eyed the man. Of course, he had a specific greeting that he was supposed to use when coming in contact with survivors. But somehow it seemed less likely to sound legitimate when he was wearing a smiley-face T-shirt. He decided to go with a simple, "Captain Harden. US Army."

The leader and apparent speaker for the group seemed to consider this, rolling it around in his mind like he was inspecting it. While the man thought things over, Lee could sense his companions from Camp Ryder behind him, ready to start shooting at a moment's notice. Lee's legs were tensed slightly, ready to dive out of the way of the gunfire if the man made any false moves.

The man tilted his head slightly. "Okay. Captain. Let's assume that I believe you. My next questions would be, where is your weapon, where is your squad, and what are you doing wandering through the woods alone?"

Lee went for blunt honesty. "My weapon is behind me in the woods, where my men are pointing guns at you right now. And I'm not wandering. I've come for the bunker." Lee readied himself to dive to the ground.

There was a ripple of shock as he told them he had men pointing guns at them, but it was silenced almost immediately when he mentioned the bunker. It was like Lee had said some secret password in a language only this group could understand. They began to look at one another and speak excitedly. Even the straitlaced man's expression softened and turned into a faint, hopeful smile.

He lowered the shovel. "Dear God...this is your bunker?"

Lee looked around at the faces staring at them. Now all eyes were on him, completely focused on the next words he was going to say, willing him to say, *Yes, it's my bunker*. Instead, he decided to address a more pressing matter. "Can we talk without holding weapons to each other?"

The speaker for the group seemed so enthralled by talk of the bunker, it was almost like he'd forgotten about the men in the woods or that his group were still holding their various bludgeoning weapons. His eyes darted for a moment and Lee thought he saw a bit of the same fear that had come out before, but it was quelled with a slight nod. "Yes. We should speak reasonably with each other. No need for any bloodshed."

Lee made a waving motion and his four men emerged from the woods. They didn't point their rifles directly at the group, but they held them tight and ready. Their eyes flitted back and forth between the dozen survivors and Lee, trying to get a feel for what was going on. At the sight of the men, the group of survivors tensed and a ripple of fearful exclamations came out. The speaker reached behind him, taking the hands of a young woman and a boy.

He turned his head slightly. "Trust in the Lord," he said to them quietly. Then he turned back to Lee, the suspicion evident in his voice. "You don't look like soldiers."

Lee glanced to the men from Camp Ryder and gestured for them to lower their weapons. The very least he could do was show this man and his people that they weren't there to murder them. "No, they're not soldiers. They're just civilians who are helping me get a job done. Please, let's be calm here. We have no intention of harming anyone."

The tension in the air eased, but only slightly.

"Can you prove to us who you are?" the speaker asked.

Lee held up a hand, his eyes narrowing. "I think I've been very accomodating so far. Let me ask a few questions."

Brief hesitation. Then, "Okay."

"Who are you?" Lee asked.

The man seemed to brace himself, as though he thought the answer might bring an attack. "I'm Father James Shultz. Everyone calls me Father Jim. The people behind me are members of my congregation."

Lee pointed to the fire, now blazing hotly between them. "Whose body is that?"

Father Jim looked suddenly very serious. "They were a few very sick people."

"Infected?"

Father Jim nodded again. "We could do nothing for them."

Lee eyed him. The man stood erect, his people behind him. They were afraid but trusting. *Trust in the Lord*. Lee had been correct in his initial assessment of the man's occupation. A priest was about on par excitement-wise with an accountant. But there was something else behind his tortoiseshell glasses that spoke of violence. Lee wasn't sure why he asked the next question, other than to see how the man would react. "And how does that sit with your beliefs?"

Father Jim swallowed. "Yes. I struggle with that."

Lee crossed his arms. "So why are you here?"

The priest turned toward his people. "We were taking shelter in our church near here, but a group of men burned it down. We lost many of our people there." He met Lee's gaze, and there was that flicker in his eyes again. "I lived there, right next to the church, and I hunted these woods for years. I remember when this bunker was built. There was nothing out here but trees. And then, suddenly, there's a bunker? Never saw the crews working on it, and it was already covered in leaves and moss when I first found it, like it had been there for ages, but I knew it hadn't been more than a few months since I passed through the area. It was always very mysterious to me.

"When our church burned down, I knew this was where we had to come. It didn't make any sense to me at the time, but I trusted the Lord." His eyes suddenly looked misty, and his voice was low and strained. "We've been here for three weeks now, hungry, thirsty, in danger every day. We have waited. And prayed, every day, that you would come. And here you are. An answer to our prayers!"

Lee shifted uncomfortably. "I'm gonna speak to my guys for a quick second."

Looking eager to know what the hell was going on, the four men from Camp Ryder quickly huddled up at the edge of the woods where quiet conversation would not be overheard. Lee stepped into the circle, that hardness now ebbing from his face.

He looked to Harper first. "What do you think?"

The older man blew air between his lips. "Well, there's not much we can do for them."

"We can feed them," Lee offered. "Give them some water and guns."

"And then what?" Doc fingered his hair back behind his ears. "Just leave them here?"

"There ain't enough room in the truck to take 'em," Miller pointed out. "Unless we don't take supplies."

"No." Lee shook his head. "That is not an option. I made a promise to Camp Ryder. The supplies are nonnegotiable."

"Then we have to leave the people here," Harper concluded.

"Can they stay in the bunker?" Josh asked.

Lee grimaced. "I really...don't prefer that."

"Well, I think your preferences might have to change," Doc said, getting indignant. "We can't take them with us, they don't have a car to go on their own, and if you leave them out here in the woods they're going to keep getting attacked until they die. That's just a fact. It's just a matter of time."

Harper cleared his throat loudly. "What if they could find a vehicle and we gave them instructions on how to reach Camp Ryder?"

"Still pretty dangerous," Lee waffled. While it was his mission to gather groups of survivors, he also had to respect the boundaries of each one. And being that he was just barely trusted at Camp Ryder, he felt it might be overstepping his bounds to start sending every survivor he met off with directions on how to get there. "And how will Bus take that?"

"The only option that isn't dangerous is letting them stay in your bunker," Harper pointed out. "And Bus will just have to trust our judgment."

Lee nodded. "I guess we should put it to Father Jim, then. We will give him supplies, and he can either go on his way or meet us back at Camp Ryder."

Miller shrugged. "Seems more than fair to me."

Josh and Harper agreed.

Doc remained silent.

Lee turned and approached Father Jim again. He looked at the priest and the hopeful faces that gathered behind him. "I can't let you stay inside the bunker, and we do not have enough room for you in the truck we came in. We are here to take supplies back to the other group of survivors, and we will be leaving first thing in the morning. We will give you directions to our community, and you are welcome to go there. Or you can remain here, and I will come back for you, but I don't know how long that will take. Regardless of what you folks decide to do, I will give you food, water, medicine, and weapons. And of course, you can sleep in the bunker tonight. The choice is yours."

Father Jim did not seem offended, but simply thoughtful. "Well, I will think and pray about this decision and tell you tomorrow morning."

Lee nodded. "Of course. Let's get down there."

Lee sent Josh and Doc to retrieve the pickup truck and pull it up close to the bunker door. While Lee wished to help Father Jim and his congregation, he did not fully trust them yet. Father Jim might be a man of God and predisposed to kindness, but he had also seen how the end of society had changed not only Father Jim, but everyone else Lee had come across. When survival was on the line, people were capable of almost anything. If Father Jim viewed the bunker as his only chance of staying alive, and Lee as the one obstacle to that goal, he didn't think it was out of the question for Father Jim to put a bullet in him, regardless of his beliefs.

He made the decision that he would arm his own group and keep the rest of the weapons locked up until they were prepared to leave. Father Jim might not come up with a seditious plan, but that wasn't to say he wouldn't take advantage of an opportunity that was dropped in his lap. It was best to play it safe.

When Josh and Doc returned with the truck, Lee went to the big bunker door. Here the multi-tiered security system became a ridiculous rigmarole of redundancy all built to ensure Lee was the only person who ever accessed the bunker.

He held up the GPS to what appeared to be another flat steel panel. The device prompted him to enter a four-digit code, which he did quickly from memory, and the panel popped out and up on hydraulic hinges, revealing a small screen with a keyboard, a thumb scanner, a microphone, and a retinal scan. He completed the thumb scan, which activated the retinal scan, which activated the keyboard and screen. He entered his information and once it had been verified, the computer prompted him to say his passcode, which was matched to his voice.

The bunker came to life with the heavy mechanical sound of bolts retracting, like a vault door being opened. The door cracked and swung open quietly, letting out a rush of cool air. For a moment, Lee and Harper and Father Jim stood at the entrance to the bunker, staring into the spacious cargo elevator that would take them down forty feet below the surface, where there was safety and security and the feeling that this was not the end of the world, that bringing them back from the brink was not an insurmountable task.

"What happens if you say the wrong code?" Harper's voice was quiet and wondering.

Lee smiled. "Let's just say we should avoid that."

"Can we go inside?" one of Father Jim's congregation asked. She was a younger girl, probably in her teens.

Father Jim looked to Lee, who gestured toward the elevator. "Be my guest."

They went down in two groups, first Lee and the men from Camp Ryder, along with a few of the men from Father Jim's congregation. Then Lee went back up to retrieve the rest of them, closing and sealing the bunker door behind him before descending down to the main level.

The elevator opened to a cement floor that took up a wide square of blank space. The entire bunker was lit by the cold but welcome glow of electric lights, and the place was not just cool but chilly, like it was turning the sweat on their bodies to sheens of ice. And Lee thought it felt wonderful.

Based on the sighs of satisfaction from many of the others, he believed that notion was widely held.

The large open area before the elevator led off into a short hallway. At the end of that hallway was a living area with a few bunks and cots, a bathroom area with showers, and a food preparation area. To either side of the hallway was a door. To the left, it led to a storage area that held all the various supplies that this bunker was stocked with. This was by far the largest section of the bunker. The doorway to the right led to a control room where Lee could monitor the bunker's systems and view surveillance footage of the area outside his bunker.

"How does this place still have electricity?" Father Jim asked with naked wonder.

Lee made his way through the crowd, counting heads as he went. "It's got a battery bank that's constantly trickle-charged by solar panels outside. It'll have electricity until the sun goes out, and a couple days after."

"Amazing," one of the people said genuinely.

"Do you have food?"

"Do you have water?"

Standing at the mouth of the hallway, Lee faced back to them. He caught Harper's eye. "Can you help me get some supplies out?"

Lee instructed the group to go into the living area where they could use the restroom and clean themselves, if they wished. Then he, Harper, Josh, and Miller began hauling out cases of water and MREs to give to the people, while Doc began making the rounds among Father Jim's people, assessing each person to see if they were in good health. Many had old wounds that were not completely healed, and some had become swollen with infection. Others had jungle rot on their feet. Everyone was dehydrated to some degree and suffering from malnutrition.

Doc treated those with infection and jungle rot with antibiotics, and a few with severe dehydration he gave an IV of lactated ringers, a diluted sodium solution. Everyone was given two MREs and instructed to eat slowly and not to overstuff themselves, especially if they were dehydrated. After everyone had eaten and Doc had seen to their medical needs, they each showered. The bunker's water supply fed from a well and was heated through a tankless water heater. It continued pumping out hot water for all of them.

Lee went last. He had disposed of the smiley-face T-shirt and old BDUs that Bus had given him. To replace them, a set of clean MultiCam combat pants and shirt sat folded just outside the shower stall. On top of them was Jack's lucky lottery ticket that had been rescued from the other pair of pants.

With the quiet mumble of survivors just beyond the shower curtain, he closed his eyes and tuned them out. He imagined that the tragedies and triumphs of the last six days since he'd left his house were like the dirt and sweat and grime that clung to his skin, something he could rinse away. He scrubbed at the blood still staining his hands and knees and watched the water running off of him turn pink. Eventually it ran clear again. And when it did, he imagined that none of this had ever happened and that life was normal again.

ELEVEN

BEST-LAID PLANS

AFTER EVERYONE HAD SHOWERED and been fed, it was almost 2100 hours and many of Father Jim's group found a bunk or a cot to fall asleep on. Lee went to the storage room and brought out several more cots, blankets, sleeping bags, and mats for the tired group of survivors to sleep on. They all thanked him profusely. A safe place to sleep with food and water in their bellies was the best thing to happen to any of them since this began.

With most of the group bedded down, Lee quietly made his way to where Harper and the Camp Ryder group were tucked away in the corner. "You guys all get something to eat and drink? Everyone get a shower?"

They all answered in the affirmative.

"Alright." Lee knelt down in their circle. "I need to speak to you guys privately for a moment."

They exchanged a few glances among themselves. The feeling they all had was that their current situation was too good to be true, and though it was unspoken, they all felt that their good fortune had been tapped and something catastrophically wrong was about to occur. Lee had to admit, he felt the same way.

"It's nothing bad," he reassured them.

That statement did little to ease the looks on their faces as they all stood and accompanied Lee to the privacy of the storage room.

"What's this about?" Harper asked quietly once they were inside.

Lee spilled it out without pulling any punches. "Before we left, Marie asked me to do something. She said she had a sister in Smithfield that she believed might still be alive, with a group of survivors at the First Baptist Church. She asked me to bring them some communications equipment so that Camp Ryder and Smithfield could get in contact and perhaps help each other. And I agreed to do that."

"But..." Miller looked at him, shaking his head.

"Let me finish." Lee held up a finger. "I made that promise to Marie, and I intend to keep it. But I don't make promises for other people, so any of you who want to go straight back to Camp Ryder, that's fine. I just ask that you drop me off at the edge of Smithfield, once we cross over I-95."

Harper hissed through his teeth. "Jesus, Lee! You're kinda putting us in a shitty situation."

Lee shrugged. "It is what it is, Harper."

Miller was still shaking his head, his eyes wide. "Naw, man. That place is gonna be crawling with crazies. I heard about towns and cities. Everyone who's come through one of them barely made it out alive. It's a bad idea...bad idea...nope... baaa-ad idea."

"You don't have to go," Lee repeated himself.

"This is bullshit," Doc put in. "If you go, you're going to die and we're fucked. If we all go, we're all going to die and then Camp Ryder is fucked." He crossed his arms stiffly. "This is a horrible idea."

"Fellas," Lee spoke with quiet command. "I'm not asking permission from any of you to do my job. It's gonna happen. I'm not gonna turn anyone down who wants to help me, but I won't hold it against you if you just want to get back to Camp Ryder."

They were all silent.

Lee rubbed his head. His hair was clean and sweat-free for the first time in what felt like ages. "You don't have to decide now, but just know what's coming so you can make your decision. Okay?" When they remained silent, Lee nodded toward the door. "Now go get some sleep."

They filed out of the storage room and Lee was alone again.

He walked to the far corner of the room, where a floor locker sat against the wall. This was his personal locker. The weapons and gear that had been stocked for the survivors was generic, fresh from the factory. In each of Lee's bunkers he had put in a personal locker that contained a set of his customized gear, set up the way he preferred.

He opened the top of the locker and looked down. At the bottom was a long, black case—that would be his M4, identical to the one he'd lost in the fighting at Timber Creek. On top of that gun case was a tan tactical vest, with pouches for twelve

M4 magazines. On each side were additional pouches, one for 40mm grenades and one for standard M67 grenades.

Lee pulled out the hefty vest—the damn thing weighed almost twenty pounds—then removed the black rifle case and opened it. He stared down at his rifle with a faint, loving smile on his face. He picked up the rifle, felt the confidence-inspiring heft of it in his arms.

"I've missed you, baby girl." Lee held the rifle like you might a long-lost lover. It was an M4 carbine variant of the M16, with an M203 grenade launcher under the barrel and an Aimpoint red-dot scope mounted on top. He'd painted the entire thing in a desert tan. The rifle had not been used after the painting and it still smelled fresh, the paint unmarred by the chips and dings of daily use.

He pulled out a soft case that contained thirteen fully-loaded magazines, which he slipped into the pouches on the plate carrier and put one in his M4. He pulled the charging handle back and let it go, feeling that satisfying slide of lubricated metal on metal, slamming a fresh, live cartridge home.

He was just putting the rifle case and vest back in the locker when he heard someone clear his throat behind him. He turned to find Father Jim standing in the doorway of the storage room. Lee gave the man a polite wave with one hand, then finished putting the vest and rifle case back into the locker. "Come on in, Father. How are your people?"

"Very good, thanks to you."

Lee smiled at the priest. "Well, I couldn't exactly tell a man of God 'no.' "

"Really?" Father Jim looked surprised. "You didn't strike me as the religious type."

Inwardly, Lee cringed. Was this guy going to start evangelizing? Outwardly he kept a look of neutrality on his face while he considered his answer. "I believe I have a mission. Whether that mission is ordained by God, I don't know. But I have to do it regardless."

"Relax, Captain." Father Jim had a welcoming grin. "I'm not going to start preaching the gospel to you. I imagine you've heard what there is to hear and have already decided whether or not to believe it. I highly doubt I'm going to be the one to sway you in either direction."

Lee had to appreciate the man's candor, and allowed a small smile to creep onto his face. He motioned toward a folding chair against the wall. "Take a load off, Father."

"Thank you." He sat down with a sigh of relief. "You don't realize how much you miss chairs until you go without them for a month. What a wonderful invention."

Lee pulled another folding chair off the wall so that they could face each other. He took a seat, laying the M4 across his lap. "Have you made a decision yet?"

Father Jim stretched his legs out and adjusted his glasses. "There's still some discussion to be had."

"I understand."

"Can I ask you a question, Captain Harden?"

Lee leaned back in his chair. "Sure."

He motioned to the walls of supplies that surrounded them. "Where did all of this come from?"

Lee told him what there was to tell. There was really no point in being coy at this point in the game, since Father Jim was sitting in his bunker, looking at his supplies in person. He told him about Project Hometown and the Coordinators in each state, the ten bunkers situated around North Carolina, and his mission to reestablish order in the region. He told him about Sam and Angela and Abby, and about Jack Burnsides, who had died fighting Milo's men, already sick with FURY. He told him about Timber Creek, Camp Ryder, and the decision to send them out to this bunker and bring back proof that Lee was in fact who he said he was.

All the while Father Jim listened, his chin resting on his hands, one finger pressed against his pursed lips, his eyes watching the expressions on Lee's face as the story unfolded. And when Lee was done, Father Jim's eyebrows raised. "Well, it sounds like you've had a rough time of it."

Lee shrugged. "I could say the same about your group."

Father Jim nodded, then took a moment to consider his words before speaking again. "There's a story about a man, during the floods in New Orleans, who took refuge on his roof from the rising water. He was a devout Christian, so once he was on his roof, he prayed to God to save him. Shortly after that, a man in a boat rowed up to the man's roof and said, 'Come on, get in! I can row us to safety!' But the man said, 'No, I trust in the Lord, and I know that he will save me.' So the man in the boat rowed off. And the man on the roof continued to pray, 'Lord, please save my life.'

"Shortly after he prayed this second time, a rescue helicopter hovered over the house and a man was lowered down in a harness, and he said, 'Quick! Take my hand! We can fly you to safety!' But the man on the roof just shook his head and said, 'No, I trust in the Lord, and I know that he will save me.' So the man and the helicopter flew off. And the man continued to pray, but the water kept rising, and eventually it overtook the man on the roof, and he drowned.

"When he got to Heaven, he asked God, 'Why didn't you save me? I trusted in you and I prayed for you to save me, but you didn't!' And God looked at him and said, 'But I *did* try to save you. I sent you a boat, and I sent you a helicopter.'"

Father Jim looked over the rims of his glasses at Lee. "Usually I tell that story to people who fail to see the hand of God extended out to them, just like the man on the roof. But in some cases I tell it to the man in the boat and the man in the helicopter, who fail to realize that they *are* the hand of God."

Father Jim didn't wait for Lee to argue or respond; he simply stood and patted Lee on the knee. "The wonderful thing about God is that he can use you whether you want him to or not."

The priest walked out, leaving Lee to his thoughts.

They woke early in the morning and began packing.

Prior to going topside, Lee checked the cameras that monitored the outside of the bunker to make sure there were no unwanted guests who had come upon the tents and pickup truck during the night. All appeared to be as deserted as they had left it.

To be cautious, Lee gave Harper an M4 from the enormous gun locker in the supply room and the two men went topside to investigate. It was warm and humid outside. It smelled mostly of rank ash from the burning bodies the night before that still smoldered in a pit of burned twigs and branches. The two of them checked around and inside the tents, and inside the truck as well. Nothing had been moved, nothing had been tampered with. Nothing attacked them as they were making their rounds.

They went back down in the elevator.

Harper rubbed his eyes and spoke in a groggy croak. "So, how much food do you think we can bring back?"

Lee sighed. "As much as we can, but still not enough."

"What do you mean?"

"I mean that pickup truck is only going to hold maybe twenty pails of food. That'll feed a group the size of Camp Ryder for about a week."

Harper's eyes went wide. "That's it?"

The elevator settled to the bunker floor and the doors opened.

"Yeah." Lee stepped through, heading for the supply room. "I've got more food in here than we can carry. Each one of these bunkers is built to supply about a hundred people for a year. But as you can see, transporting it can be difficult, and it's not a permanent solution."

"So..." Harper followed him in.

"Guns and ammo, Harper." Lee pointed to the gun locker, which was an adjoining room with a big steel door on it. Inside were two hundred M4 assault rifles and eight hundred thousand rounds of 5.56mm ammunition. "With better defenses, we can move out beyond the comfort zone of the fence. We can hunt, we can fish, we can start farming. The food stores are just a buffer to get you guys into subsistence living." Lee keyed a code into a terminal and the door to the gun locker clicked and swung open, revealing the rows of assault rifles, neatly standing at attention. "In order to reestablish industry, you have to first reestablish agriculture. Back in the day before everyone worked in an office, hawking things made in a factory, they used to work in that factory, making those things. And before that they worked on farms to feed themselves. The only reason farms still exist is because the people in the factories need to have something to eat.

"We've got to learn to live off the land again. Once humans do that, everything else falls into place. Civilization is the fruit of a tree that grows its roots in agriculture."

Harper smirked. "You come up with that on your own?"

Lee smiled wryly. "No. A sociology professor I knew."

They began pulling what they needed off the shelves. Josh and Miller both got an M4 carbine and a shoulder sling magazine pouch with six mags per, and then they were sent topside to guard the truck while the others brought the supplies up to them. Doc quietly took his corner of the supply room to accumulate the medical supplies he felt they needed. Lee provided him with a large duffel bag with foam-insert compartments so he could organize the different items he was taking.

They loaded the truck bed up as tightly as they could with rice, oats, beans, and dried milk. In addition to the five-gallon pails, they threw in a few cases of MREs and some freeze-dried and dehydrated fruits and vegetables. They were able to fit slightly more than Lee had originally thought, and with the MREs and fruits and vegetables, Lee thought they had enough food to last Camp Ryder between eight and ten days if they subsisted entirely off of the supplies. With hunting and scavenging made safer by having weapons and ammunition to defend themselves, they could probably stretch it to a month.

Lee armed Doc the same as he had the other three men from Camp Ryder. He stowed ten extra M4s in the truck and was able to squeeze in five hundred rounds of ammunition for each rifle, along with a bundle of spare mags. He took four large duffels and crammed two of them full of various sizes of BDU pants and the field jackets he had promised Marie. Though Lee preferred coyote tan and MultiCam for his own personal gear, the powers that be had equipped his bunkers with clothing all in OD green. Perhaps because it was cheapest, or perhaps simply because that was the box that some bureaucrat decided to check.

The other two duffels he stuffed with blankets, ponchos, and poncho liners. The four large duffels he was able to fit in the passenger area of the pickup truck, though they crowded Doc and Josh. Miller had just enough room in the bed to sit his butt on a pail of oats. He would not be comfortable, but hopefully they would make better time on the trip back.

Though there wasn't any room left in the truck for ordnance, Lee took a large backpack and filled it with a few bricks of C4 and some detonators, four claymore mines, and then some communications equipment, consisting of four encrypted long-range radios and two digital repeaters that looked like black boxes. He cushioned everything with a couple of poncho liners. He opened a crate of grenades and filled the three grenade pouches on his tactical vest, then swung the vest over his head and settled the weighty thing tightly onto his torso.

Father Jim's people were kind enough to help with carrying the supplies upstairs and loading them into the pickup truck. When the truck was loaded and ready, he gave Father Jim's people five M4s, five shoulder sling magazine pouches, each filled with six thirty-round magazines, three cases of MREs, three boxes of dehydrated vegetables and fruits, and five backpacks to help carry their supplies. After everyone was packed and accounted for topside, Lee sealed the door to the bunker again.

He gave Father Jim one of the long-range radios and instructions on how to get to Camp Ryder. He suggested they check the used auto lot near

I-95, as most of the cars seemed untouched, most would have gas, and the keys were probably somewhere inside the dealership. Father Jim listened carefully to the instructions. Lee expected him to object to stealing the cars on the grounds of some misguided morality, but he simply nodded and thanked Lee for the tip.

He pulled a folded piece of paper out of his pocket. "I would like to leave you with something, Captain Harden. In case we don't have a chance to speak again."

Lee shifted his weight. "You'll be fine, Father."

The priest placed the paper in Lee's hand. It was thin and waxy, and it crackled like tissue paper in Lee's palm. He opened his hand and looked down at the paper, seeing the double columns of fine-printed words and the gold inlay along the edge of the page.

Lee raised his brow. "I hope you didn't tear this from your own Bible."

Father Jim smiled and shrugged. "I didn't have a piece of paper to write it down on." He patted Lee on the shoulder. "I circled a passage for you. Don't worry, I won't make you read it right now."

"Thank you." Lee didn't really know what else to say to the man.

"Thank you, Captain. And, God willing, we will see you at Camp Ryder." The man looked incongruous with his neatly combed hair, thick glasses, and tucked-in shirt, standing there holding an M4 with six extra magazines slung over his shoulder. The image brought a quirky smile to Lee's lips.

He held the piece of paper in his fist and climbed into the passenger seat of the Dodge Ram 2500. The big machine rumbled to life and the vehicle shuddered, then idled as Lee situated himself and his gear, propping his rifle between his knees and closing the passenger door.

Through the open passenger window as the truck began to roll forward, Lee flicked the priest a salute with two fingers. "You guys be safe."

The group waved as they departed, leaving Lee feeling odd about the entire incident. He wasn't sure whether it was Father Jim's stalwart belief that Lee was guided by some divine power or the easy manner that they had accepted Lee's decisions. Lee shook his head, wondering if leaving them behind was the right choice. But as with any decision, it was better made than waffled over.

He opened his hand and spread the folded piece of paper it held. The page was small, from a pocket Bible of some sort. The priest had circled a passage that began with Romans 13:4: *"For he is God's minister to you for good. But if you do evil, be afraid; for he does not bear the sword in vain: for he is God's minister, an avenger to execute wrath upon him that practices evil."*

Lee stared at the page for a long moment, then looked up into the side-view mirror, but Father Jim and his group had already disappeared as the dirt road wound farther away from them. Eventually he folded the page up again and stuck it in the cargo pocket of his pants where it would remain next to the good-luck lottery ticket Jack had given him.

TWELVE

SMITHFIELD

HARPER BROUGHT THE PICKUP to a stop just before turning left onto the service road that led along I-95. The sun had come out briefly that morning, but the wind had kicked up as they left the bunker, and a thin gray cloud cover had set in and grown thick and dark, the sky's belly swollen with rain. The wind came in harsh gusts that whipped up dirt and leaves and pelted the side of the truck with it.

Harper looked unsurely up at the storm clouds. "It's gonna get nasty out there."

Lee didn't wait to see if anyone would join him in Smithfield because he didn't want to put any pressure on them. This wasn't what they'd signed up for, and he didn't expect them to want to put themselves in any more danger than they already had. He grabbed his backpack and pulled it into his lap.

He turned and extended a hand to Harper. "If you guys hit any roadblocks, just open up on 'em with all four rifles. They won't be expecting that type of resistance and they'll bug out. Whatever happens, you just make sure these supplies get back to Camp Ryder, got that?"

Harper nodded. "When should we expect you back?"

Lee stepped out of the truck, felt the wind tugging at him, and squinted against the flying dust. "I'd like to say a couple of days, but it will probably be longer." He pointed a finger at him. "And don't come looking for me, got it? For all you know I found some hot, single ladies who need a man, so don't spoil it for me."

They chuckled briefly.

It didn't take long for Harper to be serious again. "Are you sure you want to do this?"

"Nope." Lee slung into the backpack and cinched the straps up. "But it's what I do."

"Okay." Harper nodded. "You be safe."

Lee gave him a short wave. "You too."

"Fuck this shit," Doc said with bitter resignation. He grabbed his rifle and opened his door, stepping quickly out and slamming it behind him. "I've gotta stay with the captain."

Lee regarded him curiously. He was surprised, to say the least. Doc had argued to come with them, then whined and moaned the entire time, and now seemed resolute to accompany Lee on what would probably be the most dangerous portion of the trip. He didn't know whether to be flattered or tell the guy to get the hell back in the truck.

Harper was flabbergasted. "What? No. I'm serious, Doc. If I don't come back with you, Bus will kill me."

Doc's hair flew wildly in the wind and he had to raise his voice over the sound of it. "Then come with us, Harper. We'll all have a better chance if we stick together. And I have to stay with the captain. I've already made up my mind."

"But…"

"I'm staying with the captain," Doc repeated.

The other four men were speechless for the better part of a minute. The silence was filled with strange looks, questioning gestures, shrugs, and noncommital wandering eyes. The general feeling was one of, *Well, what the fuck do we do now?*

Miller broke it first by snatching up his rifle and standing in the bed of the truck. He stretched his legs languidly. "Well, let's get a move on. Daylight's wastin'."

As Miller prepared to jump down out of the bed, Harper shouted, "Alright! Shitfire! Everyone back in the truck!"

Lee put a thumb in the strap of his pack. "I could always use your help."

"Yeah." Harper rolled his eyes. "I'm coming along with you. But there's no sense in walking through town when we can drive."

Josh never officially voiced his opinion, but neither did he object when Doc and Lee got back into the truck and they began driving toward the heart of Smithfield.

As it turned out, the truck would only get them so far.

They were on Brogden Road, they discovered. They stayed on it until it ended into Brightleaf Boulevard, where they made a right. The intersection was clustered with a few odd businesses, such as Don Pancho's Meat Market, Biscuit Stop, and the Coffee Pot. Behind these small fronts, Lee could make out the suburban heart of the town: rows of houses built in the 1980s, some left to wither over the years, some kept in good condition. All of them looked neglected now, hunched quietly in the mess of their waist-high lawns.

The jams and pileups of collisions were sparse enough along Brightleaf Boulevard that Harper was able to easily move around them and between them. Many of the wrecks held dark shapes, slumped over against cracked glass and deflated air bags. Most of the abandoned cars had been pushed to the side, where they lined the road like a silent crowd of onlookers that had parted their ranks to allow the five men to pass.

Nearly every house they passed was draped with a white bedsheet. It hung from a gutter or flapped from a window. Some had been ripped from the houses by the storm winds and now clung desperately to trees and shrubs.

This was a sign of infection.

Stay in your homes.

Hang a white cloth outside your house so we know a member of your household is sick.

Help is on the way.

The doors on many of these houses stood open, like the gaping mouth of someone who had died in mid-scream. Like the kid Harper had gutted with that bayonet. Like the dirty redneck boys whom Lee had gunned down for killing Sam's father.

The people in those houses had stayed inside, with their white flags waving outside, slipping into madness and killing one another. Now those houses looked empty and Lee wondered whether they had lingered here in the town they had called home or run off into the surrounding wilderness and packed together like wolves.

The pickup truck swerved and Harper swore. "Lot of bodies on the road."

Looking out over the dashboard, Lee could see dozens of dark mounds, like trash scattered in the roadway. Some were curled up, others splayed out, spread-eagle. They were in varying states of dress: Some wore business suits, others wore oil-stained coveralls, some wore bathing suits, and still others wore nothing at all.

Many had dark red trails behind them, like bloody comets. Those were the ones who had kept crawling. Interspersed through these remains were pockmarks in the cement, like small meteoric craters.

Lee remembered a checkpoint outside of Fallujah where he had stood with one of his squads when an old, tan Mercedes started toward the roadblock. It happened so fast, they barely had time to fire a warning shot from the .50-cal, and the car began to accelerate toward them. Every gun in that squad started firing, and the Mercedes jerked and swerved off into a ditch, the windshield and door panels shredded with bullet holes.

When they had ventured out to inspect the vehicle, Lee remembered a hand lying in the road, sheared off by one of the big .50-caliber rounds. All around that hand were the same pockmarks, where their bullets had gouged out chunks of the cement.

Lee pointed suddenly. "Heads up."

Their progress came to a halt at Brightleaf Boulevard and Woodall Lane, where a line of cement barriers stood, concertina wire strung across the tops. Behind the hastily erected cement wall, a police vehicle and a National Guard Humvee sat with the doors open, abandoned. Lee stared at the barricade, his eyes sweeping along and piecing together what had happened.

Mashed headlong into the barricade was a small white sedan. The windshield was riddled with bullet holes, just like that tan Mercedes so many years ago. To either side of the cement barricade, the shoulder of the road had been blocked with tangles of concertina wire. In among these metal brambles were bodies, hanging in the wire, as though they had tried to blindly march through. In places, their arms or legs hung off them loosely by a thread of gristle. Blood had coagulated in stagnant pools beneath them. One section of barbed wire was choked so severely with dead bodies that they had flattened out the barbed wire, creating a bridge across.

The gusting wind made the spirals of concertina wire shiver.

A flurry of trash drifted across the road.

"These people..." Harper's voice trembled. "Were they just gunned down?"

Lee took a look at the big .50-cal mounted on top of the Humvee, tilted back and pointed skyward now. Vehicle-mounted .50-cals were hardly typical crowd-control fare. They were made for combat, and that was what they were used for.

"I don't think they were regular people," Lee observed quietly. "I think these barricades were put up to keep out the infected. Create a safe zone to evacuate out of."

"Doesn't look like it worked too well." Doc sounded nervous.

"No," Lee agreed. "It doesn't."

"Should we try to get around on some other roads?" Harper looked to the left, where Woodall Lane stretched in a straight line, deeper into the city.

Lee followed his gaze but saw only a jam of vehicles and bodies at every intersection. "It looks like they barricaded those streets as well. We could spend half the day trying to find a way to drive our truck through."

Harper tapped the wheel. "You wanna go in on foot?"

"Yes."

"What about the supplies?"

"We'll have to leave someone here."

Josh's hand shot up. "Yeah, I'll stay. I'll stay with the truck."

Lee turned in his seat to look at Doc and Miller, who was sticking his head in through the back glass again. "Someone has to stay with Josh."

"Nah, man." Miller shook his head. "I'm tired of sittin' in the bed. I'm comin' with you."

Lee turned his gaze to Doc. "You cool with staying here?"

Doc seemed to consider it for an oddly long time. Finally, he nodded. "Yeah. That's fine."

Lee dove his hand into his pack and retrieved one of the long-range radios he'd brought. He handed it over to Doc. "We'll be on system ten, subchannel one."

Doc regarded the radio like it was a tablet written in Sanskrit, but eventually he made sense of the buttons and got the thing turned on and tuned in to the right channel. When he had it switched over, Lee keyed his mic. The radio in Doc's hand burped and squelched.

Lee gave him a thumbs-up. "Looks like it works."

They parked the car facing away from the roadblock so they could make a quicker getaway if necessary. Doc took over the driver's seat, while Josh took over Miller's overwatch position in the bed of the truck, shrugging his shoulders against the wind.

Lee held up his radio. "Doc, if you guys run into trouble, call me on the radio."

Doc just nodded.

Lee turned to the barricade. He did not relish the idea of walking across the bridge of dead bodies to get to the other side of the concertina wire, but there didn't seem to be any other options to safely cross. He hitched his pack higher onto his shoulders and tightened the straps. With his rifle held snug into his shoulder and the comforting weight of his tactical vest on his torso, he made for the gap in the wire, and Miller and Harper fell in behind him.

As they disappeared behind the barricade, the first fat raindrops began to fall.

Doc sat in the driver's seat and started to sweat.

He stared straight ahead, his jaw muscles

bunching. A single bead of perspiration gathered and broke from his eyebrows, slipping down into his eye and forcing him to blink. He breathed in deep through his nose and let it slowly out through pursed lips. Doing this a few times usually helped him to relax.

Not now.

Outside, the downpour had begun, turning the blacktop into glistening snakeskin.

In the truck bed and open to the elements, Josh swore at the rain.

Doc could feel his heavy pulse starting in his heart and radiating out to his fingers like shock waves. All those electrical impulses coursing through his brain, branching out through his nervous system and triggering the beating chambers of his heart, sending all those oxygen-laden blood cells to all the organs that needed it.

It was amazing that he knew how all this stuff worked.

Right now, his brain was perceiving a life-or-death situation.

This shot a tiny signal down to his adrenal glands and they began to spew their chemical cocktail, igniting a chain reaction. The heartbeat quickened, the respiration increased, the palms began to sweat. Blood was drawn from certain organs, like those of his digestive system, and reallocated to the large muscle groups in his body. The decrease in blood to the head caused his cornea to flatten, reducing his vision down to a 2 percent field of view, also known as "tunnel vision."

This was his body gearing up for disaster.

And all he could wonder was, *If I fire a shot, will Lee and the others hear it?*

He forced his eyes up to the rearview mirror and looked through the breach in the wire. The open intersection across from that breach was empty. The other three men had moved on, but how far? A quarter mile by now? Maybe more. Would they be able to run back if they heard gunshots?

If I fire a shot inside the car, will they still hear it?

Doc had to imagine that the vehicle had a suppressive effect on a gunshot. After all, the sound of a gunblast was only a combination of the bullet breaking the sonic barrier and the gunpowder turning into a rapidly expanding gas. If the car contained the gas (and possibly the bullet), wouldn't it make sense that the sound outside the car would be muffled?

Another spike of adrenaline.

Jesus Christ…help me…

He breathed again. Slowly.

In through the nose, out through the mouth.

He couldn't think about it anymore.

He grabbed the M4 sitting in the passenger seat next to him. Then he turned to face the rear of the vehicle. Through the open back glass he could see most of Josh's legs and torso, standing up in the bed and facing forward.

Doc lifted the rifle and shot Josh in the stomach.

The kid stumbled back but didn't fall. He let out a strange mewling sound and began frantically swiping at the blooming red hole in his shirt like it was a bug he might brush off. Doc shot him three more times until Josh lay still.

His ears were humming. He stared into the back of the truck at Josh. He began to hyperventilate. He was horribly, sickeningly out of control, an astronaut who had lost his tenuous grip on the space station and was now drifting out into orbit.

"Oh, my God! Oh, fuck! *OH, FUCK!*" He tried to breathe but just kept swallowing air. The rifle dropped from his shaking hands. He fumbled for the door release and stepped out of the car, forcing himself to belch out all the air in his belly. The rain almost instantly soaked him, matting his hair to greasy-looking strands. His vision was spinning, the dead bodies all around him making laps like a gruesome carousel. He shut his eyes, felt hot tears on his cheeks, and shook the encroaching gray out of his head.

He could not lose consciousness here. This was a very bad place to pass out.

"No. No. No." He kept shaking his head. He kept saying it as though if he repeated it enough, the situation would right itself. But this fucked-up situation would never be right. There was no way to make it right. It was fucked up from the start and now he was a part of it; he was a filthy, bloody part of it.

"It's gonna be okay," he told himself.

He opened his eyes.

Josh was still lifeless in the bed of the truck. Doc swiped his eyes free of tears and raked wet clumps of hair out of his face. He felt his rain-soaked clothes clinging insistently to his chest and back as he reached into the bed and grabbed one of the kid's arms. He pulled but the kid hardly budged.

"It's gonna be okay." He grunted with effort. "It's gonna be okay."

He pulled harder, bracing one foot on the rear tire. He got the body up onto the boxes, and from there it was easier to roll him off the truck, where his head hit the ground with a dull *thwack*.

Out of breath and sobbing uncontrollably, Doc stared down at Josh's body and tried to repeat to himself that everything was going to be okay. But the tears were filtering down through his sinuses and loosening all the rotten gunk in there, and it was running out his nose and down the back of his throat, garbling his words as he gasped them out: "Ihsguhn behkay. Ihsguhn behkay."

Unable to bear the sight any longer, he ran from it, staggering into the truck and slamming the door. Panic nipped at his heels, a greyhound on the tail of a rabbit almost run to ground. He cranked the keys too long and the starter screamed. He yanked the shifter down into drive and slammed on the gas before the transmission had a chance to catch. The engine roared and finally dropped into gear. Torque spun the tires for a brief second before the truck tore off, leaving Josh among all the other dead bodies that littered the road.

THIRTEEN

House to House

THE RAIN WAS COMING in gales now.

The three figures moved through the slurry of gray, one after the other, bodies hunched against the rain, eyes darting from side to side. The splashing rain gave the effect of a low fog hugging the ground, but the humps of the dead bodies still rose out of that gray cloud like scattered islands in a misty sea.

Lee took point. His torso was like a turret: everywhere his eyes went, his rifle followed. He scanned down streets and into open windows and doors. A few short steps behind him, Miller kept an eye on their flanks, and a few steps behind Miller, Harper took rear guard, constantly twisting and checking the road behind them to make sure no one was tailing them.

Lee was grateful that the rain was beating down the stench of putrefaction that still rose from the bodies like the dense smell of a cold Dumpster. But the rain also coated the entire area in a wash of white noise, forcing him to scan more with his eyes, since his ears would never pick up the sound of running feet over the rush of the driving rain.

They moved along Church Street, one road down from Woodall Lane, where the barricades had been erected. One block over, Lee could see where the troops guarding those barricades had gone once their barricades had been breached. It was a residential street, and most of the houses were boarded up. But several were open, burned-out husks, with broken windows and bullet-riddled walls. The troops, and probably a few die-hard deputies, had used the houses to mount a defense. Each burned-out house covered an intersection. Bodies choked the lawns and cross streets. Most of them were whole, but some of them were in pieces. The bodies that were torn apart wore shreds of ACU camouflage. The rain washed away some of the blood and gave the flesh a blanched look.

In several places, Lee could see bite marks.

Miller stared at a body as they passed. "Are they...eating them?"

Lee felt the contents of his stomach press up into his throat. "I don't know." He thought about every survivor he'd met and their lean, drawn features. Everyone was starving. It was only logical that the infected were starving too. If they had been reduced to their basest instincts, what instinct was more basic than the urge to feed?

They continued on until Church Street ended at Fifth Street.

The group stopped at the intersection and looked around. To their right was a big single-story house with a large front porch and a white picket fence. The gutter spouts bubbled and spewed white rainwater. A body lay facedown at the base of the fence, a splatter of blood marring the white paint and beginning to run down the fence slats in pink trails.

"There." Miller pointed.

It appeared that Church Street doglegged and continued on about a block down. Lee could read the sign from where they stood. They made the decision to continue on Church Street because they felt it was the most logical place to find the biggest church in town. As they moved down the street, the signs of house-to-house fighting continued. The destruction, the burned-out buildings, the bullet-riddled and partially consumed corpses. This street named after a place of worship had turned into a hellish nightmare.

As they neared the intersection of Fourth Street, Lee saw the top of a tall church steeple poking up above the trees. "That's gotta be it."

The group was moving faster now, the idea of getting off the streets spurring them on. The First Baptist Church was not on Church Street at all, but took up a large portion of Fourth Street. Hurriedly, they turned the corner onto Fourth Street.

They stopped suddenly, arms spread out like burglars caught in the act.

Lee was the first to react, grabbing Miller by the collar and yanking him to the side of the street, where a large pickup truck had jumped the curb and struck a fire hydrant. The two of them scrambled to hide behind the pickup truck, but Harper didn't move. He stood in the middle of the street, staring at the front of the First Baptist Church, where a crowd milled about, an innumerable mass of dark, featureless shapes behind the curtains of rain.

"Harper!" Lee hissed through gritted teeth. "Get the fuck over here!"

Harper looked at Lee, his eyes wide, blinking away the rain dribbling into them.

The next thing Lee heard was a high-pitched howl.

Lee stuck his head around the car and felt his stomach drop.

A block away, one of the infected was racing straight toward them. It grunted and growled as it ran, its breathing so heavy and ragged that Lee could hear it from where he crouched. A thick rope of black saliva hung out of its mouth, trembling like the tail of a half-eaten snake. It was moving fast and Lee knew he didn't have time to outrun it.

He raised his rifle and put two in the thing's chest.

It stumbled, then fell. Hitting the ground, it skidded to a stop, then raised its head and began crawling toward them. Lee didn't waste any more ammunition on it—the creature would never reach them.

But the two shots he had fired had gained him all the attention he could handle. The horde of infected that swarmed the front of the church all snapped their heads in his direction and momentarily froze, like a bird dog pointing out game. The howls that suddenly erupted from them were loud and hot and hungry. All in an instant, the entire mass of bodies was churning toward them.

"Gotta move!" was all Lee could shout.

Miller was already on his feet, firing wildly at them.

Lee broke left, heading for the church. He braved a glance behind him and saw both of his companions on his heels. He jumped the sidewalk and almost lost his footing as he came down in a slick patch of wet grass. He was running blindly, but he quickly found a destination—another white picket fence cordoned off a yard and ran adjacent to the side of the church, creating a narrow alleyway that Lee thought might force the horde into a bottleneck and give the three men a fighting chance.

As he hit the mouth of the alley, he saw a window into the church, just big enough for a man to get through, and immediately changed his plan. Without thinking it through, he lunged for the window, holding his rifle in front of him. In the moment, as he hung suspended in the air, he imagined the glass not breaking. Vividly, he saw himself bouncing off the window like a bad slapstick joke, unable to get to his feet before the infected reached him and began to tear him apart, tooth and nail.

His last thought before hitting the window was, *Bad idea*.

But the glass offered almost no resistance. It was like jumping through a waterfall, but the water was sharp as razors and sliced at his arms as he landed and rolled to a stop a few feet into a linoleum-floored hallway. He looked back to the window and saw the other two men frantically push their way through and land in a heap on the inside.

A dark hand shot through the window after

them, a shard of glass catching and splitting the skin all the way up the forearm, revealing pink flesh beneath the brown skin. The infected showed no evidence of registering that pain in his ruined cerebrum but kept reaching through that window at Harper, gnashing jagged yellow teeth, his matted dreadlocks flailing.

Harper started to stagger to his feet.

Lee brought his rifle up and shouted, *"GET DOWN!"*

And Harper got down.

Lee fired once and the right side of the infected's jaw disappeared in a spray of bone fragments and flesh. Another bullet punched a hole through his neck, slicing arteries and severing the spinal column. As the thing collapsed onto the window frame, Lee scrambled to his feet, the rubber soles of his wet boots squeaking erratically on the linoleum floor.

"Get up!" He waved the other men toward him, though they did not need any further encouragement. They shuffled on hands and knees through the broken glass, their rifles clattering along on the floor with them until they finally could lurch to their feet and start running again.

Lee moved out of their way as they ran past him, then opened up his stance and squared himself to the window. Hungry faces filled the open space, screaming at him in desperate frustration, all of them trying to climb through at once. He shouted over his shoulder, "You gotta find a way through the church!"

Then Lee lowered his cheek to his rifle and

began sending rounds downrange. The dread-locked infected was ripped out of the windowsill as others tried to worm their way in, and Lee kept shooting, feeling that same trapped-animal feeling he'd felt in the Petersons' house, that dreadful feeling of *no way out*. But he kept firing, and the bodies kept falling, and behind him he could hear Harper and Miller kicking their way through a door.

The last kick was final and reverberating.

Lee found himself backpedaling down the hall, anticipating an open door.

"It's open!" Miller's voice had raised an octave in stress.

Lee turned his back on the window and sprinted for a pair of double doors as Harper and Miller disappeared inside. All along the walls, children's artwork hung in bright crayon colors that blended together as Lee hauled past them. Signs on the doors to either side announced: MS. CROUCH'S CLASS; MR. BEAKER'S CLASS, and so on.

This part of the church was a school.

Lee turned the corner into the double doors. The room they opened into was a spacious lunchroom with rows of tables and chairs and a kitchen area behind a long counter. He saw the backs of Harper and Miller, heading for a door marked EXIT.

Lee spun and dropped to his knee, snatching a fragmentation grenade from a pouch on his vest. He removed the safety clip and slid the grenade into position, sandwiched between the two double doors. He made sure the lever of the grenade was held tight in place by the weight of the door and then braced the little steel ball with one hand while he gingerly plucked the pin with his other.

"It's clear around back!" Harper sounded eager to get out.

Lee leaned away from the little explosive and spread his palms toward it, as though willing it to stay in place. When it appeared secure, he stood. From down the hall he heard the screech of infected and the tumble of feet scratching through broken glass. A fresh wave of urgency crashed over him—if the infected set off his booby trap before he got out of the lunchroom, the least injury he could hope for was perforated eardrums and probably a shrapnel wound.

Harper and Miller didn't quite understand what he'd done to the door, but he started throwing his arms, making a *get-the-fuck-out-of-here* gesture, and they understood that, turning and launching themselves through the exit. Lee was behind them, slamming the exit door and jamming it in the open position.

From inside, Lee heard the double doors slam open.

The words came out like hot, uncontrollable vomit: "Go! Go! Go!"

But they were already running, across a covered walkway toward the main church building. As the fuse on the grenade cooked down, Lee glanced to his right, toward the road, and saw a few stragglers from the main mass of the horde. These less speedy ones had taken notice of their escape and were now hobbling after them.

He looked back toward the open door to the lunchroom. After that moment he would never be able to recall the sound of the grenade detonating or the feel of the concussion in his chest. What he did remember, always poignantly, was the sight of a lunchroom chair rocketing out of that open door in a plume of white dust and smacking him in the face.

The next few moments were foggy.

His vision went from bursts of colorful sparklers and fireworks to a grainy whiteout, like overexposed film. He could hear gunshots very clearly, and Miller screaming at him to get up. He tried to tell Miller that he was okay but all that came out was an unintelligible groan. He rolled onto his side, feeling the warm, gritty cement against his head. He spit and watched red streamers splatter the pavement and a little white object skitter across the ground.

My tooth?

More gunshots.

More of Miller yelling at him.

Lee got up on his hands and knees and stuck out his tongue, watching bloody saliva dribble down. Unable to speak clearly, he exclaimed, "Mah fuckin' toof!"

He was suddenly standing upright and Miller pushed him toward the door to the main church building. His vision cleared a bit, and along with it, his nerves. His lips felt stiff and tight and swollen, and pain began to beat through his entire jaw. He probed his teeth with his tongue and found the gap where his right canine used to be.

They reached the church door and found it locked.

It was a commercial-grade door: solid wood with a steel frame.

Oh, if I only had time to rig a charge…

But he didn't.

Behind him, Harper and Miller were still firing, faster now.

The fog dissipated enough for him to realize they were stuck.

He jammed the muzzle of his rifle into the door where the latch caught the frame and fired three times. The wood splintered and the door popped open slightly. Lee put a shoulder to it and stumbled through with just enough time for Harper and Miller to squeeze in and slam the door behind them.

Something hit the door on the other side.

"Gimme something to brace it!" Harper yelled.

Miller began frantically searching for something. Lee looked at the floor and saw the same slick linoleum as in the hallway of the school. Nothing they found would gain enough traction to effectively brace the door.

Lee lent his own body weight to the door, slamming his back up against it and feeling his stitches complain. "How many were coming after us?"

Harper breathed heavily. "Maybe five."

The pounding on the other side of the door became louder, more insistent.

Lee adopted a wide stance and wedged his right foot hard up against the door. "Get back."

Harper hesitated but pulled himself off the door.

The pressure on his foot doubled without Harper's weight against the door. The infected on the other side pressed in with extraordinary strength so that the door cleared the jamb about half an inch and their screeching became louder. Urgently, Lee swapped out magazines, slamming in a fresh one, feeling that *click* as the latch caught the magazine firmly in the well. Holding the rifle at his hip, he fired off twenty rounds through the door.

He didn't wait to assess the damage, but turned and began running again.

They made their way through the vestibule and into the sanctuary.

Harper's endurance was beginning to flag. His breathing was coming in ragged gasps.

The sanctuary was as wide as it was long, with tall frosted glass windows along the sides and rows of empty pews, church hymnals and envelopes for tithing neatly tucked in the backs. The walls were painted a crisp white, the wooden trim and pews a warm brown. The carpets and upholstery were a deep burgundy, faded in the center of the aisles from the thousands of feet that had walked it during altar calls. In the front of the sanctuary was a stage, slightly raised from the rest of the floor, and the choir loft above that. In the middle of that stage stood a wooden podium of the same stain as the pews. An ornate flower arrangement adorned the front of the podium, but the blooms had long since lost their color, the leaves had dried, and the brown petals had curled in on themselves, as dead as can be.

"There." Lee pointed to a pair of double doors to the right of the stage over which a darkened exit sign hung. Lee started running for it. "I don't think there are any survivors here. We need to get back to the truck."

As he ran, he pulled his shoulder and arm free of one of the straps on his pack, swinging it around so it hung at his side. He dove his hand into the front pocket and snagged the radio there. Approaching the door, he angled his body and hit the thing with his left shoulder. The door had give, but it only went in about a half foot before something blocked it.

Lee took a step back, clutching the radio in one hand, rifle in the other. He swore and reared back, sending a boot into the door. It gave a little more, but whatever was blocking the door was heavy.

"It's barricaded!" Miller shouted, because someone always had to say something obvious.

"No shit, motherfucker!" Harper joined in with Lee by getting a running start and slamming all of his weight into the door. Whatever was on the other side shoved out of the way just enough for Harper to hold the door open about a foot. "Miller! Squeeze through and get that barricade out of the way!"

Miller clearly didn't like squeezing through a door into an unknown room, but he didn't argue, though his face set into an expression of fearful determination. He clearly knew he still had a teenager's skinny torso, made even leaner by starvation; he was the obvious choice for such a mission.

He squirmed through the opening just enough

to take a look at what was on the other side. His whole body stiffened. "Oh, shit. Oh shit, man."

Lee put a firm hand on his shoulder, ready to yank him back through if need be. "What? What is it?"

"No, it's fine." Miller loosened and edged through the opening, disappearing briefly around the door. There was the sound of some large piece of wooden furniture scraping across smooth concrete and a moment later, Miller reappeared, looking a little pale. He opened the door wide enough for them to get in.

Lee immediately felt the humid air, felt the wind eking in from outside.

He and Harper stepped through and immediately their noses curled. The double doors opened into a small entryway. To the left was a door that appeared to go behind the stage, probably to a baptismal pool, and another door to the right led outside. The door to the outside was open, the wind from the storm pinning it as far back as it would go. The rain battered and splashed the entryway but had yet to fully wash away the thick, caked-on bloodstains that smeared the door and the inside of the room. The blood smears thinned, and then in a dark corner of this dank room, they exploded across the walls. Slumped in that dark corner was something barely recognizable as human, though Lee knew that's what it was. His deduction was based on the pieces of anatomy that remained distinguishable: a foot, an ear, part of an arm.

"Holy shit." Harper seemed suddenly even more out of breath.

Lee noticed the barricade had been a damaged pew, perhaps kept back in this little room until it could be repaired. This poor dumb bastard had probably barricaded himself in this room from something in the sanctuary, and eventually something got in through the outer door.

Staring at the remains for a moment more, Lee had to admit that a lot of the man seemed to be missing. "They're definitely feeding on people now." Lee covered his mouth. The initial, visual shock was beginning to wear off and allowing his other senses to have their say. The smell in the room was very close to the overpowering smell of the infected. Where the infected smelled more like rank, unwashed body odor, this room smelled more of rancid meat. Where the two smells were similar was the heavy fecal smell, because the infected shit themselves, and so did the dead and dying.

But that's not something they tell you in the movies.

Real death is not graceful. It is not romantic. It is not a gentle sigh of breath as you float above yourself. It is bitter, and it is wretched. It smells of bowels and blood; it sounds like the strange, terrified noises of a wounded animal; and it tastes like vomit rising in the back of your throat. And here in Smithfield, it was inexorable and ever-present.

Lee covered his nose and mouth with one hand and croaked, "Let's get the fuck out of here."

Back through those barricaded doors, deep in the church, something crashed around and screamed for them.

Lee posted in the bloody doorway and scanned the outside. The drone of the rain made everything seem still and silent, but Lee knew better. He knew what threats that misting rain held. He tried to listen beyond the constant splash, tried to hear if...

He craned his neck.

Lee faced an unknown street, just a two-lane blacktop that passed between the church and a square, brick building with a storefront that announced it as AMY'S ANTIQUES. To his right, the unknown street made a *T* intersection with Fourth Street. The church took up the southern corner of that intersection, and Amy's Antiques took the northern corner.

He could hear the driving rain on the street, on the buildings, on the metal roof of the church, pouring out of drain spouts, creating that static sound, like the dead space between radio stations. But underneath that was a higher-pitched noise, steady and constant: *sssssssssssssssssshhhh*...

"Someone's coming," he said, just as the sound of an engine shifting gears rose above the rain. Coming from Fourth Street, a red Chevy Lumina hurtled around the corner of Julie's Antiques, fishtailing slightly on the rainy street. The headlights were off, but the windshield wipers beat frantically from side to side.

As the vehicle recovered from its fishtail, the engine roared and the vehicle began surging forward again. Lee strained to see who was in the driver's seat, but he could only see a dark shape through the rain-splashed windshield.

Before Lee could rein him in, Miller was out the door, waving his arms over his head. Lee's hand shot out with a quickness that surprised even himself and seized the kid by the back of his shirt collar, hauling him roughly back in the door, but the damage was done.

The Chevy Lumina's wet brakes stuttered and squealed and the vehicle came to a halt. Lee was about to raise his rifle, ready for the shooting to start, when the driver's door popped open and a man wearing bloodstained ACU trousers and a tactical vest came halfway out of the car. Across the twenty-or-so yards between them, their eyes locked, both bodies tense, each one evaluating the other.

A howl rose above the rain.

The man in the ACUs snapped his head to the left, looking down Fourth Street to the front of the church. His eyes fixed on something out of Lee's view. They maintained that cold, calculating stare, but his lips split, showing his teeth like a growling dog.

Then he looked back at Lee. "Get in the fuckin' car, man!"

There was no discussion, no consensus to be reached. All three of them burst through the door and began sprinting for the Chevy Lumina. The man in the ACUs sat quickly back in his driver's seat. Harper and Miller grabbed the back doors and snatched them open, piling inside, dripping and out of breath. Lee jumped into the front passenger's seat and the vehicle rolled forward before his boots even left the ground.

For a moment, everyone was silent, feeling the reassuring rumble of that engine carrying them away from danger. There was much breathing hard and fogging up windows and looking around at each other with curious half smiles that faded quickly. Yes, they were all happy to be alive and whole. But now they found themselves in another precarious situation: Who was this man with the ACUs? And was he friend or foe?

The vehicle made a hard right-hand turn onto a four-lane boulevard. The street sign sped by too fast for Lee to catch the name. The engine surged and the vehicle thrummed up to sixty miles per hour, then leveled off. The road straightened out and seemed to go on for a bit, and Lee caught the man in the ACUs hazarding a glance in Lee's direction.

He watched the man's eyes go immediately to the little square patch in the center of Lee's vest that held two vertical black bars. Likewise, Lee's own eyes were drawn to a similar patch on the other man's chest that bore triple chevrons. His name tape read LaRouche.

Then they were looking at each other's weapons. Lee held his M4, barrel down. The stranger had a Beretta M9 strapped into a drop-leg holster. It did not escape him that the man's right hand lay tensely against the sidearm. He looked ready to draw at any second.

The man named LaRouche turned his eyes back to the road. "We're not going to have to shoot each other, are we?"

Lee shook his head. "Who are you?"

"Introductions in a minute," LaRouche said. "What are you?"

"Excuse me?"

"What branch of the military?"

Lee pointed to his uniform. "Army, same as you."

The other man smirked. "I'm real impressed that you recognize the uniform, but that doesn't prove shit except you watch the news. You don't look like Army."

"It's a long story," Lee said enigmatically. "Let's just say I'm SF for now."

LaRouche nodded slowly. "Wow…an elitist attitude and secret squirrel talk." He smirked. "Maybe you really are SF."

Lee raised his brow and shrugged. "You can believe whatever you want."

LaRouche eyed him. "Moving on. Who are you?"

"Captain Lee Harden."

LaRouche pointed to his name tape. "It's said *Luh-roosh*."

Harper leaned forward from the backseat. "Excuse me. Where are we going?"

"Johnston Memorial Hospital." The sergeant slowed down and took a right turn. "We got a wing of the hospital secure. Army cordoned off the area to keep the infected out. They've since abandoned the place, but it's still a decent location, and we can get in and out safely."

"So there are people here?" Miller asked.

"Well, I'm here." LaRouche sighed.

Lee turned to him. "How many survivors?"

"Why do you care?"

"Because it's my job. How many?"

LaRouche considered him for a moment. Lee was not above attempting to pull rank on LaRouche if necessary, but that was a tricky card to play. Here they were, witnessing the collapse of the government, and all command and control had been stripped away. There were no consequences for insubordination, unless Lee wanted to duke it out with him, and he didn't. Lee didn't think it was his rank that finally persuaded LaRouche to shrug it off and start talking, but something in LaRouche's own mind clicked and his demeanor softened.

"One other soldier, besides myself; a Johnston County sheriff's deputy; and thirty-two civilians." LaRouche's right hand didn't hover so closely to his Beretta anymore. His eyes constantly scanned as he drove, but he seemed less concerned with Lee and his two companions now. "The other soldier's a private; he's wounded and not gonna make it much longer. The deputy—Shumate's his name— he's kind of in charge but don't really know what he's doing. And the civilians are all about as clueless and panicky as you'd expect."

Lee remembered his radio. "We might be able to help each other out, Sergeant."

"Oh?" LaRouche sounded doubtful.

Lee nodded. "I have some medical supplies and a doctor. We left them in a pickup on the south side of town, just across the barricades."

LaRouche still looked guarded. "Are you in contact with him?"

Lee nodded and keyed the radio that he still

held in his hand, waiting a few beats before speaking. He forwent typical radio protocol, because Doc probably wouldn't know what to do. "Harden to Doc—you there?"

He released the button.

Static on the other end for a brief second, then silence.

They all waited.

LaRouche drove the Chevy Lumina quickly through another set of turns, then straightened out. Up ahead and to their left, a big building loomed. Signs on the side of the road pointed arrows toward it and bore a blue square with a white *H*. Other signs teetered in the rain, their bases kept down by sandbags. These signs were labeled with that strange circular biohazard symbol and read, QUARANTINED AREA: BSL 4, and beneath that, LEVEL 4 PROTECTION REQUIRED.

A checkpoint stood up ahead. The red-and-white-striped crossing arms were tipped over, some of them broken. The white, tentlike decontamination domes were tattered and bullet-riddled and wavered weakly in the sharp winds, as though they might fly apart at any second.

Lee keyed the radio a second time, speaking very slowly and clearly: "Harden to Doc or Josh. Harden to Doc or Josh. Answer the radio. Do you copy me?"

Static, and then nothing.

LaRouche steered the sedan around the decontamination tents, between two fences strung thick with concertina wire and backed by more cement barricades. When they were around the checkpoint, he steered the sedan through a hole in the barricades and zoomed up to a parking garage entrance, then drove it up to the highest level. From there, Lee looked out over the hospital parking lot and the vast line of barriers that had been erected around it. In one far corner, he could see stacks of what looked like long black plastic bags. They were thrown haphazardly in an enormous pile. Backed up to this pile was a large flatbed truck.

Body disposal.

His stomach felt heavy, pulled down by a lead weight. Perhaps from this high vantage point, the radio signal might get better reception...

"Doc. Josh. This is Captain Harden. Can you copy anything I'm saying?"

Static, and then silence.

Miller swore quietly. "Something's wrong."

FOURTEEN

Doc

Fear and urgency forced Doc to press harder on the gas pedal than was prudent in the rain. It came in white sheets that battered the windshield with too much force and volume for the wipers to handle. Perhaps if he were going slower, he might be able to see, but the speedometer hovered between sixty and seventy miles per hour in the straightaways, dipping below that only for curves or low points in the road that might have standing water and cause him to hydroplane.

He tried to remember the abandoned cars and wrecks that dotted Highway 210, heading west, away from Smithfield and back toward Camp Ryder. They seemed to sneak up on him, jumping out of the rain and forcing him to slam on the brakes and navigate around them at breakneck speeds. A few times, he clipped the shoulder and fishtailed, but he always quickly recovered. He couldn't lose control.

Not now. Not when he was so close.

Fear and urgency.

He realized he'd been breathing heavily through his mouth and his tongue was becoming dry, so he closed it and worked up enough spit to coat his tongue again. He wanted to go faster, but if he went faster, he would crash, he was certain of it. Crash and die, and he would look like those battered, bloody messes that came into the ER, all covered in plastic tubes and oxygen masks and wires and beeping equipment. Except none of that modern technology would be there. There were no cell phones, no 911 to come save him, no medics to take him to a hospital and fix his broken body. He would lie in that smoking wreckage until the infected found him or he died from his injuries.

So the fear and urgency pushed him on, but he didn't let them push too hard.

Because he had to make it back. He had to save Nicole.

Another abandoned vehicle loomed out at him, but it was a feint—the vehicle was far enough on the side of the road that he barely had to swerve to avoid it.

He took a look at his odometer.

TRIP A: 8.7 MI

He'd zeroed it out as he'd peeled out of Smithfield. *Ten miles,* he'd told Doc. *Ten miles outside of Smithfield, we'll set it up. We'll get him when he's coming back. That'll be best, Doc. And then we'll let her go. Won't that be nice, Doc? To see her alive and well again? Just bring him to us. But don't be late, Doc, don't be late. Because if you don't show up, I will slit her open. Yeah. I'll slit her open from her pussy to her tits. Do you believe me, Doc? Do you believe me?*

And Doc did.

He believed him.

And he couldn't be late.

He slowed down now, because the odometer read 9.0 MI, and he knew the roadblock was coming soon. The staccato chatter of rain on his windshield settled to a dull drumming as his speed dropped from sixty miles per hour to forty miles per hour. The road before him came into focus a bit and he was able to see the sharp curve in the road ahead of him, maybe a quarter mile.

That would be it, he was certain.

He realized his hands hurt and he forced his grip on the steering wheel to relax, only to find them squeezing harder a moment later. His heart was pumping hard now, and the urgency was gradually being overshadowed by the fear. He did not like this. He did not like it one bit. But he had to. He had to do it. For Nicole.

He wished to God in that brief moment that he had never agreed to this. It would have been better for them both to die that hot afternoon, trapped in his parents' house, trapped like rats while a big green Hummer and a pair of pickups pulled up on his parents' lawn and men with guns started swarming the house. He should have just told them all to fuck off, then held Nicole tight for those last few seconds before they gunned them all down.

But even as he thought it, he knew it would not have happened like that. No, maybe for him it would have been quick and easy, but then again, maybe not. Maybe they would have made him watch, because they were like that. They did things like that to the people who didn't cooperate. Yes, they would have made him watch, and then they would have killed him, painfully, but not Nicole. They would have kept her, like a toy. A pretty plaything to be handed out to the men when they did a good job.

Doc's jaw was ratcheted down so hard on itself that it hurt his teeth.

No, he had to make the deal.

And here he was, completing that deal, and he just forced himself to think about Nicole. Everything would be okay in a little bit. Everything would be okay once this was over.

He realized he'd slowed to about twenty miles per hour as he crept into the turn.

The rain seemed to be letting up a bit now.

As predicted, they were waiting for him.

Two pickup trucks and that big green Hummer with the nasty machine gun on top. The Hummer faced him, glaring down the center of the road like a mean pit bull that'd just snapped its leash. The two pickups were angled in, taking up the rest of the road, like the smaller dogs that hung out with the big dog.

A man popped out of the top of the Hummer and grabbed the machine gun, swinging it in Doc's direction. Then more men started jumping out of the pickups, all of them holding rifles like the one Lee had given him. They weren't military, though. Doc knew what they were, and why they were to be feared.

Criminals. Lowlifes. People who had trouble following the rules even before the world went to shit.

Lost causes, one and all.

Out of the four men who had come out of the pickup trucks, two stayed behind, pointing guns at Doc while the others began jogging toward him. He brought the pickup truck to a stop, not wanting them to perceive any accidental acceleration as aggression. He held his hands up, touching the ceiling. The M4 was still in the seat next to him. He didn't even look at it. He didn't want to give them an excuse to shoot him, because unlike the normal people like Miller and Harper and Josh, these guys looked for reasons to shoot people and had to be convinced *not* to.

They were "not to be fucked with."

The two men stopped short and exchanged a confused look.

One of them, a tall, younger guy with a face covered in teardrop tattoos, crosses, and other nonsense, raised the rifle and shouted, "Get outta the fuckin' truck!"

Doc slowly reached for the door handle and opened it.

"Yeah…move slow!" The tattooed man nodded. "Now keep your hands up! Turn around and face away from me!"

Doc complied. He stared down the road he had just come from.

"Now start walking backward toward me!"

And he began walking backward, thinking to himself that this was actually a very professional-sounding takedown, but that these men probably had experience with them, being that they were likely the subject of several police takedowns during their lifetimes.

"Okay, now kneel down!"

Doc kneeled, and then rough hands were patting him for weapons and hauling him to his feet. The hands spun Doc around, and then he was facing the guy with the tattoos and he could see that what he thought had been a cross at the corner of the man's eye was actually a dagger pointed down. The guy grabbed Doc by the collar and got in his face. His breath stank like stale cigarette smoke and a hint of booze.

"Where the fuck's the other guy?" he demanded.

Now the tattooed man's companion joined. "Yeah! Where're the others?"

"I...uh..." Doc realized his heart was pounding so hard he could barely speak. "They're not here."

"Oh, my fuckin' God." The guy shoved Doc back. "Oh, my fuckin' God. Are you serious with this shit?"

Doc struggled to get the words out. "Yes... No...They're not here."

The tattooed man wiped rain out of his face and then pointed at Doc, shaking his head. "That's your problem, man. Not mine. Good luck explaining that shit."

From behind the two excited criminals, the back passenger door to the Hummer opened, and *he* stepped out. The source of Doc's grief. *He* had made all the commands; *he* held all the power; everything had been *his* idea. The schemes and threats and the leverage had dominated Doc's existence for so long that Doc had unconsciously built him up into a godlike status in his mind. A vengeful, hateful god. A god Doc served not because he wanted to, but because he was forced.

But he was just a man, and Doc realized it again as he watched him stride up, hunching his shoulders against the rain. He was thinner now than he had been when they'd first met. Then, he hadn't been overweight, but he'd had a slight pot to his belly and no muscle mass to speak of. His face had been drawn, his eyes dark and sunken, and his teeth rotting out from years of methamphetamine usage.

Now he looked taller, healthier. Any extra weight he'd had on him had vanished and his skin was stretched taut over cruel-looking cords of muscle. But his eyes were still dark. He'd been a harmless addict but had since become a sober psychopath.

The jeans he wore were snug on his legs, but not tight. The knees and seams had begun to fray a bit, but they were not yet torn. He wore old, black steel-toed boots—what he lovingly called his "shit-kickers"—the type you might see on a good old-fashioned neo-Nazi. On his right side was an old .357 revolver holstered in a low-slung leather gun belt. On his left side hung a giant bowie knife. He wore a faded, dirty gray shirt with a shamrock on it. His hair was shorter than Doc remembered, and his lean, angular face sported a barely healed cut that ran from his cheek to his chin. As he approached, Doc could see that the cut was clumsily stitched closed with what looked like regular fabric thread.

He walked up and stood about a foot from Doc,

his lips a bloodless line, just staring at him with those cold, dead eyes, one hand on his hip, the other on the handle of his bowie knife.

Doc unwittingly bowed his head. "Milo."

"Doc." Milo's voice was low and even. "I thought we had an arrangement."

"Well, I didn't want to be late because you said—" Doc began, but Milo cut him off, his voice gaining volume.

"The arrangement—if you recall—was that you bring me this 'supply guy' so that I can speak with him. And for this service, I give you back your beloved fiancée and let the two of you ride off into the sunset together." Milo stared silently for a brief moment, then continued. "So now, I look behind you and I can't help but notice that there are no other people inside your pickup truck. Therefore, I must ask the following question: Where the *FUCK* is my guy?"

Doc finally found his voice, but it shook when he used it. "I can lead you to him, I swear to God. I will lead you there. I just...He changed the plan and I wasn't going to be able to bring him in time, and I didn't have a way to get in contact with you. I didn't want to be late." Doc took a breath and looked around, trying to see into the windows of the trucks. "Where's Nicole?"

"Would you shut the fuck up about Nicole, for Chrissake?" Milo squeezed his eyes shut and pinched the bridge of his nose between his thumb and forefinger. "First, I am not pleased. That being said, the deal is not necessarily off, *if* you can still get me what I need." Milo jabbed a stiff index finger into Doc's chest. "Even though you royally fucked me over and I should gut you where you stand."

Doc nodded. "Okay."

"I notice the truck is full. Are those supplies?"

"Yes."

Milo regained his cold composure. "Are there more?"

Doc hesitated for a brief second, but he saw Milo's fingers slowly wrapping around the handle of that bowie knife, so he spoke up. "Yes. The guy is legit. He's got supplies. Shitloads of supplies."

Milo looked down his nose at Doc. "What type of supplies?"

"Everything. Food, water, medicine, weapons, radios. You name it."

Milo appeared thoughtful and looked up at the sky. Doc noticed that it had all but stopped raining. The last few raindrops were falling in brief smatterings, but the brunt of the storm appeared to be passing, or at least pausing to gather its strength, as the summer storms often did.

"Okay." Milo crossed his arms and Doc was just happy his hand was away from that bowie knife. He'd seen the man use that thing and didn't want any part of it. "Do you remember where the supplies are? Can you take us back there?"

"Well." Doc was not sure how to break the information. "I can. But it won't do you any good. The captain has to physically be there to open the door to the supply bunker."

"The captain, huh?" Milo scoffed. "Well, I guess we need to get the captain, then, don't we?"

Doc didn't respond.

"Where is he?"

"Smithfield," Doc said slowly. "It's a little town up—"

"Oh, I know Smithfield." Milo smiled. "Yeah. We're great friends with Smithfield. Really great friends."

Everyone in the Chevrolet Lumina stared out the windshield at the small city below them, wondering why Josh and Doc were not answering their radio. The wind was gone and the rain had all but died. Far to the south, a corner of the thick gray storm clouds folded back and the sun broke through, like it was fighting to beat back the clouds but was eventually overwrought and covered up again. It was close to midday.

"It's a good distance from here to where you left them," LaRouche observed. "You sure the radios can reach that far?"

Lee looked at the radio in his hand. "Yeah. The distance shouldn't be a problem on these."

"Maybe the storm's interfering with the signal," Miller suggested.

Harper shifted around in his seat. "We need to go back."

"Uh-uh." LaRouche shook his head vehemently. "You can't go out during the day."

Lee and the men from Camp Ryder looked confused. "I thought you didn't go out at night."

Now it was LaRouche's turn to look confused. "You don't go in the woods at night, and you don't go in the city during the day." He hiked an arm up on the passenger seat so he could twist around and look at the others. "Jesus Christ, guys. You don't know that? How are you still alive?"

"You were out during the day," Miller said, as though it were an accusation.

"Yeah." LaRouche raised his voice. "Trying to get some fucking diesel for the hospital generator before it runs out."

Lee raised a placating hand. "We're not arguing here. Sergeant, can you explain to us what the difference between the city and the woods is—besides the obvious."

LaRouche seemed indignant for a second, giving everyone a look that made it very clear that he didn't like being called into question. "Yeah. You got 'hordes' and you got 'packs.' The city crazies tend to gather in one big horde. There doesn't seem to be a single leader; they just all go where the others go. Mindless. Like cattle. The ones out in the woods tend to be in smaller packs, though they can still get pretty big. They seem to have one 'pack leader' that they follow, and they tend to be a little more clever."

Lee remembered the horde that had attacked them at the Petersons' house, and he remembered the Shovel Guy who had almost killed Angela. He'd seemed to be the leader of that group, and they were large, probably around eighty strong. Lee said as much to LaRouche.

The sergeant answered with a shrug and upraised hands. "I don't know, Captain. I'm just telling you what I've seen. I've heard the same type of stories from a couple of others. Keep in mind I'm not a scientist. I don't know how this shit works. That being said, these crazy people, they still have to eat, right? So what happens when these hordes in these cities have picked clean everything there is to eat in the city? I don't think they'll just sit around and wait to starve to death. I think they start... migrating, I guess."

Lee didn't know about LaRouche's theory on migrating hordes, but the sergeant was at least correct that they didn't have much information about the infected. Everything they knew was based on anecdotal evidence. There were no officials anymore to tell them what was normal and why. Strange shit was happening, and they just had to deal with it and worry about the reasons later when there was time.

"So." Lee tapped his lips with the radio antenna. "Why is it more dangerous to go out during the day if you're in the city? What difference does it make?"

"Again, I can't tell you why, because I just don't know." LaRouche seemed to be losing patience. "All I can tell you is that the ones in the woods get way more active at night, and their senses are like an animal's. They'll sniff you out and I swear to God they can hear a squirrel fart from three hundred yards away." He shook his head. "The ones in the city are the exact opposite. They get lethargic or something at night and just stand there, hundreds of them, standing there in the moonlight. It's creepy as fuck. But their senses aren't as tuned as the infected in the woods. They rely more on their eyesight, I think. Like regular people. So we try to avoid them during the day when they're moving around a lot and can see much better."

Harper's voice was quiet. "They've changed a lot since a month ago."

The implication was obvious, and everyone knew exactly what Harper was really saying, because they had all just had the same thought. First the bacterium burrows through the brain. People get sick. Then they lose their minds. They don't appear to have any will to survive, and they throw themselves in harm's way. They are simply full of aggression toward everything around them. Then they form groups, and the aggression toward other infected subside. These groups turn into hordes that threaten survivors simply by their massive numbers. Then the infected begin to develop a pack instinct. They are on the brink of starvation, so they begin to hunt the easiest prey for a human to catch—another human. And they begin to feed.

A cycle of instinctive survival.

All in a little over a month.

If the infected were capable of evolving this far, what would life be like for the survivors in another month? In two? What about a year? The unspoken hope in everyone's mind was that winter would come and wipe out a large portion of the infected, killing them with exposure, hypothermia, and starvation. But if they could think enough to hunt, if their survival instincts were reigniting inside their brains, what was to stop them from hibernating or developing some other method of coping with the cold?

"So what do we do about Doc and Josh?" Harper asked.

Lee breathed deeply, trying to rid his stomach of that leaden feeling. "I guess we have to wait until dark."

LaRouche opened his door. "That would be advisable. In the meantime, I'll introduce you to Deputy Shumate and maybe we can talk about helping each other."

Lee felt strange to simply dismiss the situation like that. But he could see the sergeant had a point. As Harper and Miller and Lee had just witnessed, the hordes were too large to contend with. It would be impossible to kill them all. The only present solution was to wait until dark and sneak out to check on Doc and Josh.

"Okay." He opened his door and stepped out.

Reluctantly, Harper and Miller followed.

LaRouche pointed to their rifles. "Let's go ahead and leave those in the car for now. I'm sure Deputy Shumate won't mind you guys havin' them, but he likes to have the say-so. You don't want to start on the wrong foot with him."

The other two men looked to Lee for approval.

Lee nodded, depositing his own rifle in the front seat.

When all the rifles were secured in the car, Lee realized he was tense, expecting LaRouche to use that moment to betray them, pull his sidearm, and capture them. But LaRouche only nodded. "Alright, come on in."

FIFTEEN

THE HOSPITAL

THEY FOLLOWED THE SERGEANT to a steel door where he knocked twice.

"Who is it?" a muffled voice demanded.

"LaRouche, asshole." The sergeant leaned on the doorframe. "Grapefruit."

The door clanked open. Lee assumed "grapefruit" was some sort of code word. The man on the other side of the door was a tall, rat-faced man, with strangely long fingers wrapped around a shotgun. He looked at the men from Camp Ryder with narrowed eyes, still standing in the doorway.

"Who're they?" His voice was gravelly.

LaRouche threw his thumb over his shoulder. "Couple more survivors."

"More mouths to feed." But it sounded like *mo mahths*.

A Cajun accent, perhaps?

LaRouche just stared for a long moment. "So, can we come in?"

Still staring at them with his beady rat eyes, the man stepped out of the way and allowed them to pass. They entered a stairwell where the air was slightly dank and cooler than it felt outside, almost like a cellar should be. The party descended two floors and stopped at a door marked with the number four. Beyond that landing, the stairwell below them was blocked with jumbles of concertina wire, ostensibly to prevent anyone from coming up.

LaRouche opened the door and they all stepped inside the hospital.

It was dim inside, but not dark. They were on the floor of a nondescript ward, the outer walls bearing large windows that let in the diffused light from the cloudy day outside. Adding to the muted glow were red emergency lights, the kind that popped on when the hospital was completely out of power.

"Did your genny run out?" Lee asked, looking at the emergency lighting.

"Not just yet." LaRouche led them to a nurses' station. "One of the guys here is an electrician. He rigged up the wiring so we wouldn't use so much fuel burning lights and bullshit like that. Now these fucking emergency lights are on all the time. They'll start to get on your nerves." LaRouche sneered. "But we only use the genny to keep electricity running to the sliding doors on the bottom level. They're designed to open in case of a power outage, so we have to keep a current running through them at all times or we might get some unwanted guests."

It finally made sense why LaRouche had decided to risk a day trip to get the diesel fuel. The alternative was to run raggedly close to the "E" line and possibly lose power to the doors. What didn't make sense was why LaRouche had ventured out on his own. Lee thought about what the sergeant had said about his fellow survivors. It seemed that maybe LaRouche just didn't trust any of them enough to accompany him.

At the nurses' station, LaRouche put his hands on the countertop and nodded to two men on the other side. They were both middle-aged with pistols stuck in their waistbands. One was a little shorter than the other with dark hair, and the other was taller and leaner looking, with a mop of straw-colored hair. They both looked less than enthusiastic, and Lee guessed that they were on guard duty.

LaRouche raised two fingers as a greeting. "Gentlemen. Where's Shumate?"

The short, dark-haired guy eyeballed the three newcomers and then jerked his head back behind him. "He's down the hall with Darryl, tryin' to figure out the power situation."

"Diesel fuel, right?" Lee asked, giving a side-long look at Harper, who returned a discreet nod.

The short man quirked his brow. "You say that like you know where to find some."

Lee plastered on a dimwitted smile. "Can we speak with Deputy Shumate?"

The tall man and the short man exchanged a look, and then they both shrugged.

"Sure," the tall man said. "I'll get him."

He turned and walked down the hall, his movements like that of a stork.

Lee stretched his tired back and shifted his weight, leaning on the counter with one arm. He learned the name of the shorter man was Javier.

For the most part, the people seemed accustomed to new faces. There was a slight level of interest in Lee and the other newcomers, but nowhere near the scrutiny he'd received at Camp Ryder. Perhaps they had survivors joining their ranks with more regularity than Camp Ryder did, or perhaps they had a lot of people pass through.

To Javier, Lee said, "So, do you know most everyone in your group?"

Javier placed his palms on the counter and smiled. He was affable, but he also wasn't volunteering much information, and when Lee asked for it, he became guarded. "I know a few."

"I'm looking for a specific person."

Javier's face remained stolid.

Lee continued cautiously. "There's a woman in the group I came from. Her name is Marie and she thinks her sister, Julia, is here in Smithfield."

Rather than answering, Javier looked to LaRouche. "These guys straight?"

LaRouche looked at them and shrugged. "They seem okay to me."

Javier looked back at Lee. "Yeah, we got a Julia, but I don't know if she's the one you're looking for." He paused for a moment. "I'll talk with her."

From around the corner came a man in a dirty white T-shirt tucked into brown pants with a gold stripe that immediately pegged him as a sheriff's deputy. He wasn't wearing a gun belt, like Lee had expected, but instead just had his service pistol shoved in the front of his waistband like the others. At first glance he seemed like an okay guy, perhaps a little young, maybe somewhat naive. But as he got closer Lee could see into his eyes and didn't like what he saw there. It was the look of scared prey, the look of someone barely holding it together. Someone on the verge of cracking.

He walked up and put his hands on his hips, not bothering to greet them. He made eye contact with each of them and started nodding the type of nod that says, *Okay, I see how it is.* The man's upper lip quivered like he was barely controlling a snarl. Then he turned his gaze on LaRouche.

"These some friends of yours?" The words were spat out.

LaRouche stared straight ahead blandly. "Yeah. Old army buddies."

Lee decided to step in, since it seemed there was bad blood between LaRouche and Deputy Shumate. Whatever was between the two of them, he didn't want it to affect his relationship with Shumate. He extended his hand. "Sir, I'm Captain Harden of the United States Army and these are my friends from another group of survivors." Shumate took Lee's hand somewhat reluctantly while the captain continued. "I'm here to see what type of assistance I can render to your group."

That gave Shumate pause. He released Lee's hand and retracted it back to his hip. His eyes squinted with suspicion. "Yeah, that's what the last guy said, and that ain't been nothing but trouble since."

Lee's brow furrowed. "The last guy?"

Shumate looked like he was calculating an answer, but LaRouche took over. "Captain, you were asking about our diesel fuel situation. Are you just curious, or do you have something to offer us?"

Lee took a small step back so that Harper was by his side. "Well, that's not my deal to make. This is Harper—he's kind of the second in command at the other camp." Lee looked at him. "Harper?"

Harper took a moment to think, and Lee hoped he would choose his words carefully. They still didn't know how this group operated, and there was always the possibility that once they learned that Camp Ryder had diesel fuel, they would just attempt to take it by force.

Harper finally spoke. "We may have a way of getting a significant supply of diesel fuel to you."

Shumate's jaw worked back and forth. For a group of survivors like this, the hospital likely had stores of food and water and medicine. That made finding diesel fuel their biggest survival priority, and Lee could see that even the mention of a "significant supply" of diesel fuel was enough to make Shumate more cordial.

"Diesel fuel, huh? You want to trade diesel fuel." The deputy rubbed his stubbled chin. "How much do you have?"

Harper shook his head. "We'll talk numbers when you put something on the table."

Lee leaned in to Harper. "Talk to you real quick?"

They took a few steps away and huddled together, conferring in hushed tones. Miller was excluded from the deals, but he didn't seem to care and was just leaning against the counter, looking about as bored as LaRouche.

Lee whispered first. "How do you want to work this?"

Harper grimaced. "I don't like making a deal without Bus."

"Too bad," Lee said simply. "Bus ain't here and you are."

Harper hung his head. "Shit, I'd just as soon pay it forward. We're getting loads of supplies from you, so there really isn't anything they can give us that we can't get from you."

"True, but that's not advisable." Lee took a glance over his shoulder, where Shumate and LaRouche stood, staring at them. Javier and his friend were no longer there. "We're trying to make a deal here, because no one wants to feel like they owe someone else. Mutual support is what you want. A fair trade."

Harper looked lost. "But what do we need?"

"How about a safe place?" Lee suggested. "We're going to be making supply runs back and forth for a bit until Camp Ryder can get on its feet. Smithfield could be very useful if we were welcome to crash here anytime. They're very secure from what I can tell, and they seem to have their shit together for the most part. In the long run, if we can power this place, we might be able to actually use some of the medical equipment here."

"We're not really using the diesel fuel. So we could do the diesel tanker in exchange for safe lodgings whenever we need them," Harper clarified.

"It's up to you, but I think it'll be a good deal."

"Okay." Harper seemed resolute now. "We'll do it."

The two men stood and walked back to the nurses' station. Shumate tapped his foot impatiently as they stepped back up. "So? What's going on? How much fuel can you get your hands on?"

"The getting will be the easy part," Harper said truthfully. "Basically, we want our groups to be friends. We want to give you some communication equipment so we can talk back and forth. And we can supply you with plenty of diesel fuel. In exchange, we would like to be able to use Smithfield as a stopover point whenever we need to."

"How much diesel?" Shumate repeated.

Harper clearly did not want to be pinned down to a number, because if he just blurted out that they had seven thousand gallons of diesel fuel, it would be obvious that it was in one location. Then all Shumate would have to do was find out where. Instead, Harper put it in terms of time. "Let's just say we can get enough to keep you going indefinitely."

"*Indefinitely* is a big word." Shumate's face pinched up. "Can you be more specific?"

"Two years," Harper said finally. "Give or take some."

It was obvious that Shumate would have liked to say something about that but that he didn't want to reveal how ecstatic he was about even the possibility of getting enough fuel to last for two years. Finding supplies of diesel fuel could not have been easy for the Smithfield group. Having such an enormous amount just dropped into their laps was like winning the lottery.

But Shumate played it cool. "Two years, and

you want to just drop in unannounced anytime you want and receive a warm welcome?"

Harper shook his head. "If you take some radio equipment, we'll be able to maintain contact, so there won't be any dropping in unannounced. And we won't come in to clean out your food and water. We just want a safe place to stay if we need it."

Shumate pretended to consider it further, but Lee could see in his eyes that the decision was already made. He couldn't give a shit about letting people stay here, as long as they were bringing him that precious liquid gold.

He was extending his hand to shake on the deal when Javier reappeared around the corner. The shorter man's eyes darted to Lee and gave him a look that Lee didn't like, causing his stomach to tighten. "Hey, Shumate..."

"What is it?" Shumate turned, annoyed.

"Yeah, um..." Javier mumbled, still staring at Lee. "Can I talk to you in private for a moment?"

Shumate followed Javier's eyes and looked the three newcomers up and down briefly, as though sizing up whether they were a threat or not. Then he shrugged and followed Javier partially around the corner. Lee could still see Shumate's back and hear the hushed and urgent tones, though he couldn't make out the words.

Harper raised an eyebrow. "What's going on?"

Lee kept his words quiet. "I don't know, but I don't like it."

"Me neither."

Lee cleared his throat and looked around the

room, breathing evenly to maintain his calm and trying to keep a look of neutrality. He counted six men with guns, including LaRouche, Shumate, and Javier. They all had pistols. Two of the others in the room held shotguns, and the last a hunting rifle. They were all staring at Lee and his two companions.

LaRouche turned and rested his elbows on the counter, paying more attention now to Shumate and Javier and their whispered conversation. The sergeant inclined his head as though trying to eavesdrop.

Be calm, Lee told himself. *It's probably nothing.*

But to Harper, he murmured casually, "Still got the .22?"

Harper spoke casually. "Yup. You?"

Lee nodded. He'd almost left the pistol in the truck but decided it might be a nice backup weapon, so he'd squirreled it away underneath his tactical vest. Of course, they were still woefully outnumbered and outgunned. If it came down to that.

It won't come down to that, Lee told himself.

Then why is my pulse skyrocketing?

Lee watched Shumate as the deputy leaned back around the corner, just slightly, and glanced at Lee. They were giving an awful lot of attention to him, and not to Miller or Harper. Lee thought about the GPS device he'd stowed deep in his backpack. Protectively, he cinched the straps of his pack a little tighter. The tension in his gut became a sick feeling. That feeling of knowing what was about to happen but stubbornly hoping that it wouldn't.

Maybe it was just paranoia.

It appeared the conversation between Shumate and Javier had ended. Shumate seemed to stand there, as though he were weighing his options. Finally, Shumate turned and began walking back to the nurses' station, his head down as though still deep in thought. Lee watched him closely as he approached and saw the movement of his eyes, glancing to the men with shotguns who sat behind Lee. That little look was followed by the slightest of nods, and Lee knew that it was not just paranoia.

Lee's hand swept to his vest, but Shumate was quick with his service pistol and in a flash Lee was staring down the barrel.

"Put your hands up!" Shumate yelled.

Lee complied, because he could see the deputy's finger tight on that trigger.

"What are you doing?" Lee tried to keep his voice even. As he spoke, he thought about snatching the gun away from the deputy. But Shumate was no fool and had distanced himself so that Lee was just outside of arm's reach. Behind him, Lee could hear the other men approaching quickly, and Lee recognized that his options were rapidly dwindling.

He couldn't just lie down without a fight.

He felt a rough hand grab him by his arm.

Lightning quick, Lee seized hold of whoever had grabbed his arm and then swung around so that his attacker was between him and Shumate. He reared back and planted a boot in the man's chest, sending him sprawling into Shumate. The two men cried out and tumbled to the ground in a tangle of limbs.

The force of the kick set Lee off balance and he had to turn and plant his feet to recover, but then the momentum was already carrying him toward the door. Trying to keep his feet under him, he noticed out of the corner of his eye that Harper and Miller were standing stock-still.

Why weren't they moving?

Why weren't they moving?!

Lee twisted to see, as his hand reached out to throw the stairwell door open. Harper's hand was hovering over his hip as he looked to his left. There, LaRouche held Miller firmly by the collar, the muzzle of his Beretta touching just behind Miller's ear, and the sergeant looked at Lee, his lips moving rapidly.

"Stop or I blow his fucking brains out!"

Lee's hand wavered in empty air where the door should have been, eyes still locked on LaRouche. The sergeant's expression was born of both confusion and determination. Hanging there in that split second, still waiting for his hand to hit the door, Lee wondered to himself, *Is this for real? Is he really going to shoot Miller?*

What his hand finally found was someone's chest, and then it was sliding off and Lee felt his feet go out from under him and his vision turned briefly gray. Strange how even as he could only see sparkling whorls and eddies in his vision, he could still hear someone shouting.

"Don't kill him! We need him alive!"

When Lee's vision cleared, he was on his back,

looking up at the rat-faced Cajun man, standing over him with a sneer. The side of his face began to throb where Rat-face had hit him with his shotgun. Had he not paused for just a moment to think, Lee would have swung his legs up and clamped them around Rat-face's neck, then punched him in the groin and slammed him to the floor.

But he did pause.

Because LaRouche was still screaming that he was going to shoot Miller, only now, Miller screamed too. Screamed that he believed LaRouche, that Lee had to stop or the sergeant was going to shoot him in the head.

And that pause was all it took.

Immediately, Rat-face descended on him, snatching his arms up and flipping him over onto his stomach. Then there were others, grabbing his legs, and someone was sitting on his back, someone heavy who made it difficult to breathe. Rat-face put his knee in Lee's neck, crushing his face into the floor. Someone yanked his arms behind his back and screamed for tape.

The hands were rough. These boys were pissed, and they meant to show him. But the fight was over, and Lee knew it. He might have gotten away if it were only himself to worry about, but with Harper and Miller still staring down pistol barrels, fighting to escape would only lead to bloodshed. He didn't know what the fuck Shumate wanted with him, but he could only assume it had to do with the GPS.

Lee received a quick elbow to his ribs and he grunted, but was relieved not to hear a bone break.

His hands were held tightly behind his back, and someone had returned with tape and began wrapping his wrists in it, binding them together.

LaRouche shouted, "Don't you two fucking move! Just stay right there!"

Lee struggled against the knee in his neck and managed to twist just enough to see Harper and Miller both prone on the floor. Their feet were spread wide and their hands were clasped over their heads, their eyes looking up across the floor at Lee. Miller looked blank, clearly still trying to work through what the hell had just happened. Harper's eyes were angry slits and his lips were peeled back, showing his teeth. Between the two of them, LaRouche stood, pointing his pistol first at Miller, then at Harper.

For a moment, LaRouche's eyes flicked up and caught Lee's stare.

"Why are you doing this?" Lee yelled at him, feeling hot anger and frustration like lava boiling up inside of him. "Fuck you! You fucking traitor!"

Someone punched Lee in the side of his head, causing his ears to ring and his head to bounce off the floor. He wanted to struggle against them, but LaRouche still stared at him, his pistol pointed at his companions and his finger on the trigger. A warning note passed over his face, like a cloud briefly blocking the sun, and Lee restrained himself. He would not let Miller or Harper come to harm because he wanted to escape. They were in this together now.

When the men from Smithfield finished with his hands, they snatched him to his feet and shoved him against the wall. They all yelled things in his ear, but he wasn't listening. He set his jaw and went to that cold place in his mind where pain became anger, and anger became a warm blanket that you pulled over yourself.

It registered with him that they were trying to take his backpack off, but they'd already taped his wrists together. Someone finally decided to just cut the straps. Lee felt the heavy pack fall to the floor and someone snatched it up and began riffling through the contents. Someone else worked on getting his tactical vest removed.

When Harper and Miller were secured, LaRouche holstered his pistol and spun on Shumate. "What the fuck is going on?"

Shumate seemed uncomfortable. He glanced at Lee for a moment but quickly looked away. He rubbed his sweating brow. "It's Milo. Javier just received a call on the radio from him."

Milo? THE Milo?

LaRouche holstered his pistol. "Fucking Milo? What the fuck does that asshole want with them?"

"I don't know!" Shumate snapped. "I don't even think he cares about the other two." Shumate pointed at Lee. "He wants that guy."

Lee's head spun, like someone had thrown a jigsaw puzzle up into the air, and he was trying to put it together as the pieces fell. Rat-face pulled him up off the wall and began dragging him back over to the nurses' station, where Shumate and the others were. After a moment of shock, Lee's legs began moving.

On the floor, Harper screamed, "You're with

Milo? You're with fucking Milo? You murdering sonofabitch!"

LaRouche and Shumate exchanged a quick, uncertain glance.

LaRouche's eyes darkened. "Are you really going to hand him over?"

Shumate looked lost again. "What do you want me to do about it? Huh? Tell him 'no'? He'll kill us all."

"What are you doing, Deputy?" Lee growled at him.

Shumate couldn't even look at him. He waved his head toward the hallway to their right. "Just go put them in a room. Milo will be here shortly. He's already on the way."

Lee remembered what Jack Burnsides had told him about the group that had attacked them. How they were either a rogue military unit or a group of survivors that had taken military equipment. Just like Jack had told him, Milo was making the rounds, using the brute force of his stolen military equipment to extort groups of survivors and get what he wanted from them. If you gave them what they asked for, they would let you live. If you denied them, they would wipe you out.

And now they were asking for Lee, because somehow Milo had figured out that Lee had supplies. What other reason would he have for wanting to capture Lee alive? Lee racked his brain trying to think where he'd made a mistake. And then he thought of his house, and beneath that ashen rubble, the bunker where he'd stayed that contained so many supplies. Lee's pickup that they had taken and the registration in the glove box, leading them back to his house. They must have found the door that Sam had left open. They must have gone inside and found the bunker, found the supplies inside.

Rat-face began pulling him down the hall.

Lee struggled to stay put, his voice rising. "Don't do this, Shumate! We can help you! If you do this, he's just going to keep using you. He's never going to go away until you fight him!" Rat-face was yanking him down the hall, Harper and Miller being pushed along behind him. "You've got to fight him! You've got to end it!"

And then the three of them were being shoved into a hospital room, and the door was slammed and locked from the outside.

SIXTEEN

MILO

Doc SAT IN THE rear of the Humvee, crammed against the sloped backend. All around him were boxes of ammunition, MREs, and jugs of water. There were stacks of canned goods as well, "contributions" from groups of survivors that Milo and his band had come across. Your life for a can of fruit cocktail. The only thing they didn't have much of inside the Humvee was gas, and Doc could only assume it was because Milo didn't want to breathe the fumes. Doc had seen all the red gas cans, stacked up in the bed of one of the other pickup trucks.

But the smell in the Humvee had its own overwhelming flavor. It was obvious to Doc that none of the men in the truck had cleaned themselves within the last month, and that rotten-onion rank of body odor and sweat had nearly caused Doc to retch. The rain soaking through the rags of clothing they wore had made them all smell like wet dogs.

He looked around for something that he might use as a weapon, but there was nothing. And then, with dawning self-loathing, he realized he wouldn't fight them, even if he did have a weapon.

Because Milo still had all the power over him. He was still that evil demigod. He still had Nicole.

The driver was a large man with short gray hair and a long goatee. He had a face that would be described as a "mug" and meaty hands that would be described as "mitts." He wore a pair of Oakley sunglasses, like the times were still normal, like he was still out riding his Harley around. Beside him, in the front passenger seat, was some strange kid, a taut-skinned bundle of bones that apparently was not fond of wearing a shirt, perhaps to proudly display the webwork of scars (self-inflicted, Doc thought) that adorned his chest. He had wide, insane eyes that generally stared off into nothing, but occasionally he made eye contact with Doc and caused him to feel off-balance and uncomfortable.

Behind the driver was a dark-skinned man with the beginnings of filthy-looking dreadlocks forming from his unkempt Afro. He was twisted in his seat, head cocked to one side, regarding Doc blankly and covering him with a pistol-grip shotgun.

And then in the back passenger seat was Milo himself, looking as intensely focused as Doc had ever seen him. His eyes glittered euphorically and he turned in his seat, still holding the handheld CB radio that he'd ripped from a Johnston County medic truck. It gave him an open line of communication to Deputy Shumate and his little band of survivors, currently holed up in the Johnston Memorial Hospital.

"They've got him," Milo announced, his voice tense with excitement. "Shumate's got him."

The big man in the driver's seat was more

reserved. "I wouldn't get excited until we have him in hand. Shumate's an idiot, and this fucker's been slippery."

Milo's face fell into a thoughtful repose. "Mmm..."

He turned and faced Doc, his dark, hollow gaze like that of a shark.

The look made Doc's skin crawl and his stomach flip-flop.

Milo pointed the antenna of the CB radio at him. "Well, that's where Doc is going to become useful to us once again."

Doc clenched his jaw, feeling his guts twist up inside of him. He tried to speak but found his mouth dry.

"What's that, Doc?" Milo inclined his ear. "Got a question?"

"What do you want?" Doc croaked out.

"Ah, yes. What do *I* want." Milo wobbled his head exasperatedly. He brought the radio up and keyed it. "Shumate, answer your goddamned radio. This is Milo."

There was a long pause.

The radio squelched and a shaky voice came over. "What do you want, Milo?"

"I would like for you to inform your prisoner that we have his friend—Doc is his name—and that if he attempts to escape, or is not there when we arrive, or otherwise makes my life difficult, I will be forced to execute Doc."

Another long pause. "I'll tell him."

"I appreciate your cooperation, Mr. Shumate." Milo smiled beatifically. "We will be there shortly."

There was no response.

Milo rolled his eyes at the silence. "They judge me, Doc. They judge me because they themselves do not want to do that which needs to be done, but they will not complain when my men and I risk our lives to do it. Someone has to dispose of the infected, but we need supplies to do it with. Is it so much to ask that people contribute a little to the war effort?" He shook his head. "What the fuck is this country coming to?"

Doc's heart was pounding in his head. He wanted to make a demand, but Milo was so off his rocker that Doc wasn't sure whether he would oblige his request or slit his throat. He thought there was an equal chance of both. Finally he managed to squeak: "I'm not doing anything else until you let me see Nicole."

The expression on Milo's face barely changed, but somehow it became something entirely different. He whipped around to the front. "Big G, stop the vehicle, please."

The driver, who Doc assumed was Big G, didn't utter a word. He just slammed on the brakes, causing Doc to lurch forward and catch himself on his hands. He very suddenly regretted his decision to make the demand. He didn't want to be here anymore. He didn't want to be a part of this. He just wanted to go home.

You have no home.

He closed his eyes as he heard Milo and Big G stepping out.

After a brief moment of silent darkness, the rear hatch of the Humvee was yanked open and Doc forced himself to open his eyes. Outside, Big G and Milo stood there, staring at him.

"Get out," Milo commanded.

Doc shook his head, his hair flying in his face. "I'm sorry..."

"Get the fuck out of the car!" Milo screamed, stamping his feet like a child throwing a tantrum.

Doc tried to command his unwilling body to cooperate, but he was too slow. Big G reached in with his giant bearlike paws and grabbed Doc up like a sack of groceries and dragged him out. Doc screamed and found his body losing control. Warm piss spread through his already rain-soaked pants and his arms and legs flailed about in a panic.

He's gonna kill me! He's gonna kill me!

And then Big G was standing him up, the massive bulk of his body huddled close behind him, each of his hands holding one of Doc's arms, and no matter how much Doc tried to fight against it, he couldn't move. And out of the corner of his eyes, Doc could see the glint of Milo's bowie knife sliding out of its leather sheath.

Milo pointed at the doorjamb of the rear hatch with the big knife. "Grab it!" he hissed. "Grab it or I'm gonna spill your guts on the street."

Doc didn't want to grab it. His heart was like a jackrabbit trying to get out of his chest. He tried to pull his left arm back, but Big G kept forcing it inexorably forward. Doc breathed in short, shallow breaths as he fought. "I'm sorry! I'm sorry!"

His hand touched the smooth metal and he tightened his fist into a ball.

Milo was suddenly there beside him, his breath

hot on his ear. "Open your hand, Doc. Open your fucking hand or I kill you. Do it!"

Doc closed his eyes and bared his teeth.

He opened his hand and grabbed the doorjamb.

The old metal hinges on the back hatch creaked just slightly as Milo slammed it down. Doc could hear the popping of his fingers, so quick in succession that they sounded like someone stomping on a pile of dry twigs. Doc felt the air come out of his lungs like an explosion and he began madly trying to yank his fingers free, but they were smashed in too tight.

Air found its way back into his chest.

He screamed.

Milo's hot breath on his ear again. "Shhhh. Stop screaming. Be quiet."

Doc tried to contain it but the pain was coming out of him in short, sharp barks with each rapid exhalation. Milo's voice was strangely, horribly soothing. He didn't want to fight it anymore. It was easier just to give in. Do what he was told.

Milo stood in front of him, looking him in the eyes. "Doc, calm down."

"Okay." Doc nodded, tears making dirty paths down his face.

To his right, one of the pickup trucks had stopped and the driver and passenger were looking on at Milo's handiwork. Their eyes showed dim amusement and faint smiles tweaked their lips. Like they were watching a mildly entertaining sitcom.

"I really wanted to cut your fucking hand off at the wrist, but I'm not sure I could stop the bleeding if I did that." Milo tapped Doc's hand with the knife. "But I think you need something very permanent to remind you—"

"No!"

"So I'm going to cut off one of your fingers."

"No! Please!"

"Doc, listen to me," Milo droned on. "It's for your own good that I do this, because if you ever back-talk me again, I'm just gonna fuckin' kill you. Just remember, it could have been your whole hand."

Doc sobbed, the words coming out in strangled syllables. "Please. Don't."

But Milo had already set the edge of his blade to Doc's flesh, at the very base of his index finger. "It has to happen, Doc. Just go with it."

And then the blade was sawing through his finger, not a quick chopping motion but an agonizing back and forth, quickly sliding through the skin and then grinding against bone—Jesus, he could feel that sensation all the way up his arm—and then tendons were popping, the ligaments snapping, crimson spurting out in perfect time with Doc's thundering heartbeat and dribbling down the back of the Humvee.

Doc screamed until he had no more left in him. The pain seemed to keep increasing, like a plane rocketing into the sky until it stalled, and the pain finally crescendoed and his hand began to feel numb. It was still there, but it was almost as though his brain couldn't process it all, so it turned the volume down. Brokenly, he thought to himself, *At least he didn't cut off my whole hand.*

The bloody knife was pointing at him now.

"Did you learn your lesson?" Milo asked.

Doc's eyes squeezed shut and he nodded. Spit and snot and tears ran down his face, combining and dripping off of his chin. "Yes."

"Are you ever going to back-talk me again?"

"No."

Milo smiled, just as pleasantly as though they were two old friends who had just resolved a minor squabble. He looked at Big G. "Great! Get him back in the truck and let's hit the road."

Lee stood for a long moment in the glow of the red emergency lamps that were the only source of light inside the hospital room. Across from him, he could see the faint apparitions of Harper's and Miller's faces. They both stared at him, shocked. Confused. Lost. They needed Lee to do something, to take control of this situation, but it was spiraling quickly away from him and there was a knot of panic growing in Lee's throat that threatened to choke him.

He paced the dark room, looking for anything he could use, but they had emptied the room out, almost as though they had anticipated having to hold prisoners there. Lee didn't really believe they had planned this. Not judging by the looks on their faces. Milo was using them, and fear of reprisal was keeping them in line. Shumate had wanted to make a deal with Camp Ryder, but he wanted to stay alive more, and he genuinely believed that Milo was going to murder their group if his wishes were not obeyed.

For that matter, Lee believed it as well.

Lee didn't personally know Milo, but he could surmise based on what he'd heard. One did not come to be the leader of a band of criminals and feared by so many by being merciful and kind. Cruelty and brutality were the traits that earned that position. Anything less was weakness.

After pacing the room three times, looking for anything useful and coming up empty-handed, Lee returned to the hospital room door and gave it a swift kick in frustration. The thing was solidly built. Industrial, with a steel frame. No amount of kicking would break this door in. He tried the handle, though he knew it would be locked.

He swore in the darkness and tried to force an idea to spring forth in his mind. He pulled and yanked and contorted his wrists, but the layers and layers of tape they had tightly spun around them were too solid to stretch or break. His circulation was cut off, and his fingers and palms were beginning to feel cold and numb.

One question blocked out any new ideas: If he escaped, what would Milo do to the Smithfield group? They had successfully detained him, showing Milo that they intended to do what he said, but would Milo hold them responsible if Lee managed to get away? And if he did, what would the punishment be? An even better question was whether or not Lee gave a shit about what happened to Shumate and his group at this point. Lee could not help deeply resenting Shumate and everyone in the hospital for the situation he now found himself in. He came in peace, trying to offer a deal, and he got imprisoned and turned over to the local warlord.

Objectively, Lee recognized the situation that Shumate found himself in. As the leader, everyone was looking at him to keep them safe, not to make alliances with other groups of survivors. There was no doubt that Milo outgunned them. Standing up to him would almost certainly result in massive casualties and possibly complete destruction. Standing with Lee and disobeying Milo was a bad bet for Shumate at this point in time.

Subjectively, Lee did not see the point in keeping the Smithfield group alive if it meant he was going to be dead. Of course, he didn't know what Milo's plans for him were, but he doubted they involved handshakes and friendship. He anticipated that Milo planned to get into his bunkers by any means necessary, which would include torturing him and torturing or killing others like Harper and Miller to get Lee to talk.

So what do I do about it?

Lee's thoughts were interrupted by the sound of voices outside. All three prisoners turned and faced the door. The voices grew louder as they drew closer and Lee could hear two men's voices contending with a female's. Just from the sound of the men's voices, he knew their fight was lost. The woman's voice was clear and demanding and carried with it a note of command.

The door was unlocked and thrown open.

Even the subdued light from outside made Lee squint.

The voices continued their argument and Lee

now realized the two men were LaRouche and Shumate. He didn't recognize the female voice but saw the three figures in the doorway, Shumate and LaRouche trying to keep a pissed-off woman from barging into the room.

"Get your fucking hands off of me!" She shook Shumate's hand from her arm and pointed a finger in his face. "You touch me again, I swear to God I'm gonna kick your nuts into your mouth."

Shumate made a face that looked like steam might come out of his ears, but he only balled his fists at his sides and didn't touch the woman anymore. On the other side of the woman, LaRouche held his hands up as though to surrender.

"Just let her talk to him." LaRouche put a staying hand on Shumate's chest.

The woman glared at the two men, then turned her attention to the three prisoners. She stood all of five feet and six inches, but she put her hands on her hips and glowered like she was in charge of the damn place. She wore only a pair of jeans and a white tank top and Lee immediately recognized the same corded, hard-work muscle he'd seen on Marie.

"Which one of you was talking about my sister?" she demanded.

Lee raised his head a bit. "You must be Julia."

She turned her attention on him and Lee thought for a second she might just hit him for the hell of it. But she approached him without hesitation and appeared to be looking over his injuries with a skeptical eye. When she spoke again, her voice was somewhat softer. "Is she still alive?"

Lee nodded once.

"How do you know her?"

Lee looked to his left, where Harper and Miller were still leaning up against the wall. "She's in a camp—the same one these guys are from. We left to get supplies and Marie asked me to see if I could make contact with you." Lee turned an accusatory eye on Shumate. "She wanted me to make sure your group of survivors was okay and to leave them with communications equipment so the two groups could help each other. Obviously, Mr. Shumate here has a different idea."

Shumate bristled. "You know I don't have a choice."

"We all have a choice," Lee snapped.

Julia turned back to Shumate and LaRouche. "You have to let them go."

LaRouche didn't respond, but Shumate threw his hands up in the air. "Jesus H. Christ, woman! Are you insane?" He jabbed a finger at Lee. "Milo wants that guy, and if he don't get him, we're all fucked! Would you think about everyone else for a change?"

That set Julia off. "Think? What about you? Have you *thought* about why Milo wants him so badly? Have you bothered to ask him? Don't you think that's something we should know about before we just kowtow to every whim Milo comes up with? Or maybe you're just too fucking dickless!"

Shumate fumed and growled something unintelligible, but he turned his gaze on Lee. "Why does Milo want you?"

Lee thought for a long moment whether or not he should spill the truth to Shumate. Given the current situation, Lee didn't think it could make things any worse.

Shumate took his silence as a refusal to speak. "You see? He ain't gonna say shit!"

Lee laid it all out, quickly and concisely. "I have access to supplies. Things people need. The US government gave me these caches so that I could help restore order to the region." He tossed his head toward the two men from Camp Ryder. "They can attest to that. I've been helping their group, and we were on the way back with the supplies when we stopped in here."

Shumate stared at him dubiously, then looked at Harper and Miller.

Both men nodded.

"Oh, you've got to be kidding me." Shumate shook his head. "What a crock of shit."

Lee felt frustrated laughter bubbling up in his chest. "That's what everyone says."

"Prove it," Shumate challenged.

"Prove it?" A tiny chuckle escaped Lee's throat. "Have you fucking looked in my backpack? Have you seen anyone else carrying live grenades, 40-mike-mikes, and claymores? Anyone else got a bunch of brand-new long-range radios in their pack?" Lee looked down at his clothing. "Even my goddamn clothes are brand-fucking-new! Everything we have is fresh from the supply cache!"

Shumate looked at the uniform Lee wore, then rubbed his face. "It doesn't *prove* anything."

This time Harper spoke up. "There's a pickup

truck full of supplies just outside the barricade on Brightleaf Boulevard. We left it there because we couldn't get it past the barricade. You can go and see for yourself. All those supplies came from Captain Harden's bunker."

"Now it's a fucking 'bunker,'" Shumate muttered.

Julia stepped toward him. "You've got to let them go!"

LaRouche seemed to side with them. "It explains why Milo wants him so badly."

"He can help you!" Harper said urgently.

Lee cleared his throat. "Deputy, you at least need to let these other two men go."

A brief moment of silence before Harper objected. "Captain…"

Lee spoke more forcefully. "You've got no reason to keep them here. And those supplies need to get back to the other camp. The people there are starving. They need help. If you don't let these men leave, you're killing them just as surely as if you shot them yourself."

Shumate's eyebrow twitched up. "You know what doesn't make sense? Who the fuck leaves a pickup truck full of supplies just lying out in the open, unguarded?"

"We left two men there," Harper explained. "Their names are Doc and Josh."

At the mention of the names, Shumate and LaRouche looked at each other with a dreadful silence that made Lee feel rubbery. Shumate suddenly avoided eye contact. "By the way, Milo called me on the radio. He wanted me to tell you that he has a guy named Doc, a friend of yours, and he's going to execute him if you aren't here when he arrives."

Lee wanted to feel what should have been shock, sucking the wind out of him, but instead all he felt was a sinking, wretched disappointment, a positive knowing, a confirmation of dreadful things you already knew but didn't want to admit to yourself. That was why Doc hadn't answered the radio. Milo had found them. And he hadn't mentioned Josh, which meant he was probably dead or dying. And the pickup truck, full of supplies they had risked their lives and killed to get, was all gone, sucked up into a tornado named Milo.

And inside of Lee, he didn't know whether the fire was so hot it felt cold or whether he just wasn't feeling anything at all. He didn't know whether to be crushed with the disappointment or explode with rage. The two equal and opposite forces pressed at each other and sandwiched Lee in the middle so that he just stood there, staring at the red emergency lights above the door and wondering why ever in the fuck did he take this job? Was the destruction of humanity the will of God and Lee was just a modern-day Jacob, wrestling stubbornly and fruitlessly with an angel over the wreckage of America?

Maybe Father Jim would have an answer for him.

Lee found himself looking at Shumate again, and when he spoke he heard his voice like he had water in his ears. "Let Harper and Miller leave. You've got no business with them. You've got me. You've got what Milo wants. Unless you're going to stand and fight with me, then let them go, and leave me the fuck alone."

Shumate seemed unsure, an expression that crossed his face often and seemed to fall into place there like a wheel finding a well-worn rut. He looked at LaRouche, who was staring at him intensely.

"I can take them," LaRouche said. "Milo doesn't know about them, so he can't be mad."

Julia stepped forward. "You have to let them go. My sister's there. We can help each other."

Shumate finally nodded. He pointed a finger at LaRouche. "But Milo's gonna show up any minute. You need to move them out before he gets here."

LaRouche didn't waste any time. He produced a big knife from his vest and instructed Harper and Miller to turn around. The two of them looked stunned, but they didn't argue. Lee didn't want them to argue. He wanted them to be gone. The less they said the better.

LaRouche cut through the duct tape binding their hands together. The two of them looked at Lee, rubbing the stickiness off their wrists. When they seemed like they were trying to find something to say, Lee just shook his head. "Go. I can take care of myself." Lee looked at Shumate. "Let them take my pack, but keep that black box you got out of my pocket. I'm just going to assume Milo knows about it anyway."

Shumate seemed to consider this for a moment while LaRouche ushered them out of the door. Eventually, he nodded. Perhaps the deputy figured that if he was trusting Lee this far, and if Julia and LaRouche thought he was being truthful, he may as well go with it. Lee also assumed that Shumate might be trying to remedy as much of the relationship between him and Camp Ryder as possible, in hopes of still getting his hands on some diesel fuel.

Everyone had their motives.

Julia turned to him before she walked out. "Thank you."

Lee didn't respond, and she left the room.

Shumate was the last one. Before he closed the door, he stopped and looked at Lee. "I'm sorry about all this."

Lee thought about choice words, but in the end only stared at Shumate, his eyes full of hatred. When Lee once again had nothing to say, the deputy sheriff looked down with that familiar look of shame and uncertainty and closed the door, plunging Lee back into the dim red darkness.

SEVENTEEN

BREAKING POINTS

HARPER AND MILLER FOLLOWED LaRouche as he marched back down the hall toward where they had first come into the hospital. Both men walked along with their hands clasped together as though they were still bound, their gaits no longer confident but subdued. To their right, the woman that was apparently Marie's sister rushed past them and fell in step with the sergeant.

"How far are you taking them?" she asked.

LaRouche looked at her, as if he already knew where this was going. "You've got too many people here relying on you."

"I don't want to be here anymore." She lowered her voice. "Shumate is going to get us all killed. I know he thinks he's saving us, but you know as well as I do what happens with people like Milo. They keep taking and taking until there's nothing left to give, but by then we won't have anything left to fight him with."

LaRouche stopped and spun on her. "You want to fight Milo? I'm with you on that. But running off to another camp is not the way to do it. The people here need you, Julia. And if you truly are serious about fighting and not just trying to get away from Shumate, then you'll stay here. I think your sister has some pull in the other camp, but she'll have no basis to send help if you're there with her."

Julia considered this. "Leave me one of the radios from the captain's backpack, then."

LaRouche regarded Harper as though he maybe should ask them permission. But he didn't. He just nodded. "Fine."

They walked to the nurses' station where Javier and the man with the Cajun accent stood. They'd emptied the contents of Lee's backpack onto the counter and were poking through everything, handling the explosives with caution, well aware of what they were.

LaRouche spoke with a bite of anger. "Pack that shit back up."

Javier pointed to the array of gear. "He's got fuckin' grenades, man! We could really use those!"

LaRouche took a warning tone. "Pack it up, Javier."

Javier shrugged and began placing the items gingerly into the backpack. "Alright, alright. I'm just saying...we could have used them."

The Cajun spoke up. "What's goin' on?"

"I'm taking these gentlemen back to their camp."

"And what about the other guy?"

LaRouche shook his head. "Milo wants him. And Shumate plans to give him up."

The Cajun snorted and spat. "Fucking weasel."

Harper watched the exchange in silence. It appeared to him that Shumate was losing control here at Smithfield. As well intended as his actions were, people did not want to labor under the threat of violence from Milo. Harper knew if he were in their position, he would feel that it would be better to fight Milo and get it over with than to wait until all their strength had been bled dry.

Yes, Shumate was losing control of this group.

But LaRouche was gaining every inch of it that slipped out of the deputy's fingers. LaRouche might not view the other survivors as equal—likely he had been part of the detachment that was meant to protect them until evacuations could be made—and he probably viewed them as pitiful civilians. But those civilians looked to him for answers, the same way Harper found himself looking to Captain Harden.

It was strange for Harper, thinking so callously of his own family. But Milo was family by blood only. Their relationship had been strained ever since childhood and it had not improved with age, as Harper once believed it would. Instead, with the end of everything, Harper found himself thinking of the man named Milo less as his brother, and more as a man who was responsible for many of the bad things that surrounded Harper's life.

When the pack was full again, with the exception of one long-range radio, LaRouche handed it to Harper. He noticed that someone—probably Javier—had rethreaded the straps that they'd cut. He swung into it, shocked at the weight of it. Captain Harden had made the pack look like it weighed no more than twenty pounds or so, but it was at least twice that.

Harper felt not only the physical weight but the figurative weight of the burden of Camp Ryder's survival being passed over to him. Only Harper was not a soldier. He did not know what to do in these situations. And now he would be returning empty-handed once again, without the rifles and ammunition and food and medical supplies that would have brought Camp Ryder back from the brink.

Harper thought he might break down right there.

But then Miller was next to him, patting him on the back. "Let's get the fuck out of here, Bill."

LaRouche led them forward. They exited through that same door that led to the stairwell, then up two flights of stairs to the last landing. LaRouche took the stairs quickly, and when he opened the door at the top, he moved through with urgency, his eyes scanning the horizon. Harper assumed he was looking for signs of Milo's arrival to gauge how much time they really had.

They moved swiftly to the car and piled in, Harper sitting up front this time, where he had to move Captain Harden's rifle out of the way. As he sat, he looked at the rifle and all of the switches, buttons, and levers. It reminded him somehow that he was not up to the task, that he could not fill the shoes of the man who had come before him.

But he would try, dammit.

LaRouche cranked the old Chevrolet and it started faithfully.

The tires on the car chirped slightly as he rushed the vehicle down the several levels of the parking garage to the bottom. As they sped out from underneath the shadow of the garage, they were all silent and focused, eyes trained as far out as they could see, dreading a glimpse of Milo's convoy rolling up to the hospital. None of them wanted to think about what Milo would do to them or the survivors inside the hospital if he caught LaRouche smuggling them out.

Up ahead, Harper saw the skeletal remnants of the decontamination domes and the checkpoint they had passed through on the way in. LaRouche slowed down just enough to navigate these safely, but then sped back up when he hit the main drag. He took side streets that Harper didn't recognize from their trip in. They made a right on a two-lane street, the tilted sign declaring it North Street. Harper watched ransacked houses on his left, a wide-open cemetery to his right. Among the tombstones were bodies, lying as though they had found a suitable place to rest and were now awaiting burial.

They made a left-hand turn on Third Street and it was more houses to either side, a mishmash of styles, old and new and recently renovated. The hazards were light on this road and Harper got the impression LaRouche knew which streets were clear for quick traveling and which were not. They approached the intersection of a main thoroughfare and it was at that moment that an old habit saved their lives.

Lost in a tumult of thoughts, LaRouche drove on autopilot. The same way Harper could remember he would drive home from work, thinking about different things both good and bad, and then suddenly he would be home with no recollection of the drive he had just made. Somehow, without thinking, he'd managed to avoid collisions, stay on the road, and stop for all the stops signs and traffic lights.

In the dead world of Smithfield, there was no need for traffic safety, as there were no other cars to worry about but the one you were driving. But in that state of instinctive driving, LaRouche's subconscious mind registered the intersections, the traffic signals (even though they were dark), and the broad white line where you were supposed to stop.

And LaRouche applied the brakes, slowing down for that stop.

With a faint note of curiosity, Harper asked, "Why you stopping?"

LaRouche realized what he was doing, even as he looked both ways down the intersection—first right, then left—and prepared to take his foot off the brake and continue on, when he saw the movement far to their left and several blocks down.

He straightened in his seat and squashed the brakes. "Shit!"

Harper and Miller were instantly alarmed, grabbing up their assault rifles.

Several intersections east of them, moving in the opposite direction, there was a green Humvee rumbling past, with the distant figure of a man on top, pointing the .50-caliber machine gun dead ahead. Following this were three pickup trucks.

"It's fucking Milo," LaRouche whispered, as though he could be heard.

As the last of the pickup trucks passed through the intersection, Harper's hand shot out, jabbing at the air with a pointed finger. "That's our truck! That's our truck! Milo's got our truck!"

Miller was beside himself. "We gotta get it back, boss!"

LaRouche looked at them both like they were crazy. "Are you kidding me?"

Harper didn't realize he was grimacing. The thought of trying to get their pickup truck back was horrendous—it spiked his blood pressure and reminded him of those days in the office when something bad came down the pipeline. But oh, this was so much worse. The juxtaposition almost choked a weird laugh out of him. A stressful day two months ago was when the boss was mad at you because you fucked something up. A stressful day today was when you had to get in a gun battle so you could feed your family.

My, how times change...

"We gotta get it back!" Miller repeated, as though Harper hadn't heard him the first time.

It would be so much easier to return to Camp Ryder—as a coward, but as a coward with no bullet holes in him. It would be easier, and it would be safer. Just to give up. Give in. Resign yourself to your fate. Gather your family around you and starve to death eating dirt and twigs and all the stupid shit people do when they are trying to ease that gnawing ache in their stomachs. Yes, even that seemed better than trying to get the truck back.

But it wasn't about him.

It was about Marie, who stretched a couple bags

of rice and beans because she had the stalwart belief that help was on the way. It was about Bus, who stood like a proud stone monument but inside was scared to death of failing so many people, because they were all looking to him, and he was looking to Harper. It was about Captain Harden, with eighteen stitches in his back and a missing tooth, sitting in a dark room with his hands taped behind his back, who did it all for no other reason than he believed in something bigger than himself. Captain Harden, who fought like a wild animal to save a few innocent lives, who even now prepared to face a madman alone, having released his companions with the simple promise that he could take care of himself. And if it were possible to die of shame, Harper was sure it was the fate that awaited him should he go back to Camp Ryder empty-handed.

It was do-or-die time.

"Yeah," Harper said. "We gotta get it back."

Everything has a catalyst. Lee knew this from personal experience. Anyone who said he was the same unchanged person he had been a year prior was either naive or lying. That held true for people before everything fell apart, as well as for the entirety of human existence. People changed. Every minute, every experience, it eroded you like eons of wind and water made canyons through solid rock. Sometimes those experiences were small, almost imperceptible, changing you in ways you couldn't quite put your finger on. Other times those experiences were nuclear blasts that reshaped you in an instant. Whatever the catalyst for change, no one was the same person he had been.

The catalyst for Lee was the day he found out that his morality, his code of ethics, and all the strong ideals that he'd held as a young man could be turned on and off like a lightbulb. Like every human being who had ever lived, there was a savage little animal stuffed deep down inside of him, kept under lock and key by society's views of "good" and "right." And it only took the right catalyst to bring it out.

When he had been twelve years old, he'd body-checked Rudy Stovall during a pickup game of flag football after school. Rudy Stovall had gone sprawling. This was unacceptable because he was a year older and had a girlfriend who, unfortunately, happened to be watching at the time. His ass and pride hurt, Rudy immediately jumped up and the two of them got into a little scuffle, at which point, a teacher walking to his car broke it up.

Lee had thought that was the end of that, but Rudy's pride needed further vindication. So the next day when Lee walked into the locker room to change for PE, Rudy slammed him from behind and began pummeling him in the face. Lee remembered first the shock, as he bounced off his own locker, and then the burning indignation when he suddenly realized what Rudy Stovall had just done.

He'd attacked him from behind! Didn't even give him a fair warning!

As the bigger kid's fists were smashing into his face, Lee remembered thinking quite clearly, *This isn't fair! He's not fighting fair!* Because a fair fight when you were twelve years old was when you arranged the time and the place and you duked it out—no biting, kicking, or scratching—in front of the flagpole, surrounded by a ring of your chanting peers.

And that was when the switch was thrown, and Lee realized that fairness and truthfulness and honor and morality were all excellent ideals to espouse and to practice in times of peace. But when the shit hits the fan, there's no such thing as a fair fight. There're only winners and losers, and the only way to win is to be quicker, more aggressive, more *psychotic* than your enemy. To act with brutal decisiveness and end it as soon as possible.

So that twelve-year-old Lee sank his butt down to the ground and then uppercut Rudy Stovall right in his groin. As Rudy toppled into the locker with a groan, Lee scuttled out from underneath him and slammed the locker door in Rudy's face three times, breaking his nose, popping out both of his front teeth, and splitting his upper lip all the way to his nostrils.

Rudy and Lee were both expelled and sent to separate schools.

It was the first and only fight of his childhood, but it had taught him a valuable lesson about human nature—how people were just another species of animal, and, like any animal, from the biggest predators to the smallest scavengers, most human beings could only be pushed so far before they lashed out.

Lee ruminated on this in the stale darkness

of the hospital room. He sat against the far wall, staring at the door directly across from him and feeling strangely calm. Save for his thoughts and memories, his senses were tuned outward, listening, feeling the vibrations as people bustled past the door, hearing their hushed conversations.

"He's here!"

"Shit! Get the fuck in your room!"

"I don't wanna be anywhere near that psycho."

He listened and he waited. He waited like a trap-door spider, tucked underneath its little rock, huddled in its dark space, nothing but patience and instinct. Waiting for the right moment. For an opportunity. For a mistake.

The movement outside reached a crescendo and tapered off.

There was a long and empty silence in the hospital. The sound of a dark house, everyone inside asleep. Only they weren't sleeping; they were waiting. With the hospital quiet, Lee twisted himself onto his feet and began looking around once again. The length of time he'd spent in the dark room with only the red emergency lights had given his eyes time to adjust, and now with the relative certainty that no one would be barging in for the next minute or so, as they were all laying out the red carpet for Milo and his crew, Lee felt it was a good time to search the room for anything he could use.

The room had been completely emptied—even the curtain that partitioned the room had been torn down. The phone had been ripped off the wall, and for the life of him, Lee couldn't figure out why. Even if they did use the room as a holding cell—which he was beginning to think they did—there were no working phone lines. Perhaps they were concerned that someone would use the cord.

But Lee wasn't looking for a cord. He was looking for something sharp. Anything with a point or a jagged edge. They had used several layers of duct tape to bind his wrists behind his back, and while strong and unyielding to his efforts to stretch it and break it, duct tape was relatively easy to shear. If he could poke a hole in it or cut through even just a bit of it, he might have enough to rip it off his wrists.

Because that was step one: Get your hands free.

He had already tried pulling his hands underneath his feet so he could at least have them in the front, but he was not as flexible as he would have liked. So he was back to square one.

Find a sharp object.

Four times he circled the room, staring up and down the walls, thinking to himself that there must be something, *something* he could use to cut through the tape. A piece of plastic he could break into a jagged edge or a corner of some piece of metal...

Somewhere farther in the building, a door slammed shut.

Voices.

Lee growled to himself, "Only fucking hospital room in the world with nothing sharp in it."

The voices drew closer until Lee could make out several distinct speakers involved in a heated discussion, though he couldn't quite make out the words. They stalled and Lee imagined they were somewhere around the nurses' station. Frustrated, he quickly crossed the room and sat on the same wall as he had before, the plaster still warm from his body heat. He continued to wait.

Whatever the voices were talking about, someone had the final word and the conversation ended. The shuffling sound of several pairs of feet replaced the talking and trundled down the hallway, where they stopped in front of the hospital room door that Lee stared at. Someone whimpered pitifully. The lock clacked and the door handle quivered. Lee squinted, preparing himself for the daylight to come lancing through.

The door opened and he could see that the hall was full of figures that milled about in front of the doorway. He tried to count heads, but the backlighting and Lee's own slitted eyes obscured what he was looking at. He licked his lips and for the first time realized his mouth was dry.

The whimpering continued. Now the voice was familiar. "Why won't you let me see Nicole? What did you do to her?"

The shapes in the doorway shifted and Lee opened his eyes a bit more, bringing things into focus. He saw the scrawny back, the long and scraggly hair, wet with sweat and body oils and rain. Doc had his back turned to Lee and was speaking to someone, but clearly not receiving the answer he wanted.

And then Doc was being pushed out of the way, and a tall, thin man stepped forward. Lee still could not make out the man's face, but Lee could tell the man was looking directly at him. Then the man spread his arms out and laughed. "Jesus, Mary, and Joseph! Ha ha! Could it be? Do my fucking eyes deceive me?"

The man's voice was strangely melodic, but there was something in there that didn't sit right with Lee, like the one violin in the orchestra not tuned properly, a discordant note floating out among the rest and lending the whole thing a sour tone.

Lee felt his heartbeat increase.

He's crazy...

The thin man sauntered forward, his hands still outstretched as though he were about to embrace Lee as an old friend, and all the while that giddy chuckle kept coming out of him, like the kid who knew the secret no one else knew. He reached the back wall where Lee remained motionless and knelt down.

Now the red emergency lights played over this stranger's face, revealing a fresh gash across his cheek that had been stitched closed with black thread and eyes that seemed to glow in the dark with some great and sordid mirth. He spoke again, this time quieter, more reserved, as though he were trying to control his satisfaction. Like he didn't want to be rude.

"You must be the 'Captain.' That is what everyone seems to call you."

Lee nodded. "You must be Milo. No one really likes you."

Milo shrugged and placed a hand on Lee's shoulder. "People are..." He considered his words.

"Small-minded. I'll be the first to admit I won't ever win a popularity contest. But I do what needs to be done, and I don't ever let my humanity stand in the way of my survival." He smiled and his teeth seemed to glow crimson. "I'm sure that's something you can understand."

If he was waiting for Lee's answer, there was none forthcoming.

He leaned in a bit closer to Lee, his voice conspiratorial. "I understand at this point in time, you may not like me, Captain. But I assure you, I don't come to cause harm to anyone. Unfortunately, sometimes they force my hand and I'm sure that has resulted in some...hmm, inflated stories concerning my methods. However, I hope that you, as a reasonable man, can see that we both have something to gain from being in a mutually beneficial relationship."

Lee turned his back slightly. "Can you get this tape off my wrists?"

Milo laughed. "No. No, we won't be getting too comfortable with each other just yet. I'd like to make this situation work, but you have a track record of causing me problems. I'd just as soon keep you restrained."

"That's probably smart," Lee admitted.

"Before I waste any more of my time attempting to build a rapport with you..." Milo rubbed his palms together. "Do you have any intention of cooperating with me?"

"Cooperating how?"

A brief swipe of sweat from his face and Lee could see the thinly veiled impatience there. "Yes, well, it's my understanding that you have a device. A device that allows you to locate and access bunkers that contain items. Items that I need."

"Oh." Lee frowned. "No, those aren't for you."

Milo's face became deadpan. "But they are. Because I own you, Captain. Whether you like it or not." He cleared his throat. "I would truly—*truly*—like to be civil with you. I bring you the device, you show me what there is to see, I go collect the items that I need, and I leave you alone. It's just that simple."

Lee shook his head slowly. "That's a lie."

The two men stared at each other in silence.

"You're a broken man, Captain." Milo spoke almost with pity. "You're fighting a fight you can never win for a country that no longer exists, in a manner that has become outdated. You cling to your goodness and righteousness and all the comfortable teachings you grew up with, but have you bothered to look around lately? Have you noticed how different things are? These are violent times, Captain. These are cruel times, and no one hates it more than me." He looked away from Lee. "I would like to be idle, as I have been for the last years of my life, and let myself slip quietly back into a life of addiction and dependence. Because it's easy. But there's no room for it now. There's no one else to depend on, so I have to outgrow that part of myself. We have a job to do; you must see that. The infected threat must be eradicated before we can rebuild. Or do you plan to skip that step altogether?"

"No." Lee worked enough saliva into his mouth

to moisten it. "You're right. It is necessary. But you're just a criminal, Milo. Just a thug. No one wants you, and they certainly don't need you. And I won't help you."

"Fine." Milo stood, his voice cold now. "I hate that you forced me into this situation. I wish we could have worked something out."

Lee matched his tone. "We can't work anything out."

"Noted." Milo spun on his heels and strode for the door.

Lurching from a dark shadow, Doc tried to grab his arm. "Where's Nicole? Where is she?"

Milo jerked away from him and backhanded him in the face. Lee noticed for the first time the bloody bandaging wrapped around Doc's left hand and wondered what was missing underneath all of that. A giant man stepped in and threw Doc to the floor, and then there was the distinct sound of duct tape being pulled from the roll, and Doc's hands were secured with tape behind his back as he lay facedown just a few feet in front of Lee.

Doc didn't resist, and he didn't look at Lee. His face was covered with stringy hair, so that Lee couldn't see his eyes. He just kept mumbling to himself, droning on and asking incessantly for whoever this Nicole lady was. All the while, Milo stood and watched with a vacant stare. When the men were finished restraining Doc, Milo nudged his arm with the toe of one of his boots.

"Doc." Milo sounded far away. "I take no pride in this, but I've been using you for the last few weeks. Nicole guaranteed your cooperation, and you were such an enormous help to us that I simply didn't want to lose you. But I suppose all good things must come to an end." Milo bent over Doc's prostrate form. "Come on, now. Surely you suspected. Pretty girl like that, in with a bunch of lowlifes like Big G here. What did you think was going to happen?"

It seemed as though the life had left Doc.

He remained as still as a corpse on the floor.

Milo patted Doc on the back. "Yes, I'm sure you knew already. You just didn't want to admit it. I think it was Big G who had her last, and I'm sure he would tell you that she was . . . well, she was probably too fucked-up on pills to remember much of anything. Or feel much of anything. So I hope you can take some comfort in that."

Then Milo turned and cast a smile and wink at Lee, as though they were old college pals, and the desecration of Nicole was just another good time to reminisce about. Huddled in the doorway, some faces Lee didn't recognize stared on in vague amusement, while others, like Shumate and Javier, stared uncomfortably at the ground. Doc simply breathed slow and steady breaths and didn't say anything. The air coming in and out of him made him sound hollow.

"Ah, well." Milo shook his head in disappointment and walked through the door, leaving Lee and Doc alone.

EIGHTEEN

FIRE

IN THE STILLNESS OF the room, there was only the sound of Doc's breathing.

Against the wall, Lee cringed, waiting for that moment to come crashing down on Doc and squeeze the screams out of him. Lee didn't know who this Nicole was—Doc had never mentioned her before—but it was obvious she was important to him. After long minutes, Lee realized that the emotion wasn't going to come. Doc didn't start crying or yelling or sobbing or anything else besides continuing to take those long, deep breaths. Gradually, even those subsided until he just lay there, face pressed against the floor.

Just existing.

"Doc," Lee murmured.

He gained no response. Not even a movement.

"Doc," Lee tried again. "Who's Nicole?"

Doc budged finally, rolling onto his left side so that he now faced Lee, his head lolling. His eyes were lost in the darkness, just sunken orbs. A clump of his hair stuck to his lips and stirred as the air moved between them.

"You've gotta tell me..." Lee began, and almost missed the whisper.

Had it not been for the slight movement of his lips, Lee wasn't sure he would have registered anything at all. But what he did register didn't make sense.

"What?" Lee leaned forward. "What did you say?"

Doc's eyelids fluttered closed as he gathered the strength to form a few words. When his eyes opened again, there was a glistening there in the dark hollows. "It was me. I did it. It was all me."

"I...uh..." Lee shook his head like he was trying to clear it. "I don't understand."

"Because I thought they had her, Captain." Doc's voice became louder, more insistent. "I did. I thought they had her, and I thought that if I didn't do what he wanted me to do that they would kill her. He promised he wouldn't kill her. He promised."

"What did you do?" Lee asked warily.

Doc waggled his head and rolled onto his back so he was staring at the ceiling. "He told me to do it, Captain. I didn't have a choice. I didn't mean for it to turn out like that, but it did. It did, and I couldn't stop it. I couldn't stop anything." He suddenly spoke so forcefully that spittle flew up from his lips. "I couldn't save Kara! And I couldn't fucking save Nicole!"

"Jesus," Lee said with dawning comprehension.

"I cut the fuckin' fence, man." Doc's face twisted up. "I cut the fence, and I put the CD player there. I thought—I really fucking *thought*—that I was gonna get you. I was gonna take you and your little device at gunpoint and I was going to escape fucking Camp Ryder and bring you back to Milo. And I was gonna save Nicole. That's what I was gonna do. Save Nicole."

He cut the fence. He cut the fence because he knew that everyone would gather in the square and no one would see him kidnap me. But what he planned on doing once he got Lee outside the fence was a mystery. Perhaps some of Milo's men were waiting nearby for Doc to deliver Lee into their hands.

"Doc…"

"But you weren't there. Nothing happened the way it was supposed to. You got up like you were fine, and you started fighting the infected like you hadn't just been knocked out for hours, and you ruined the whole fucking thing. Fucking ruined it."

Lee's voice cut through the mad rambling. "Doc, where's Josh? What happened to Josh?"

Doc was eerily silent for a long time. Then: "I shot him. I shot him in the gut and I left him on the road. Like an animal. Like roadkill. I wish I hadn't. I wish I knew that Nicole was dead. I wouldn't have shot him. I wouldn't have cut the fence. I wouldn't have even"—his voice exploded—"*COME ON THIS FUCKING TRIP!*"

"Oh, my God." Lee felt a tightness in his gut. "You…"

There was a moment there when Lee pictured it all. He pictured Doc putting a bullet in Josh and watching the kid squirm around and die. He saw the blood, smelled the opened bowels, heard the pathetic screams, all like he had been standing there when it happened. And through it all, in his mind's eye, he could see Doc, watching but doing nothing. Doc, the weakling. Doc, the coward. Doc, the complainer. The one who convinced everyone to let him come on the trip and the whole time was scamming them. The one who killed Josh and gave all those hard-earned supplies to their enemies. The liar. The traitor.

Doc.

But Lee found any further words were caught in his throat. There was such a tidal wave of thoughts that he just sat there with his mouth open, trying to find the language to express himself but couldn't, as though he'd suddenly been struck mute. Through the hazy shock of disbelief—or simply not wanting to believe—it began to make sense to him. Little details began popping back up in his mind, like wreckage from a sunken ship that floated to the surface. Doc's insistence that the people of Camp Ryder would eventually blame him for Kara's death. How eager he was to come with them on the trip but how unwilling he seemed once he was there. How he volunteered to accompany Lee into Smithfield. Lee had to wonder if there'd ever been a genuine moment between the two of them, or whether every decision he'd made had been for the purpose of getting Lee to walk into a trap.

Two competing notions fought for control.

The first was pure hatred. The sting of betrayal, the humiliation at realizing how utterly duped he had been, and the nearly all-consuming desire to lash out because of that. The childlike instinct to repay mental pain with physical pain that turned into the very adult will to stomp Doc's head into a pulpy mess.

The second was a kind of morbid curiosity. The

never-ending desire to know *why* something happened. To seek some fact that might explain it all away. Something that might absolve Lee of any responsibility. Something that Lee could point to and say, "See? Anyone would have been tricked by that. It's not just me. It's not my fault."

Instead, what eked out was simply, "How?"

Doc didn't ask for any clarification. He just started talking again. "We went to my parents' house when all of this happened. We were both students at Duke. But my parents were gone by the time we got there; I think they'd already been evacuated. I think everyone had already been evacuated. So we just stayed there, not quite sure what to do, thinking the government would come back for us. Thinking that someone would come to save us.

"But the only people who came were Milo's people. They knew we were in there, even though we hid and stayed as quiet as we could. I think they'd been watching us. Or maybe just Nicole." His voice fought back a break. "When they came in after us, I didn't fight. I should have done something. Anything. But I just stood there with my hands up. I was sure they just wanted food or water, or maybe they were just going to take my parents' things. I kept telling them to take what they wanted and leave us, but they weren't interested in any of the stuff.

"I remember Milo walking in and I was so terrified. The look in his eyes...he was smiling, but not in his eyes. They scared me, what I saw in them. And then he was looking at Nicole. He... he would run his fingers through her hair. I don't remember how it happened, but Milo found out we were medical students and I could see he was thinking about something. Then he had his men take Nicole out to that big green Hummer and from inside the house I could hear her screaming.

"And Milo described Camp Ryder to me. He told me where it was. He told me they would take me in because they needed a doctor, but that I would be working for him, in exchange for keeping Nicole alive. So they drove me to Camp Ryder and dropped me off a mile from the gate. I was so scared of walking alone, but all I could think about was Nicole. When I came to the gate, Bus was there. He took me in. Fed me and gave me water. I told them about my medical training, and they were so excited. They were so happy to have someone to help them. But I wasn't there to help them. I was helping myself. Trying to help Nicole."

Lee took a deep breath and forced his voice flat. "How long ago did you get to Camp Ryder?"

"I don't know. Two weeks ago? Maybe a little more. I lose track of time..."

"But Milo must have continued to talk to you."

"Yeah." Doc sounded far away. "There's a tree that grows against the fence. He would leave instructions on pieces of paper and hide them under a rock at night. Or at least *someone* would. That's how he maintained contact with me. That's how he told me to watch out for you."

"So this whole time..."

"I've been trying to trap you." Doc nodded. "I didn't want to, I really didn't. But they didn't give me a choice. They set up a roadblock to catch us on the way back from the bunker. I was supposed to have you there by twelve o'clock today or they were going to kill Nicole. That's what they said, anyway."

"How did he know about me?" Lee demanded.

Doc made a small shrugging motion. "I don't know. He never said. Just said to keep my eyes out for a soldier accompanied by a female and two kids. He said he wanted to speak with you. That you had access to supplies. But he never said how he found all of that out."

"Had to be my bunker," Lee mumbled to himself.

Doc looked at him. "I know you probably want to kill me."

Lee stared back at him, considering that for a long moment. Did he really want Doc to die? It was a difficult question to answer. Lee knew that he would not feel bad for Doc if they blew his head off right then and there. He knew watching Doc die would only leave him with a sense of fulfilled justice. He had murdered Josh in cold blood, whatever the reasons might be, and he was also responsible for Kara's death. A death that he allowed Lee to take the blame for. And even though Doc had killed two people, he hadn't been able to find it in himself to fight when they needed him during their engagement at the roadblock the previous day. Instead he froze up and stood there. Worthless.

No, Lee had no great love for Doc. Ten minutes ago, he had still been an ally, albeit an annoying one. Now he was just some sad, broken creature, and for all his righteous anger of only moments ago, Lee felt that pent-up fiery feeling in his chest beginning to deflate. He wanted to be angry with Doc but found himself simply disgusted instead.

Lee shook his head. "No. I don't want to kill you. Because you're going to help me."

Doc made a drowsy sound. "I don't care anymore."

Lee worked his way up onto his feet. "It doesn't matter. You're going to help me get out of here if it's the last thing you do," he hissed, spittle flying from his teeth. "You fucking owe it to me, Doc, and you owe it to Josh and Kara and everyone else at Camp Ryder that you've fucked over with your bullshit."

Lee crossed to him and pushed Doc into a sitting position with his foot. "Sit up," he commanded. "Quit rolling around and feeling sorry for yourself. Nobody did this shit to you; you made this situation yourself. Now you have to deal with it. At least be useful for something."

Doc sat lazily, apparently unconcerned with whatever Lee had planned. And that was fine. If Doc did this one thing and then keeled over and died, Lee wouldn't shed a tear. But he needed him right here, right now. With Doc sitting up, Lee turned his back on him and pushed his bound wrists toward Doc. "Now start chewing through that tape."

With nothing further to say, Doc began chewing.

Trevor Schlitz was mentally unstable.

Or "bat-shit crazy," if you were his father.

Whatever the terminology for it was, Trevor didn't view it as a weakness or a problem to be overcome. He hurt people, so they had to slap him with a label, qualify and quantify him, and attempt to "cure" him in their various ways, both through the court system and through mental evaluations that ended with him attending hours of counseling and having all kinds of weird medications shoved down his throat. Uppers, downers, all arounders. He had to admit, the drug cocktail was the most fun part of being "cured," because it got pretty trippy sometimes. Sadly, his medications were no more, because pharmacies and pharmaceutical companies were no more.

What a shame.

But at the end of the day, there wasn't a cure for what Trevor had. Simply put, he loved knives. All the talking and the blah-blah-blah psychiatrists tried to make it sound like more than it was, tried to make it sound like he had "anger issues" and told him he was "paranoid schizophrenic" and displayed "sociopathic tendencies." But he just loved knives. It wasn't that he was angry at the people he hurt, but he just enjoyed the feeling of skin parting under a blade. Clearly, it wasn't that he disliked his victims, because he'd cut his own skin just as much as he'd cut them. He rarely wore a shirt, because he liked to display the strange crosshatch pattern of scars that marred his chest. He liked to show it off. Like a masterpiece.

But it was okay now because the world was ending and nothing really mattered anymore. Court dates and probation violations and involuntary commitment paperwork—all things of the past. Frankly, Trevor loved this new world and all of its freedoms. With all the dead bodies he could cut to his heart's content and no one would ever say shit to him. Even the living were fair game, though sometimes they moved around too much and spoiled the moment. Why, just the other day he'd shot an old man in the chest and then spent hours working his body over. Then, for no other reason than that the whim popped into his head, he poured gasoline on the body and made it into a stinking bonfire, and he danced around in the glow, laughing and hollering like a wild man. Just because he could.

He loved knives, and he loved this new world.

Gone were all the people of old who judged him with their shifting stares and chose never to even attempt to understand the machinations of his mind. All of that was wiped out and replaced with this amazing new playground where no one could ever get in trouble for anything and he was sur- rounded by people who—though they might not be considered "bat-shit crazy"—still accepted him for the person that he was.

They even started calling him Slitz, which he found delightful.

For the first time in his life, Trevor Schlitz was happy.

The smooth-faced black man they called Roc (it was the only name he answered to) passed him what was left of their last cigarette they'd cobbled together from the leftover tobacco they'd found at the bottom of cigarette boxes and butts. It had been a collaborative effort on their part and had resulted in three horrid-tasting cigarettes. They agreed to both take one and split the third.

Trevor nodded his thanks, and Roc hocked and spit on the ground.

The two of them never said much, but that was

why they preferred each other's company. And to be honest, Trevor thought that Milo and Big G were a bit creeped out by them. Maybe that was why they had been told to stay outside and watch the trucks while everyone else got to go inside and look at the trim.

Trevor shrugged, keeping his own counsel.

That was fine with him. He had no qualms with standing atop the upper level of the parking garage adjacent to the hospital and enjoying the view. Most other people would find the view cold and disturbing, as it was mostly battered barricades, concertina wire, and dead bodies. But to Trevor it was just another reminder that he was free to be himself, liberated from the constraints of a suffocating society that refused to give him room to breathe.

No, he had no problem with it at all.

"Hey." Roc nudged his arm and motioned to the western side of the parking garage, where it overlooked the old decontamination domes. They were all aware that this was the only way past the barricades erected around the hospital, and watching it was part of their job when they were hanging around Smithfield.

Navigating the domes and cement barriers was a red sedan that struck Trevor as being kind of familiar. He had never been good with cars and couldn't name the make or model, but he was pretty certain he'd seen it around there before. It navigated the barricades deftly, as though it had done it a thousand times.

"I think that's one of their guys," Trevor murmured, speaking of the Smithfield survivors.

Roc grabbed his shotgun. "You never know."

Regretfully, he set the little remainder of his cigarette in a crack in the cement and hoped it wouldn't be burned out by the time he got done dealing with these folks. He still had a few good lungfuls of acrid, nicotine-laced smoke that he could coax from it.

The sedan drew closer and they could see that there were three people in the car. Then it was quickly out of sight underneath them and they could hear the faint squeal of the tires as it took the corners just a little too quickly and rose up the levels. The growling of the engine grew louder and louder until it finally crested that top level.

Trevor and Roc stepped out, brandishing their weapons at the car, and it slowed down to a stop on the other side of the parking deck from them. Through the reflective surface of the glass, they could barely make out the three faces staring at them.

A little thrill worked its way up Trevor's spine.

Maybe he would get to shoot them, and then maybe he could cut them up.

"Who the fuck are you?" Roc yelled at them.

No response but the engine idling.

Trevor and Roc exchanged a suspicious glance.

This was exciting!

When it was clear that the occupants of the vehicle were not going to continue forward, Trevor and Roc began to approach. Though they were approaching from the front, neither of them was dumb enough to walk directly in the path of the vehicle. They both walked in line with the sides of the vehicle—Roc on the driver's side and Trevor on the passenger's side—so they could dive out of the way if the crazy bastard inside decided to run them over.

When they were within about twenty-five yards of the vehicle, Trevor noticed what he thought was a weird green license plate strapped to the grille of the car. As he got a little closer he realized that it must be some type of style plate, because it was too thick to be a regular state-issued license plate, and it had a slightly convex shape. He could see some sort of writing embossed on the front, but it was the same olive green color and difficult to read.

Trevor loved to read vanity plates and style plates. He laughed, even at the airbrushed ones that said I LOVE JESUS or R.I.P. SHAWN because it was hilarious to him what people thought was important enough to display on their car for total strangers to read.

Distracted and curious, with a small smile on his lips, Trevor couldn't help but lean forward and get a little closer. He just had to read what this idiot put on his car.

"Don't rush up," Roc said from several yards behind him.

Trevor hadn't realized he'd gone that far in front.

He wasn't worried. He was pretty sure these guys were with the Smithfield group.

He was about fifteen yards away from it when he finally made out the lettering. As he did, he barely noticed out of the corner of his eyes that all three individuals in the car had ducked down behind the engine block. Trevor Schlitz's brows narrowed in confusion as he read the words aloud: "Front toward enemy?"

And just before dozens of one-eighth-inch steel balls ripped through his body, he thought, *I don't get it*...

LaRouche and Harper stared at each other, cringing as the whole vehicle rocked with the detonation of the M18 claymore mine they'd strapped to the grille. Admittedly, LaRouche wasn't sure it would work or if they would even be safe behind the engine block, as he had never been so close to a claymore mine upon detonation. They all hoped that the hood of the Chevrolet Lumina would soak up any shock wave or bouncing shrapnel.

When the vehicle stopped rocking back and forth, LaRouche straightened in his seat, still holding the "clacker" in his hand, attached to the conspicuous wire that trailed out of the driver's side window and into the engine compartment. He had imagined that the windows of the Lumina would have shattered, simply based on the proximity to the blast, but whoever had invented the claymore mine knew what he was doing, and the convex design of the explosive had projected all that energy outward at their attackers.

Front toward enemy...

Harper sounded half excited and half disgusted when he spoke. "Holy shitfire..."

Looking through the unmarred windshield, LaRouche didn't even recognize the bodies on the ground. He knew there had only been two men approaching the vehicle, but there were three mounds of bloody flesh on the ground. One of the men had been torn in half.

The back passenger door opened up and Miller got out, clutching his rifle. "Come on, guys, we gotta move."

The other two men quickly exited the vehicle. LaRouche snatched up Lee's rifle as he left, but Harper didn't mention anything. This was a fight now—no time to squabble about what weapon belonged to whom. The blast from that claymore mine had been pretty attention-getting, and they would have company rushing through that door any minute now.

As they sprinted toward the four vehicles that made up Milo's convoy—the big green Humvee, the two pickup trucks, and now the truck full of Camp Ryder's supplies—the air was choked with gasoline fumes. Not of exhaust or the old lawn-mower smell of spilled and dried gasoline, but the fresh, sweet stench of it. As LaRouche ran, he searched for the source of the smell, and it didn't take him long to find it.

The closest enemy truck to them was full of gas cans, and the blast from the claymore mine had peppered the bed and the cans inside with those little steel balls, punching holes through the thin plastic gas cans and letting that precious fluid spill out onto the ground, like another wounded casualty spilling his blood.

Harper swore when he saw it. "Woulda been nice to have some of that gas."

"Fuckin' leave it," Miller huffed. "Let's get our truck and get out!"

The two men from Camp Ryder split for the Dodge Ram 2500, still stocked and strapped with white food pails and boxes of dehydrated fruits and vegetables. The sight of the truck within their grasp was hopeful and tantalizing, but they couldn't ignore the black dread inside of them that this would never work, that they would never manage to get this thing out of there alive. They weren't soldiers; they weren't heroes. They were just an old businessperson and a young kid.

At the Humvee, LaRouche yanked open the door and jumped in, thanking God that the keys were dangling from the ignition. Apparently Milo had assumed their posted guard would be enough to defend the vehicles. His hubris irritated LaRouche and exhilarated him at the same time. It always tasted sweet to pull one over on the person you hated most in the world.

LaRouche cranked the truck up and slammed it in gear. He nudged the gas pedal with his foot and the diesel monster leaped forward, smashing its ram bar into the side of the concrete wall of the stairwell, jamming the door to the hospital closed. Then LaRouche put it in park and hopped out.

No one would be coming through that door.

Harper had already positioned their pickup, facing away from the hospital and ready to roll. The big V8 engine rumbled mightily and Miller looked at him through the open passenger-side window and waved his hand.

"Let's go!"

LaRouche slung into Captain Harden's M4 and shook his head. "I can't leave these people, man."

"Are you fucking kidding me?" Miller nearly screamed.

LaRouche waved at him. "I have one of your radios. If you don't hear from me by tonight, things haven't gone well. Now get the fuck out of here!"

Harper tossed him a salute and slammed on the gas, not waiting for further argument, but Miller stared at him through the window even as the truck pulled off. LaRouche watched it for a brief moment as it dipped down into the parking garage and began making its swift descent to the ground level, and from there, away from Smithfield and back to Camp Ryder where it belonged.

LaRouche began jogging toward the ramp to the lower level. He popped the magazine out of the M4 and checked the chamber. The mag was full, plus one in the chamber.

It was time to find Captain Harden.

Behind LaRouche, the punctured gas cans continued to slop the pickup bed with gasoline. That gasoline pooled and began to dribble at first, and then to flow through the tailgate and down the bumpers, splashing on the ground in little pools. Those little pools quickly turned into big pools with tiny streams that meandered away from the back of the pickup truck, following the slight downslope of the concrete. Like a half dozen dark snakes slithering away from the tailgate of the truck.

The first two narrowly passed by what remained of Trevor Schlitz's cigarette, but the third found its mark, connecting with the bright red cherry at the tip of the cigarette. An almost-invisible blue flame erupted and spread, quickly consuming the entire writhing pool of snakes.

The first thing LaRouche noticed wasn't heat or flame but the *whoosh* sound behind him that grew rapidly and suddenly into a roar, like a jet taking off. Then there was the sensation of running against the wind at the same moment that LaRouche attempted to draw a deep breath and found the air in front of him devoid of oxygen.

Then came the searing heat, like a harsh slap on the back, and he immediately felt hot and sunburned, like his skin was shrinking on his skull. The air was on fire, burning his face, burning his mouth, hot and dry on his tongue and stinging in his lungs like he'd just inhaled pepper. He spluttered and coughed, and then fell to his hands and knees, scrambling forward a few feet and looking behind him.

A tower of flame rose above a fully engulfed pickup truck, red and menacing, thick tongues of it licking angrily and leaving behind black smoke. LaRouche stared in wonder at the giant fireball that swelled in the sky above the truck, turning black and obscure as it rose.

On hands and knees, the sergeant began scrambling for the ramp that led to the lower levels of the parking garage. In the wake of the lashing heat, his face seemed cold and stiff. Eventually he got his feet under him and began running again. He felt a deep, black certainty coiling up in his stomach. The hospital and the adjoining parking garage were two of the tallest structures in town. From that top level of the parking garage, LaRouche could see almost all of Smithfield.

And all he could think was, *Now everyone in Smithfield can see us...*

NINETEEN

UNWANTED ATTENTION

LEE HEARD THE BOOM from inside.

He and Doc both sat extremely still, waiting for something that might explain the loud concussion that shook the floor under their feet. Out in the hall, beyond their locked door, there were a few cries of surprise. Then came urgent shouts and the sound of running feet.

"What the fuck was that?" Doc's voice was a whisper.

Lee tossed him a sharp look. "Some kind of explosion. Keep going—I'm almost out."

Doc set back to picking and gnawing at the duct-tape bindings. Lee could feel his teeth grabbing at the edges and tearing, layer by layer. Every time he heard that little popping noise as Doc's teeth made it through another layer, he would strain against his bindings, hoping that they were weak enough now to break, but they hadn't been yet. However, the tape was loose enough now that feeling was returning to his fingers, so that was at least something good.

Out in the hall, a door slammed.

The yelling and scrambling around seemed to quiet for a bit.

Another popping sound. Lee tested his bindings, felt some give.

"Keep going. Almost there." Lee began to sweat now, his jaw clenching and unclenching rapidly and his eyes fixated on the door. It was only a matter of time before someone came and checked on them. Because he knew that if he were in their shoes and heard an explosion, his first thought would be, *Prison break*.

A moment later, there was another odd noise from outside, like a sudden rush of water. It lacked the harsh, jarring slap of the explosion a few moments earlier, but it still rumbled the building like distant thunder.

"What...?"

"Keep going!" Lee snapped.

The sound of boots in the hallway. A flashlight flickered, strobing the space underneath the door with cool white light. Lee felt another rip in the tape and pulled, groaning with the strain as he fought to pull his hands free.

The door flew open and the light rushed in.

"What are you doing?" someone demanded, though Lee could not see his face past the blinding flashlight. All he knew was that the man was getting closer, stepping into the room to investigate. Now only a few short feet away from Lee. He saw the flicker of the flashlight on gunmetal, the faint outline of a pistol pointed at him.

Doc had stopped tearing at the tape, too afraid to continue, but Lee still strained hard. The man with the flashlight must have seen the effort in his features because he shook the flashlight at them.

"I said, what are you doing?" he demanded again.

Lee girded himself up. He could feel the give in the tape and it was to the point of no return. He flipped the switch in his mind, shut off that comfortable, moral code of humanity, so he was just a mean dog trapped in a cage. He stared at the dark shadow of the man's face and kept repeating in his mind, *I am going to kill this man. I am going to kill this man. I am going to kill this man…*

The tape snapped.

Like a greyhound shooting out of a stable, Lee dived forward, dodging to his left as he grabbed the pistol with both hands and shoved it to the right. The flashlight dropped, the beam causing the shadows in the room to shift. In the ghostly light diffusing off the walls, Lee could see the man's face, eyes wide with terror, lips spread apart, teeth gritting together.

Lee pulled the man close and put a knee in his gut, doubling him over. He felt the struggle for the pistol ease a bit as the man lost some of his strength, and Lee hammered his fist twice into the man's forearm, crunching the radial nerve and causing the man to cry out in pain and drop the weapon. Lee head-butted him sharply, felt the sting of the man's teeth slicing into his scalp, and heard the crack of the man's nose breaking.

The ferocity of Lee's attack had driven the man back so that Lee had him pinned against the wall. To their left, the door still hung wide open, and Lee knew he had to end it quickly before someone showed up to help the man out. Lee had the initiative now and he didn't want to lose it. He could feel the man struggling against him, trying to get off the wall, their hands and arms scrabbling back and forth, blocking each other from grabbing any holds.

Lee reared back and punched the man in the throat.

His wide eyes closed to a squint and he made a choking noise. His hands flew up to his collapsed larynx, and that was the last mistake he ever made. With both hands free, Lee drove his thumbs into the inner corners of the man's eyes, felt them pop and give way under the intense pressure, felt the anatomy wriggling against his fingertips. Lee was instantly repulsed and fought the urge to simply jump back and begin wiping off his hands. He had to stuff down that feeling and force himself to curl his thumbs inward, hook the insides of the man's head, and rip them out.

The man convulsed, twitched, then sank to the floor.

Shaking now, Lee flicked his wrists and felt something warm and wet leave the palms of his hands and splatter against the floor. He had no time to think about what he had done, to self-recriminate. Those were feelings that were saved for long, sleepless nights when faces swam up from the dark parts of your mind, like the depths giving up their dead.

Shoving it all aside, Lee bent down and snatched up the gun and the flashlight.

He put the beam of light on Doc's face, found him staring slack-jawed at the dead body lying against the wall. Lee hated him in that instant, hated him for the look of shock and disgust on his face. "I'm not sticking my ass out for you," Lee growled at him. "You want to escape, you keep up with me and don't say a fucking word."

Doc looked at him and slowly sat back on his heels. Lee shook his head. "Fine."

He turned his back on Doc, and the last image he ever had of the man who had betrayed him was a stringy clump of hair obscuring his face as he hung his head, looking too ashamed to even save himself.

Lee stuck the flashlight in his pocket and checked the pistol he'd picked up. It was some cheap and shitty make that Lee didn't recognize, with a gaudy chrome plating, chambered for 9mm. It contained a single-stack magazine with eight rounds out of fifteen left and one in the chamber. He took a quick moment to make sure the safety was off.

He moved to the right side of the open door and gained a good angle down the hallway. A few people were at the end of the hall, with their faces pressed against a window, pointing at some spectacle that Lee couldn't see. They didn't look like they were with Milo; they just looked like regular people. *Some of the Smithfield group of survivors*, he thought. He forced himself to stay in that position, take a breath, and think about the layout of the hospital and where he intended to go. Overall, he needed to get back to Camp Ryder, but he needed to break it down. Manageable portions. He needed to compartmentalize.

The first step: Get some time to think. He

needed to leave the hospital room, because somebody would eventually come looking for the man he had just killed, and Lee didn't want to be around when someone did. He needed to find some dark corner where he could take the time to slow down his mind and think clearly about the next step, which was getting out of the hospital completely.

Lee looked down at himself to make sure he wasn't covered in blood—it wasn't bad—and jammed the pistol in his waistband. He figured if he just walked out casually and closed the door behind him, no one would really take notice of him. He was banking on the Smithfield folks avoiding contact with him, thinking he was one of Milo's men.

He stepped out, pulling the door closed on his heels. He heard it latch and looked to his right, where the hallway led to the nurses' station. He could see a few men there, and all of them were armed, but they did not appear to be looking his way. Their attention was instead focused on the door to the stairwell, which one of them was holding open. From inside the stairwell, Lee could hear shouts and grunts and expletives. Whatever was going on at the top of the stairwell, it wasn't going well for them.

Lee turned away from them and started walking, fast but not too fast. If you moved too slowly, it was obvious you were trying to appear casual. If you moved too quickly, it looked like you were trying to escape. You had to just look like you had really important business to get to. Lee held that picture in his mind and tried to imitate it as best he could, but the fear of discovery kept banging at the back door of his mind, demanding attention.

He marched past the group at the window.

One of the men looked at him, but only briefly. Then he cast his eyes downward, as if he had made a mistake by looking at Lee, and put his arm around a young woman standing next to him, as though Lee was going to snatch her away.

As he passed, Lee risked a glance out the window at what everyone was staring at. The window gave a good view of the western-facing side of the parking garage. Over the concrete wall, he could see the tops of two pickup trucks, parked close to the building, one behind the other. The one in the back was a charred skeleton of a vehicle and it belched fire and black smoke. Lee realized his jaw was hanging open and snapped it closed. He kept walking.

His head buzzed with questions.

Who set the fire? Whose truck is that? It looks like a gasoline fire. That had to be a lot of gasoline. That was the rumble I felt inside the room—all that gas going up. Was that all Milo's gas? Is somebody sabotaging Milo or was it just an accident? What are they struggling with in the stairwell?

The loop went on, dizzyingly.

Lee found a door and tried the handle. It was locked. He moved on.

More doors. Lee didn't stop for each one, but he tested the handles as he went by to see if any of them were unlocked. It seemed the people of Smithfield were as paranoid about Milo as Camp Ryder was. They were all buttoned up tight, waiting for him to leave.

Gotta find a room. Gotta find a room.

Finally, a handle gave and Lee slipped in, not even checking to see who was in the room. His instinct to hide was so strong that he didn't even think about it until he closed the door behind him and realized he was in total darkness—this room didn't even have the red emergency lights.

Plunged into blindness, Lee felt the fear turn into a brief bout of panic, and he fumbled quickly for his flashlight and flicked it on. The room leaped out of the darkness in stark relief. Buckets. Mops. Industrial cleaners and solvents. Spray bottles.

Janitor's closet.

Lee put his back to the wall and let himself close his eyes and think.

Step two was getting out of the hospital. If he knew the hospital better, he might know a good way out, but in his current situation, he only knew two: the stairwell to the parking garage and the exits on the ground floor. Obviously, the stairwell to the parking garage was a no-go. All of Milo's men were jam-packed in there and trying to get to the parking garage. Lee had faith in his abilities, but he also knew he wasn't Superman.

Exiting by the ground floor might be safer but presented its own set of problems. Thinking back to every hospital building he'd ever been in, Lee knew that most doors from the ground floor to the outside would be electronic sliding glass doors so the sick and injured could get inside without too much trouble. Some of them would have key-card or code-security locks, but Lee had to assume that even on the unsecured doors, they would have dismantled the motion sensors to keep the doors from opening up to anything that wandered past. And usually they were constructed of bullet-resistant and shatterproof glass, which meant he couldn't shoot or bash his way through.

They might have them barricaded as well, but he wouldn't know that until he got down there. If it were impossible for him to pry open the doors, he would just have to find the hospital's diesel generator and start pulling parts until it stopped working. He figured the best bet for finding the generator was either on the ground floor or the basement level, if the hospital had one. In either case, it looked like he needed to go down.

Lee shut off the flashlight and replaced it in his pocket. He eased the door open an inch and peeked out through the crack. The curving hallway was clear. He stepped out and closed the door behind him, like he had every reason to be inside the janitor's closet, and began making his way down the hallway. He searched the walls for placards indicating the direction of an emergency stairwell that might take him down to the bottom floor.

The hallway he walked in was on the outer wall of the hospital, which was where the emergency stairwells were usually situated, so it didn't take him long to see the little black placard on the wall with a rudimentary picture of stairs, a flame, and an arrow pointing to a door.

Lee looked behind him to see if he were being followed, but the hall was deserted as far as he could see. The sounds of struggling from the parking garage stairwell had grown muted and faraway.

He pushed through the door and into a dimly lit space. To his left, the stairs led down into darkness. The smell in the stairwell was dank, like an unfinished basement, but he didn't detect anything foul. He flicked on his light and began moving down the levels, taking the stairs two at a time. His earlier guesstimation about which floor he was on turned out to be fairly accurate, as he only had to travel down four flights before reaching the ground level.

As with all emergency stairwells, the ground floor had an exit door that opened to the outside world. Lee pushed on the door but found that it would not budge. He played his light around the edges and discovered the sloppy chunks of soldering that bound the steel door to its metal frame. Someone had been in a rush to weld the damn thing shut.

"It can never be easy," Lee mumbled to himself.

Behind him, he found another door, this one leading into the hospital. It was unsecured. He opened it slightly and looked through to what appeared to be the main entrance to the hospital. The smell of the lobby eked through the open door, heavy and rich with decomposing flesh. Lee gagged but forced himself to stay in the door and keep surveying the room.

The place had clearly been a madhouse in the last hours before Smithfield fell apart. Muted daylight bathed the room, coming in through the bank of windows and sliding doors at the front. The room was wider than it was long, with white linoleum floors and heavy-looking white pillars topped with green accents. Trash was scattered everywhere and shoved into corners to make narrow paths for gurneys to get through. The trash was a mix of food wrappers, bottles, and the sterile packaging of innumerable medical supplies. Directly across from Lee, a corner of the lobby was crowded with gurneys draped with white sheets. On several of them, the white sheets bulged into swollen, discolored mounds. Here and there a hand or foot poked out from underneath.

Lee watched, and the moment stretched. Nothing moved in the lobby, so he stepped out slowly, keeping his eyes trained on the front as he navigated around one of the large white pillars that blocked his view of the outside. When he could finally see around it, he froze. Fear mounted a comeback and seized the breath in his chest.

Outside the thin wall of sliding glass doors, just past the cement barricades and loops of concertina wire, the parking lot and the street beyond had been swallowed by the approach of hundreds upon hundreds of infected.

Doc stared at the dead man for a very long time.

The man's mouth was open in a scream that Doc couldn't hear, staring back at him with eyes that Doc couldn't see. The feeling that the dead man gave him was as raw and empty as the holes in his face that glistened darkly in the bloodred light. It was a ponderous, horrid feeling, but it was something Doc had never felt before, and for that reason only, he could not take his eyes off the dead man. The feeling that wormed around in his gut, the feeling that he had never felt before was true and pure. It was unadulterated hatred.

Eventually, Doc moved.

He leaned forward and got his legs underneath him. Then he staggered three steps so that he was looking over the dead man. Who was it? Some stranger. Some person. Another random event. Another act of violence. Another dead body.

He mustered what frothy spit he could in his dry mouth and let it fall from his pursed lips as he hung over the dead man. The white globule landed with a wet smack in the center of the man's forehead. The glob seemed to wiggle, as all the tiny bubbles it was made of popped and dribbled down the man's forehead and into the gaping wound of his left eye socket.

Doc knelt. For once in his life, his skin-and-bones build was a blessing. He was able to pull his hands around to his side, despite the duct tape that bound them. He went through the man's pockets, found half of a granola bar wrapped in a napkin and a pocketknife.

Doc sat back, satisfied with his find, and opened the pocketknife, feeling his way through cutting at his bindings. His face was a mask of concentration as he focused and visualized his own hands behind his back, twisting and contorting his wrists to get the knife edge to the tape and begin to slowly saw back and forth. The process was long and particularly difficult with a missing finger, but after about five minutes of breathless focus, he freed himself.

He brought his hands to his front. Ripped the remaining bits of tape off his wrists, not wincing when they took his hair with them. He balled up the tape and tossed it to the side. He worked his shoulder and neck, trying to get some life back into the stiff joints. Then he inspected the pocket-knife. It was about a three-inch blade. Solid wood handle with brass fittings. He took the knife, blade up, and made three quick stabbing motions with it.

He looked at the knife and nodded.

He leaned over to the dead man and took a breath, as though preparing himself. He put the tip of the blade against the dead man's stomach, then seemed to reconsider and moved the point to the neck. Cringing slightly, he pushed the blade into the neck. He pulled the knife out and regarded the blade curiously. The silvery steel was marred only by a small smear of blood near the base of the blade. He was familiar with the weird sensations that went along with putting a blade through flesh. Being a premed, he'd done some work on cadavers. But he'd never simply stabbed someone in the neck.

This was a new sensation.

Doc settled himself into position in front of the dead man and stabbed him in the neck again, three times in quick succession. When he was done, he took a moment of self-evaluation, then finished with a firm nod. He wiped the blade off on his pants and closed the knife. He folded his legs underneath him and picked up the granola bar, regarding it unsurely, but unwrapped it, sniffed it, and did not find it offending. He ate the granola bar slowly, still watching the dead man lie there.

When he had finished the granola bar, he picked up the knife and opened it again, then he moved to the door and tested the handle. Captain Harden had left it unlocked. He opened it without regard for what was on the other side and stepped through. The hallway to his left was beginning to fill with people, but they paid him no mind. Their eyes and their fear were focused out the windows and down to the cement and barbed-wire barricades that encircled the hospital. Even Doc paused for a moment to stare down at the view. It was amazing and terrifying all at once.

Pushed tight against the barricades and stretching to either side, beyond Doc's line of sight, a horde of infected scrambled at the defenses. They climbed and clambered and tangled themselves in the wire, trying to get over. Trying to get to the hospital. In several places they had already choked the barbed-wire defenses with so many bodies that they had managed to create more human bridges across, just like at the outer barricade. Like storm waters through a crack in the dyke, the encroaching horde was beginning to trickle through. There were so many of them, it was breathtaking in an almost awe-inspiring way. A bacterium, something smaller than the width of a hair, had brought humanity to its knees and had turned them all into a surging mass of lunatics.

Incredible.

He kept walking down the hall, toward the nurses' station.

Several of Milo's men and a few of the survivors from the Smithfield group were crowded around the door to the stairwell. As he approached, he could hear a shouted conversation between two familiar voices that he eventually realized were Milo and Shumate.

Milo had a finger in Shumate's face. "Tell me how to get the fuck outta this hospital!"

"There's only one way in." Shumate looked scared, his voice a panicked whine. "We did that on purpose so we didn't have to guard all the other entrances and exits."

"Well, what the fuck did you do to those exits?"

"They're all on the ground floor!"

"And there's no other way to get in the parking garage?"

Shumate's face clouded with thought. "We might be able to jump across from the roof, but by the time we do, the parking garage is going to be full of them." He pointed out the windows. "They're breaking through already!"

Milo had had enough. He drew out his bowie knife and grabbed Shumate by the collar, slipping the blade easily under his chin and growling so low that Doc almost couldn't hear it. "This is your fucking fault. This was one of your fucking people who did this, because you're weak, and you have no fucking control."

Shumate's terrified eyes were squeezed shut. "I didn't know; I swear to God! It had to have been LaRouche. He's had it in for me and you since this all started!"

At that point, Doc had lost interest in the conversation. He strode forward, heading for the big man with the goatee standing close behind Milo with his arms crossed. Big G. Didn't Milo say that Big G was the last person with Nicole? Yes. Doc believed those were his words.

He pushed through the crowd, and for some

reason, no one stopped him. Maybe because they didn't recognize him; maybe because they just didn't expect it coming from Doc, because he had always been such a puppet for Milo that they simply couldn't wrap their brains around him doing something Milo wouldn't approve of. Whatever the reason, they moved out of his way when he nudged them aside and strode up, just to the right-hand side of Big G.

Big G must have felt the burning stare, or perhaps he noticed the movement out of the corner of his eye, but he managed to turn his head just as Doc reached him, and he uttered a weak syllable of surprise before Doc plunged the pocketknife into his throat.

It was odd how everyone stood around and did nothing.

Like they couldn't believe this was actually happening. Big G. The mighty giant, slain by Doc, the weakling. Surely Big G was just going to toss Doc off of him and beat him to a pulp. They all just watched and waited in those brief few seconds, as though it were some sort of stage play put on for their amusement.

But it was not a play.

Doc felt the crunch of all the little bones and cartilage in Big G's throat as the blade slipped into his larynx. The man's eyes went wide and his mouth opened and emitted a strange, raspy shout that turned into a gurgle as blood welled up in his throat. Doc held the back of Big G's neck as he kept the blade pressed firmly inside him. Big G's hands scrambled about, first going to his throat, then trying to shove Doc off of him, but they were panicked and ineffective. Doc stared into his eyes, his skinny arms corded tight by manic strength, a grimace of pure hatred on his face.

"Where's my Nicole?" Doc whispered.

Big G sank to his knees and there was a collective gasp from those who crowded around. Even Milo seemed too shocked to move for a moment.

"Where's my Nicole?" Doc's voice grew to a bellow. "She was mine! She was mine!"

The shout seemed to jar Milo into movement. He released Shumate and sprang for Doc's slender frame, plunging the bowie knife into the man's back, all the way up to the hilt, nearly running him through.

The only reaction that Doc gave was to pull the knife from Big G's neck and begin repeatedly stabbing him in the same spot, screaming as he did. It was not pain that wrenched that sound from Doc, but a purity of rage that froze everyone else in the room.

Milo pulled his bowie knife out and stabbed again and again into Doc's back, but it was as though Doc had completely disconnected from his body. The entirety of his mind was focused on Big G, who was nearly dead even at that point in time, and he just kept sticking that pocketknife into his neck until the heavy body fell backward, taking Doc down with it.

Doc rolled onto his back, looking up at Milo with wild, insane eyes. The skinny man smiled and blood pooled behind his lips, staining his teeth. It was a wicked smile, a sneer that said he knew something they didn't know.

His voice was a thready whisper. "You're all gonna die. You're all gonna die...tonight... tonight..."

And with those last words, Doc faded away.

When he died, everyone stood in silence for a moment.

A heavy breath bubbled out of Big G's mouth and speckled his face with red. Then that big man died as well, right alongside the skinny little medical student that no one thought would ever do something like this.

Milo stared at the two dead men, flabbergasted. Then he threw his hands up, still holding the knife. "Fuck!" He stared at the two bodies in bewilderment, tapping the blade of his knife against his thigh. A thought seemed to occur to him and he pointed to two of his men. "If he's out, Lee's out! Check the room!"

The two men hauled off to the room down the hall.

Milo pointed his knife at Shumate. "How much longer until your generator runs out of fuel?"

As if on cue, a steady hum that had gone unnoticed up to that point suddenly ceased to vibrate the air, and just for a second, the emergency lights flickered. Milo's men looked around, stupefied, while every member of the Smithfield group let out a collective gasp of dismay, because they knew exactly what that meant.

Shumate began to visibly shake. "I think that was it."

TWENTY

OVERRUN

LEE WAS HALFWAY ACROSS the lobby when the power went out.

He hadn't noticed the constant hum that filled the air until it died and left him feeling like his hearing had just gone out. When that happened, he stopped in his tracks and looked around. The ubiquitous red emergency lights flickered and then dimmed.

A subtle *whirr*ing sound came from the front of the lobby and instantly the lobby was filled with the maniacal screams of the infected as they fought to get over the barricades. When Lee spun, he found himself exposed to the outside world. The thin wall of shatterproof glass that comprised the main entrance to Johnston Memorial Hospital had used its last bit of battery power to slide open, ignorant that its safety function was not saving the occupants of the building but dooming them.

Beyond those gaping, open doors, at least a hundred infected had managed to get inside the barricade, and when the doors slid aside, a hundred pairs of eyes locked on the opening like a predator picking out the sick antelope in the herd.

Without pausing to think—because they didn't think, they just acted—they all began sprinting for the opening.

It was almost like Lee's adrenal glands had been tapped out. The only thing he felt was a dull ache of disappointment and his earlier words echoed in his mind: *It can never be easy.* He looked desperately around the room as the dark shapes of the infected loped toward him, sodden tatters of clothing hanging off of them in ribbons, trailing behind them like kite runners.

Lee crossed the room in three quick steps and grabbed one of the gurneys huddled in the corner. He didn't have time to be respectful of the body lying beneath the darkly stained sheet. He twirled the bed around and shoved it at the door to the stairwell, constantly glancing to his side as he ran, checking to see how close the infected were.

Too close.

He slammed the gurney into the door, flinging it wide and causing the body to jitter and nearly topple off. Some horrid gas trapped in the corpse was jarred by the impact and came out of the thing in a gush of warm, noxious air that nearly made him retch. The gurney barely fit into the bottom landing of the stairwell, the head of it jamming against the door that had been welded shut. There was maybe an inch of clearance between the foot of the gurney and the frame of the door to the lobby, so the gurney was effectively stuck in that position. If Lee wanted to get the lobby door closed, it was going to take some jostling.

Behind him, a feral growl echoed, and he knew

without having to look that they had made it inside. Lee leaped over the gurney and into the stairwell, landing hard on his shoulder, feeling a pop and a tingling sensation in his fingers. He rolled onto his back just as the first infected hit the open door, its eyes wide and wild, trying to climb over the gurney after him.

Lee let out an involuntary cry and yanked the pistol from his waistband, firing three times into the infected's chest, knocking it backward off the gurney and directly into a second infected. This second mad creature tried to scrabble for purchase by grabbing the doorframe but couldn't quite get a grip and fell back, hissing.

Lee jumped to his feet and yanked the gurney out of the doorframe, then reached across the putrid-smelling body still strapped to it and slammed the stairwell door closed. The door hadn't even closed completely before it shot open again, stopping only because it slammed into the corner of the gurney as Lee tried to push the damn thing in place to block the door. A wiry hand shot through the narrow opening and grabbed hold of Lee's arm, trying to pull him through.

Lee stuck the muzzle of the pistol into the opening and fired three more times without looking. The hand on his arm didn't let go, but the grip loosened enough that Lee was able to extricate himself. He slammed the door closed on the arm with as much strength as he could muster and heard bones crack. The infected's arm spasmed and slipped back out through the door. Breathing heavily, Lee shut the door with both hands and used his hip to nudge the gurney in place. Now the foot of the gurney was wedged against the inner door and the head of the gurney against the outer door, effectively blocking the door off. It wasn't a tight enough fit and would eventually rattle out of the way as the infected on the other side continued to assault the door. But it would buy him some time.

Lee squeezed past the gurney and bolted up the first flight of stairs. When he reached the landing and turned the corner, someone was standing at the top, pointing a rifle at him. Lee nearly fell backward off the stairs but caught himself on the banister as he brought up his pistol, finger already squeezing the trigger.

"Captain?"

The only thing that stayed Lee's trigger finger was the gray-and-tan digital pattern of ACU camouflage, which in the recesses of Lee's subconscious mind still meant "friend." Lee gasped as he lowered his pistol, realizing how close he'd come to putting two holes in LaRouche's head.

"Sergeant!" He sucked in air. "What the fuck?!"

LaRouche ported the rifle—Lee's rifle, he realized—and took two steps down from the landing he stood on. "Jesus Christ, Captain! I almost fucking shot you!"

"What the hell is going on out there?" Lee bounded up the last few steps. "Where're Harper and Miller? Did they make it out?"

"Yeah." LaRouche put a hand to Lee's shoulder to steady him. "They both got out, and they got the supply truck too. That was the fireball that went off. It was an accident, but it happened when we came back to get the supply truck."

"What?" Lee realized he sounded furious, but he actually felt a measure of pride for what Harper and Miller had pulled off. What a couple of regular G.I. Joes. "Are you kidding me?"

LaRouche smiled. "Naw. We used one of your claymores; hope you don't mind."

"Shit." Lee rubbed his face, trying to process everything. "So how'd you get back inside?"

"Busted a window on this floor. Radiology, I think." LaRouche moved to the door that led to the second level of the hospital. "No one comes down here. I was just getting back inside when I heard the gunshots from the stairwell and came running over. Man, I'm glad to see you."

Lee nodded rapidly. His plan was changing even as he stood there and processed what he had learned. Escaping the hospital was being moved to the back burner. The lobby below them was filling with infected even as they spoke. Those infected would eventually find ways to get upstairs.

Lee looked at LaRouche. "How many other emergency stairwells are there?"

"One other in this wing of the building." LaRouche pointed through the doorway to the opposite side of the building. "It'll be on the east side."

"None of the stairwells are secure?"

LaRouche shook his head, then seemed to register the banging below. "Aw, fuck...they're in the lobby, aren't they?" And then louder, "Dammit, we ran out of fuel, didn't we?"

Lee pushed him through the doorway and onto the second floor, letting the door swing closed behind them. "I got the door blocked, but they're gonna find the other stairwell soon."

LaRouche paced, shaking his head. "It was the explosion and the fireball. It must've attracted every infected in the city."

"I know." Lee smacked his shoulder. "It's done and over. We need to figure out a way to get out of here."

LaRouche pointed above them. "We gotta talk to Julia. She's got the radio to Camp Ryder. We can get them to help us."

Lee grimaced. "I don't know how much help they can be."

LaRouche began walking. "I still need to find Julia. I'm not gonna leave all these people here to get ripped to shreds by infected or shot by Milo's goons."

Despite Lee's desire to get the fuck out of town, he had to admit that LaRouche was right. The average survivors taking refuge in the hospital weren't responsible for Lee's incarceration, nor did they wish to align themselves with Milo, from what he'd seen. On the contrary, they all seemed to loathe him, and they seemed to loathe Shumate even more because he subjected them to Milo's whims.

"How many floors up is Julia?" Lee asked.

"Just one." LaRouche poked a thumb up. "Right above us."

"Alright." Lee glanced between the pistol in his hands and the M4 in LaRouche's arms, and the look did not escape the sergeant.

"You want your rifle back?" He held the weapon out to Lee.

"Yes." Lee smiled like he was being reunited with a friend. He handed the pistol over to LaRouche and grabbed the rifle. As he reached out, though, a shock of pain ran down his arm from his shoulder, causing him to nearly drop the rifle. "Shit!" His free hand instinctively reached up to touch his shoulder.

LaRouche held his hands out as though he were preparing to catch Lee if he passed out. "You okay, Cap?"

Lee rolled his shoulder a few times to loosen up the tense pain there. "Yeah, I'll be all right." It felt like soft-tissue damage. Nothing serious. He jerked his head down the hall. "We need to roll. You lead the way."

LaRouche slipped the extra pistol in an empty pouch on his vest and went to his Beretta M9, which he obviously felt more comfortable with. Moving with controlled speed, he led them through the floor cautiously. Lee's bad tidings of hordes of infected one floor beneath them had made LaRouche think that perhaps radiology was not as abandoned as he thought.

They passed the ever-present cream-colored medical devices that stood only as memories of a time when a hospital wasn't a place for people to hide but a place for people to heal. Each one of these unknown devices that Lee passed by was probably worth several thousand dollars, but now they lay discarded and gathering dust in a dark and empty radiology department that would probably never see the amount of electricity that had made it useful to begin with. At least not for a very long time.

They reached the other side without incident and approached the eastern emergency stairwell. They stopped at the door and listened to what lay beyond, but it was only dark silence huddling there, holding its breath.

Lee covered him while LaRouche opened the door and stepped through. This stairwell was as dark as the other and Lee had to again use his flashlight to illuminate the hollow space above and below them. When the white light pierced the still redness, nothing reacted by screeching or rushing toward them.

LaRouche's voice was a low whisper, fear taking the volume out of him. "Should we go down there? You know...block off the door?"

"No," Lee said. "I don't see anything we can use to barricade the door, and we don't have time." He thought about using a gurney like he had on the other stairwell, but there was no way in hell he was going back into the lobby now. "We need to focus on getting everyone out of this place."

LaRouche didn't look like he was in love with the idea of turning his back on a door that might burst open at any moment and let through a horde of infected, but he turned and took the stairs to the next level without further comment. Behind him, Lee followed, still shining his flashlight down into the gloom.

The next level up held another door. LaRouche pulled it open slightly and poked his head through. From the other side, Lee could hear the sounds of people, the steady murmur of urgent conversations. They weren't shouting, because they weren't panicked just yet, but it was clear that many people were expressing many viewpoints. The sergeant took in whatever he saw and seemed to decide that it was safe. He pulled open the door and the two of them stepped through onto the third level of the hospital.

The smell was the same as the building in Camp Ryder: dirty clothes, dirty bodies, and a faint sewer smell underlining everything. This level was slightly better lit than radiology, due to a large bank of eastern-facing windows to the right. The layout was different from the fourth floor where Lee had initially come from. The whole wing of the hospital was a rectangular shape, the short sides facing approximately north and south, and the long sides facing east and west. Offices occupied the south-facing side, a bank of elevators on the north-facing side. The outer walls of the east and west sides were just windows, while the inside was a block of hospital rooms. A nurses' station was at the mouth of a hallway that bisected the block of hospital rooms.

The nurses' station seemed to be the natural meeting point for the people living on this level. They had all gathered there, perhaps twenty or thirty men and women, and were engaged in a hushed but animated conversation. As LaRouche stepped toward them, Lee felt like he should hang back, but the sergeant motioned him forward. The gathering at the small nurses' station did not take notice until they were standing among them.

A man looked around at them, almost annoyed. He was middle-aged and wore a tattered old baseball cap with the Browning logo on it and a dirty white T-shirt and jeans. When his eyes focused on LaRouche, a sudden and hopeful smile broke out across his face. "Sarge!" he exclaimed, immediately grabbing LaRouche by the shoulders. "You're back! They said that you'd left us!"

LaRouche didn't return the smile, but he shook his head by way of response. "Where's Julia? We really need to speak with her."

"I'm right here!" The lady who had wheeled and dealed brazenly with Shumate to get Harper and Miller released pushed her way through the crowd and latched onto LaRouche with ferocity. "Jesus Christ! What's going on out there?" Her eyes traveled to Lee. "You're out? How the hell'd you get out?"

Lee shook his head. "Don't worry about it." He pointed to the stairwell door behind him. "I'm sure you folks heard the power go out. The doors are open downstairs and infected are inside the building. We need to start getting you guys out of here."

There was a chorus of exclamations and the air became almost palpable with fear.

The man in the Browning hat swore. "Well, what are we fuckin' waiting for? Let's grab our shit and get the hell outta here . . ."

But Julia was shaking her head. "No."

Lee took her arm and looked into her face again. "We don't have a choice. This place is about to get swarmed. On top of that, Milo's men are still in the building and it's only a matter of time before they come looking for me. It's not safe here. We gotta get out."

She jerked her arm away, looking between him and LaRouche. "You don't understand! I have people here who need me, people we can't just move! They're sick and injured and I sure as hell can't leave them lying here."

The gathering at the nurses' station mumbled, but now it seemed split down the middle, half of them agreeing, the other half wanting to make a run for it. Lee could imagine that those who agreed were the ones with the sick and injured in their families. Those who wanted to leave were the single ones with no ties and no reason to linger.

When the crowd realized it was divided, it got louder.

Lee cut it off before it got nasty. "Can you give me a rough estimate of how many immobile people you have?"

Julia raked hair out of her face. "It's not just about immobile. The only way out now is down the elevator shaft and into the maintenance crawlway that leads out back. I have six injured people who won't even be able to make it down the shaft, not to mention a few old folks and some of the younger kids."

The man with the Browning hat looked incredulous. "You've gotta be kidding me, Julia. So you're just going to sit here and not even try? We can at least *try* to get them out."

"And what are we gonna do if we even make it out?" Julia demanded. "I don't know if you've looked out the window, but we're completely fucking surrounded!"

LaRouche stepped in and looked at the man with the Browning hat. "George, we can continue this conversation in a second. Right now, help me barricade the doors to the eastern stairwell."

"The doors open into the stairwell," George observed halfheartedly. "How we gonna barricade them?"

LaRouche was already moving down the hall. "We stack up a big pile of shit. It won't hold them forever, but it'll buy us some time."

"What about the western stairwell?" someone asked.

"And what about Milo's guys?" spouted another.

Lee raised a placating hand. "Western stairwell is blocked from the bottom. As for Milo's men, we'll just have to cross that bridge when we come to it." Then he looked at Julia. "Where's the radio to Camp Ryder?"

Julia reached over the counter of the nurses' station and snagged the radio from the other side, handing it to Lee. He spoke to her quietly as he turned it on. "If I can get ahold of someone from Camp Ryder, we might be able to get help to clear the back. Then at least we'll know we have a safe way out."

Julia looked exasperated. "I already told you—"

Lee put a hand on her shoulder and leaned in so the others could not hear his low voice. "You can't speak for everyone here. There might be people who want out. If you choose to stay here and fight, that's up to you. But I think you need to start thinking of ways to get your sick and injured down that elevator shaft. I'm sure we can figure something out."

Julia looked back at the smattering of gaunt-faced survivors huddled at the nurses' station. Slowly, she nodded. "Okay."

Lee keyed the radio. "Captain Harden to Camp Ryder. Captain Harden to Camp Ryder. Harper or Miller or anyone from Camp Ryder. Does anybody copy me?"

He released the push-to-talk button and waited. A short burst of static filled the air, but no response came. Everyone jumped at the screeching sound of metal on tile floors as LaRouche and George shoved a big filing cabinet up against the door to the eastern stairwell. They grunted and groaned and finally got the thing in place. It had to weigh at least three hundred pounds, but it was top-heavy. With enough infected pounding at it and trying to climb over it, the thing would eventually tip over. LaRouche and George turned and began looking for other heavy objects to stack in the doorway.

Lee repeated his attempts on the radio, receiving the same response.

Nothing.

"What do we do now?" someone moaned.

Julia pointed to a redheaded woman. "Barb, do you have any rope?"

She looked briefly flustered. "I can try to find some . . ."

"Do that," Julia instructed. She raised her voice. "Everyone, we need to find rope. And some soft-restraint straps—like the kind they have on the gurneys—and some backboards. The backboards are usually orange or yellow and they look like a little surfboard with handles on the sides."

Then she pointed at Lee, every bit in charge. "You keep trying that radio, Captain. And keep those stairwell doors secure..."

Her last few words were drowned out by the sound of LaRouche and George suddenly shouting as the eastern stairwell door was thrown open and dozens of mad voices began screeching at them from the other side of the barricade.

TWENTY-ONE

THE ONLY EASY DAY...

LEE SPUN AND POINTED at Julia and the group of survivors standing stock-still behind her with big eyes and open mouths, frozen in terror. He had to shout to make himself heard over the ear-splitting feral screams of the infected. "Gather what you need! We'll hold them off!"

She nodded once and turned on her heels. The stillness in the group of survivors behind her broke into frenzied motion, everyone shouting and pointing this way and that. Two men broke off from the group, one of them with a scuffed and bloodstained baseball bat, the other with a classic wood-handled AK-47. Lee was surprised to see it, as mostly he'd seen nothing but hunting rifles and sporting shotguns in the hands of the average survivor, but the AK-47 was the most manufactured firearm in the world. He should have been surprised that this was the first one he'd come across.

"We're with you, Captain," the man with the AK-47 said.

Lee didn't respond to him but turned and made for the stairwell, where he could see LaRouche with his back braced up against the filing cabinet and George struggling to push another, slightly smaller one into place to bolster the first. The first cabinet covered the edges of the door with room to spare but left about a two-foot gap on top. The whole thing was shaking back and forth as the infected on the other side pounded and tried to climb over. A pair of greasy, gray hands gripped the top of the filing cabinet, pulling desperately, and a horrific visage squirmed out of the murky darkness of the stairwell, all sinews and gnashing teeth.

Lee stamped his feet to a stop about twenty feet from the creature on top of the filing cabinet and raised his rifle. Behind him, the two tagalongs skidded up short to avoid running into him. It would be an uncomfortably narrow shot: LaRouche's head was only a foot from the infected's gaping maw.

"Heads up!" Lee yelled.

The little red dot settled, and Lee fired three times in rapid succession.

The infected jerked a bit, then lay still atop the cabinet with its toothy jaw still working like a fish out of water. After a second or two, its grip on the cabinet faded and it fell back into the stairwell. LaRouche stared indifferently at a bullet hole in the side of the cabinet, not six inches from his head.

Lee slapped his shoulder as he took position next to the sergeant. "You'll be all right." He planted his feet and pressed his back against the cabinet, mimicking LaRouche's position. "I got this. Cover the top."

LaRouche bounced off the cabinet, drawing his

sidearm again and pointing it over Lee's head at the gap. The other three men slammed into the second cabinet, breaking the inertia and shoving the thing into place with a heavy metallic *crunch*. The two cabinets were now perpendicular to each other, forming a *T* shape, the smaller bracing the larger.

Lee pulled himself upright. "That's not gonna hold forever, but it'll give us some time."

LaRouche breathed hard. "Any more of those filing cabinets?"

"Yeah." George pointed to a room behind him with the door hanging open. "There're two more in—"

George's right eye exploded.

Lee heard the *zzzip-snap* of a bullet passing close to him.

Salty warmth on his lips and tongue.

George pitched forward, dead before he hit the ground.

Lee reached out and grabbed the person nearest him, who happened to be the man with the bat. He hooked his arm around the man's chest and dove sideways. As Lee flew sideways, he saw LaRouche and the man with the AK-47, their eyes following George's lifeless descent, their faces plain and unamazed, not having realized what was happening.

Lee would never know if that bullet was meant for him or if Milo's men had decided to kill everyone for the sake of simplicity. He would wonder about it later, but he didn't have time for it now. He hit the ground and scooted up against the wall.

He registered rapid gunfire.

The unmistakable chatter of an M249 Squad Automatic Weapon erupted from down the hall— Fuck, he should have remembered that Milo's crew had one! It chewed the floor and walls, sending drywall and chunks of tile into the air. A cluster of holes suddenly appeared in the filing cabinets, but LaRouche dove out of the way.

The man with the AK-47 wasn't as quick.

He tried to leap, but a few rounds zipped him through the legs, spinning him around. He flopped to the floor, his legs limp and useless behind him. He looked down, suddenly aware that something irreversible had just happened to him. His mouth opened but he had no words so he just started screaming. Another blast of 5.56mm projectiles silenced him.

The guy with the bat was yelling. "Dale, get up! Dale! Hurry!" He tried to stand and go to his dead friend.

Lee grabbed him by the shoulder and pushed him against the wall. "He's fucking dead, man! Leave it!"

The M249 fell silent and in its place was only the ringing in their ears.

LaRouche was up on his feet but crouched down low, with one hand on the ground, like a sprinter on the starting blocks. Lee followed the sergeant's gaze to where it was fixated on the AK-47 lying between its owner and George, just out of their reach.

Lee edged up to the corner and grabbed a handful of LaRouche's sleeve to get his attention. When he had it, he said, "On me," and got a single, curt nod by way of response.

Lee stuck the barrel of his M4 around the corner and started cranking off rounds blindly in the general direction of their attackers. He knew he wasn't going to hit anything but walls, but he hoped it would keep their heads down long enough.

LaRouche didn't need to be told to move. As soon as Lee started firing, he darted out into the hall, snatched up the AK-47, and then launched himself back into cover. Not a second after he had cleared the corner, the hall flared up with automatic fire once again. It inaccurately sprayed the walls on the far side of the hall and Lee figured their attacker was blind firing, just like he was.

LaRouche scooted himself between Lee and the man who clutched his baseball bat. He checked the ammunition level on the AK-47 while the man with the bat began to whimper. The magazine was full. LaRouche pointed down the hallway. "The hallway wraps all the way around. I'll keep 'em busy; you flank 'em."

Lee made a circle out of his thumb and forefinger and then hauled himself up to his feet. He felt exposed going into a gunfight without his vest. It wasn't the first time, but that didn't make him feel any more comfortable. It just made him feel like *eventually my luck will run out*.

He flew quickly down the hall to the nurses' station and turned the corner. The hallway there would cut through to the western side of the building, where he could come in from the side of their attackers. But when he turned the corner, a man was standing in the middle of the hall, hunched over and holding a big black shotgun. The man turned just as Lee brought up his rifle and their eyes met.

The man didn't react. He just stood there.

Lee pulled his finger off the trigger at the last second, realizing it was one of the survivors. He further realized with a sharp feeling of anxiety that he would never be able to tell the difference between one of Milo's men and one of the survivors. They were all just tired, skinny, dirty-looking people with guns.

Lee glared as he passed, though he knew the man had done nothing wrong.

"What's going on?" the man asked dumbly.

"Just sit," Lee commanded and moved on.

Past the nurses' station, another jumble of unused medical equipment had been shoved to one side of the hallway. At the end of the hall, Lee could see the western-facing bank of windows. Through those windows he could see the edge of the parking garage, and to the left of those, the stretch of trees and housetops that comprised the small town of Smithfield. All he had to do was turn left at the end of the hall and he would have those bastards dead to rights.

Behind him, echoing up the eastern hall, he could hear the heavy bark of the AK-47 shooting slow and steady. LaRouche was smartly pacing himself to stretch his ammunition. You didn't need to throw a thousand rounds downrange to keep an enemy's head down. One round every second or so would usually do the trick.

Lee reached the corner and started slicing the pie, dividing up the 90-degree turn into small, manageable portions. There at the end of the hall, he could see two men huddled at the corner; one was standing, and one was prone. They both cringed from the corner each time the AK-47's big 7.62mm bullets tore another chunk out of the wall they hid behind. Lee approximated their distance at twenty yards.

Callously, Lee thought that with the men bunched so close together, he might be able to take both of them out with fewer rounds. He braced his hand on the wall and rested his rifle's quad-rail on it to steady his aim. Then it was five quick shots, punching neat holes in the back of the one standing up. He lurched and toppled forward onto the one lying prone, who began to shout and panic, attempting to scramble away from the noise of Lee's gunfire while his buddy smothered and bled on him. In his panic to escape Lee, he squirmed himself right into LaRouche's line of fire. Lee heard the old soviet rifle report twice. He could see where one of the rounds went low and kicked up bits of tile just inches short of the target, but the second round smacked into the top of the man's head and, Lee thought, probably all the way down through his body.

"Moving to you!" Lee shouted as he raced down the hall.

"I hear you," came the response from around the corner.

Lee slid to a stop on the floor, which was already slick with blood. The man LaRouche had caught on the top of the head was hemorrhaging badly, his facial features swollen and deformed by the shock wave of the heavy projectile that had passed through him. LaRouche came around the corner and looked at his handiwork with a wrinkled nose, as though he'd just gotten a whiff of garbage.

Lee hefted the M249 off the ground with something akin to reverence. While it was no .50-caliber ass-beater, it still held plenty of ammunition and a high rate of fire. It was fed from a plastic box underneath the chamber that held up to a two-hundred-round belt of 5.56mm ammunition. Great for suppressive fire. Or raking hordes of infected. The downside was that the damn thing weighed about twenty pounds. A quick glance revealed that it had about half of its original two-hundred-round belt still sitting in the ammunition box.

"That's a fuckin' game changer," LaRouche said eagerly.

Lee nodded and held the weapon out to him. "Trade up."

LaRouche happily accepted the trade. "Probably about fifteen rounds left for the AK."

Lee swung his M4 around so it was resting against the back of his leg and held the clunky-feeling soviet rifle. "It'll work. Let's move back."

At the eastern side, the man with the baseball bat stood, dividing his attention between trying to see what Lee and LaRouche were doing and watching the barricade at the door. The screeching had died down as the infected beyond had lost the fervor of the chase, but it was clear they weren't giving up just yet. Even from down the hall, Lee could still hear dozens of them growling and muttering senselessly and occasionally striking out at the filing cabinet with a loud metallic *BANG*.

"Will!" LaRouche hollered at him. "Move back to the nurses' station!"

The man with the baseball bat—aka Will—nodded, clearly scared out of his mind, and began backing away.

They jogged back to the corner. Lee pointed to the ground for LaRouche's benefit. "You post up right here with that SAW. Anything comes through that door, you let 'em have it."

"Roger that." LaRouche went prone and propped the M249 up on its bipod. Only the gun and the side of his head were peeking around the corner; the rest of him remained in cover.

Beyond the nurses' station, pandemonium had broken out. The shooting and the infected trying to get through had sent almost everyone into a panic, and they were taking the lull in the shooting as an opportunity to bolt from their rooms. They carried children over their shoulders and clutched what little things they owned, stuffed into backpacks, but sometimes just loose, like a blanket or a bottle of water. They were all heading away from the fighting, toward the back of the hospital where the elevator shaft was located.

Julia came around the corner as Lee fished the radio out of his back pocket where he'd stuck it earlier. "Did you get in contact with them?"

Lee shook his head sternly. "About to try again. Did you get your contraption set up?"

Julia wiped sweat from her forehead and closed her eyes shakily. "I tied some ropes and soft restraints to the backboards so we can lower the sick and injured and anyone who can't climb down on their own. I don't know if we have enough rope to get to the bottom of the elevator shaft, but we'll try." She opened her eyes and there were tears. "You were right. We can't stay here. Whether your friends come or not, we can't stay here."

"Just get the healthy ones down first." Lee tried to sound encouraging but felt like he failed. "They can help the sick and injured through the maintenance tunnels. Just tell them not to go outside until we know it's clear."

"Okay." She seemed like she wanted to say something else but turned instead and disappeared into the crowd of panicked survivors.

Lee keyed his radio and tried to make contact again but got nothing. He could feel that heavy dead weight in the pit of his gut, the suffocating feeling that all of his efforts, all of his trying, no matter how hard, no matter how desperate, were all going to count for nothing in the end. The situation seemed insurmountable, with infected below and Milo's thugs above.

But you gotta do it.

You gotta compartmentalize.

Step one: get the survivors off of this floor.

Fighting back those edges of fear and doubt trying to creep into his mind like a dark wolf slinking through the forest, Lee keyed the radio again and spoke, perhaps a little louder than he needed to. "This is Captain Harden. Does anyone copy me?

We need help. Right now." And then, with a bit of frustration, "Does anyone fucking copy me?"

Will was suddenly standing next to him. "What do you want me to do about the stairwell?"

Lee shot him an angry look. "Keep a goddamn eye on it!"

The man jumped and scooted over to the corner opposite LaRouche so he could watch the eastern stairwell. The creatures inside had managed to create a few inches of give between the two filing cabinets by their constant smashing and rocking the barricade back and forth. Their excited calls had died down, but they were being replaced by the loud crash of the two cabinets banging together.

Impressed wasn't quite the right word, but Lee had to admit that the infected were persistent. Perhaps they lacked the ability to reason, but like any animal, they could recognize cause and effect, and their efforts seemed to be reinvigorated by their small victory of inches.

LaRouche called out, straining to be heard. "Contact right!"

A clipped, three-round burst belched out of the M249, the brass casings and metal couplings that made up the links of the ammunition belt went tumbling across the ground, and in the same instant the tile floor to LaRouche's right shattered.

LaRouche yelped and jerked back into cover, his hands over his eyes, blood seeping between the fingers. "Fuck! I think they shot me!"

Lee was on his knees in an instant, blindly sending a burst down the hallway to keep them occupied for a brief moment. "Calm down! Calm

down!" He pulled LaRouche's hand off of his face.
The right side was streaked with three deep cuts
from his cheekbone all the way back through his
shredded ear. Speckled in with the lacerations were
tiny red pockmarks that oozed a steady trickle of
blood, but nothing looked like a gunshot wound.
"I think it was just the shrapnel from the tile. Can
you see?"

LaRouche tried to open his eyes, but his right
eyelid was already swelling shut disobediently.
"Ah...I can't see out of my right eye..."

"Fuckin' A..." LaRouche would do no good
covering the hall if he couldn't see. Lee rolled the
sergeant out of the way and shoved the AK-47
and the radio into his arms. "Keep trying to make
radio contact." Then Lee sprawled out on his belly,
making sure that his tidbits were behind cover,
and pulled up tight with the M249.

Down the hall and to the right, the western
emergency stairwell was open and a man in a black
T-shirt was hanging his ass out in the wind, trying
to get a look at Lee. Purely out of reaction, Lee
squeezed the trigger, letting off a few rounds that
tracked high over the man's head but forced him
to jump back into the stairwell under a shower of
drywall dust.

Short, controlled bursts, Lee reminded himself.

That was how you shot an M249, or any automatic weapon for that matter: short, controlled
bursts. Ammunition—even half of a two-hundred-
round belt—went very fast if you didn't take your
finger off the trigger.

To his left, LaRouche spoke into the radio,

loudly and clearly, but got nothing back. Lee heard a gasp of surprise and shot a quick glance over his shoulder only to find Julia kneeling down next to LaRouche.

"Oh, my God." Her hands hovered around his face, seemingly unsure whether touching him would make it worse. "What happened?"

"Just some shrapnel from the floor," LaRouche mumbled.

"We don't have a whole lot of time," Lee warned, refocusing on the stairwell. The door still stood open, but he couldn't see anybody. "How we comin' with getting people down the shaft?"

"Uh…" She blinked rapidly. "I've got eight people left to lower down. They're working on that right now. Almost everyone else is already down in the maintenance tunnel."

Lee was about to respond when the guy in the black shirt leaned out of cover again and fired rapidly from an M4. Lee felt the rounds pass uncomfortably close and gritted his teeth, letting out a burst from the M249, but not before another man darted out of the stairwell and around the far corner where the two bodies of his comrades lay.

He heard someone screaming from down the hall.

Had he landed a hit on one of them?

"One might be tryin' to flank left!" Lee called out.

LaRouche handed the radio to Julia, who was crouched with her hands over her head and covering her ears against the assault of noise that poked mercilessly at their eardrums. He tucked the

AK-47 into his left shoulder, though he was right-handed, since he would not be able to sight with his dominant right eye.

"I got it." The sergeant moved to the corner, taking watch directly over the huddled form of Will, who was pressed so tightly against the wall that he looked less like a man and more like a child clutching his mother's bosom.

Whether he was hit or not, the man in the black shirt dipped into view, slightly lower than Lee expected, and began firing. Lee felt Julia smack him in the shoulder, trying to get his attention, but he focused through the sights and pulled the trigger, giving the man in the black shirt two heavy bursts to think about. The man jerked and flopped, clutching at his neck, his rifle clattering to the floor. Lee felt Julia pressing a finger against his right shoulder, and she was really digging it in deep.

"What the fuck?" Lee snapped his head to the left, but Julia was just staring at him. He could see both her hands, and yet the pressure on his shoulder was becoming painfully intense.

Julia suddenly pointed at him. "They...they shot you!"

Lee rolled onto his side and craned his neck to see his shoulder. The hard pressure was becoming fiery, and he couldn't help growling low through his gritted teeth. *It can't be much more than a graze*, he told himself, but the patch of blood on his shoulder was beginning to spread. He wanted to take off his shirt and check the wound, but he didn't have the time.

"It's fine," he said stubbornly, because there was nothing else to do. He didn't have a combat medic, he didn't have any supplies to fix himself, and looking at the wound wouldn't do him any good at this juncture. He told himself that it wasn't that bad, despite the pain. Sometimes pain could be deceiving. Superficial wounds often felt the worst.

There was a brief lull in the overwhelming noise, and Lee could hear the two men from down the hall. The exchange was one-sided, as all the man in the black shirt was doing was gurgling, desperately trying to get oxygen to his lungs and sucking in blood instead. He kept blubbering and coughing, and his comrade across the hall from him kept yelling at him, as though he were going to get a different answer.

"Wes! Wes! Get your fuckin' ass up! Come on, man! You okay? Snap out of it!"

Lee didn't think he was going to snap out of it.

"Wes? Can you hear me?"

"Gggllrrgullpgrg."

"Come on, man! Don't leave me by myself!"

"Gaaaghagllulpgggl."

Lee was so fixated on the strange and macabre conversation that he almost didn't hear the tiny voice right next to him. When it finally registered, he turned to face Julia and found her holding the radio out to him as though it were some foreign device she knew nothing about.

Lee snatched up the radio and keyed it. "Is someone there? Can anyone copy me? This is Captain Harden."

There was a burst of static, and Lee thought it was just a cruel joke, that the airwaves would go dead again, leaving him hopeless. But almost immediately after the static, the mic crackled again and he heard Harper's voice, and he didn't think he'd ever been as happy to hear another man talk to him.

"Captain? Is that you? This is Harper!"

Lee couldn't help but grin. "I copy you loud and clear, Harper. I'm at the hospital. We are pinned down by infected and Milo's men. We need help here, buddy, and we need it yesterday."

"Alright, Captain." There was shuffling on the other side and Lee thought he could hear the sound of a vehicle's engine accelerating to a roar. "We're coming down the boulevard now, and we got help with us. Just hang on. We're almost..." There was a long, interminable silence, followed by, "Holy shit!"

And then the sound from the radio was gunfire and screaming.

TWENTY-TWO

. . . WAS YESTERDAY

LEE TRIED TO KEY the radio, but Harper was still transmitting and the radio only gave back a negative tone, as if to say, *You can't do that yet . . . Please wait . . .*

"Motherfucker!" Lee squeezed the radio in his hand and shook the thing around. Finally, the transmission ended with a quiet whisper of static. Julia was staring at him with her hands over her mouth. Will was looking at the ground with his head resting on his baseball bat, as though all hope was lost. Even LaRouche's face was half turned to him, but it was the wounded and sightless side, and he quickly looked back down the hall.

Lee keyed up, trying to stay calm. "Harper, this is Captain Harden. Are you okay? We heard gunfire. Harper, are you there?"

To his credit, Harper took the time to respond. It was short and clipped and barely audible over the gunfire in the background, but it told them he was okay, at least for that moment. "Can't talk!"

Lee snatched the M249 off the ground, peeking around the corner as he did and seeing the man who had run across the hall now darting back into the stairwell as though fleeing for his life. It gave Lee a savage sense of satisfaction. That was, until he heard LaRouche's voice and realized it wasn't Lee the man was afraid of.

"They're comin' through! We gotta go!" And then he fired once, twice, and then *three-four-five*. From the direction of the eastern stairwell, Lee heard something heavy fall and slide on the tile ground.

Lee shoved the radio in his back pocket again and brought up the M249, the bullet wound in his right shoulder screaming. He moved to LaRouche's corner and gave the sergeant a hard slap on the shoulder to indicate he was taking over. Still sighting down his rifle, LaRouche shoved off the corner and moved out into the middle of the hall.

Lee aimed his weapon down the eastern side of the building. The infected horde had manage to shove the makeshift barricade far enough that there was about a six-inch gap between the filing cabinet and the doorframe. It was narrow, but it was an opening. Lee watched an infected with long and dirty hair shove herself through, headfirst, and then squirm past the barricade. He was briefly reminded of something his father had said when they were surprised to find a raccoon in their garage after leaving the overhead door cracked just a few inches.

If they can get their head through, they'll find a way to get their body through.

The infected was doing just that, pulling her chest through, showing no sign of pain at how it crushed her breasts, and then she had her torso through and the rest was easy.

Lee stepped out into the hall, because there was no purpose in taking cover when there was no one shooting back at him. He yelled over his shoulder, "Get the fuck out of here!" and started shooting. He zipped the infected woman with a five-round burst, every shot finding its mark except for the last one, punching holes in her from her left hip all the way to her right shoulder, and down she went.

Behind him, he could hear rapid footfalls as Julia and Will and LaRouche beat a hasty retreat for the elevator doors. Lee started to back up, keeping his weapon trained on the breach in their barricade and thanking God that it wasn't bigger. In a way, it was a blessing that the infected had managed to shove the barricade only six inches. It distracted them enough that they appeared to no longer be attempting to push the barricade, but it was narrow enough that only one fit through at a time.

Lee was foolishly taking solace in this when he heard gunfire coming from the western side. It was the nasty sound of LaRouche's AK-47, followed by a short pause, a shotgun blast, and then the popping sound of a small-caliber pistol. Had LaRouche already run out of ammunition on the AK-47 and transitioned to his 9mm?

Lee waited until the next infected was trying to shove itself through the breach at the stairwell, and then he popped its head right where it was stuck between the cabinet and the doorframe, creating a nice blockage in the already tight space. Lee was about halfway from the nurses' station to the northern end of the hospital wing where the bank of elevators stood. He turned and made up the last thirty feet at a dead sprint. When he hit the back wall to stop, the scene at the elevators was mass confusion.

The elevator doors had been pried open. Three men were standing in a line in front of the yawning hole of the elevator shaft. Their feet were braced wide, and their arm muscles bunched as they all held tightly to a rope that looked like it bore a heavy load. The rope was secured to a hospital bed that was wedged in an open door behind them and, little by little, they released the slack, lowering someone down the shaft. All three of them looked scared, but the lead one was completely focused on the elevator shaft while the other two looked around fearfully, trying to see where the threats were coming from.

Around them, a cluster of people scrambled about. They were trying to find a safe place to hide, but there was no escape except down the elevator shaft. One of the men kept moving to the open shaft and looking down with his hands clenched in his hair, as though he were contemplating how badly injured he would be if he made the jump.

Behind it all, LaRouche and two other armed men were covering the western hall and taking potshots at whatever was down there. In Lee's back pocket, he could hear Harper squawking, but he couldn't talk right now. He worked his way through the panicked cluster of people and managed to get LaRouche's attention by screaming his name.

Whatever they were shooting at down the hall

seemed to be taking a lot of firepower, while the breach in the barricade was only leaking one or two infected at a time. It only made sense for them to post the M249 on the most troublesome corner. Lee made the call and LaRouche did what was asked of him without hesitation and moved to cover the eastern hall.

Lee took the corner as the others vacated the area. Bullets split the air close to his face and smacked the wall behind him. The acrid smell of cordite stung his nose. Numerous voices yelled from behind and in front of him, each vying for his attention. The senses became overwhelmed.

This was combat. You created the chaos, but at the same time, tried not to be a part of it, tried not to be affected by it. It was a strange mix of hot-blooded instinct and cold-blooded logic. It was fighting with emotion but thinking with your head, almost as though your mind were the handler and your body the beast, the two of them at odds and yet oddly the same. And when the two forces fell into step with each other, it was sickening and exhilarating all at once.

These were not things that Lee thought about in the moment; they were just things he instinctively knew—the same as when you drop a ball, you know it will fall to the ground. In his mind there were only priorities—*Move to the corner, evaluate the threat down the hall, deal with the threat down the hall, reevaluate where the M249 needs to be, get the survivors to safety*—and then a slurry of thoughts and experiences underneath it all that guided his actions.

When he turned the corner, he found the man who'd been Wes's partner running straight at him, with no weapon in his hand. He had almost reached the hallway that bisected the hospital rooms and led to the nurses' station. Their eyes locked, and there was nothing in that man's expression but fear and pleading. Behind him and pouring out of the western stairwell were dozens of infected.

Lee realized that though they had barricaded the entry to this level, all the infected had to do was go up one more floor. They must have been running through that floor, attacking Milo's men and forcing them back into the stairwell. The man had either dropped his rifle because it ran out of ammunition or felt it slowed him down.

He waved his empty hands and screamed, "Don't shoot! Don't shoot!"

Lee gritted his teeth and pulled the trigger anyway.

His first burst took the man's legs out from under him. The man looked shocked and dismayed as he fell to the ground, and no matter the steel of Lee's cold resolve, the look on that man's face would always be a crystal-clear picture in his mind of what he was capable of when it was Us versus Them.

An infected teenage boy leaped nimbly over the fallen form, completely ignoring the easy kill and still heading straight for Lee, his eyes wild with aggression. He caught Lee's second burst and veered off to the right, where he smacked the wall and then fell to the floor, still breathing but not moving.

The man Lee had shot in the leg started screaming and Lee thought it was more in fear than in pain. Two skinny, wraithlike creatures pounced on him, smothering his screams. To Lee's surprise, one took hold of the man's arm and one grabbed his head and they dragged him back around the corner where they could feed in relative safety. Did they recognize that Lee could kill them if they stayed out in the open, or did they simply view him as competition for food? Whatever their reasons, they wiggled backward and fixed Lee with an animal stare that communicated the same message as a growling dog: *Don't come any closer... This is mine.*

Lee felt his skin prickle into goose bumps.

Their kill safely behind the wall, more infected turned off into the hall and Lee could just make out flailing arms and legs as their prey screamed hoarsely. This time it was pain that Lee heard. The scene affected Lee on a visceral level, causing his arms to shake and his stomach to feel hollow and weak. He began firing indiscriminately and had to force himself to get under control. He sent more rounds downrange, each burst raising the muzzle of his weapon, then he would level it and let it burst again.

You did that, Lee thought. *You own it.*

From the other corner, Lee could hear the sporadic popping of LaRouche's pistol and the occasional blast from a shotgun. A quick glance over his shoulder revealed that only LaRouche and two other men remained. One of the other men was helping LaRouche cover the corner with his shotgun, and the second was positioning himself to rope down the elevator shaft.

"How you lookin'?" Lee yelled to LaRouche.

"Clear for now..."

Three more infected burst out of the western stairwell. Lee raked the hall with fire, killing two of them instantly and taking the third one down to the ground, where it scrabbled forward with one working arm and one working leg, its screech of fury turning to a pathetic coughing, yelping noise.

"Move out!" LaRouche yelled, and from the corner of his eye, Lee saw the man with the shotgun making a run for the elevator shaft. The sergeant followed up his command with a quick double tap from his pistol, and the slide locked back, empty. "I'm out!"

"Got you covered. Move!" Lee called out.

LaRouche spun and made for the elevator shaft. The man with the shotgun was standing at the edge and looking down, calling to someone before dropping his shotgun down to him. Then he swung onto the rope and slipped out of sight. LaRouche knelt down quickly and took hold of the rope. Lee didn't see him descend because he forced his attention back to the hallway.

Five more were coming out of the western stairwell, and another staggered out from the hallway where the man had gone quiet, a stringy piece of flesh hanging from its chin. It tottered around like it was drunk until the other five raced past it, and then it turned and followed suit, like any good herd animal.

Lee let out burst after burst, but they were fast, and they were getting closer. The last one collapsed nearly at his feet, causing him to jump back and let out a yelp as his mind prepared for the filthy thing to sink its teeth into his leg. It raised its head, still alive, and reached out in a slow, deliberate grab for Lee's feet, and Lee lost his cool for just a moment. He held the trigger down, the hallway flashing bright like a strobe as each of the bullets did their damage and left a mess of broken floor tiles and gore.

More were coming from the western stairwell, and more were coming out of the hallway, no longer interested in the fresh kill. The eastern hallway, now abandoned and unwatched, screamed for his attention. He knew how these things liked to attack from both sides.

He backed up so that his feet were just inches from the drop-off of the elevator shaft and he could cover both corners. His mouth felt full of sand, his rapid breathing like a harsh desert wind, sucking all the moisture out of him. His pulse stretched the arteries in his neck almost painfully. In the back of his mind, he registered tunnel vision setting in, and he forced himself to scan back and forth, back and forth. His whole world became the gun sight of the M249 with a background of the right corner, and then the left corner. Right corner. Left corner.

They came from the western hall first, running like they knew exactly where he was. There was no hesitation as they turned the corner and were instantly upon him. He couldn't back up— all he could do was fight. They screeched and he screamed back and held that trigger down like he wasn't supposed to do, but they were so close to him now that it really didn't matter.

The air in the hallway seemed to dim with a thin pink mist erupting out of dark, polluted flesh, and Lee closed his mouth and held his breath, though his body ached for more oxygen. Vaguely, he registered the sound of his radio squawking and could hear people at the bottom of the elevator shaft calling his name.

Three more infected from the western hallway, and one from the eastern hallway.

Even as they rounded the corner, only twenty feet away from him on either side, he knew he wouldn't be able to continue this fight. He was only delaying the inevitable.

He swept the hallway with another gale of chattering machine-gun fire, hoping to stall the encroaching infected for just a beat. Still holding the M249 with his right hand, he used his left to wrap the rope around his forearm twice and gripped it hard in his left hand. He knew this was going to hurt, but he didn't have the time to formulate a better plan, and any plan was better than no plan at all.

With the rope in hand, he leaped backward.

The last clear image he saw was two hands reaching out for his face, long, dirty fingernails and skin caked with unimaginable grime. And then he was falling into that dark abyss and he could feel the acceleration of his own body through the air, and it felt similar to a combat jump: dark and noisy and terrifying.

Then the slack on the rope ran out.

The cord went tight, ripping and sliding across the flesh of his left arm. He felt explosions in his joints—first his wrist, then his elbow, and the burning sensation was so intense in the palm of his hand and in the coil around his forearm that it nearly masked the tearing of his ligaments. He felt like he fell forever, building up heat as he went, like a meteor breaking the atmosphere, and he was convinced his arm was catching fire. No matter how hard he tried, he couldn't get a grip on the rope tight enough to stop his body from plummeting to the ground, and toward the end, the burning was so hot, he almost didn't care.

He didn't feel it when he hit the ground.

TWENTY-THREE

Fight

NO PLAN SURVIVES FIRST contact with the enemy.

This was a concept drilled into any soldier from day one as a recruit. It was reinforced mentally and physically, officially and unofficially, through indoctrination and through the military subculture. Nothing you did as a recruit was right, even if you were right. The instructors were always striving to achieve the sensation of failure, because it was imminent and inevitable that every soldier, every warrior would someday find himself in a position where even his best efforts were not enough and the greatest plan in the world still didn't work out. That failure could bring out two things in a man: forfeit or fight.

A normal man forfeits where a warrior fights.

The psychological evaluation for candidates of Project Hometown placed heavy focus on that very concept. They recognized that there would be no leadership, that the entire command structure would be eliminated, that the Coordinators would be operating in a vacuum. So they set out to find the warriors, the ones who just kept fighting because there was a fight to be fought. The ones who wouldn't ever forfeit. The ones who were too fucking stubborn to know when they'd been defeated. Because it was not the measure of a warrior whether his plan went off without a hitch, but how he reacted when that plan inevitably failed. Because the real plan for victory wasn't what you put down on paper; it was the heart of the man you put in the fight.

So when consciousness suddenly returned to Lee's mind, he fought. Through the agonizing pain in his left arm, through the throbbing in his freshly broken tailbone, through the inability to catch a full breath through his three cracked ribs, he found himself batting away LaRouche's hands as though the sergeant were an infected, and then punched him square in the face.

"Fuck!" LaRouche bent backward, warding off Lee's next blow and covering his broken nose with his other hand. Lee recovered his senses, realizing he was not being attacked, and stopped trying to beat the snot out of LaRouche. "Fuckin' A, Captain..."

Lee tried to say his name, but it came out jumbled. "Laharoof?"

And then he rolled onto his hands and knees and discovered all his new injuries as each movement brought out the pain in different places. They all jostled for attention and became just a white noise of pain, almost making it easier to ignore.

"You're hurt; you need to stay down." It was Julia speaking now.

"No..." Lee forced one foot to the ground, and

then lurched unsteadily to his feet. "Fi-fine...I'm fine."

The radio was still going off in his back pocket. It was a small miracle that it had even survived the fall. Lee tried to grab it and found his left hand somewhat uncooperative, so he tried his right hand and succeeded, though twisting his torso sent waves of sharp pain through his ribs. Harper spoke frantically on the radio, trying to reach him.

Lee keyed up. "Lee here." He blinked rapidly to clear spots from his vision as unconsciousness tried to mount a comeback. Above them, the elevator shaft rose up to a small square of light. That was the opening Lee had just jumped from. Crowded around that opening, the dark shapes of the infected were screaming at them in frustration, but they did not make the jump themselves. "Harper, where are you?"

"Where the fuck are *you*?" came the panicked reply. "I've been trying to...Fuck! Forget it!" Harper took an audible breath. In the background, a roaring engine but no gunfire. "We got plenty of attention when we rolled up to the hospital. We turned and ran, and almost all of them followed. But we lost 'em, so we're swinging back around. Where are you?"

Lee managed to pull intelligent thought from the fog hanging around his brain. "We're gonna be on the backside of the hospital. The north side. But listen..." Lee turned and looked into the maintenance tunnel, lit only by the glow of a few flashlights interspersed throughout the group. It illuminated enough of them for Lee to make a

quick head count. "Shit...I got about thirty survivors. All you got is the pickup."

"Well, God's on our side, brother!"

Lee looked at the radio, not comprehending.
"Yeah, that's nice, Harper. How are we gonna
move these people?"

"You remember Father Jim?"

Hope swept the fog right out of his mind. He
found himself smiling tentatively. "Yeah. What
about him?"

"I'll explain later. We're coming back up on
the hospital, near those big white tents. Where
are you?"

"I'm gonna hand you to Sergeant LaRouche so
he can guide you in." Lee shoved the radio into
LaRouche's hands.

Still stifling blood flow from his nose, LaRouche
took the radio and spoke with urgency. "When
you get inside the barricade, go to the left of the
parking garage, all the way around to the back of
the hospital. You'll see a bunch of utility boxes and
a brown door marked MAINTENANCE. We're right
on the other side of that door. Just tell us when
you're here and we'll make a run for it."

"Okay, just hang on for a second."

Lee pointed everyone forward. "Get up on that
exit, folks!"

The group turned obediently and, in tense
silence, moved to the door. The maintenance tunnel was not long, but it was tight, so two people
could barely walk abreast of each other. Both sides
were crammed with panels and power boxes and
other things Lee couldn't even name. Over their

heads ran a snakelike jumble of pipes and cables. As the group moved down the tunnel, Lee stooped to grab the M249 off the ground and it felt like every muscle and joint in his body was broken.

As they reached the door, LaRouche called out from behind them all. "Don't open the door yet. Wait for our ride to get here."

Lee regarded the sergeant's broken nose with a remorseful look. "Sorry about your nose."

LaRouche waved him off. "Five-second rule. No worries."

Lee almost smiled, remembering life in the barracks where pranks were common and often involved rudely waking someone from sleep. If you woke someone up and he beat your ass, you couldn't complain about it, because the rule stated that he wasn't responsible for anything he did within five seconds of waking up.

Lee's mind turned back to the situation at hand and he found himself wondering what the hell Harper and Father Jim had managed to bring that would help them get all the survivors out. And where had Father Jim even come from? Harper had gone back to Camp Ryder. Had Father Jim beat them there? And then Lee thought, *Harper didn't even have time to get back to Camp Ryder...*

Harper's voice sparked with static. "Okay. We see the door. We're outside. We got company, so let's haul ass."

"Move!" Lee shouted to the group.

The door flew open. Coming from the dark tunnel, even the waning daylight, diffused by cloud cover, seemed blinding. Lee's excitement and hope were replaced by dread as he heard the sound the survivors made as they broke out of the door and found themselves in daylight. All heads seemed to instantly look to their right and there was screaming and pointing and everyone started running much faster.

Spurred on, Lee tried to move through the crowd but found his tailbone and left leg sending electric shocks of pain up his spine with each step. His teeth were set in a rictus grin and he could feel the sweat going cold on his brow. He broke from the tunnel and spun to the right.

About a hundred yards out from them, a group of about twenty infected had taken notice of them and were coming in fast. Lee took a knee, almost passing out with the agony of the movement, but forced himself to steady his aim. One quick pull— five rounds downrange—and two creatures fell. Another pull, another target down. But they were fanning out, making it difficult for Lee's bursts to catch more than one target at a time, as though they knew that bunching together made them more vulnerable to machine-gun fire.

They can't think, Lee had to remind himself. The logical parts of their brains were gone, eaten through to nothing. Anything that looked like reasoning was either a coincidence or some random firing of leftover synapses.

Right?

He kept firing, picking his targets as they drew closer and closer and he kept pulling that trigger every time the sights lined up. Someone was yelling his name from behind him when finally the M249 ran out of ammunition and became a twenty-pound paperweight. Lee decided to drop the gun in the very spot that it ran dry.

There were still about ten infected running for him.

Maybe less, maybe more.

Things were getting a bit hazy now.

He turned and noticed the world having to take a second to catch up with him. When he had focused and was hobbling as fast as his damaged body could handle, the vision of the road cleared and he saw the most unlikely of vehicles sitting in the roadway, with Harper hanging out of the open door and waving at him like a madman.

Somewhere, they had picked up an activity bus.

It was a big white machine, not quite the size of the huge yellow school buses, but with plenty of room for all of the survivors if they crammed in tight. On the side of it, underneath the bank of windows, Lee could read in big blue letters, FIRST BAPTIST CHURCH, and he almost laughed at the strange coincidence of it all. Where the hell did they get that thing?

Idling in front of the church bus was the Dodge Ram 2500, its bed still packed full of supplies, and it didn't look like a single package or pail had been touched. In the driver's seat of the pickup truck, Miller looked beside himself with the desire to leave the area and seemed like he might peel out at any second.

Lee reached the church bus and Harper and LaRouche hauled him in even as it started rolling. One of the infected tried to jump at the front of the bus but only smashed its head against the windshield, leaving a bloody mark and a wide crack in the glass before tumbling to the side and becoming a small speed bump.

"You all right, Captain?" LaRouche yelled.

Lee found himself leaning against the driver's seat, his M4 squashed uncomfortably against his back, his legs dangling into the small steps down to the bus doors. He craned his neck to see who was driving the bus and discovered Father Jim looking down on him with a genuine smile.

Lee expected some platitude or scripture about the Lord rescuing them, but the priest just nodded knowingly. He must have seen the look in Lee's eyes, the disbelief that somehow Father Jim had been at the right place at the right time with just the right equipment to save their asses, and so Father Jim said nothing. Instead, he patted Lee on the shoulder and steered the bus in a wide left-hand turn, banking around the northeastern side of the hospital as a few infected stragglers chased madly after them.

"Are you okay?" LaRouche repeated, kneeling down so they were on eye level with each other.

Lee tried to take a deep breath, felt the pain spike through his ribs, but managed to control the wince and give a thumbs-up. "All good here, Sergeant."

The bus listed slightly as they cornered, reaching Brightleaf Boulevard again and turning south toward Camp Ryder. Toward safety. Lee felt an immense relief like a warm blanket being pulled over his drowsy body. Out to the right of the bus, the parking lot of the Johnston Memorial Hospital stretched, empty save for a few bodies and a few cars. The enormous horde that had occupied it so recently had disappeared, running off into Smithfield to chase Harper in a vehicle they would never catch. To the left of the main hospital wing, Lee could see the parking garage and the still-smoking ruins of the pickup truck that LaRouche and Harper and Miller had unintentionally lit on fire. Behind the smoldering ruins was the hulk of the big green Humvee, and it looked like it was smashed into the wall of the hospital, right where the door had been.

Staring at the scene, Lee couldn't help but laugh, though the pain it brought quickly stifled it. That must have been what Milo and his men were struggling with in the stairwell. To keep them from being attacked while they stole back their pickup full of supplies, LaRouche, Harper, and Miller had wedged the Humvee against the door so no one could get out.

Lee had to admit that was clever thinking.

Too bad in a way, though.

It seemed like a waste to leave the Humvee there.

Lee was about to close his eyes and relax for a brief moment when movement from the rooftop of the hospital caught his eye. He sat up, gritting his teeth, his eyes narrowing. LaRouche noticed the intense focus and spun to look out the window.

"What? What do you see?"

Lee pointed to the top of the building. "Is that..."

A dark figure was sprinting along the rooftop. The weird, loping gait was a dead giveaway to anyone who knew him, and LaRouche almost immediately responded. "Fuck! That's Milo!"

"What?" Harper snapped his head around. "How the hell did he get out alive?"

LaRouche jabbed a finger out toward the hospital. "He must have escaped to the roof somehow."

It was clear what Milo's objective was. The top level of the garage was only a short drop from the roof of the hospital, and without a doubt he was heading for that. He was making a run for the Humvee.

TWENTY-FOUR

THE RIVER

LEE PULLED HIMSELF UPRIGHT, looking through the windshield at the pickup truck driving just ahead of them. "Tell Miller to stop."

"What?" LaRouche put a hand to his chest. "We can't stop! You're injured! You need to—"

"Tell him to stop!" Lee shouted, causing both LaRouche and Father Jim to jump.

The sergeant must have heard something in Lee's voice that told him this was not the time to argue. He put the radio to his mouth. "Miller, this is Sergeant LaRouche. Stop right there. We're going to stop."

The response was instant and high-pitched. "We can't stop now!"

Lee snatched the radio out of LaRouche's hands. "Fucking stop the truck, Miller! Milo's getting away! He's got my fuckin' GPS!"

Realization dawned on the faces around Lee. Without the GPS, their safety, their security, the presence of food and ammunition and medical supplies would be limited once again. They all seemed to realize how much they had believed in Lee, that he could rescue them, that he could rebuild them. But without the resources, Lee was just a good soldier. Someone you'd like to have in a fight but not much else.

Ahead of them, Miller applied the brakes sharply.

The bus lurched as Father Jim pulled to a stop to avoid slamming into the pickup truck.

Lee was off the bus before anyone could stop him, hobbling toward the Dodge Ram, trying to keep the pressure off his left leg. Stiffly, he pulled his M4 off of his back as he approached the driver's door and yanked it open.

"Scoot over," he barked.

Miller threw the truck in park and jumped over into the passenger seat.

"Hold this." Lee shoved his M4 into Miller's hands and struggled for a moment to get himself into the driver's seat with much grunting and swearing and rapid, shallow breathing that hissed through his clenched teeth. Through the open door, they could hear the sound of tires squealing on pavement and when they looked up, they could just see the rounded green hump of the Humvee disappearing down into the parking garage, its long antenna waving good-bye to them.

Lee put the truck in drive, then seemed to realize something. He turned and faced Miller. "If you wanna get out, now's the time to do it."

Miller didn't hesitate. "You know I'm with you, Captain."

Lee slammed on the accelerator. The engine roared and the vehicle rose up off its shocks, tearing down Brightleaf Boulevard. They watched the Humvee fly out of the darkness of the parking garage, clipping a cement barrier as it hauled toward the checkpoint and the street just beyond.

Lee found his grip on the steering wheel tenuous and had to hold it with both hands, just to make sure it didn't slip. On the good side, his hand was regaining some range of movement. The speedometer swelled up to sixty-five miles per hour before he had to slam on the brakes to make the right turn onto North Street. Just ahead, the Humvee emerged from the checkpoint onto North Street about two blocks ahead of them.

It seemed that Milo knew he was being pursued.

More than that, it looked like he was trying pretty damned hard to get away.

Not so brave now, without his pack of goons.

"Tell the bus not to follow us." Lee's voice was loud and strained. "Tell them to go straight back to Camp Ryder. We'll meet up with them there once we deal with Milo."

Miller seemed to realize what sticking with the captain entailed. "Shit. Okay." He keyed the mic. "Miller to anyone on the bus. Don't follow us. Captain Harden says go straight back to Camp Ryder. We will meet you there."

There was hesitation in LaRouche's response. "I read you. Be careful."

From the tone of his voice, Lee could tell that LaRouche didn't want to leave the fight behind him, but it was too late now. He couldn't follow Lee into battle and bring all the innocent civilians with him. Lee knew from watching LaRouche that he wasn't one to back down from a fight. But sometimes one had to swallow that down and do what was right for other people.

Miller's voice broke through his reverie. "You okay, Captain? You look pretty banged up."

Banged up?

He'd been blown up, lost a tooth, shot through the shoulder, and had taken a three-story fall with a rope wrapped around his wrist that kept him from dying but ripped nearly every ligament in his left arm. He could barely breathe through his cracked ribs, barely walk with his left leg, and barely sit with his busted tailbone.

Yeah. Maybe he was a little banged up.

"I'm still breathing," Lee said stubbornly, perhaps more to convince himself than Miller. He recalled instructors in his survival course taking a half gallon of corn syrup with red dye in it and spilling it out on a patch of pavement. They had pointed to the big puddle and said, *Take a good look at that, gentlemen. Remember the size of that puddle. That's how much blood the average male can lose before he's in danger of dying. If you feel like dying before you see that much blood on the ground, you're just being weak.*

Don't be weak.

They were gaining on Milo when the Humvee hit the brakes hard and laid rubber trying to make the left turn from North Street onto Second Street, nearly losing control and planting the big green vehicle in the living room of a house.

Lee slowed in time to make the turn and then accelerated again. Milo's choice of the Humvee as a getaway vehicle was probably not smart. If he'd taken the Chevrolet Lumina, he might be putting distance between them, but a military Humvee peaked out around seventy miles per hour and accelerated like a tired old warhorse compared to the quick acceleration of the Dodge Ram. After a moment of pressing the gas pedal to the floor, they were right on his ass.

Milo swerved back and forth in the roadway, trying to wait until the last second to dodge abandoned cars. Lee's reactions were quick and he kept the pickup right behind the olive green tailgate. So when Milo hit the right-hand turn from Second Street onto an inviting four-lane stretch of road, Lee followed, thinking that the four lanes were going to give Milo room to maneuver and possibly get away.

Lee noticed it immediately. The way the land sloped off just slightly but the road elevated just a bit. The way all the businesses and houses just suddenly stopped. How the sides of the road went from barren shoulder to concrete abutments.

"Look out!" Miller pointed.

"I see it." Lee applied the brakes just a second before Milo did.

It wasn't the bridge up ahead that stopped them but the concrete barricades that spanned from abutment to abutment, barring anyone from entering or leaving by crossing the river that flowed underneath it. As had become the usual thing, the barricades were topped with concertina wire, and on the Smithfield side of the bridge, a single sheriff's vehicle sat abandoned.

The pickup truck came to a screeching halt.

It only took the briefest of seconds for Milo to start moving again. The Humvee lurched forward and to the right, hitting the curb and heading for the steep, muddy embankment that led from the road down to the river.

"What the fuck?" Miller sounded bewildered. "Can he make it across in that thing?"

Lee took a glance at the river and knew the answer to that question without too much thought. "There's no fucking way."

The water underneath the bridge was high and angry and brown. The heavy summer rain had swollen its banks so that they licked the edges of a paved jogging path that ran alongside the water. Some sections of the jogging path were just barely submerged under roughly an inch of murky water.

But despite the ugly look of the river, Milo appeared to have made up his mind. The Humvee rumbled quickly down the embankment, ran along the wet jogging path for less than a hundred feet before finding a gap in the trees big enough to squeeze through, and made for the water.

"Oh, my God," Miller murmured.

For a brief moment, Lee thought the vehicle was going to make it. It hit the water with a mighty splash and surged forward as though it were built for amphibious operations. But then the front end rocked forward, dipping below the waterline and not coming back up. Lee wondered how many people had attempted this very same maneuver as they tried to escape the horrors of whatever had occurred in Smithfield, only to drown in their vehicles.

Perhaps it was one of these submerged vehicles

that the Humvee landed on, because it stopped sinking after a moment, leaving the top of the vehicle above water. Lee could see about six inches of the doors, but there was no way Milo was going to be able to push them open with the water rushing against the sides of the vehicle.

"He's gonna be trapped in there," Miller observed coldly.

But he spoke too soon.

A pair of wiry arms reached out of the circular opening of the gun turret, and after a brief moment, a waterlogged figure dragged himself out of the interior of the Humvee, one hand on the roof, one hand on the .50-caliber machine gun on the back end. And then Milo looked right at them.

Lee knew what was about to happen and opened his door, simultaneously reaching for his M4 only to discover that Miller was no longer in the passenger seat and neither was Lee's rifle. The younger man had already stepped out of the car and was raising the M4 to his shoulder even as Milo swung the big gun on them and gripped it with both hands.

Miller took the shot.

The bullet hit Milo with a wet *smack* that Lee could hear even from fifty yards away. He could see the spray of misting blood and water come off of Milo's back as the man pitched backward into the river.

Miller let out an audible breath.

"Holy shit." Lee raised his eyebrows at the impressive shot but really couldn't come up with anything else to say.

From behind the bulky green vehicle, Lee spied the splashing water, something moving around just outside of their view. He began hobbling as quickly as he could toward the embankment. "If he's still alive, he's gonna try to run."

Lee managed to get himself to the side of the road, Miller walking right at his side. They had just begun picking their way down the embankment to the jogging path when they saw Milo lurch away from the sunken truck, splashing through the water with one hand clutching the left side of his chest. His dark T-shirt was already soaked and it was impossible to tell where the shot had landed or whether it had gone all the way through, but it had obviously not debilitated him.

Miller broke into a run, still holding Lee's M4. "He's gonna get away!"

"Wait!" Lee reached out and tried to snag Miller's arm, missing by inches.

But Miller was focused, like a dog running down a rabbit. He hit the bottom of the hill and all semblance of caution was thrown to the wind on the level pavement of the jogging path. Holding the M4 in both arms, he sprinted after Milo with everything he had.

Lee decided the embankment would take too long for him to navigate on foot. He took two painful running steps and then jumped, hitting the ground on his already broken tailbone and sliding down the slick mud of the embankment. He shouted after the stupid kid running in front of him.

"Miller! Get the fuck back here!"

If Miller even heard him, he gave no response.

Lee tumbled to the bottom of the embankment and rolled onto the jogging path, feeling his body surrounded by cool, shallow water in this small patch of submerged concrete. For a moment, he couldn't feel anything. He stared up at the mottled gray of the sky, moving and swirling in the atmospheric winds. It was almost peaceful.

He coughed and picked himself up.

Down the path, Miller was about twenty-five yards in front of Lee, and Milo was another ten yards in front of him. Miller's feet pounded the shallow water, causing white crowns of glistening water to explode up around his feet with every stride. Lee was oddly reminded of his childhood; playing in the rain in his yard, he would pretend he was a soldier in Vietnam and would run around, slamming his foot down in each puddle he came across to give it the effect of an explosion at his feet. But the explosion never brought him down, and he just kept running, an invincible man. And Miller ran through the rain with that same mindless resolve to keep going, as though he couldn't be hurt.

Milo was obviously wounded and was trundling along about as quickly as Lee. Miller gained ground rapidly, and the quick glances that Milo threw over his shoulder said that he knew what was coming.

Lee saw it, even from where he was, almost thirty yards behind them. He could see Milo reach for something on his right leg, and then he stopped running. Lee was too far away to do anything but yell out to Miller.

"He's got a gun!"

Finally, Miller saw the gun in Milo's hand, the big .357 revolver he always carried. Miller staggered to a stop as the revolver swung up at the same time, leveling the M4. The two men were less than twenty feet from each other, Milo extending his right arm, the end of which was only a big silver revolver, and Miller leaning back, with the stock of the rifle tucked under his arm, almost aiming from the hip.

The two men began shooting at each other.

It all happened in the span of a second.

The .357 fired. Miller jerked backward as the slug passed through his chest, but he didn't lose his footing. He fired twice in response, the first round splashing the water at Milo's feet and the second piercing him in the gut. The revolver roared again, and this time Miller did lose his footing. He staggered backward and fell to his knees, where he swooned like a drunkard but managed to fire three more times. Two of the three shots found their mark—one in Milo's leg and another into his right side, traveling up as it went through his body and smashing through his shoulder blade.

And then it was over.

Lee moved forward, and he could hear the rising groan of pain coming from Miller. Beyond Miller's sprawled form, Milo squirmed like a fish on the deck of a boat, trying to get his legs under him again. He was still trying to make a run for it, not yet realizing that the last bullet had pulverized his spleen and pierced his left lung before it had exited out of his back. No amount of running was ever going to save him.

Lee reached him just as he succeeded in rolling onto his hands and knees, still holding that silver revolver in his left hand. Milo seemed to realize that Lee was almost upon him and tried to spin, bringing his weapon to bear, but Lee swiped at it with one swift hand and knocked the thing clear across the jogging path and into the deeper water. Milo watched it leave his fingers with a hiss of pain.

There was nothing momentous about it, no poetic justice, nothing artful. Lee did not use Milo's own words against him or have anything sharp or clever to say. There was just a brief and violent struggle, during which neither made eye contact with the other. Milo tried for a moment to scratch at Lee's eyes, but Lee pinned his arms and then took hold of Milo's neck with his good right hand. He slammed Milo's head back into the concrete repeatedly, until the hard crack of the skull hitting pavement became a much softer, wetter sound.

Milo's body went limp.

Lee released his neck, breathing hard.

He looked up at the sky, not wanting to look at what he'd done. Far above him, the pattern of clouds was nearly indiscernible. It was all just one big gray blob, backlit by a sun that couldn't quite break through.

A weak cough from behind him brought Lee's attention back to the here and now. He quickly searched Milo's body and located the GPS in Milo's back pants pocket. The sturdy construction of it had kept it from being damaged and had sealed it against the water. Lee put it in his pocket.

Then he walked back to Miller, who no longer moaned, because he struggled even to breathe. All around him, the shallow water had turned red. Long tendrils of it were caught in the current and gliding slowly downstream. Lee thought he could hear the wet wheezing noise of a sucking chest wound, but he couldn't be certain over Miller's labored breathing.

Lee knelt down next to him, looking up at the pickup truck with all of their medical equipment, parked at the top of the embankment. It seemed farther away than Lee remembered it. He stared back down into Miller's face and tried to look and sound confident. "Alright, buddy. I'm gonna run up to the truck to get something to fix you, okay?"

Miller looked scared, and he nodded. Tears were running down the sides of his face.

Lee grabbed his rifle off the ground and slung into it. He moved as quickly as he could to the embankment and worked his way up on his hands and knees. Going up was much more difficult than going down, and twice he slipped in the mud, nearly losing all the progress he had gained. And when he reached the top, feeling somewhat relieved and triumphant, he realized that his little journey was nothing more than a waste of time, because he would never be able to get to the truck with the hundreds of infected coming toward him.

TWENTY-FIVE

The Return

LESS THAN THREE HUNDRED yards down the four-lane road on which their pickup truck was parked, Lee could see the massive throng of infected, stretching the entire width of the four lanes, from building-front to building-front. They were not sprinting, but neither were they taking their time. They had heard the gunfire and were coming to investigate.

Is gunfire something they've begun to equate with food? Lee wondered. Or was it simply a loud stimulus to respond to? Lee knew that animals, even the less intelligent ones, were quick to pick up on anything that meant they could eat.

Lee would have to cross two wide-open lanes to reach the pickup truck. The horde would see him, and then they would charge. He looked desperately for something he could use as concealment to get to the truck, but the road was bare of even the trash and bodies that Lee had seen plentifully elsewhere in the city. It was almost a mockery.

His only chance was to hide until the horde passed. Since they were moving with less haste than usual, Lee thought he might have enough time. He slid quickly down the embankment and limped over to Miller's form. They needed to hide, and the closest spot to do that was the half-submerged Humvee. He immediately grabbed the kid's arm and struggled to hoist him up onto his feet.

"Come on, buddy. We've got company."

"No..." Miller managed.

"Yep." Lee struggled and finally pulled Miller into the water, where he became much lighter. The current was strong, but Lee fought against it, towing the younger guy behind him as he worked his way toward the front of the Humvee, trying to keep Miller's head above water. If he could make it to the front, the vehicle would hide them from the view of the infected, and he hoped they wouldn't venture out into the water.

The current was much stronger at the front of the Humvee. The vehicle's bulk had shielded them from much of the river's pull, but now Lee felt it in all its rushing anger, as though it had been sent by nature for the sole purpose of sweeping him away. He hooked his right arm through the ram bar at the front of the vehicle. The other arm he wrapped around Miller's chest, keeping it as tight as he could with his damaged wrist.

Miller moaned.

"It's okay, man." The kid's head rested on Lee's shoulder, just above the water. His skin was cold. "Just hang on. We only have to wait until these crazies are gone and then we can get you some help. Just stay strong for me and don't fall asleep. Can you do that for me?"

Miller didn't respond.

Lee felt his stomach drop and he shook the kid slightly, eliciting another moan. Good. He was still there, still fighting.

From behind them, Lee could hear the growing sound of the approaching infected. When they were not excited, they issued strange guttural noises back and forth, and Lee could have sworn they were communicating on some instinctive level. The grumbling noises grew to a loud rumble, but Lee could not see them from where he clung to the front of the Humvee. In his mind he could imagine all of them, hundreds of them, packing the banks of the river, milling mindlessly back and forth.

Their growling grew excited as they found Milo's body and fed on it. A brief but ferocious fight broke out between a couple of them that sounded like a pair of dogs in a pit. Lee could only imagine that they were fighting over scraps of Milo's flesh.

The sunlight grew dim.

Lee wasn't sure how long it had been. The infected still milled around behind them, but it sounded as though they had finally finished feeding on Milo. Lee hoped they would leave in search of other food. He wondered to himself how much normal food the infected scavenged out of trash bins and whatever convenience and grocery stores still had products in them. Marie had mentioned that they were drawn to the smell of cooking food. Then, Lee had to wonder how long a horde this size could survive on the scraps and dead bodies that littered the city streets. Perhaps the hordes were the first step when food was plentiful, and the packs only came afterward when they realized on some subconscious level that they needed to hunt to survive.

Hours passed.

It was now completely dark out. The cloud cover had dissipated in the last hour and the moon was nearly full, illuminating everything in a cold chrome light. Lee's thinking became muddy. Thoughts would seem important and poignant and then they would be quickly forgotten, only to leave him confused and frustrated. The water was not what he would consider cold, but after hours of exposure in it, the river was beginning to take its toll, making his whole body shake. His muscles ached with the strain of holding onto the Humvee's ram bar and holding onto Miller.

The infected were quiet now but not gone. He could still hear them muttering behind him, sometimes their voices so low that the sound of the water overcame them, and other times they barked loudly at each other.

Lee went in and out of consciousness. He wouldn't define it as sleep or passing out, because he never once let go of Miller. But he would open his eyes and have the sense that his last jumble of confused thoughts had been the rambling of his dreaming mind, and that time had passed.

The whole night, he had been afraid to stir Miller for fear that he would yell or moan and draw the attention of the infected, sending them into a frenzy. So he stayed quiet and still and hoped and prayed that Miller would stay alive just a little while longer.

It was sometime in the early morning, just as the sky above his head had begun to turn a deep, melancholy blue, that he realized Miller was stiff in his arms. Lee pressed his face against the side of Miller's and felt the chill that wasn't just cold skin but the tombstone coldness of death.

Lee held on a little while longer, though he couldn't explain to himself why. Perhaps he didn't want to simply let Miller go and be discarded like all of the other bodies in Smithfield. Perhaps he saw himself in this kid. He had seen him fight with everything he had and still come up short, and that sense of impending mortality scared Lee more than anything else.

But eventually he let Miller slip out of his arms.

The current took him, much gentler now that the water had receded some. Lee watched him, floating on his back in the pale half light of dawn, and pictured him as a boy, just spending a warm summer night floating away on the river.

It was full light by the time Lee could no longer hear the strange noises of the infected. He moved for the first time in hours and felt the screaming pain of his stiff muscles and injuries. He drifted slowly to the edge of the Humvee and looked around at the riverbank, where he could see a bloody mound of clothing and gristle that used to be Milo.

Other than Milo's remains, the banks of the river were empty.

Slowly but surely, he made his way to the riverbank. Steam was rolling up off the water as the sun began to crest the trees and buildings and beat down on the river's surface. His skin felt flimsy and waterlogged, though his mouth was parched. He'd been thirsty all night but knew better than to drink the river water, especially with all the dead bodies decomposing in the streets. His left wrist was swollen badly, though he thought that the buoyancy of the water may have helped alleviate some of the pressure and pain in his ribs. What the dirty river water had not done for him was help the bullet wound to his shoulder. The skin around it was tight and hot and Lee could feel fever settling in as an infection took hold. As he crawled out of the numbing water, all of these injuries began to grumble more loudly.

He wanted to rest, but this was not the place.

Not with so many infected nearby.

He made his way with much pain and effort back up the embankment, cresting it with caution this time and peering down the four-lane road but seeing nothing. He lay there for a moment, his torso on the flat ground and his legs hanging off the embankment. He was tempted to close his eyes, but he knew that if he did, he might fall asleep right there. He knew he had only been awake for close to thirty hours, but the physical pain sapped strength and stamina. The body needed rest to heal itself, and it made its demands known by causing the mind to be fuzzy and drowsy.

Don't be weak...

He blinked rapidly, thinking he may have just fallen asleep for a moment.

Were the shadows different? He didn't think so.

He slithered out of the embankment and used the concrete abutment of the bridge to haul himself to his feet. He felt the weight of his M4 tapping him on the back of the leg. It was still slung faithfully around his shoulders. After being in the silty river all night, he was sure it would be clogged up with grime. It would probably still work, though.

He hitched across the road to where the pickup truck sat. It wasn't until he was almost touching it that he realized he had left it running. Swearing under his breath but too tired to put much effort into it, he gently closed the front passenger door that Miller had left open, then crossed in front of the car, taking a moment to inspect the inside and make sure that no maniacs had taken up residence in the backseat during the night.

It was empty.

He found half a bottle of water in the backseat of the vehicle and guzzled it. It was warm, but it was clean and at least moistened his dry tongue. He discovered several of the rifles were missing, possibly handed out to Father Jim's people in case there was a firefight during the rescue. Or possibly looted by Milo's goons. He decided to swap his personalized M4 for one of the fresh and clean standard-issue M4s in the back. His M4 would probably still function with the dirty river water in it, but why take the chance? He appropriated one of the shoulder-sling magazine pouches, since his vest was now lost somewhere in the hospital. He loaded four magazines, placing three in the shoulder sling and one in the brand-new M4. He put his dirty, silt-clogged rifle on the floorboard of the truck.

He sat down in the driver's seat and closed his door, again making sure not to slam it. Looking at the fuel gauge, he saw that the needle was hovering just above the "E" line but the gas light had not yet come on. It took him a moment to figure out how it could be that the truck was not completely empty by now, but finally remembered that Milo's crew had stolen it and incorporated it into their little fleet of trucks. There was a good chance Milo liked his fuel tanks topped off, and they'd had plenty of gas that they had confiscated from groups of survivors.

At least until Harper and Miller and LaRouche blew it up.

He stowed his M4 in the passenger seat next to him and then put the vehicle in gear, spinning a wide U-turn so that he was heading directly into the rising sun. He drove with an empty mind, his thoughts so knotted that he could not possibly untangle them in the exhausted state he was in. So he simply ignored them and watched the white lines on the road pass him by.

At Brightleaf Boulevard he stopped and looked in both directions. He saw no sign of the massive horde that had populated the area only so recently. He recalled those sinewy grabbing hands with their fingers like claws and the way their ripped and tattered clothes hung off of their emaciated bodies. The horde of infected that populated Smithfield was starving, he was sure of it. The question that remained was whether that would cause them to die off. Or would they simply adapt, breaking into packs to more efficiently hunt for food?

He recalled the barricades farther south on Brightleaf Boulevard. However, two blocks down the road, he could see a small bridge where a set of railroad tracks passed over, running parallel to the boulevard. He was fairly confident that whoever was responsible for the Smithfield quarantine had not barricaded the tracks. Lee wasn't sure if this was the fastest way around the barricades, but decided he didn't want to waste fuel looking for another way out. A short and bumpy ride later, he passed the barricades on Brightleaf Boulevard and found his way back to the road.

He brought the truck up to forty-five miles per hour and headed south for Camp Ryder.

The roads seemed empty, as though they lacked the teeming danger of the previous two days. Lee knew it was his own exhaustion causing complacency and he forced himself to approach the abandoned cars and possible roadblocks with vigilance. But he never saw a soul. It was as though all the small-time crooks had heard that Milo was going to be in the area and had packed up their little operations until they were sure he was gone. Lee could only imagine what Milo would have done to them if they'd tried to attack his convoy.

The only living creatures he passed were three infected that stood by the side of the highway, just outside of the woods that bordered the road. When Lee saw them, he sped up, but they merely watched him pass without making a move to chase him. For a brief second, as the truck was parallel to them and Lee was looking out the passenger-side window at them, he thought that perhaps they were not infected at all. But he could see the wild eyes, the ripped and tattered clothing, the dried blood that ran down their chins and necks, and the way their clawlike hands worked convulsively as though strangling the air at their sides.

Looking at them staring back at him with indifference, Lee felt almost as though it was a safari and he was passing a pack of hyenas that knew he was only prey when he stepped out of the big metal canister he was in. Or perhaps they had already eaten their fill.

Lee sped away from them, a cold feeling in his gut.

It was still morning when he pulled down the dirt road to Camp Ryder.

In his mind, he braced himself. The last week had not been kind to Lee. He had learned that this world he was in was much different than the one he had operated in previously. Even a combat zone was nothing compared to the randomness of this turmoil. At least when he had been deployed, he knew that he had a base to go back to that would be standing there when he returned from his patrols. Here, he didn't know what to expect and so he feared the worst. He pictured the gates of Camp Ryder ripped from their hinges, all the shanties burned to smoking rubble, and the bodies of all the survivors stacked up like cordwood in the big fire pit in the center of camp.

But when he turned through the last curve of the dirt road, the gates still stood intact, with a guard who stared at the approaching truck like he couldn't believe his eyes. Lee could see his mouth moving suddenly, and all the people behind him, who were busying themselves with their everyday tasks of survival, simply stopped what they were doing and all heads turned to see the approaching truck.

Then other people were running.

Bus was the first to the gate, flinging it open. Harper was close behind him, with LaRouche in tow. Lee felt at first elated to see friendly faces, and then sickening disappointment as he knew what he would have to tell them.

Miller died. I couldn't save him. I tried my best, but my best wasn't enough.

I couldn't save Miller.

Lee drove through the gate with a heavy heart. When he put the truck in park, he opened the door and stepped out slowly and gingerly. Bus was there with tired, distraught eyes, and Angela appeared next to him. She hesitated for a brief moment, but then, as though she couldn't contain herself, she threw her arms around him and squeezed him so tightly that he nearly cried out. He felt her body, warm against his still-damp clothes, and her hair brushed against his neck.

It was a strange and altering feeling for him that he couldn't quite explain. He wouldn't call it love or attraction or anything even close. But it was a unique sense of comfort, of human closeness. It was something his life had lacked, even before the fall. Like any human being, he craved that connection and he found himself putting his own arm around her and holding on to her. But the embrace lasted for only a brief second before Angela pulled away, her face flushed with embarrassment. She didn't meet his eyes, but she smiled tightly as she stepped back away from him.

"We were very worried about you," she said simply.

When she was out of the way, Bus swooped in to support him by slipping Lee's uninjured right arm over his broad shoulders. He had clearly seen the pain on Lee's face when Angela had embraced him, and that Lee was favoring his left leg.

"You gotta stop getting injured," Bus said as lightly as he could.

Lee winced as they moved. "I just love the attention."

Then Harper was there too. Lee could see him looking back at the truck with a grave sort of certainty in his eyes. They glanced at each other and neither spoke a word because none needed to be spoken. Harper was no blood relation to Miller, but it was clear even to Lee that the two had formed a bond. They had watched out for each other. Like a father and son. Harper didn't ask about Miller in that moment, though he would later ask Lee how he had died, and Lee would tell him the truth: He died fighting with everything he had, and Harper would have been proud. But in that silent moment between them, Harper simply put an arm around Lee's waist to help support him as they walked, and Lee could see the redness in his eyes and the brine that welled up but never spilled over.

They sat him on the same cot that he had occupied before, when Doc had patched him up.

Doc...

Lee started to tell them about Doc. At first they told him to rest and that he could explain things later, but eventually they were quiet and they just listened while Jenny wordlessly began to clean the gunshot wound to Lee's shoulder. She wept silently as she worked, her hot tears landing on Lee's arm. He told them about Doc's betrayal, but also about how he'd been given no choice, that he had done it for his fiancée, whom Milo had captured and held for ransom.

He told them that Milo was dead, and most of his men with him, though no one knew what had become of Deputy Shumate. LaRouche had already told them about the gasoline explosion and the shoot-out inside the hospital, but they all appeared relieved to learn that the ringleader was no longer going to be a problem. Without Milo's fanatical leadership, the rest of his crew were just individual sociopaths, people to be avoided but without a common bond to unite them.

When Lee had nothing else to report, Harper told him about how he and Miller had returned to steal back their truck full of supplies. He told them about how LaRouche had rigged the claymore mine to the grille of the Chevrolet Lumina and used it to take out the guards. Harper seemed very proud of this, though he choked up when he spoke of Miller. He went on to explain how they had headed out of Smithfield, using the same rail-road tracks that Lee had used to get around the barricades, and how just as they were turning onto Highway 210 to return to Camp Ryder, they saw the church bus pass them by, full of Father Jim's people.

Father Jim, who had come in to check on Lee, laughed good-naturedly as he told Lee how Harper had driven up behind them so aggressively, honking his horn and flashing his lights, that they almost opened fire on him, thinking he was a desperate raider. Luckily, one of the children in the group recognized who was inside the truck before that happened, and they pulled to the side of the road, where Harper told them about what had happened in Smithfield.

Father Jim smiled and placed a gentle hand on Lee's shoulder. "After what you did for us, there was no possible way I could turn my back on you. And all of my people felt the same way." His voice grew more serious. "We were lucky we were able to help without having to kill anyone, but I want you to know that we were fully prepared to defend you, whatever that entailed."

Lee nodded, wondering once again what the background of this priest was.

Julia also came in, with Marie close behind. Marie spouted profuse thanks, but Julia, who appeared to have some medical training, set to work helping Jenny put Lee back together again. They cleaned and patched up the shoulder wound as best they could. It was too old to immediately stitch closed, especially since they agreed that infection had set in. They quickly gave him a round of Cephalexin, an antibiotic that they appropriated from the medical supplies Doc had packed for them. They gave him plenty of water while they poked and prodded him, explaining that they did not want to use one of their indispensable IV packs, since his dehydration was not severe.

After much discomfort and answering questions like, "Does it hurt when I do this?" and, "Can you move your fingers like this?" they explained to him that, from what they could tell, he had torn the ligaments in his wrist and elbow and had been lucky that his shoulder had not been pulled out of its socket. They further concluded that his tailbone was indeed broken, his right collarbone fractured or badly bruised, that three of his ribs on the right side were either broken or badly bruised (without an x-ray machine it was difficult to tell for sure), and that he had a pretty severe high ankle sprain on his left leg. For good measure, several of the stitches that Doc had put in his back had ripped out and needed to be replaced, and he had managed to get them infected.

As they worked, his friends silently trickled out of the room. Eventually it was just Julia and Jenny fussing over him, and then it was just Jenny, testing his temperature and asking him if he needed anything. When he said that he was fine, she only smiled, clearly knowing that he was far from fine but too proud to admit it.

TWENTY-SIX

―――

THE ROAD AHEAD

HARPER APPEARED AFTER A short time. His eyes were dry now, but the redness at the rims and the rawness around his nose gave him away. He carried a long, straight branch of some hardwood. He had affixed a crossbeam at the top so it made a tall *T* shape. The crossbeam was wrapped in cloth to pad it.

"Made a crutch for you." Harper handed it to Lee.

Lee felt humbled by the gesture. "Thank you, Harper."

Harper stuffed his hands in the pockets of his pants. "It'll hurt like hell with your cracked ribs, but knowing you, you won't be wanting to sit in bed for long."

Lee smiled. "Yeah, I guess you're right."

He took the crutch with his right hand, because they'd wrapped his left up with enough ACE bandages to keep it from moving too much, and pulled himself to his feet. It seemed that the less he used his left foot, the more tender the ankle became, but he also knew he needed to rest it. He got the padded crossbeam under his left arm and held it in there tightly. Lee tested it out, keeping pressure off of his left foot as much as possible, and walked around the medical trailer with it. Jenny kept a watchful eye on him but didn't object. Harper had been right on both counts: it hurt like the dickens on his ribs, and Lee definitely wasn't in the mood to sit in bed until he healed up. Survival was a twenty-four-hour job, no days off and no vacations.

"It's good." Lee nodded.

"One other thing I thought you should see." Harper pointed out toward the Ryder factory, just to their left. Lee moved forward with his crutch to the edge of the medical trailer so he could see what Harper was pointing at. The two-story build-ing stood in dark relief against the sky. Hanging from the tall awning over the entrance to the fac-tory was Old Glory, flapping gently in the breeze. Beneath her colors, a few people walked in and out of the building, occasionally looking up with wist-ful smiles.

"It's the one you took from the car lot," Harper said. "Just a little reminder for everyone."

They looked at the banner for a long time before Lee finally broke the silence. He would never admit it, but he needed that moment to swal-low the lump in his throat and steady his voice. "Thanks again."

Before Harper could respond, Bus appeared with a familiar face beside him.

Lee's expression changed a bit, as though he'd just tasted bad food.

Jerry, wasn't it? Yes. Jerry the Politician.

The very same Jerry who had insisted that

Lee prove to them he wasn't with Milo, who had turned a large part of the crowd against him, who had convinced them to send Lee out with half as many men accompanying him as he'd originally planned. Lee felt his chest swell with bitterness. If Jerry had kept his goddamn mouth shut, would things have been different? Would Miller and Josh be alive now?

The look on Bus's face was that he clearly knew this was not the time for Jerry to come speak with Lee, but Jerry had likely insisted. Lee also got the impression from Bus's uncomfortable body language that he knew what Jerry wanted to talk to them about and knew Lee and Harper were not going to like it.

Jerry opened his mouth, but Lee cut him off. "What the fuck do you want?"

He couldn't contain his hostility. Frankly, Jerry should be glad Lee didn't beat him to death with his crutch.

Jerry held up his hands, but he still had that stupid smile on his face. That placating politician's smile. The smile of a man who thinks no one can see through him. "Captain, I stand corrected. Clearly, from all accounts, it sounds like Doc was the person responsible for the breach in the fence. I was wrong to accuse you of being with Milo."

The apology did nothing for Lee. It didn't take away his injuries, and it didn't bring back Miller and Josh. Just to watch him squirm, Lee said, "I bashed Milo's skull in with my bare hands, Jerry. So yes, you were wrong to accuse me."

Jerry gave a sidelong glance at Bus, as though

looking for some help, but Bus had crossed his arms and regarded the other man with a look that said, *I told you not to come down here.*

"Yes, well..." Jerry trailed off, then appeared to find his train of thought again. He seemed to come to the conclusion that Bus had been right and this was the wrong time to confront Lee over whatever he felt was so goddamn important. Maybe he would have walked away and left it where it was, but Lee wasn't going to let him off that easy.

"Was there something you wanted to talk to me about?" Lee asked.

"Well." Jerry appeared extremely uncomfortable now, shifting his weight back and forth and touching his ear nervously. "I had just wanted to extend my apologies to you...and..."

Bus came in this time. "I believe you had a question about why Captain Harden invited a busload of survivors to join Camp Ryder without first getting clearance from us." Bus said it in such a way as though he were simply trying to help Jerry remember. "By the way, Captain Harden, I agree with your decision."

Jerry looked at Bus with venom in his eyes but didn't respond directly to him. He realized that a small gathering had followed them over to the medical trailer and was eavesdropping on the conversation. With an audience to watch him, his demeanor changed and he drew himself up, like his dingy shirt and pants were a three-piece suit.

"Yes." Jerry cleared his throat and spoke louder, like he was on a stage. "I was going to ask you about that. I understand that you did an excellent

job getting supplies for Camp Ryder. However..."
He glanced around, making sure all eyes were on
him. "Let me be frank with you, Captain. Those
supplies aren't enough to go around, and I feel
that we should have the final say on how to split up
those supplies, because they're ours—"

Lee's blood boiled. "They're yours?"

"Yes, they're ours. We paid for them with our
blood!"

Is he serious? Lee thought. *Is he really saying this?*

"We sent you out with four of our men and you
only returned with one!"

*I'm going to kick the shit out of him if he doesn't
shut up...*

"I think I speak for everyone when—"

Harper saved Lee the trouble and punched
Jerry square in the jaw with a vicious right hook.
Jerry dropped to the ground, where he wiggled
around for a moment, twitching and groaning in
that weird way that people do when they've been
knocked unconscious. When he came to a second later, Harper stood over him with one finger
pointed directly in his face.

The crowd had gasped suddenly but was now
silent and transfixed.

Harper's entire balding head had turned beet-
red. "Where were you, motherfucker? Where were
you when we were fighting? Where were you when
Josh was murdered? Where were you when Miller
died? You didn't pay for shit! We were the ones
who bled. We were the ones who sacrificed. So
don't you ever fucking open your mouth to the
captain again! If I ever so much as see you look in

his direction again, I swear to God I will fucking knock every tooth out of your mouth!"

Dazed and shocked, Jerry put a finger to his mouth and then looked at the blood on his fingertips as though it were the first time he'd ever seen himself bleed. He looked scared and disgusted, and then his look became one of indignation. He turned to Bus, again searching for support.

Bus shook his head. "I told you not to come over here." But he extended a hand and helped Jerry up off the ground. Jerry staggered back away from Lee and Harper, who were both looking at him like they might start into him again if he didn't back off.

He pointed a trembling hand at them. "You're both nuts. You've lost it."

Disembodied voices came out of the crowd.

"Give it a rest, Jerry."

"Yeah, why don't you fuck off?"

"Shove it up your ass, Jerry!"

Jerry turned his glare on the crowd but must not have seen who had spoken. A small contingent of people that clearly sided with Jerry surrounded him and seemed to escort him away like bodyguards for some dignitary, casting disdainful glances over their shoulders. Lee was dismayed to see that Jerry's supporters were more than a dozen strong.

The rest of the small crowd began to dissipate. Several of them clapped for Harper, while others shouted thanks to him, and one younger man threw him a thumbs-up and said, "I've been wanting to do that for weeks!"

Bus, Harper, and Lee watched them leave, dark foreboding settling on them like a cloud. Jerry and his supporters had gone right, and the others had gone left. Some people remained in the middle, still milling about, not quite sure what to do with themselves.

Bus was the first to put it into words. "This place is divided, guys."

"I'm sorry, Bus." Harper shook his head. "I shouldn't have lost my cool like that."

"He deserved it," Bus said simply.

"The food is going to make things worse," Lee observed. "It'll calm things down at first, keep everyone's bellies full for a little while. But we have no crops to harvest. We're going to have to work hard to get through the winter."

"Even harder with this many people," Bus agreed.

"Once the food starts running low again, the divisions will become more obvious unless we do something about it now." Lee shifted his weight on the crutch. "How bad is it?"

Bus scratched his bearded chin. "Jerry wants us to be a cloister. He wants to reinforce our defenses and stay here and not let anyone in or out. He thinks bringing any more people into the group is going to make it too difficult to survive. And there are a lot of people who agree with him. Not just the people you saw walking away with him."

"And what do you think, Bus?" Lee asked.

"I think I agree with your plan. Jerry wants to batten down the hatches and wait it out, like it's all eventually gonna blow over. I think he's wrong. I think this is our life now, and we need to start adapting to it. More survivors only give us more manpower. We're just going to need more resources to support them."

"We're going to have to start hunting." Lee nodded. "There's plenty of game around. And we need to start scavenging. There're things we can use out there; we just have to find them. With better weapons and more people, it'll be safer to do. We'll need to find a bigger place, fortify it better. Someplace with enough land to plant some crops come spring."

All three men nodded. They agreed, but what about the other people? What about Father Jim's group? And the group from Smithfield? Now there were three distinct groups all jammed into one place together. They would have different ideas and different people whom they trusted. Even in Camp Ryder they were split, and Lee could only imagine it was the same for the Smithfield group—some would trust LaRouche simply based on his military knowledge, and some would trust Julia because she took care of them. Father Jim's group was clearly united in their opinion that he was in charge, but they were the smallest group by far.

"It's gonna be a bumpy road, gentlemen." Lee looked at their faces and saw only determination. "I hope you know what you're getting into."

Harper nodded, still looking out at Camp Ryder, and it sounded like Miller when he said, "We're with you, Captain."

Bus took a deep breath. "Yep. We're with you."

TWENTY-SEVEN

A DEAD MAN'S WISH

THE TWO MEN COLLAPSED at the base of a tree.

One wore jeans with holes in them and a plain white T-shirt with sooty smudges all over it. The other wore an ACU-pattern uniform with a heavy tactical vest and an M4 slung around his shoulder. They both breathed hard as they lay at the base of the tree, but the man in the uniform was obviously not well. His breathing was more labored and it rattled in his chest wetly. His skin was unnaturally pale in the moonlight, and he was sweating profusely. His eyes seemed vacant when they were open, which wasn't often now. A bloody bandage was wrapped around his thigh.

"Jacob," the man in uniform whispered.

"I'm here." Jacob took hold of the other man's shoulder. This was a rare moment of lucidity, when Captain Mitchell was not only able to form a coherent thought but speak clearly. In the past few hours since the firebomb, Captain Mitchell had only spoken twice. Once was to ask for water, and the second time was a rambling and slurred lamentation about some predatory fish called an oscar that he used to keep in his bunker. Except he didn't call it a bunker. He called it "The Hole."

Now his fevered eyes were open wide, as though sensing the impending end of himself. Not his physical death, so to speak, but the death of the person he was. Staring at him in the moonlight, Jacob thought of that efficient little bacterium working its way through the captain's brain, eating away all those nonessential human affectations and leaving behind...what? An insane person? A wild animal? A new species, perhaps?

Captain Mitchell coughed and his eyes lost some of their focus. That look lasted for the better part of a minute until his eyes snapped back into reality and he pinned Jacob with that intense stare of his.

"Jacob, where's my knife? I need my knife."

Jacob's eyes flashed down to the blade strapped to the front of the captain's vest. He spoke coherently enough, but was it wise to give him a knife when he was almost gone? "Why do you need your knife, Captain?"

"I...uh..." The captain lost his train of thought again.

Jacob thought he knew the answer to the question anyway.

Thought recaptured, the captain spoke again with urgency. "I need my knife. You have to help me. I don't want to be like that."

Because a gunshot would only attract the thousands of them milling about only a mile or two from where they were. The captain wasn't willing to risk Jacob in that way. Jacob was an oracle now, something to be valued and protected. That was why they were in the situation they were in. Because the captain had been protecting Jacob. At the cost of everyone else.

Jacob slid the knife out of its sheath and placed it in Captain Mitchell's open palm. He tensed when he released his grip on the knife, wondering if the captain would turn and begin slashing at him with it. But the captain only looked at the cold edge of the blade and spoke haltingly. "You gonna 'member what I told you 'bout?"

Jacob nodded. "I remember. I'll get there. I promise."

With some effort, the captain removed the sling of his M4 rifle, followed by his tactical vest, and laid them in a pile next to Jacob. When words escaped his tongue, the captain just pointed to the items and then to Jacob.

"You want me to put it on?"

The captain nodded weakly. He was beginning to twitch.

"I can't leave until dawn," Jacob said, looking around at the dark woods. "You know how they hear at night. Do you think you can make it through the night?"

Captain Mitchell shook his head. The twitching was beginning to turn into full-body spasms. There were only minutes left now. The captain realized this; some part of him was clear enough to know he had to die and knew it had to happen soon. And he knew he'd already made Jacob promise that whatever happened, Jacob would not let him turn into one of them.

Jacob had made that promise, as the captain had made that promise to him.

The captain held the knife back out to Jacob and fought for his garbled words. "You," was all he managed to choke out. "You."

Jacob tried to be clinical. How do you kill a person painlessly with a knife? It didn't work. As he reached out to take the blade, the question turned into something different: How do you kill *your friend* painlessly with a knife? And when his fingers closed around the handle of the blade, he began to weep.

The captain's tenuous grasp on reality slipped and his head began lolling around, his eyes tracking hallucinations in the darkness. His legs twitched as though kicking out at something. The fingers of his hands opened and closed. His breathing became rapid and shallow.

Quick. He had to do it now.

Jacob looked around for something heavy and found a rock a little bigger than his hand. It would do. He got up on his knees, unable to control his hitching chest and the tears that streamed down his face. Nor was he able to control the nausea curling in his stomach, and he was certain that he was going to vomit, but he forced himself to wait until he had completed his promise.

The captain was not all there anymore, but he wasn't violent just yet, and he allowed himself to be lowered to the ground by his shoulders with his head jerking spasmodically on the ground. Jacob set the tip of the knife against his temple with one trembling hand and gripped the rock with the other.

"I'm sorry," he whispered.

But Captain Mitchell wasn't there. His gray eyes had gone vacant and though they were open, they were not seeing, and they surely did not recognize Jacob. *He's already gone*, Jacob thought to himself. *So I'm really not killing him.*

It didn't help.

He gritted his teeth and swung the rock down on the handle of the knife like he was driving a nail. The blade slipped in with surprising ease. The captain twitched a few more times and then lay still in the leaves at the base of the tree.

Jacob leaned back against the tree and wept bitterly and quietly for a little while longer. The vomit didn't come after all, and the nausea in his gut was replaced with a deep, unforgiving grief. When the cold feeling in his gut was all that was left, he gathered up the captain's things and began to put them on. The vest was still slightly warm and damp with the captain's sweat. It felt heavy and cumbersome, but he knew it would protect him. He slung into the rifle, feeling marginally better that he had a weapon now, though he was unfamiliar with it outside of its basic functions.

To the north, Jacob could see the little twinkle of orange firelight where their compound on the edges of Petersburg, Virginia, continued to burn. It made his heart ache to think about all of the dead people turning to ashes in that fire, all the men and women and children he had known, whom the captain had tried so hard to protect.

He never closed his eyes even once during the night but kept scanning the trees for the black shadows that would be stalking him. Throughout the entire night, he heard the howls and screeches of the infected. Sometimes they sounded close, and other times they were far away. They were searching for him, combing the woods for him.

He waited for the gray light of dawn before standing and facing south.

South, because there was nothing left for them up north.

Stay off the roads, Captain Mitchell had told him. *And you'll have to walk. I know it's a long way, but you have to do it. They need the information you have. They can still make it. They still have a fighting chance.*

His other words rattled around inside Jacob's head, so much information that he had a hard time holding on to it all. It was all random and disjointed in his mind, none of it neatly organized according to category: Don't drink anything but fresh rainwater; full auto just wastes ammunition; follow the interstate, but don't get too close to it; always be aware of your surroundings; don't make contact with anyone until you've watched them for at least a day; don't ever tell anyone why you're looking for him...

He wished he'd written it all down.

He looked over his shoulder one last time at the body of Captain Mitchell, lying at the base of the tree. Then he checked his watch. It was six o'clock now.

Time to get a move on.

It was a long walk to North Carolina.

extras

orbit

meet the author

D.J. Molles is the bestselling author of The Remaining series. He published his first short story, *Darkness*, while still in high school. Soon after, he won a prize for his short story "Survive." The Remaining was originally self-published in 2012 and quickly became an Internet bestseller. He lives in the southeast with his wife and children.

introducing

If you enjoyed
THE REMAINING: AFTERMATH,
don't miss the next book in the series

THE REMAINING: REFUGEES

by D.J. Molles

CHAPTER 1

KILLBOX

The two men worked quietly.

In the cold morning light, diffused through a thin veil of clouds, their breath came out of them in bone-white plumes. Thick beards covered both of their faces. The shorter, balding man crouched over a single-burner camp stove and attached the small green propane tank. As the shorter man worked, the taller man held his tan-coated M4 rifle at a low-ready and scanned the derelict streets around them.

The concrete surrounding them sparkled with a thin sheen of frost. Squat buildings stared down over them like empty and plundered tombs. Their windows were either boarded up with graying plywood or smashed through, leaving only jagged glass teeth protruding from the window frames. Directly behind where the two men worked stood a two-story brick building, and as the tall man scanned, he could see dark figures atop the roof, silhouetted against the sky. The figures peered over the side and watched intensely.

The two men worked in the center of a four-lane street. Along the edges, trash had gathered at the base of the buildings and the gutters, where wind and rain had swept them. All of it was old and sun-bleached and melded into anonymous heaps. From these mounds of trash, hastily disguised, small green rectangles poked up. Wires ran off of them and trailed up the side of the building to where they dangled from the rooftop.

A lighter clicked.

Lee looked down to see Harper setting the lighter's tiny butane flame to the gas grill and slowly turning on the propane. There was a shallow hiss, and then blue flames jumped from the burner, sending up a wave of heat that felt pleasant on Lee's face. Harper adjusted the flames so they quivered low and then set a grungy-looking aluminum pan atop the grill.

"Your turn." Harper stood, his knees popping.

Lee took one last look at his surroundings and bent to the ground, where he had laid a small canvas satchel. He opened the top and retrieved the only item it contained: a gallon bag full of deer guts, the pale coils of intestines steeping in a marinade of blackening blood. His nose wrinkled as he bent over the grill and dumped the bag into the heating pan. The air smelled immediately of a stagnant slaughterhouse.

Harper growled low in his throat and shook his head. "Disgusting."

Lee nodded in agreement and gingerly zipped the plastic bag closed, stuffing it back into the canvas satchel. Letting his rifle rest on its sling, Lee pointed to the building where all the thin black wires trailed up to the roof. "Let's go."

Harper snatched his own M4 off the ground and they headed for the open door at the base of the building. Lee matched his pace, just barely showing the limp in his left leg. The ankle had never healed properly from his fall down the elevator shaft three months ago. His back hadn't been the same either, and it had become quite a process to get mobile in the morning.

They picked their way through the ransacked interior of the building—an old mom-and-pop pharmacy. The shelves had been tipped over, everything emptied and looted. Refugees and scavengers had taken what they needed, leaving behind the pill bottles and packages. At the back of the pharmacy, where a sign that read COLD REMEDIES hung over empty white shelves, a door opened into a stairwell that led up to the second level, and from there to the roof. The door was in splinters from when Lee had kicked it in earlier that night. The place still smelled of death. They had not moved the bodies of the pharmacist and his wife. They remained huddled in the dark corner of this shit-stained storage area.

The only light in the upstairs area came from an open skylight with a pull-down ladder to provide roof access and from the three glow sticks lying on the dark floor like a strewn-out constellation leading to the ladder and creating an eerie green glow across the floor.

Harper went up first and Lee followed.

On the roof, he found the other eight members of his team with their backs against the brick abutment of the roof and their rifles lying across their laps. Seven men and Julia, Marie's sister from Smithfield. She had insisted on being a part of the team and working as their medic. After she had explained her background as an EMT, Lee welcomed her to the team.

He crossed the tar-paper roof and sidled down between Julia and LaRouche. The sergeant's old tactical vest was worn and grimed to a grayish tan, and some of the edges were frayed from the constant hard use. His light brown hair was about as overgrown as Lee's, but he kept his reddish beard hacked shorter with his knife. As Lee sat down next to him, LaRouche dug a packet of Red Man out of his cargo pocket and stuffed his cheek with a giant chaw. He'd found a box of the stuff squirreled away in a house earlier that week and had been so overjoyed that Lee thought he might shed a tear.

LaRouche offered Lee the pouch, but he declined.

Lee turned his attention to his right, where Julia sat. Her skin was pale to the point of looking green and her lips were seized down to a short, flat line across her face. She avoided eye contact with Lee.

"You gonna be all right?" he asked.

She nodded but didn't speak.

He leaned back and stared up at the granite skies. "It has to be done."

She closed her eyes and shook her head. "I just can't find a way to make it right, Lee. I'm sorry, but I don't think I'm ever going to be comfortable with it like you are."

Lee didn't respond for a moment, just watched his breath drift up into the air. *It's going to be a cold winter*, he thought. *Not usually this cold by November.* He moistened his lips. "Just because I do it doesn't mean I'm comfortable with it."

"They're people."

"I don't know."

"They're people," she repeated.

Lee looked at her again, and this time she met his gaze.

He nodded. "Okay."

The smell of burning innards began to drift up to them from where the bloody mass boiled and smoked on the pan below them. He turned to his left where LaRouche, Harper, Father Jim, and the rest of the group were lined up, their hands resting on the grips of their rifles.

"Everybody locked and loaded?"

Thumbs-up from everybody.

Silence and grim faces.

Lee rose to his knees and peered over the abutment to the street below.

The downtown area of Lillington was spread out over a few small blocks. The building they were perched on stood at the southwest corner of Main Street and Front Street, where they had set up the small burner, letting the smells of dreadful cooking waft across the small town. Opposite them was a collection of small businesses: a barbershop, a diner, the Lillington Chamber of Commerce, and a few boutiques. Everything stood gray and dead and falling apart.

Still, there could be some salvage there.

Lee rested his bearded chin on his hand as he knelt. He watched and waited and remained silent along with his group as the minutes dragged themselves by like wounded animals, slow and painful. One of the group checked the chamber of his rifle, and then snicked the bolt back into place. LaRouche spit out a stream of tobacco juice that hit the tar paper with a sharp *splat*. Somewhere the lilting voice of a winter bird called out from a barren tree.

"Cap," someone whispered.

Lee looked over and saw Jeriah Wilson, the stocky black kid fresh out of the Air Force academy. He'd been a running back throughout high school, and his build showed it. His face bore only patchy wisps of hair across his chin, but his once-regulation crew cut had now become shaggy.

He tapped his ear and pointed out to the east toward Main Street.

Lee strained to hear, and for a brief moment as the steady cold breeze lulled, he could hear the patter of numerous feet coming from the streets below them. He looked at Jeriah again and nodded, then leaned up slightly over the abutment so he could see Main Street. Everything looked empty and devoid of life, and yet Lee could hear their soft footfalls just around the corner.

They were coming.

He shifted slightly and his hand came down slowly to touch the comforting grip of his rifle. His eyes stayed locked on the intersection.

The footfalls were louder now and interspersed with short, breathy snorts that could have been mistaken for some other noise from nature, if Lee were not so familiar with it. It was the noise they made when they were tracking something. Especially when they were tracking by smell.

The first one came around the corner quickly and then slowed.

Seeing it made every muscle in Lee's body stiffen.

Staring at it from his concealed vantage point, Lee thought it was a young boy, dark-haired and short of stature. He wore a stained pair of jeans and what had once been a white T-shirt, now tattered and darkened with gore. Steam rolled off the boy's shoulders, his body still hot from whatever wretched hovel he and his hundreds of den mates had packed themselves into for warmth. They liked low places, like basements and cellars, and they all huddled together during the night in one giant, twitching mass.

The thought of it made Lee's skin crawl.

"Eyes on," Lee whispered.

"Eyes on," LaRouche repeated down the line.

In the street below, the boy trotted out cautiously, now hunching down, now standing erect. His squinted eyes surveyed the scene but always came back to what had drawn him to this intersection: the scent of the deer guts, steaming atop that single-burner grill.

Marie had been right. The smell of cooking drew them in quickly. It tickled some tiny memories in their violently rearranged brains that promised food. It worked better than anything else.

The boy sniffed the air and eyed the grill again, then began to move closer. Behind him, his den mates appeared, a bedraggled horde of them. They began to chitter back and forth to each other excitedly. As they drew closer, their calling got louder, and they began to bark and screech and growl. They worked their hands reflexively and snapped at the air with their jaws. Lee counted as they moved onto Front Street, measuring them in segments of twenty-five, up until he reached approximately a hundred and fifty. The old and the weak and the nearly dead straggled in, taking up the rear of the column.

Lee crouched there on the abutment and breathed very slowly so that the fog of his breath would not give him away. His pulse was strong and quick, and he could feel the tightness in his stomach and in his throat.

He lowered himself very slowly and touched LaRouche on the shoulder. The sergeant looked up and Lee whispered, "You ready?"

LaRouche moved his chaw around in his mouth and nodded, his lips stained brown. He reached down to his side and held up a little green box with a wire running off of it.

Looking out onto the street again, Lee watched as the horde gathered around the boy. Now others were on the scent, and they were less cautious and quicker to move in on a possible source of food. This was a herd, not a pack. There was no leader, only the instinct to stay together, to move together. The stink of the burning entrails began to mix with the pungent living odor of the infected and it lifted up on the breeze and made bile rise in the back of Lee's throat.

"Little closer," he whispered to no one in particular, his lips barely moving.

Now the tip of the crowd had reached the bubbling pan of guts. They stood back perhaps three feet away or so and circled around, wary of the heat but certain there was food there. They were all on the verge of starvation, their skin stretched taut over their bones and their ribs standing out like the rungs on a ladder. The rest of the horde bunched up behind them, fanning out and filling the street.

Almost there, he thought.

The sweat on his palms chilled in the air.

The first of the infected leaned forward and took a swipe at the pan, knocking it off the grill and spilling the hot, bloody contents into the street. They screeched and jumped forward, their clawlike fingers rasping across the concrete as they grabbed chunks of organs and long strings of intestines. The horde pressed in, compacted, became one blob of flailing, grasping limbs, and the screeches became desperate as the feeding frenzy began.

"Now," Lee said.

LaRouche counted out the three clicks from the detonator: "One, two, *away*."

Lee watched as the four daisy-chained claymore mines exploded from where they were hidden in the piles of trash, scattering tatters of white paper that billowed out into the crowd like some violent confetti cannon.

The outside of the horde appeared to wilt as the hundreds of steel balls shooting out of the four simultaneous detonations cut them down. With the dust and smoke still hanging in the air and the horde of infected still unsteady on their feet, as their eardrums bled and their animal minds attempted to comprehend this thunder that had struck down their den mates, the rest of Lee's team crested the abutment with their rifles at the ready and barrages of withering fire erupted along the rooftop.

The creatures below howled in rage and pain. They turned in mad circles, striking out at each other in the smoke, biting and slashing at anything before them. They began to scatter, but then they bunched up again as their instinct took over, and they ran this way and that as the rifle fire echoed off the storefronts and confused them.

Their screeching began to lessen as more and more of them fell. The horde became a few stragglers trying to cling to life, and then only a dozen or so wounded that crawled and moaned and growled. The rifle fire became sporadic until there was only one infected left.

It was the same small boy who had come around the corner. His left arm was sheared off at the shoulder and he clutched his belly with the hand he had left and made a hideous noise.

Calmly, LaRouche raised his rifle while all the others ported theirs, smoke rising from the barrels. The boy writhed and moaned as LaRouche squinted through his sight and fired. Then there was silence.

LaRouche spat. "That's the last one."

The group looked down at their handiwork.

In the street lay the sprawled remains of what was left of Lillington's populace. Some of them stared up into the sky with glassy eyes while others lay facedown in their own muck. The spaces between their bodies glistened darkly as thin streams of red meandered away from the road and toward the trash-clogged drains.

LaRouche slapped Harper's shoulder and pointed. "Shit, Harper. I think your grill is still going."

Harper nodded slowly and looked slightly nauseated. "Yeah."

LaRouche was clearly impressed. "Damn thing's indestructible."

Lee grabbed his pack up from the floor and slung his arms into it. "Everyone refresh your mags."

Those who had not done so already put fresh magazines in their rifles and stowed the half-full ones in the pockets of their field jackets. They stooped and gathered their empty magazines and put them in a different pocket.

Julia remained still during this.

She hadn't fired a shot.

"Wilson." Lee pointed to the Air Force cadet. "Get your guys and pull the Humvees around. Let's start setting up shop."

Wilson nodded and headed for the ladder down, his three companions falling in behind him.

The two Humvees that Lee had repossessed from Milo were parked around the corner. The block of buildings that they stood in created a perfect square around an empty parking lot. With some measures to fortify the doors and windows of these buildings, the interior parking lot could be used as a base and the buildings as a wall. A little concertina wire and some barricades, and Outpost Lillington would be secure.

Wilson and his team slid quickly down the ladder and disappeared into the empty pharmacy below. Lee thought about telling them to be cautious—there would be others lurking in the city. But it was unnecessary. Everyone was already cautious. They all jumped at shadows and slept lightly, always anticipating the next round of misfortune.

"Let's go down there and check it out." Lee put a hand on LaRouche's shoulder. "You mind keeping overwatch again?"

The sergeant shook his head. "Nope. I got it."

They went down and emerged from the pharmacy onto Front Street. It was Lee, Harper, Julia, and Father Jim. They were a good team, Lee had to admit. Though Julia refused to take part in the traps they set to clear the small towns of infected, she still did the training and pulled her weight along with everyone else. Plus, her medical knowledge made her invaluable. Lee had spent a lot of time training his team, and they were practiced and tested almost every day. They were still a far cry from professional soldiers, but they were fluid, most of them were decent shots, and they got the job done.

Standing on the sidewalk in front of the shop, they stared at the carnage in the streets.

"Jim, Harper..." Lee pointed to the front of the shop. "Post up here. We'll strip the pharmacy."

The two men nodded. Julia followed Lee back into the building. The interior already looked ransacked, but most things did these days. There wasn't much left, but they managed to pull a few large bottles of medications that Lee was unfamiliar with, along with some prescription pain relievers and some over-the-counter items such as antidiarrheal medicines, ibuprofen, acetaminophen, and antibacterial ointments. Julia piled these items into her pack just as the Humvees rumbled into the back parking lot.

Lee called out to Jim and Harper and they all headed for the back lot.

The two Humvees sat in the interior parking lot, one behind the other. The lead Humvee had been outfitted with a dozer blade that now sat angled up so as not to impede the vehicle's ground clearance—a bit of creative welding. Wilson and his three teammates were already offloading spools of barbed wire, some of which they had taken from the barricades in Smithfield and some they had found in various farm equipment stores.

The back lot was half paved and half dusty gravel. Two small sedans and a pickup truck sat abandoned, parked along the rear of the buildings. There were two entrances into the back lot, one from the south and one from the west. The western entrance was only wide enough for one vehicle to pass through at a time, while the southern entrance was much bigger. For this reason, Lee made the decision to block the southern entrance. The materials to barricade it would be harvested from the refuse around them, including the cars already parked in the back lot, Dumpsters, and any other heavy objects they could haul into place.

While the rest of the team finished offloading the Humvees, Lee sat in the passenger seat of the lead vehicle and grabbed the handset to the SINCGARS—Single Channel Ground and Airborne Radio System—mounted inside. He dispensed with proper radio protocols and used plain English when he spoke.

"Captain Harden to Camp Ryder. How do you copy me?"

A hiss of static.

A gravelly voice answered. "Yeah, I got you, Captain."

Lee smiled. "Morning, Bus. Haven't had your coffee?"

"Don't remind me. Haven't had coffee in months." Bus cleared his throat. "Did you get Lillington cleared?"

"Yeah, it's clear."

"Anybody hurt?"

"Nope." Lee looked out at his team, now in the process of breaking into the abandoned cars in the back lot so they could be moved and used as barricades. "They're just getting everything set up right now."

"Sounds good. I know Old Man Hughes won't tell you, but everyone from Dunn really appreciates what you're doing out there. It's been cramped quarters over here."

Lee nodded. Old Man Hughes was the leader of nineteen other survivors from the town of Dunn to the southeast. He was a crotchety old bastard, but for some reason the Dunn survivors loved him. Due to overcrowding at Camp Ryder, the twenty from Dunn were slated to move to Lillington and establish an outpost there, along with another twelve from Fuquay-Varina.

"Not a problem," Lee said simply.

"I'll let Old Man Hughes know. They'll be on their way shortly. Any trouble on the roads?"

"No, the road was clear. Make sure they stick to the route we planned."

"Will do. What time should we expect you back?"

Lee thought out loud. "I think we'll leave most of the scavenging for the new residents. My guys need some sleep and I need to restock some of our ordnance. So we'll probably head out shortly after they get here." He clucked his tongue. "I'd say around noon at the latest."

"Sounds good. See you at noon."

"Roger. Out." Lee put the handset back on its cradle.

As he stood from the Humvee, he watched Harper exit the back door of the pharmacy. The older man's face was clouded, and he approached Lee with a purposeful walk, avoiding eye contact until he was standing right in front of him.

Lee felt that old familiar certainty of the worst case scenario creeping up on him. "What's wrong?"

Harper squinted one eye. "Not really sure."

Lee stared at him blankly.

"Take a look at something." Harper began walking back toward the pharmacy, and Lee followed. "Jim just pointed it out to me. I hadn't noticed it before but... Well, just come look."

They made their way through the pharmacy to the open front door and out onto Front Street. In the middle of the road, mired by bodies lying two deep in places and surrounded by the overwhelming stench, Jim stood and looked around at the corpses, a finger pressed thoughtfully to his lips. Lee turned to catch a glimpse of the rooftop behind and above him and saw LaRouche resting his elbows there on the abutment. The sergeant met Lee's eyes and gave a minimal shrug, as though Father Jim's actions mystified him as well.

Lee stood at the edge of the bloodbath. "Jim?"

The man in the tortoiseshell glasses looked up and nodded by way of greeting.

Harper put his hands on his hips. "Tell him."

Jim looked around hesitantly, as though he were in the process of some complicated calculation, confident that his math was correct but somehow coming up with the wrong answer every time. Finally he gestured to the bodies around him. "There are no females."

Lee's brow narrowed.

He looked around as though he might prove Jim wrong. He stared down at the pale limbs covered in dried and fresh blood. Their clothing barely clung to them in tatters. It was difficult to determine gender by a glance—malnutrition robbed them of most of their distinctions so that all that remained were bony sacks of flesh. Lee had to look at their faces and see the grizzled, mangy beards, clumped together by clots of blood. Some of them were too young to have beards, but they were male as well. He searched and searched but could not find a single female to discount what Jim had said.

"That's weird." Lee spoke slowly. "But…"

"There were none in the last two traps we set in Smithfield either." Father Jim looked at him with fevered eyes. "Or at the university. Or at Dunn. In fact, when was the last time you saw an infected female, Captain?"

Lee didn't respond.

He had no answer.

"What do you think happened to them?" Harper asked quietly.

Jim began carefully stepping between the bodies, making his way toward Lee and Harper. "Not sure," he said simply. "Could be that they aren't as strong, so the male infected feed on them."

Lee thought back to the young girl, the first infected he'd encountered as he stepped out of his house and into this new reality so long ago. She had been a scrawny thing but shockingly powerful. "I don't know about strength being the issue," Lee said. "Besides, if that were the case, why not kill and eat the young ones too?"

Jim shrugged. "I have no idea. I'm just making an observation."

Lee stared down at the bodies for a moment more. He could find nothing further to say on the subject, so he nodded back toward the buildings. "Let's get rid of these bodies. I don't want to give the assholes from Fuquay-Varina anything else to bitch about."

They drove the Humvee with the dozer attachment out to Front Street and lowered the blade so that it was only an inch off the ground. Lee watched from the sidewalk as Harper moved the vehicle in slow, broad strokes, the blade gathering up a tumble of pale bodies and pushing them toward a vacant lot at the northeastern corner of the intersection. Then Harper put the vehicle in reverse and backed slowly through the thickening blood, the tires slinging droplets of it down the sides of the vehicle. The thought of all that infected blood still gave Lee cause to worry, but over the last few months, several survivors—including Lee—had come into contact with infected blood and had not contracted the plague. They'd determined that simple blood-on-skin contact didn't contribute to infection.

After nearly an hour of back and forth, Harper had managed to clear Front Street of most of the bodies. The ones he couldn't get to—the ones that were huddled behind trees and in the corners of buildings—were picked up by hand and placed in the path of the dozer so he could push them into the growing pile. They mixed in pallets and pieces of wood and doused it all with diesel fuel and set it on fire with a road flare. Lee stood back from the blaze and watched the acrid black smoke curl into the sky as Harper drove the Humvee-turned-dozer back into the parking lot behind the buildings.

The use of fuel was a shame, but they didn't have the equipment to dig mass graves, and leaving rotting bodies out in the open was not only offensive to the senses but a serious health hazard, even if they were uninfected. An expired human body became a petri dish for diseases of all types. On top of that, the rotting meat had been known to draw other infected into the area. It was best to dispose of them quickly.

Beside him, Father Jim looked down Main Street. "They'll see the smoke, you know."

Lee shrugged. "Nothing I can do about it, Jim."

"I know." He put a hand on Lee's shoulder. "But you know that asshole White is going to say something."

Lee smiled and looked shocked. "Father...such language."

Jim waved him off. "To call Professor White anything but an asshole would be to lie. And lying lips are an abomination to the Lord."

LaRouche joined them in the middle of the street, his cheek still bulging from tobacco.

Lee nodded to him. "How long you keep that shit in your mouth?"

LaRouche spat. "Gotta conserve."

Both Jim and Lee shrugged and nodded. It was a valid point.

From the north end of Main Street they could hear the rumble of a bus downshifting, muted by distance. Main Street dipped down into a slight grade and leveled out as it crossed over the Cape Fear River. Lee could see clearly in the winter air, and from the other side of the bridge, he watched the big white bus come into view, led by a blue sixteen-passenger van. Those two vehicles would contain all that was left of Dunn and Fuquay-Varina, along with all the worldly possessions they had managed to carry out with them. Which wasn't much.

Lee remained standing in the intersection as the vehicles approached, his hands folded and resting on the buttstock of his slung rifle. The gray skies washed the windshields out to a pale reflection of nothing, and he could not see who was driving either vehicle. He supposed the Fuquay-Varina group would be in the van, as there were only twelve of them compared to Dunn's twenty.

LaRouche smiled at Lee. "Can't wait to hear what the great Professor White has to say to you this time."

Lee smiled wanly but didn't feel much humor in it.

The van crested the hill and began to slow, the brakes on it squealing as it pulled to a stop in the middle of the intersection with the driver's side window rolled down. Sitting in the driver's seat was an aging man with longish salt-and-pepper hair, pulled back into a ponytail. He looked over the rims of thick glasses as though Lee were one of his pupils who had spoken out of turn in class.

Lee met his gaze and fought to keep his face neutral. "Mr. White."

Professor Tommy White of the once-prestigious Chapel Hill University pursed his lips. The rumbling of the engines at idle filled the silence between the two men. Lee watched as the professor's eyes flicked to the burning pile of bodies. They stayed there and the man's face seemed to wilt. Then he just looked straight ahead again. Someone in the van began to weep loudly.

Lee sniffed and smelled charred flesh.

He pointed down Front Street. "Take your first left onto Eighth Street. Entrance is on the left."

A teary-eyed girl, perhaps twenty years old, appeared in the front of the van. She stared accusingly at Lee and bawled at him. "Why? Why'd you do it?"

"So you can be safe," Lee responded with thinly veiled annoyance.

The girl began to speak but Professor White held up his hand and shook his head. "It's pointless, Natalie. You won't convince him." White looked at Lee again. "We'll be going now."

Lee nodded. "Please do."

The van lurched forward quickly and made the right-hand turn onto Front Street, followed by the quick left turn onto Eighth Street. Lee watched them go with a small shake of his head and kept telling himself, *You don't get to choose who you rescue. You don't get to choose...*

The bus lumbered after the van. From the driver's window, Lee could see Old Man Hughes standing in the center aisle while a younger survivor from Dunn piloted the bus. The old man tossed Lee a salute and a nod of thanks.

"Hey." LaRouche put a hand on his shoulder. "At least someone appreciates us."

Lee made a chuckling sound that was born of frustration and anger. "It just never ends with these fuckers, does it?"

LaRouche flicked his hand dismissively. "Those fuckers have been living off of guys like me and you for centuries. They love their safety and security, but they'll never stop bitching about how we accomplish it." The sergeant shrugged. "Ain't nothin' you can do about it."

Lee nodded. Without further words, they began to walk toward the newly created Outpost Lillington. They had nearly reached the door to the pharmacy when Jeriah Wilson burst through. His eyes found Lee and he raised his hand to flag him down.

"What's up, Wilson?"

"Hey, Captain." Wilson looked confused, maybe a little curious. "Just got a call from Camp Ryder. Outpost Benson made contact with a guy, some survivor, and they're bringing him into Camp Ryder right now."

Lee's eyes narrowed. "Okay. And why are they calling for us?"

"Well, they're calling for you," Wilson corrected.

"Did they say why?"

"The guy says he's from Virginia." Wilson met Lee's gaze. "And he asked for you by name."

CHAPTER 2

THE HUB

Lee stalked to the Humvee as quickly as he could without showing his limp, ignoring the young college kids from Fuquay-Varina that sided with their old professor and grumbled about him as he passed. A few of the middle-aged survivors from Fuquay-Varina murmured their appreciation to Lee, and he nodded to them politely but distractedly. Not everyone from Fuquay-Varina was opposed to him, but as a whole they went along with whatever Professor White said. Jeriah Wilson had been the one major exception.

At the big green truck, Lee ripped open the passenger door and snatched the handset from the cradle, keying it up before he even had it to his ear. "Captain Harden to Camp Ryder."

A click. Someone whose voice he didn't recognize came on. "This is Camp Ryder. Go ahead, Captain."

"Is there someone asking for me?"

"Uh..." Shuffling, and then the radio clicked off for a brief moment. "Yeah, let me get Bus."

Lee waited quietly, leaning his elbow on the frame of the Humvee and chewing at the inside of his lip.

"Bus here."

Lee looked at the radio as though he might see Bus through it. "Is there some guy looking for me?"

"Yeah, two of our guys from Outpost Benson are bringing him to Camp Ryder." Bus sounded bewildered. "From what they described, the guy's at death's door. Dehydrated, starving, but they say he's wearing a vest, like a military one. Says his name is Jacob."

Lee racked his brain. "I don't know a Jacob."

"Well, he knows you."

"Was he armed?" Lee pinched the bridge of his nose and squeezed his eyes shut.

"When they first found him, yes," Bus said. "But they said he wasn't hostile. Surrendered immediately and laid down his weapon. They said it was an M4, but they're also saying this guy doesn't seem like military at all."

Lee could think of plenty of people he knew in the military who didn't look the part. Not everyone was a lean, mean fighting machine. Many of them worked behind the lines and would never see a day of combat in their entire career.

Lee opened his eyes again. "Did he say why he's looking for me?"

"Um...damn, Lee." Bus huffed into the microphone. "I haven't talked to the guy yet. I just have second-hand information. I think they said he claimed to have information for you or something. Something about Virginia."

"Virginia?" Lee said incredulously. "What the hell do I need to know about Virginia?"

Bus keyed up again. "Look, I have no idea what this guy is about. We'll get him cleaned up and tended to. You just get back here so you can talk to him and figure out what's going on."

Lee licked his lips and felt them getting chapped in the cold, dry air. "Okay. We'll be en route here shortly."

He hung up the handset, grabbed a bottle of water from the floorboard, and drank from it. The cold water ached as it filtered through the empty slot in his gums where he'd lost his right canine tooth to a flying cafeteria chair. If the memory of it didn't make him cringe, it might have been humorous.

He turned outward and regarded the parking lot, encircled by brick buildings. It was now crowded, the two Humvees, the van, and the bus taking up much of the space, but also with more than thirty survivors carrying their personal items from the vehicles and placing them to the sides of the building. Everything they owned, wrapped up in a tattered old blanket or stuffed in a ragged pack of some sort.

Looking out at all these people, he caught their sidelong glances at him, and the expressions behind those brief moments of eye contact varied greatly. The survivors from Dunn revered him as some sort of war hero. He and his team had rescued them after a hard-fought battle, and their appreciation showed. Then there were those from Fuquay-Varina, whom Lee had simply stumbled across, and their perceptions of him were much less generous.

He resented them, though he tried hard not to let it bother him.

He resented their looks and their whispers.

He resented their simplistic worldview.

But most of all, he resented being judged. He resented that every action was worthy of intense scrutiny and that some Monday-morning quarterback would always have an astounding hindsight solution for him that somehow, he should have already known. "Weren't you trained for this?" they would ask him. And he would bite his tongue and try not to think about kicking their teeth in.

This was the war he was destined to fight.

A war where victory would be measured in how many he could save, regardless of their opinions. And though he may be weak in patience and politics, he was gifted in fighting and winning. And if winning meant putting up with some assholes who thought they knew how shit should be run, then so be it. That was just a pill he would have to swallow.

He finished what was left in the water bottle and dropped it in the front seat so he could refill it later. His thoughts turned back to the stranger from Virginia who somehow knew him. From across the parking lot, he saw Harper and Jim standing together near the pharmacy entrance and eyeing him with open curiosity. He waved them over.

"What's going on?" Harper asked as he approached.

Lee adjusted his rifle sling so it was more comfortable across his shoulders. "I don't know. Some guy from Virginia is asking for me. By name, apparently. I don't know the guy, though." He craned his neck to survey all around him. "Where's LaRouche?"

Jim threw a thumb over his shoulder in the general direction of Front Street. "He and Jake are helping secure the doors and windows on the outside."

"Alright." Lee rubbed some warmth back into his bearded face. "Jim, go get LaRouche and let him know we're leaving in five. Jake can stay. Harper, relay to Wilson and his team that we'll be leaving. I want them to stay here and help for the time being. I'll radio them if I need them back over at Camp Ryder. I'm going to, uh..." Lee trailed off. "I'll be ready in a minute."

Harper and Jim nodded discreetly.

Lee turned away from them and headed into the crowd.

He found Julia making her way down the line of refugees, checking everyone for illness before they let them cram together in tight spaces and get the whole outpost sick. Cold, flu, and the ensuing pneumonia promised to be a problem for them this year. People simply couldn't sanitize like they used to. There was now a full generation of people who had been addicted to sanitizing gels and wipes, whose immune systems were not quite as robust as they should be for this type of lifestyle.

Julia was easy to spot by her tawny hair, pulled back into some practical arrangement Lee didn't know the name of. It was darkened now with sweat and oil and smoke from three days in the field, and it was plastered back to her skull because she constantly worried at it with her dirty hands.

He fell in step behind her as she worked her way through the thirty or so refugees.

"How are you?" she asked one of them, an older woman.

"I'm fine, just tired."

"Any persistent cough, runny nose, or soreness in your throat?"

"No."

"Any aches or chills?"

"No."

"Can you breathe through your nose?"

The woman demonstrated.

Julia held up a penlight. "Open your mouth and say 'ah.'"

"Aaahhh."

Julia shone her light around, decided everything was good except for a case of bad breath—not so uncommon nowadays—and smiled. "Thank you."

Lee nodded to the older woman as they passed to the next person. "We're heading out in five. Wilson and his team are staying. You staying here or coming with us?"

She looked at him and Lee didn't see any of the reproach from earlier.

She nodded quickly. "I'll be ready to go in just a few. I'm finishing up now."

"Okay." Lee turned partially away but felt the need to reiterate the time frame. "Five minutes."

Her eyebrows went up slightly. "Yup. I'll be ready, Captain."

He decided not to say anything else.

In four minutes they were rolling. A thin layer of clouds ranged across the horizon, showing sterling in the thickest parts, shot through with ribbons of bright sunlight like gold and silver smelted together.

The Humvee with the dozer attachment growled out of the parking lot, bristling with weapons as it exited the outpost and left the town and its new residents behind them. Harper drove with Lee in the passenger seat. Jim and Julia sat in the back, and LaRouche was crammed in the middle with the .50-caliber M2 machine gun mounted on top.

Lee turned to look out the driver's side of the vehicle and found LaRouche's dirty boots once again resting atop the radio console—a natural footrest for whoever was sitting in the turret. Lee elbowed them off.

"Keep your fucking feet off the radio, LaRouche," Lee griped for the umpteenth time.

"My bad," LaRouche mumbled from up top.

All the windows were down, letting the cold wind blow through the vehicle so that they could all rest their weapons in the window frames, pointing out into a world that had grown dangerous and alien.

"Well, I'm very pleased with Outpost Lillington," Father Jim offered up brightly. "It seems like a very secure location."

Lee looked out the passenger-side window at the passing terrain. He nodded slowly and remained introspective.

"Should lock down this section of highway," Jim continued. "Extend the patrols out a bit…Make movement a little safer…" He seemed to realize that no one else was in the mood for conversation and let his words trail off. He turned back to his own window.

Lee's mind poked cautiously at the questions that nagged him, like you might poke a stick into a dark hole in the forest floor, unsure of what lay inside. Who was the man from Virginia, and what did he want? What news did he bring? Lee wanted to believe that it could be good news but felt in his gut that it was not. Good news didn't come with a single man, sick and exhausted from miles on the road.

Underneath all of that, a question remained that seemed so inconspicuous in its simplicity but that Lee felt was just the tip of something vast and unseen, and it whispered foul omens:

Where have all the females gone?

They passed over the Cape Fear River. The water looked cold and dark, the same color as the woods that surrounded it. The weather had only been this cold for the past week, and a few trees along the banks still clung stubbornly to their brown and wilted leaves, but for the most part the forests were bare. Just a tangle of empty limbs and gray bark, splashes of emerald here and there where a lonesome evergreen stood.

Clattering over the four-lane bridge, Lee wondered when was the last time the bridge had been refurbished. Infrastructure was just another one of the many concerns constantly vying for attention in the back of his mind. Survivors were integral to the success of his mission. He had to rely on them to assist in rebuilding.

But there were so few.

Far fewer than he had ever imagined.

Engineers were at the top of his list: civil engineers, electrical engineers, mechanical engineers...the list went on. At this point, he'd take any kind of engineer he could get his hands on. But it seemed that they were lucky to find survivors at all, let alone someone with a specific skill set.

"Heads up," Jim said suddenly from behind him.

Lee's eyes snapped into focus and he looked out the passenger side of the vehicle. The grade of the earth coming off the road sloped down into a deep ravine that cut toward the Cape Fear River and ran parallel to the roadway. On the other side of that ravine, the ground rose up in a steep incline, and it was there, about midway up the face of that hill, that Lee could see what had drawn Jim's attention.

"Movement! Right side!" Lee called.

"I don't think..." Jim pushed his glasses up on his face and squinted to see farther.

There were four of them in all. Two large ones and two small. They were strange and bulky in their appearance, and it took a moment for Lee to realize that all of them were heaped with heavy coats and blankets to keep them warm.

LaRouche swiveled in the turret, bringing the fifty about.

Jim slapped at LaRouche's legs. "Don't shoot! I don't think they're infected!"

"Relax!" LaRouche dodged his legs about. "I'm not gonna waste 'em..."

"Stop here!" Jim spoke with urgency.

Harper looked back incredulously. "I'm not stopping here."

The sound of Jim's door unlatching.

"Close your fucking door!" Harper barked at him.

"Hey!" Jim leaned out the window, his door still hanging partially open. "Hello!"

Lee reached across and slapped Harper's shoulder. "Stop before he falls out."

The Humvee screeched to a halt, causing everyone inside to lurch forward and LaRouche to slap the top of the roof, trying to gain his balance again.

"It's okay!" Jim yelled again.

The figures were now almost to the top of the hill. One turned and Lee could see the face peering at them with dark, suspicious eyes, his jawline shadowed by the scraggly beginnings of a beard. It was a younger man with a tan complexion, possibly Hispanic, but difficult to tell from this distance. The unknown man turned back around and pushed the others ahead of him—they appeared to be a dark-haired woman and two small children.

"What are you doing, Jim?" Lee said with a note of caution.

From behind him, Lee heard the loud creak of the dry, rusted door hinges as the ex-priest flung his door open. Lee twisted in his seat and tried to reach through to the back and grab a fistful of his jacket, but Jim was already out the door.

"Hey!" Lee growled. "Get the fuck back in here!"

Father Jim completely ignored Lee, even left his rifle in his seat and stood outside the Humvee with both arms raised above his head. "It's okay, we're here to help! You don't have to be afraid. We won't hurt you!"

They continued to clamber up the steep embankment.

Lee kicked his door open with force and slid out of his seat, bringing his rifle to his shoulder. He resisted the urge to simply grab the other man and stuff him back in the Humvee. Warning Klaxons were blaring in his head and he could feel heat rising up the back of his neck. He reached out and put a hand on Jim's shoulder. "What are you doing? Leave it..."

Jim shrugged the hand off and continued waving his arms. His voice took on a desperate quality. "We're here to help you. It's okay! You don't have to be afraid!"

The four strangers reached the top of the hillock and dipped over to the other side, the man pushing the woman and the two children over before disappearing himself. Just before vanishing onto the other side, he turned and looked at them again, and this time his eyes locked onto Lee. He appeared to hesitate for the briefest of moments, but then ducked down over the top of the hill.

Jim stood in the street with his hands still raised.

The look on his face was one of complete confusion.

The breath came out of him in a long blast of steam.

Finally he let his arms drop to his sides.

"What the heck?" he said indignantly.

He turned back around and found the rest of his squad looking at him. From the driver's seat of the Humvee, Harper shook his head just slightly and then studiously avoided eye contact. Julia held his gaze a bit longer, showing a measure of concern. Lee looked at him severely and grabbed his shoulder again, this time more firmly.

"What the hell was that?" Lee demanded.

Jim looked over his shoulder toward the hill, but they could see nothing. "I dunno...I just thought that...I thought..."

"Come on." Lee pulled him toward the Humvee again. "Let's go."

"I thought they needed help."

"They probably did. But we're an armed vehicle—would you have stopped?"

"No," Jim mumbled.

LaRouche sighed and let the barrel of the fifty rise up and point at the tops of the trees. He leaned over and spat. "Maybe I shouldn't have pointed the Ma Deuce at 'em."

Lee looked back into the woods. Faintly, he thought he could hear them crashing through the forest, just barely audible above the grumbling Humvee at idle. He ushered Jim back into the Humvee, the ex-priest seeming deflated and limp. He closed the door and then got back into the front passenger's seat and pointed on down the road.

"Let's keep moving."

There was a moment of silence, thick and uncomfortable.

Then Harper put the vehicle in gear and they continued on.

From the backseat, barely audible over the sound of the engine and the wind rushing by the open windows, Father Jim murmured, "I'm sorry. I thought we could help."

They arrived at Camp Ryder before noon.

In the span of a few months, Camp Ryder had undergone some extreme changes. Some of the ramshackle huts were gone, and "The Square" had graduated from an empty area with a fire pit in the center to a noisy open-air market. Those who scavenged would set up spots inside the Square to barter items they had found—anything from dental floss to batteries or canned food. While everything Lee and his group gathered in their scavenging operations went into a pool to be distributed evenly through the group, scavenging had quickly become a livelihood for those with the impetus to go outside the gates.

The influx of Lee's rifles and ammunition had played a large role in making scavenging possible. Since accessing Bunker #4 three months ago, Lee had emptied it in the course of several trips to and from. The outposts they had set up at several key locations in the area ran patrols along the major roads, keeping them mostly clear of raiders and their roadblocks. He had distributed a rifle and five hundred rounds of ammunition to every member of the community who wanted them, provided they were over the age of sixteen. This was a defensive measure. If the community came under attack from infected hordes or from a human threat, Lee wanted each and every adult man and woman to be able to join the fight.

While the area was safer now than it had been after the initial collapse, it was still dangerous and they'd taken some losses. Infected were a constant threat, and the patrolling of the roads did very little to limit them. The previous week, two scavengers had been killed before they could make it back to their vehicles and flee. The infected had them almost completely surrounded by the time the scavengers knew what was happening.

Last month alone they'd lost five.

The month before that, seven.

But even with the constant danger, the scavengers had successfully created a thriving trade economy right there in the heart of Camp Ryder. They traded among themselves frequently, but people came in from the other communities that had been incorporated into the collection of towns and neighborhoods that was being called the "Camp Ryder Hub," and every so often they got visitors from the two groups of survivors that had decided to remain independent of Camp Ryder: Newton Grove to the southeast and Broadway to the west.

Speak of the devil... Lee thought as he noticed the red Isuzu Rodeo pulling in just past the gate.

The driver would be Kip Greene from Broadway. He came to Camp Ryder for two reasons: to talk with Bus and to trade with the scavengers. The Broadway survivors were almost all farming families, and they had continued to tend their crops as best they could after the collapse. They used what they could spare of their harvest to trade at the Square.

Harper pulled the Humvee up to the gate, where a group of three scavengers was preparing to leave and receiving white armbands from the sentries posted there. Every day had a randomly assigned color. An appropriately colored strip of cloth would be given to the scavengers as they left so they could quickly identify themselves as friends when they approached the gate later.

The three scavengers hustled out of the way as the sentry pulled the gate open for the Humvee as they rolled into camp. Harper pulled their Humvee to the right and parked it out of the way. Behind them, Lee could hear the chain-link fence rolling shut. Recently reinforced with scrap metal and hanging heavy on its hinges, it rattled and clanked noisily as it closed.

Lee eased his way out of his seat and took a moment to work some blood back into his stiff ankle. Feeling a little more limber, he walked to the rear of the vehicle and hauled his heavy pack onto one shoulder. As he stood up, the hollow feeling of hunger seeped into his midsection and his stomach growled noisily. He glanced across the dusty parking area and could see Angela standing there with Sam by her side. They both waved to him when he looked in their direction.

Inwardly, he could not shake how strange this made him feel, still the impostor living another man's life. But outwardly he smiled, waved back, and made his way over to them.

Angela looked at him brightly, her pale skin flushed at the nose and cheeks against the chilling wind. She pulled her jacket closer around her. "Good to see you back, Lee."

She reached one hand out, and Lee took it. Not a handshake, but a quick and heartfelt squeeze. What there was between them was a mystery to Lee, but he had long ago decided to go with it, because despite his reservations, it was something real. It was something he could come back to. Something to ground him so that his entire existence was not an unending slough of death and conflict.

"Where's Abby?" Lee asked.

"She's learning how to sew with some of the other kids."

Abby hadn't warmed up to him, and it didn't seem like she was going to.

"Did you hear about the guy who's asking for you?" Sam broke in, peering up at Lee with one eye squinted against the sun.

"Yeah, I heard," Lee said and glanced at Angela, who returned a quizzical look. To Sam again, Lee said, "Did you learn anything new the last few days?"

"Mr. Keith taught me how to shoot his .22 rifle," Sam nodded with a smile. "We went out and got a couple rabbits. He said I was a natural. Showed me how to skin them and cook them and everything."

"Wow." Lee's eyes went up. "He took you outside the fence?"

"Is that okay? We didn't go very far."

"Yeah." He pictured the old man and Sam running through a field with wild-eyed and shit-covered crazies sprinting after them, screeching and howling. Then he saw blood and entrails smeared across the grassy earth. He swallowed. "I'm sure Mr. Keith was smart about it."

Angela spoke up. "Where're you off to now?"

Lee pointed a thumb toward the Ryder building. "I gotta get up with Bus and figure out what's going on with this guy from Virginia. You hear anything about it?"

She shook her head. "Last I heard he was in the medical trailer, passed out. He was in pretty bad shape."

"How so?"

"Jenny mentioned dehydration, dysentery, mal-nutrition..."

"He must've been on the road for weeks."

"Yeah." Angela nodded.

Lee craned his neck toward the medical trailer. "I should probably see what's going on with him."

"Of course. See you at dinner?"

"Yeah," Lee said, slightly distracted. "I'll be there."

Harper met with him as he made his way toward the Ryder building.

Ahead of them, people gathered at the entrance to the medical trailer to peer in curiously at the man from Virginia. While the novelty of newcomers had faded somewhat as contact was made with more and more survivors, this particular newcomer had caused a stir. A man who showed up out of the blue and asked for Captain Harden by name was an immediate subject of interest, if not downright suspicion.

Lee and Harper stopped there in front of the medical trailer, and the passersby watched as though they believed there would be some great reunion between Lee and the stranger. Inside the trailer, a nearly shapeless form of skin and bones lay crumpled like a discarded piece of paper upon one of the cots, a white bedsheet draped over him like a body in a morgue.

Lee could smell the man from outside the trailer. Most of the people managed to bathe regularly now, but they all still smelled of hard work and body odor, Lee probably being the most offending of them, since he'd been in the field for the past few days. That Lee could smell the stranger over his own stink was a feat in and of itself.

"You recognize him?" Harper asked.

Lee shook his head. "Don't know him."

They didn't linger. The man was clearly passed out from exhaustion, and they could not expect to have a lucid conversation with him until he was rested.

They continued on to the Ryder building.

A short series of cement steps led up to a pair of steel double doors kept closed to block out the cold air. Pushing them open, the pair was immediately inundated with the overwhelming smell of the place and the noisy clamor from inside. The building had once been a service bay for Ryder trucks, and the smell of oils and car parts was forever steeped into the concrete floors and walls. However, it was now home to several families and Marie's kitchen. There was always a slight haze of smoke in the place, and it bore with it the heavy scents of people and cooking food.

Immediately upon entering the building, they could see a metal staircase to their right that rose up to a second level that overlooked the floor below, with a series of metal catwalks that led to a roof access point, a few utility closets, and what used to serve as a foreman's office—a twelve-by-twenty-foot room that housed a desk, a filing cabinet, a few folding chairs, and a large corkboard with a map of North Carolina pinned to it.

In the office they found Bus and Kip Greene standing in front of the map. Bus wore the same OD green jacket as Lee and Harper—actually a Gore-Tex parka—and a pair of jeans with the beginnings of holes in the knees, twice patched and twice ripped. Stress had drawn some of his size from him, but he was still an imposing figure, especially next to Kip Greene, who stood all of 5'8", with wiry arms and a thin neck.

"Captain…Harper…" Bus greeted them as they walked in.

Lee clasped hands with him. "Good to see you, Bus."

"How was Lillington?" Bus ventured cautiously.

Lee dropped his pack to the floor. "Nothing worse than usual."

"Glad everyone came out all right." Bus nodded.

Lee turned his attention to the man from Broadway. "Kip...how are ya?"

"Decent. You?" Kip nodded, his hands planted deep in the pockets of his tattered old Dickies coveralls.

"Good. But we could still use some help." Lee looked pointedly at him.

Kip smiled grimly. "Funny enough, that's what I came to talk about."

"Oh?" Lee perked up a bit. He took a seat at the edge of the desk. "I sense there's a caveat."

Kip nodded.

Bus folded his arms across his chest. "I've been trying to explain to Kip that we need to use Broadway as a launch point for Sanford—"

"My people aren't interested in being a base for you guys," Kip said steadily.

"It's not just about us, you know." Lee pointed to the map. "You guys have been catching all the shit leaking out of Sanford since this started. You're doing an admirable job, but if you let us go in and clean house, you'll be able to focus more on your farming and less on watching your back."

Kip shook his head. "Not an option at this point."

Lee let his hands drop to his lap. "Okay. Why don't you explain what you want with us, then?"

Kip looked up at Lee from underneath his eyebrows. "We've been taking a lot of heat from Sanford. More and more lately, in fact. I'm not sure why, but they're coming out of that place in droves. I don't know, maybe they're running out of food in there. They all look pretty lean." He adjusted the brim of his cap. "Anyway, we've been getting them as they try to go down 421, but..."

Lee waited.

Kip seemed a little abashed. "But we're running out of ammunition."

Lee folded his hands. "Ah."

"That's why I'm here. To set up a trade."

"And what are we trading?"

"Food for ammunition. We've got corn, wheat, peanuts, and tobacco. We'll trade any of them, in any combination, as long as the deal is fair."

Silence blanketed the room.

Lee was the first one to speak. "Kip, you mind if I talk with Bus and Harper for a moment?"

Kip shook his head. He stepped out and closed the door behind him as the three men from Camp Ryder gathered in close so they could speak in hushed tones.

Lee spoke first. "I think this is a good opportunity to build up some goodwill by making a generous trade with them. Keep in mind, they'll probably need rifles as well, since most of what we can give them is 5.56mm and I doubt they have many rifles that are chambered for that."

"We could play hardball," Bus suggested. "If they need the ammo badly enough we might be able to break him down and let us use Broadway to get into Sanford."

Harper made an ugly face. "I don't know if playing hardball is a good idea. That might just piss them off, and then Broadway is out as a source of food *and* as a base."

Bus rubbed his eyebrows. "I just want to avoid a repeat of Smithfield. I sure as hell don't want you guys camping in the woods outside of Sanford while you clear it. We need them."

Lee spread his palms. "Ammunition is a finite resource. We can have the best of both worlds. Let's make a small but generous deal with him now so he's forced to come back soon. Then we can play hardball. If we have some goodwill built up with him and his group, we're less likely to scare him off when we do. Plus we'll get a little fresh food out of it."

"We need the wheat," Harper nodded. "Cornmeal would be good too."

"Any value to tobacco?" Bus questioned.

Harper and Lee both shrugged.

"As a trade item, yes," Lee said. "But I wouldn't worry about it for now."

Harper grinned. "Don't tell LaRouche."

Lee stretched his arms. "So what's the offer?"

"You're in charge of guns and ammo," Bus pointed out. "You tell us what we can afford."

Lee considered it for a short moment. "How about we trade five rifles and six hundred rounds total. That'll be six mags per rifle. Depending on their level of contact, that could last them one or two weeks."

"That's a good time frame for us," Harper noted.

"Alright. Everyone agree?"

"Agreed."

"Yup."

Lee headed for the door.

He was about to reach for the handle when he heard shouting and the sound of footsteps pounding rapidly up the metal staircase. Someone cried out in alarm. The steps thundered as they drew closer. He didn't recall grabbing it, but Lee's rifle was suddenly in his hands and addressed toward the door.

The door burst open and a madman with sunken eyes and sallow skin tumbled in. The strange creature's eyes landed on Lee and the captain's finger went to the trigger. The thing reached forward and sank down to its knees and seemed about to scramble at Lee on all fours.

Lee was about to pull the trigger when it spoke.

"You're Captain Harden!" the man said and clasped a hand over his face. "I found you...I finally found you!"